"I live with pain all the time," he said.

"And there's a part of you that likes it." Kye sat back.

Kasabian came up on his hands and knees, facing her. "The Shadow part of me craves all kinds of feelings." Like a cat, he prowled closer to her, until his face was only inches from hers. In his eyes, the Shadow flashed. "Pain. Sex." He moved even closer, forcing her to lean back. "And you, Kye. It craves you."

Her heart pulsed at his nearness, his words. "Is the Shadow in me, too? Because of the bond? Ever since we did the Cobra, I feel...different."

"Hungry? Horny? Afraid? Afraid is good. You should be pushing me away, heading to the door. But you're not."

She knew she should be, but the Shadow in his eyes held her. "No. I'm not."

Also by Jaime Rush

Dragon Mine
Dragon Rising
Dragon Awakened
Magic Possessed

ANGEL SEDUCED

A Hidden Novel

JAIME RUSH

FOREVER

NEW YORK   BOSTON

Copyright © 2014 by Tina Wainscott
Excerpt from *Dragon Awakened* copyright © 2013 by Tina Wainscott
Excerpt from *Magic Possessed* copyright © 2014 by Tina Wainscott

Forever
Hachette Book Group
237 Park Avenue
New York, NY 10017

www.HachetteBookGroup.com

Printed in the United States of America

First Edition: February 2014
10 9 8 7 6 5 4 3 2 1

OPM

Forever is an imprint of Grand Central Publishing.
The Forever name and logo are trademarks of Hachette Book Group, Inc.

The Hachette Speakers Bureau provides a wide range of authors for speaking events. To find out more, go to www.hachettespeakersbureau.com or call (866) 376-6591.

The publisher is not responsible for websites (or their content) that are not owned by the publisher.

*To all of the amazing people in the South Florida
Romance Writers chapter. You have been my friends,
confidantes, and cheerleaders. And especially to Joyce
Henderson, who is one of our founding members and now
watches over us from above.*

Acknowledgments

Thanks to Mary Pat Dailey for her help with information
on therapists.

My gratitude to the Hachette Books team for their guidance, fabulous cover art, and everything they do to take a
book from words on a computer screen to a finished product.

Chapter 1

Kye Rivers bypassed the velvet rope that corralled the line of people waiting to get into the Witch's Brew. Too bad the handful of Mundane humans didn't know this exclusive Miami nightclub allowed in only Deuces like her. Of course, they knew nothing at all about Crescents, humans who carried the DNA of gods and angels. Kye traded a greeting with the bouncer and entered the jam-packed cave of a building.

Sarai raced over, her serving tray tucked under her arm. "Kye, wait 'til you see the new bartender! His name is Kasabian. He's totally hot. And"—she gave her the *wait for it* grin—"he's Caido."

"No way. Maybe it's a Deuce illusion, like his gimmick."

"He couldn't hold it for two whole shifts. Plus, he's healed a couple of people with some kind of angel-essence thing." Sarai cracked her gum. "There was quite a stir at first, as you can imagine. The women were all gaga, and the guys were all 'why's the pretty boy Caido working here?' But people are starting to warm to him. He's nice. Not snotty like Tad or slutty like Donnie was. He's politely turned down overtures from every woman who's come on to him."

Kye's gaze went right to the new face behind the bar. The gorgeous new face. Red lights within the thick glass counter cast a glow over the angles of his cheeks and the gloss of his dark-blond hair. Kasabian might be new to the Brew, but he was clearly not new to tending. He flipped bottles, poured, and returned them to their places with the speed and grace of a juggler. The relaxed smile on his face indicated that he was enjoying it. So were the people watching him in rapt awe. Of course, that could be the Thrall, the way Caidos could hypnotize with their preternatural beauty. Because of what Kye did for a living, she'd learned to shut out that allure.

But damn, fascination stirred deep in her chest. *Whoa, cut that shit out.*

Kye shrugged. "Just another gorgeous Caido." She pushed her long, blond hair back over her shoulder. "Think I'll order a drink now."

"Hah. You are so totally checking him out—" Sarai's teasing smile disappeared. She gripped her arm, the mist in her eyes stirring like storm-tossed clouds. "Don't do it!"

"You're freaking over me ordering a drink from the guy?"

Sarai shook her head. "I'm feeling a lot more than a drink. First, I sensed that there could be something good and hot and sexy between the two of you. Which was crazy enough. Then I got a really bad feeling."

Kye splayed her hand on her chest. "Uh, remember who

you're talking to. The girl you're always giving a hard time because I never date."

"Remember who's doing the talking. I had a feeling about that guy Katie was dating, and he ended up being a drug dealer. I warned Rhea that her brakes were going to give out, and the mechanic said they wouldn't have lasted another day."

"I don't doubt your forecasts. Maybe something good and bad *would* come from getting involved, but I'd never get romantic with a Brew employee." She patted Sarai's hand. "I need to meet him. He's in my world, after all." The Brew was her second home, the employees a sort of family.

But yeah, it was odd that a Caido was working at a Deuce nightclub. All three classes of Crescents traced their ancestry to a mysterious island in the Bermuda Triangle, where humans had procreated with gods, but none intermingled much socially. Caidos, who were descended from fallen angels, were downright reclusive.

Kasabian looked up, zoning right in on her as she approached. His hazel-green eyes held the Caido glitter, like sun on early morning frost. Each of the three classes held their unique magick in their eyes, visible only to other Crescents.

He watched her, even as he shoved limes into two Coronas and pushed them across the counter to the men waiting for them. "What can I get you, love?" he asked when she reached him. *"Love"? What kind of Caido was this guy?*

The smooth edge of the counter pressed into her palms as she leaned forward. "Know how to make the Whis-Kye?" she called out over the pounding beat of Katy Perry's "E.T."

His mouth curved into a heart-stopping smile as his gaze lingered on the patch on her black leather jacket that read NO DOES NOT MEAN CONVINCE ME. "You must be Kye. Before he left, Donnie filled me in on the special customers. From what I've heard, you're quite special." He held out his hand. "I'm Kasabian."

A strange twist of anticipation and fear overtook her, but she slid her hand into his—and instantly knew why. A jolt like a low-level electrical surge went through her. She pulled her hand back, heat flushing over her. He was watching her as though he expected her to react, so she did her best not to.

He turned and pulled down the bottle of Johnnie Walker Black whiskey with one hand, a highball glass in another. There were no available stools, but the couple beside her shifted so she could settle in more comfortably. Which she shouldn't do. Which she did.

Kasabian mixed the drink Mike, the club's owner, had concocted for her years ago. Whiskey, Mountain Dew, and a splash of lime, just enough liquor for a tiny buzz. He snuggled a wedge of orange on the rim and slid the glass in front of her. Someone farther down the bar flagged Kasabian down.

"Don't go," he said, moving away to take an order. He made three different drinks and pulled one draft. His tight black shirt showed off a physique he got doing more than tossing bottles. Not bodybuilder thick, but lean and well defined. He returned to her. "Mike told me you're a Zensu Deuce, that you pick up people's sensual pathos and fix them. He thinks you're a goddess."

Embarrassment stung her cheeks but warmed her heart. That was a lot more appreciation than she'd ever gotten from her own family over her gift. She couldn't go into how she'd helped Mike with his sexual dysfunction, discovering it stemmed from an impotency spell cast by an ex.

"I'm a certified sex therapist," she felt compelled to say. "With a doctorate in clinical sexology."

"Plus a dash of magick."

She lifted one shoulder. "To be honest, it's mostly the magick."

Kasabian regarded her with a curious expression. "You pick up people's feelings?"

"It can work that way, if someone asks me to open the door. I don't make a habit of eavesdropping. In fact, I keep the psychic door closed most of the time."

He gestured for her to lean closer, then leaned in himself. She had the bizarre notion that he was going to kiss her. Even more bizarre, she involuntarily licked her lips in anticipation. His mouth moved close to her ear, brushing the shell of it ever so slightly as he said, "So, what do you get from me?"

She tried to stifle her shiver at his touch. He leaned back, and she saw that his question was a challenge, maybe a test. She opened the door and...holy Zensu, a wave of desire, pain, and heat washed over her. Desire for her. *He's Caido. This can't be right.* She'd never picked up anything like that before. It spiraled inside her like a vine, a dark hunger twining through her until she slammed the door shut.

She worked to mask her surprise, along with the flush on her face. She had to lean close to him now. "I got nothing, but that's no surprise. Caidos don't have sexual pathos...or sexual anything. You're all shut down." She grabbed her drink, intending to turn around and leave.

Kasabian's raised eyebrow and smile said, *I don't believe you.* He gave her a wink and tipped his chin toward the dance floor. "Go dance, give me something to watch."

Was he serious? His playful smile could go both ways.

A woman tugged her sleeve. "Are you Kye? I was told you could help me with...a problem."

"Yes, yes, I can." Kye gratefully led her to her usual table. Damn, did she need a diversion from the way his smile still tingled through her.

A RESERVED sign sat on the shiny black tabletop. Mike let her conduct business in the club, and she insisted on giving him a cut. Some people felt more comfortable talking about their sexual issues in loud, smoky surroundings. The club had become her second office.

It was damn annoying how Kye's attention kept straying to Kasabian through the night, how her mind kept replaying their conversation. Women gawked and flirted, but he didn't flirt back. She was glad to see him leave while she finished up with a client session after closing time.

Her relief evaporated when she stepped into the well-lit parking lot and spotted him leaning against a deep yellow sports car. As though he were waiting for her. The thought fluttered in her chest. Not helping, the Lotus's license plate read NOANGEL, and black angel wings spread across the hood. Caidos in particular were drawn to fancy, fast cars, funded by the good investments many had made in real estate before the boom.

But the man himself was far sexier than his car. His arms were loosely crossed in front of his chest, which made his biceps bulge nicely. She told herself it was enough to enjoy the view. Men who took care of their bodies, working out enough to build muscle without looking jacked up, were eye candy. No calories in looking.

The thick, black heels of her boots clunked on the asphalt. She felt such an odd pull toward him that she gave him a brief smile and made to continue on.

"Aren't you hot in that?" he asked, gesturing as though he were wearing a jacket.

She slowed to a stop in front of him. "Only when I dance." No matter how warm she got, she never took off the black leather jacket with her patches and studs.

"And you didn't dance." He tilted his head, giving her an oh-my-gods-stop-my-heart pout. "Pity."

"Are you flirting with me?"

He arched an eyebrow. "You make it sound like a crime."

"What you're hearing is surprise. I know it's painful for Caidos to feel desire, punishment when your forefathers fell to human temptation. Don't worry. As a therapist, I'm sworn to secrecy," she added. "Caido clients tell me it's easier to shut down their desire. Yet you do . . . feel desire."

"Ah, so you did sense it."

"You threw me off back at the bar. First that you were flirting, then that you asked me outright to feel you." She had an instant visual image of her hands sliding down those biceps. "I mean, to sense your feelings. You're different."

"Very. I don't usually flirt." He let his gaze drift down over her black leather skirt and fishnet stockings. His eyes met hers again, jumpstarting her heart. "You have a strange effect on me."

Ditto, buddy. Which made her all too aware that they were outside alone together.

His chuckle rolled across her skin. "Don't worry, I'm not waiting out here to pounce on you."

"But you are waiting for me."

"Yes, I am."

"You're not going to ask me out or anything, are you? Because I don't date." He didn't say anything, which made for a really awkward few seconds. "It's a general rule, nothing personal. If…that's what you were going to ask." She would *thwap* herself on the forehead if it wouldn't look stupid.

And, of course, as a Caido, he picked up everything she was feeling, which put a sexy smile on his face. "As much as I'd love to hook up with you, it's not feasible. Or wise."

He'd love to hook up with her. She tried to stanch her reaction.

He gave her a sympathetic smile. "The love guru doesn't date? That's sad."

She debated being obtuse but decided it was better that he knew she wasn't just playing hard to get. "Being involved with someone interferes with my abilities. The drama and distraction, even if things are going well, takes over my mind. All I get is noise when I read someone."

He cocked his head. "And that terrifies you. Why?"

She really hated that he could read her. "Helping people is important to me."

"Which leads beautifully to the reason I'm waiting for you. The Caido/Deuce couple who came in and greeted you like you were their best friend, who danced together, and kissed…you helped them, didn't you?"

Kye had watched them snuggling together on the dance floor with just a tiny bit of longing. "Sorry, client confidentiality."

He rubbed his chin. "So you did help them. The only way they could be together is by doing the Essex. I assume you know what that is."

She had been shocked and saddened to learn that the emotions Caidos picked up from others cut through them like a knife. It was a secret they held very closely, for their own well-being. Kasabian was testing her. She knew he wouldn't volunteer the information. "That's when a Caido exchanges his magick essence with a Dragon or Deuce. It's how a Caido heals other Crescents' emotional or physical pain. Unbeknownst to those Crescents, our essence has a balancing effect on him so he's not as sensitive to others' emotions. Or desire."

He nodded. "But it only temporarily eases his pain. So a long-term relationship would eventually deplete her essence, because he would have to do it with her every day. No self-respecting Caido would endanger someone he cares about. So how is it that they're together?"

"I can only give you a general answer. Not one specific to any couple in particular. I've come up with a way to make the Essex permanent."

He pushed away from the car, interest crackling off him as he came closer. "Tell me more."

She fought the instinct to back up a step. "I've had a few mixed-Caido couples approach me about circumventing the pain. They hadn't meant to fall in love, but now they wanted to be together. I tried several different spells and magick devices, but nothing worked."

He crossed his arms in front of him and rocked back on his heels. "And you take it very hard when you can't fix someone."

"You get that from me, too?"

"I suppose we both bear a similar burden in picking up feelings we have no business sensing. How does your permanent Essex work?"

She laid one of her hands on top of the other and let her fingers barely settle between each other. "With the Essex, you're limited to how much essence you can exchange, kind of the way my fingers aren't fully locked together. That's why it's temporary. The Cobra, which I named for the tantric position, surrounds the Essex process with magick that acts as a conduit, allowing both essences to reach fully toward each other, like this." She laced her hands together, fingers straight so that they formed an X. "This starts the bonding process. The last step is when both parties actually pull each other's essence into their souls, permanently locking them together." Her fingers wrapped over her hands as though in prayer. "At least, I think it's permanent. The first couple did it four months ago, and it's still holding strong."

"Why haven't I heard about this magick of yours? The Caido community should be buzzing."

"I haven't made it public yet. There are some side effects I'm still working out. The Caido is bombarded by every emotion he's ever repressed. It can be intense. One Caido had to, as he put it, get deprogrammed. It was a fail, and yes, I took it hard. Another effect: the couple is emotionally bonded, perhaps permanently. And one Caido experienced a resurgence of buried memories."

Kasabian's eyes shimmered. "Buried memories?"

"It apparently caused some big problems, but he couldn't give me any details beyond that. He just wanted me to know that it happened."

Kasabian went silent for a few moments, sliding his

fingers across his mouth. "Can you do it so a Caido can simply experience desire?"

"Only if you have a committed partner who wants to be permanently bonded to you."

"That would not be a good thing. For any woman."

"Why?" The mystery of him pulled at her, the dark desire she'd sensed.

"Oh, love, there you go, needing to help even though you know you should run the other way." He lowered his chin, the street light reflecting off his razor-sharp jawline. "And you should run. I'm forty ways fucked up."

She swallowed. No one had ever made her this off balance. "I do want to help. Too many messed-up people are not only suffering but also inflicting their misery on others."

"I assure you that I'm not inflicting my anything on anyone." He reached out and brushed the back of his hand down her cheek. "As much as I'd like to."

She stumbled back, his touch curling throughout her body. "I should go."

Hunger flashed in his eyes. "Yes, you should."

Go, run, and never look back.

Chapter 2

"Another game, Mr. Grey?" one of the Youth Harbor kids called out as he ran the basketball down the court.

Kasabian dropped down on the bleachers, catching his breath. "I'm done."

"Getting old, Kasabian?" one of the kids chided.

"Yeah, thirty-two and over the hill." Of course, that was old to these kids. They couldn't yet comprehend how long Crescents lived, how those years would drag on. "Five hours straight, and I can't take a break without getting harassed?" Had he been this relentless when he lived here? Yeah, probably, in his eagerness for a grown-up's attention.

Most of the Harbor kids were Caidos, but some were Dragon or Deuce orphans. Here, there was none of the separation that eventually happened between the Crescent classes. They all belonged equally. And while Kasabian had felt safe and accepted here, he had never truly belonged.

"I'm done, too." Daniel Portofino, another volunteer,

flopped down beside him, panting. "Man, I can't believe you do this and then work until three in the morning."

"Helping out here is recreation for me." He liked giving back to the place that had taken him in after his mother's murder when he was twelve. "Actually, so is bartending."

"I don't know how you do that, either. All those emotions, people getting hot for each other, jealousy...that's got to kill you."

Even joy felt like a thousand razor blades across his soul. "I'd rather suffer than shut myself off from humanity." Kasabian wasn't about to tell anyone he craved emotions. He leaned back on the bleacher behind him. "Ever been in love, Daniel?" At his surprised look, Kasabian added, "Not seriously in love, but crushing on someone even though you knew it wouldn't work? Because we're Caido." *An innocent crush*, he wanted to add, but his thoughts about Kye were far from innocent.

Daniel stared at him for a long second, some odd emotion flashing behind his dark blue eyes. "Once. Long time ago. You?"

Kasabian chuckled, shaking his head. "There's this Deuce chick who hangs out at the Witch's Brew, and she's freakin' amazing."

"A *Deuce*?"

Caidos couldn't pick up the emotions of other Caidos, but Kasabian didn't need supernatural ability to see that the idea annoyed Daniel. Who cared? It felt good to talk about her. "Long blond hair, the creamiest skin I've ever seen, dresses all biker-chick in black leather and fishnets." He thought back over the last few nights that he'd seen her at the Brew. "Last night she finally danced within sight of my bar, and man, can she move. She kept checking to see if I was watching." And he had been, every spare second. It had been a long time since he'd desired a woman, and then only fleetingly. With Kye, he couldn't seem to stop.

"You going to act on it?"

"I have to do the Essex twice a night to dull the pain. But wanting her is as far as it goes." The only thing he and Kye could ever do was exchange furtive glances.

"Smart. That kind of thing never works."

"Actually, it could." For normal Caidos, anyway. "She's a Zensu Deuce, and she's come up with a permanent Essex so the Caido is immune to his lover's emotions." Then he remembered that it wasn't public knowledge yet, so he added, "But keep that to yourself."

"Caidos should stick with their own."

It was easier for Caidos to get together. Desire didn't hurt as much if they were in angel form, nor did any emotion, a layer of protection that allowed them to heal others. Caidos could Invoke and partake in carnal activities with a non-Caido, but the numbness also muffled the excitement. And, unfortunately, holding on to angel form for the sole purpose of getting off was difficult. After a while, it was easier—hell, necessary—to douse desire altogether.

Until someone like Kye came along.

"Yeah, and that would be fine if there were plenty of Caido females." Part of the curse their forebears passed on was relatively few females in their Crescent class. At least that was the theory.

"That's why some males turn to each other. Ever considered that?"

Kasabian shook his head, wondering if Daniel was making a pass at him. "I like women way too much. Their curves, the soft mounds of their beautiful breasts..." Kye popped into his mind again, and desire prickled through him. Yeah, she had some nice curves, all right.

Daniel's mouth tightened, like he was preparing some kind of lecture, but his sulk turned into a speculative look. "A permanent Essex, you said? How does it work?"

Kasabian demonstrated the way Kye had.

"Who is she?" Daniel asked, not so judgmental anymore.

"Kye Rivers." Damn but he liked the way her name rolled off his tongue. "But remember, she's not offering this magick to just anyone. In fact, I probably shouldn't have mentioned it."

"Kasabian!"

Hayden Masters approached from the end of the bleachers. He acknowledged Daniel with a nod but focused on Kasabian. "Can I talk to you for a sec?" He glanced at Daniel. "Sorry, but it's confidential."

Kasabian pushed up, excusing himself. He bumped knuckles with the big Caido, and they headed out of the gym.

Hayden lowered his voice. "Something came up at work that you need to know about. Even though you're not supposed to know."

"Gotcha."

Hayden was a Vega in the Guard, the Crescent's police force. He'd shared some of his cases, mostly hunting down Crescents who broke the laws of the Hidden. Rule Number One was to never reveal the magick of the Hidden to Mundanes. Other rules focused on not using fangs, orbs, or other magickal weapons on either Mundanes or Crescents. Not that everyone obeyed.

They stepped out into the humid air, the afternoon sun

cooking them until they moved beneath a tree by the tennis courts. Two Harbor residents were batting a ball half-heartedly back and forth.

Hayden braced his hand against the tree trunk. "A five-year-old Caido boy was picked up this morning, just wandering the streets. The kid was weak, disoriented, and mute. Whatever he'd gone through traumatized him pretty bad. And he had this." He yanked up his shirt to reveal a faint gray starburst over his diaphragm.

Kasabian felt a squeeze where his own scar was. "Hell. Whoever kidnapped us more than twenty years ago is still doing it." He remembered the group of kids who'd escaped with him, none with any memory of their captivity. Once sexual abuse had been eliminated, based on physical exams, all they had were questions. Four years of captivity were locked away in some part of Kasabian's brain that no magick or hypnosis could touch.

Kye's voice echoed in his mind: *One Caido experienced a resurgence of buried memories.*

"Did you talk to the kid?" Kasabian asked.

"Yeah, for about three minutes. My sergeant called me in because he knows about our ordeal and recognized that it was the same type of scar I have. He thought if I showed the kid, maybe he'd open up. And I think he would have, only my sergeant pulled me out of the room. He said the Concilium was taking over the investigation. Sensitive matters and some such bullshit."

Hayden smacked the tree, making leaves float down. "Within minutes, the kid's sucked into the system. My boss wasn't happy about it, but what's he going to do, fight the Elders, who are like the United Nations of Crescents? Hell, we don't even know who's in the Concilium, and they're supposed to be representing us. My guess is that someone knows what these marks mean. Wouldn't be the first time something was covered up *to protect society*," Hayden added with finger quotes.

"Five years old." Kasabian shook his head in disgust. "Even younger than when we were taken."

"If it's like last time, the bastards are taking kids from hookers or drugged-out mothers who either are accepting a payoff or are too scared to report their kid missing." A shadow passed over Hayden's features.

When they were able to track down the mothers, they got a story about how some government official had offered to send the boy to a camp and get him away from the situation while the mother got sober. Pressure had a way of cracking people with magick. Crescents had to worry about being incinerated by Dragons, stalked by demons, hurt by spells. Exposing their magick.

Hayden pushed away from the tree. "I'm going to do some digging."

"I'll check around, too." Kasabian headed back into the building.

Cory, one of the guys who ran Harbor, was going over some details for the middle school kids' overnight trip to the Everglades. Maps and brochures were spread out all over the desk. Cory looked up. "I keep expecting the headmaster of the Deuce Academy to postpone the trip, what with all the talk of the solar storm effects hitting as early as Thursday. Even the Mundane news is reporting on possible GPS distortion and electric outages. We'll feel it in deeper ways. Some of the younger Caidos are already experiencing headaches and bad feelings."

"We've weathered them in the past. We'll get through

this one." The solar storm was the least of Kasabian's concerns. "Have you heard about any kids going missing recently?"

"You know Lyle?"

"Skinny Caido with the choppy hair? Came here, what, a year ago? Keeps to himself."

Cory nodded. "He's barely hanging on to his required grades. I've suspected him of running drugs, maybe Abyss. I hate to even think it, a twelve-year-old doing that. Caught him sneaking out a few times, though I couldn't find anything on him but a bunch of pictures of the same kid. His missing brother, he said. I wasn't sure if he was telling the truth or using it as a cover."

"I'll have a chat with him, see what I can find out."

Kasabian found Lyle at a computer in the library. The kid quickly closed the browser screen, a suspicious move. Kasabian decided not to call him on it, turning a chair at the next computer and sitting down backward. Although it was obvious that Kasabian was there to talk to him, Lyle opened a new screen and pulled up one of the curriculum programs, ignoring him. His eyes were bloodshot, face gaunt.

"You came from the Vale, didn't you?" Kasabian asked, finally getting the kid's attention. The Vale was a run-down area populated by the addicts.

"Yeah." Lyle kept his gaze on the computer screen, but he was working really hard to do it.

"I'm investigating some disappearances. Have you heard anything about kids going missing from there?"

Lyle turned to him, his mouth working. He pulled back whatever words he was going to say and affected a nonchalant shrug. "I'm not sure you could call it disappearing.

They supposedly went to some kind of camp, while the mothers moved to this weird neighborhood for a better life."

Kasabian considered what angle to use. "But they lied." Not a question. "How do you know?"

The kid was clearly in a war with himself: tell the nosy guy the truth or distrust him as he did everyone else.

Kasabian knew how he felt. Sharing didn't come easy for him either, but he needed to if he was going to get anywhere. "I was kidnapped when I was eight. I was lucky. I escaped. The people who took me, I think they're still taking kids. I want to stop them. Maybe it has something to do with this camp. I need to find out more."

Lyle's expression slowly revealed his pain. "My brother went a year ago. They said I was too old to go with him."

"How old was he?"

"Four."

"And you never saw him again."

Lyle chewed his lip, his eyes staring at nothing. Finally he shook his head. "We moved to the Bend soon after."

"Is that the weird neighborhood?"

Lyle nodded.

The Bend. Kasabian had heard about the gated community that housed middle- and low-income Crescent families, particularly single mothers. It was touted as being safe and claimed to help the drug-addled clean up their lives.

"They never returned your brother," Kasabian said gently.

"They said three months. Then it was six months. All my mom kept talking about was our beautiful house and wasn't our life so nice now? She didn't even seem concerned."

Because she knew the kid wasn't coming back.

"When I threatened to go to the Guard, she admitted that Jonathan had been adopted by another family." Lyle met Kasabian's gaze with a fierce expression. "She said it was kind of a trade-off. I accused her of selling him, and then she was all like, 'I didn't say trade-off!' I ran away and came here."

The pieces were coming together. "You sneak out to the Vale to search for him."

Lyle searched Kasabian's face, sensing whether he could trust him. Finally he nodded. "I ask around, talk to people. But no one knows anything."

"Can I help you?"

"No. But thanks. I can do it on my own."

Just like Kasabian, not wanting to involve anyone else. The poor kid had been dealing with this alone, driving himself to exhaustion.

"I understand. No one cares about your situation like you do. But sometimes what you're after is more important than your need to do it on your own. I'm going to look into this for my own reasons. It would help if I had a picture of your brother."

Lyle pulled out his worn nylon wallet and extracted one of many color copies. On the back was the boy's name, age, height, and weight, along with the date he'd gone missing. The boys looked nothing alike; Jonathan had straight brown hair while Lyle's was dark blond and wavy. Lyle's face was lean and sharp, Jonathan's round, his eyes soulful.

Kasabian ran his thumb along the edge of the photographic copy paper. "Thanks."

"I should be thanking you."

"Don't thank me yet."

Kasabian left Lyle in the library, feeling the unease sympathy caused in his body. Caidos didn't feel pain at their own emotions, only a sense of discomfort. He let the tightness in the chest come as he gathered information from both the kids and the counselors. Nothing conclusive, just tidbits here and there that added up. It wasn't just the camp. One kid was thought to have drowned in a canal. No body was ever recovered. One kid wandered off and was never seen again.

Kasabian found Cory on the worn-out chair in front of his desk. "Lyle's not running drugs. He's trying to find his little brother. Give him space, okay?"

Kasabian saw Cory's reaction in a quick-fire burst: surprise, guilt, and then a nod. He didn't stick around to say more. Cory would have questions—so did he—but answers, well, he was painfully short on those.

You have the answers…

Buried in the recesses of his mind. He rubbed the scar. He would always be fucked up, and it wasn't only because of his abduction. But he could help these kids, get to the bottom of the abductions, and put a stop to them once and for all.

Good thing for him he knew a chick from a bar with just the kind of magick he needed to unleash the repressed memories in his mind. He'd vowed to stay away from her. But now he needed to get close. Very, very close.

Chapter 3

───

"You want me to do *what*?"

Kye stared across her table at Kasabian, where he'd sat after closing his bar. She was sure that the echo of the night's pounding music was distorting his words.

"It's not a want. I need to do the Cobra with you."

His words catapulted through her body. "Uh...no." She swallowed. "Remember what I said about it bonding."

No longer in the tight shirt encouraged by Mike for the purposes of being eye candy, Kasabian wore one of those urban shirts with angel wings on the back. He smelled like limes, clean and citrusy.

He took her hand and mirrored her earlier gesture of hands on top of each other. "So we take the Cobra to the second step"—he slid his fingers between hers—"but don't permanently take each other's essences." His touch, along with what he was proposing, shook her.

As much as she knew she should pull her hand free, she couldn't. "Just so you can lust without pain? No way."

But he didn't look like a man in search of physical pleasure. His expression was somber, his eyes intense. He turned her hand and traced a circle on her palm. "When I was eight, I was kidnapped and spent four years in captivity. I escaped, along with four other children. Three of them were Deuce or Dragon, and they were dreadfully weak. I heard they survived, but I never saw them again. There were two of us Caidos."

He unbuttoned his shirt and pulled it open to reveal what looked like a gray starburst tattoo at his solar plexus. "Whatever they did to the Caidos left these scars...and made us crave feelings. What they did to the other kids depleted their essences, leaving them in the same shape as someone who's left Miami for an extended period."

The god essence inside Crescents needed *Deus Vis*, literally the "god force," that radiated from the Bermuda Triangle. If Crescents were away for too long, their magick essence withered away, and so did they. "But I doubt we walked far, not with the kids in such bad shape. The problem is, we don't know anything because we think they memory-locked us. That's a Caido ability to lock away a period of time or event. So when you mentioned that the Caido's buried memories returned, you got my attention." He buttoned his shirt again.

Kye's hand continued to tingle from where he'd touched her. "You want me to help you remember."

This was not at all what she'd expected, not children in danger. She saw the pain of what he'd gone through and his fear for those kids. "I'm sorry that happened to you, but doing the Cobra just to revive those memories, well, I can't even guarantee it will work. And if we accidentally bond, I have no idea how to unbond."

"I dismissed approaching you for those reasons. But now there's more at stake. The Caido who escaped with me works for the Guard. Hayden told me a boy was found with the same mark." Kasabian tapped the starburst through his shirt. "He may have escaped from the same people who had us. Before Hayden could get the traumatized kid to talk, he was whisked away by someone connected to the Concilium. Whatever the people who took us all those years ago were doing...they're doing it again. There are secondhand stories about Crescent social workers taking kids to camps so the mothers can get back on track. No one ever hears from the kids again. Others have simply disappeared."

Kye shuddered. Who knew what horrors those children were exposed to? She looked at Kasabian, really studied him. For a moment, she was tempted to pry, to delve deep and glimpse the pain he'd endured.

He raked a hand through his hair. "Because of the Concilium's involvement, we don't know who to trust. We're on our own with precious little to go on. Remembering our captivity might help us figure out who's behind this. Will you do the Cobra with me? I've done the Essex enough to know how to control it. Once you set your magick in place, we touch, back off, and hope it's enough to trigger the return of my memories. I promise not to take in your essence."

She thought of the boy, of children in danger, and found herself saying, "All right."

"Tonight. Now."

Her fingers curled in the fabric of her skirt. "I always perform it at the Caido's residence so he'll be comfortable. The bombardment is pretty intense. I have to monitor that part. His girlfriend stays with him through the night in case anything happens. Is there someone who can stay with you?"

Kasabian shook his head. "I'll handle it."

Kye would have argued further, but she could see that he wouldn't be swayed. Or maybe he didn't have someone who could stay with him. "All right, let's go then."

She followed his yellow Lotus all the way to SoBe— South Beach. *Why am I doing this?* Her fingers tightened on the steering wheel as she pulled into the parking lot of an old Florida-style apartment complex. *Children. I'm doing this for children.*

Kasabian gestured to a parking spot, then pulled his Lotus into one farther down. Kye slid out of her jacket, folded it, and laid it in the trunk of her BMW coupe. The black-and-red patch with vampire fangs was on top, an ominous portent. She quickly shed her fishnets and black boots and changed into black and red flip-flops.

Kasabian rested his hand on her shoulder as he guided her through a gated entrance into a lush courtyard. The pool was lit, and a few people lounged around. They all greeted Kasabian and gave her a curious look. One couple was getting all kissy-face in the corner of the pool. The woman's nervousness glowed a pale yellow and made Kye's stomach churn a little as it reached for her. It was not dissimilar to her mother's gift of mediumship, as she described it, the way spirits sensed and migrated to a receptive soul. Kye closed the psychic door.

They took the stairs to the second level. Kasabian unlocked the door and gestured for her to precede him. He flicked a switch, and three corner torchieres threw soft light over the living area. Nice place, with polished wood floors and moss-green walls. Plants in dark wicker baskets accented the natural feel.

He waved toward a dry bar in the corner. "Want a Whis-Kye?"

"Maybe just a splash of whiskey straight up."

Her gaze went to a picture of a little boy held by an alligator magnet to his fridge. He had haunted brown eyes and a smile he was obviously forcing for the photographer's sake. She walked over to it. "Who's this?"

Kasabian stepped up behind her, his presence nearly overwhelming. "Jonathan. He's the younger brother of one of the kids at the youth home where I volunteer, and he went to one of these supposed camps. The mother said he was later adopted, but Lyle is suspicious. And hurting. He hasn't seen his kid brother in a year." He stared at the picture, anger and pain in eyes that were now more hazel than green. The shade of whiskey. "The need to find him is eating at my soul. Maybe it's because I imagine my mother looking at my picture the way Lyle looks at his."

"You volunteer at a youth home?" The thought gave her a whole different impression of this sexy bartender.

He handed her a glass of amber liquid, dark gold in the ambient light. "It's where I lived for a few years. I like to give back." He shrugged, downplaying it.

She took the glass, inhaling the smoky scent. He started making an absinthe, pouring water over a melting sugar cube into a glass of opaque green liquid. The menthol aroma filled her nose and made her eyes water.

She leaned against the black granite counter and watched him. "Every Caido who's done the Cobra had one of those first."

He lifted his glass up, and when she touched hers to it, he said, "Here's to liquid courage."

Kye felt no speck of courage as she threw back her splash and a half. *You have control over this.*

He finished his drink and came to stand in front of her. "Tell me what to do."

He was at her mercy. It gave her a weird sense of power she'd never felt before. "The Caidos dropped fast once the process was complete, so you want to be on carpet. The bombardment lasts anywhere from one to two hours and then you pretty much pass out for the night. The Caido who recovered his memories woke with them the next morning."

"Hopefully it won't be as bad for me. I haven't stuffed away my emotions as much. In fact, I crave them: joy, heartache, jealousy, anything. That's why I work in a club, so I can soak them all in."

"But don't they hurt you?"

"I have to do the Essex every night to manage the pain."

Now she understood that strange twist of emotions she'd picked up from him that first time. "So you're an Essex addict?"

"I'm an emotion addict. But I guess since I need the Essex to manage the emotions, that assessment would be apt. Working in a bar gives me an array of people who need healing, and who can ease my pain as well." He gave her a soft smile. "And you want to know why I crave emotions."

She started to say no, that it was none of her business. Might as well be honest. "Of course."

"I think it has something to do with what they were doing to me while I was being held captive. Hayden feels the same."

"So that's why you're forty ways fucked up." Finally, she had an answer.

His smile darkened. "Part of it."

Great. *Part* of an answer.

He led the way to the living room, where he moved the coffee table away from the thick, contemporary-style rug beneath.

"Get comfortable," she said.

He raised an eyebrow. "That usually means being naked."

The mental picture of him standing naked in front of her sent an odd tingling right down to the core of her belly. She blinked, pushing it away. "Stop that," she said to both him and her wild imagination.

"Just saying." He stripped out of his shirt, which made his pecs and biceps move in all kinds of interesting ways, and tossed it on the couch. His torso was golden tanned male perfection. He undid the top button of his jeans, kicked off his shoes, and stood in the middle of the rug. "You going to catch me when I fall?"

Her gaze, which had centered on the faint hairline that went down to those undone jeans, snapped to eyes with a smile in them. She almost said, *I could ask the same of you.* She blinked. *Whoa, where had that thought come from?*

"I'll try." With a hard swallow, Kye stepped up in front of him. "How does the Essex work on your end? Can you see the exchange?"

"No, I feel it. I pull in a little of the essence of the person I'm doing the Essex with and send mine into her." He demonstrated, weaving his long fingers through the air and making her think of an orchestra leader. His actions, along with his words, sent a shiver through her body.

She cleared her throat. "You'll send your essence out to me. Then I'll take over. Get into the same state that you're in right before you do the Essex."

He held out his hands. "We need to connect physically."

His hands slid against hers, his fingers locking around her wrists. Why did his touch always jolt her deep inside? He blinked, obviously feeling it, too.

"Close your eyes," she ordered, completely unnerved and unable to tear her gaze from his. When he complied, she studied him for a moment, the planes of his cheeks, the thickness of his lashes, a mouth made for sin. Frigging gorgeous. It seemed surreal, him standing in front of her like this, them about to do this.

She closed her eyes and summoned her magick. In her mind's eye, it manifested as a beautiful column of dark pink. Then she pulled her own deep yellow essence toward the column. "Send your essence to me." Cool, silvery smoke floated toward hers, and she directed it toward the column as well. "We're going to start with the Essex, our essences barely touching."

Even that mere brush took her breath away. She focused on the pink column, sending it to wrap around their essences. It required a part of her, that small extension of her essence, but nothing too intense. Here was that sought-after addictive state where a Caido could feel without pain.

But Kye was beginning to feel something, too.

Kasabian's essence was powerful, his magick strong and compelling and...sexy. It spiraled in languid, sensuous circles, and her essence began to wind around his of its own volition.

A slow smile spread across his handsome face. "Damn, I wish we were doing this for different reasons." His eyes opened for a moment, glowing brightly with such blatant hunger that it made parts of her ache. "This feels incredible with you."

Better than with anyone else? she wanted to ask. *No, don't ask.*

"Like a sensual dance," she heard herself saying. She was a Zensu Deuce, versed in sexual pathos and magick. She knew the chemistry between them was rare. But that was a path she could *not* tread. She caught herself physically leaning toward him and pulled back her body and her essence with a soft inhalation. "Which it shouldn't. Close your eyes and focus."

"Don't worry, love, I won't be forgetting that this isn't about sex. Or about us. It's about those kids."

"It's not as though we'd forget. Right? Get caught up in this and lose our minds." She shook her head, sending her hair washing across her shoulders. "Of course we wouldn't. Right now our essences are resting against each other, the way my fingers laid on top of each other. We're going to the next step now. Our essences are going to slide together like my fingers did, but remain straight like an X." She felt the sensuality of the two colors sliding against each other throughout her body. Lord, but she wanted to let them intertwine, the way her body wanted to intertwine with his. "We can't go to the final step. Let's stay here for a few seconds and see if that will trigger the bombardment."

Mmm, it felt good in a way that it shouldn't. Like lying naked in bed with an achingly beautiful man and not being able to touch him. Heat began to generate wherever their essences met, slowly filling her entire being.

"I think it's beginning," she said on a soft breath. "I

don't know exactly how it feels, since I haven't done it myself, but my subjects reported heat right before things started."

His fingers tightened on hers. "I feel it, too, heat and pressure building inside me. And..." His voice changed to a puzzled, concerned tone. "Something else."

Like a sudden storm, his essence darkened and whipped into a fury. Its tendrils grabbed on to her, wrapping her in a tight hold. She tried to pull back, but he surrounded her. In the same moment, it felt seductively powerful and suffocating. Heat exploded between them, and she lost all sense of where he ended and where she began. *No!* She struggled, both psychically and physically, to free herself. She stumbled back, landing bottom-first on the coffee table. She was free of him. Except...no, she wasn't. She felt him inside her.

He'd bonded them.

Her eyes flew open. He dropped to the floor, caught up in the bombardment. She wanted to demand that his essence release hers, but he was lost to her now. But she wasn't helpless. She slapped her hand on his chest and summoned her magick again. *Come on, come on.* The pink column formed in her mind's eye, but her yellow was twisted with dark silver and then it vanished. She groped for it, but she couldn't muster the power to pull it back.

He had broken his promise!

As much as she wanted to run, she couldn't leave him alone. She watched him arch in pain, fingers digging into the carpet. So many emotions roared through him that she couldn't single any one out. She sank down beside him, her hand on his shoulder for support even as she wanted to scratch his eyes out.

She had never seen that darkness in a Caido's essence before. It scared her, even more so because a mystifying want pulsed through her. Part of what made him very different and, no doubt, forty ways fucked up—the part he hadn't told her about—was now bonded with her.

Chapter 4

Kasabian paced, phone clutched in his hand. He almost called Kye fourteen times to tell her he was sorry for bonding with her. And that it had worked, holy hell, his memories had returned. He could barely wrap his head around all of it, which was why he hadn't dialed her number.

He vaguely recalled waking early that morning and finding her asleep on the couch. Then he'd plunged back into oblivion, and that's when the memories had played in his mind like a movie. He'd watched through the eyes of his younger self, stunned, disgusted, and shocked by the identity of his captor. When he woke, she was gone.

A sharp knock on his door startled him out of his dark thoughts. Had to be Hayden, whom he'd summoned immediately. Kasabian snatched open the door to find Kye.

Fury and hurt emanated from her, so clear and sharp that it was like the difference between regular television and HD. "We need to talk." She pushed her way past him, stalking into the living room and spinning around to face him.

She wore jean shorts and a tank top, her hair loosely bound in a clip that left tendrils snaking down the center of her back. The scent of soap wafted from her, some light, flowery fragrance. With no makeup other than eyeliner, she was a totally different Kye than he'd seen at the club. A version he liked even more.

Her gray eyes flared with anger. "Oh, no. You don't get to look at me like that. Because if you lied about those kids to trick me into—"

Kasabian had heard of fires that rushed in and destroyed everything in their path. That's how it felt now, desire—and the thrill of experiencing it without pain or the muffling effect of the Essex—roaring through him and drowning out her words.

He pulled her to him and covered her mouth with his. She was protesting and trying to push him away. He told himself she already hated him. Might as well seal the deal and experience a taste of heaven. He plunged his tongue in and gave hers something better to do than lash out at him.

Her outrage, then shock, pulsed through him. He would give in to feelings he usually kept a rein on until she pushed him away.

Which she should be doing, oh, about now.

Which she wasn't. Her hands had flattened against his chest but stopped.

Whoosh. Just like that, fire erupted between them. That cool, fully controlled woman vanished, leaving a hot, hungry vixen in her place. Her tongue met his, and her fingers curled against his chest, nails dragging on his skin. He pulled her heat into the cool places inside his soul. His hands drew down her back and over her tight, round ass, pressing her fully against him. He drowned in the ecstasy of sensations, his hard cock aching with the need to drive into her. So this is what it felt like for everyone else. Gods, he wanted this. Wanted her.

She rocked her pelvis against him, as though she couldn't get enough contact. *Don't do that, love. Push me away before this lust feeds the Shadow too much. Before I tear off your clothes and take you right here on the living room floor.*

The moment he touched the bare curve of her breasts, the Shadow would take over. He sensed it, knew it, even though it had never happened before. Because he'd never felt this way before. And he would be a double asshole, not only letting the Shadow fuck her over by bonding, but also literally fucking her.

"No," she said, shaking her head. "No, no, no." She gave him a hard shove and stumbled back, looking shell-shocked. "I came here to light into you! To demand an explanation. Not to…to…" She rubbed her fingers across her red and swollen mouth. "I thought Caido promises were ironclad. You promised not to bond with me. Then your essence turned black and grabbed mine! Did you lie so you could get me into bed?"

The floor would do just fine. Thank gods he hadn't spoken those unbidden words. He should let her believe he was a snake. She would call him names and stomp out, hating him forever. That would be good. But what he said was, "I didn't initiate the bond."

Her laugh sounded caustic. "You're telling me it was, what, your evil twin?"

"I suppose that's as good an explanation as any I have."

She gave him one of those nods that meant *I don't*

believe you. "And that was the evil twin that just very inappropriately kissed the daylights out of me?"

"I think that started with me, but the evil twin kicked in quickly after that." She seemed so angry, he had to throw in, "Was it *your* evil twin that had your tongue dancing with mine?"

She narrowed her eyes, even as he could feel her embarrassment. "No, I think it was some kind of Thrall trick. I am so pissed at you, but it was like I had no control over myself. Do you even realize what you've done? We are bonded." She jabbed her finger at him. "I could frigging feel your bombardment last night. And when I was in the shower a little while ago, I felt some mix of feelings I don't know how to describe. Damn it, I can feel you right now. You're…" She clamped her mouth shut and took a step back. "You're serious about the evil twin thing, aren't you? It scares you. And since I don't think much scares you, that scares *me*."

He leaned against the back side of the maroon chair. "That dark part of my essence you saw is something I call my Soul Shadow. It's hard to describe because I don't know what it is. I've had it in me for as long as I can remember. When I was a kid, I dreamed of this black creature inside me." He forced out words he'd never uttered to anyone. "It rears up when I'm enraged or aroused. But I am rarely either, so it's usually dormant."

She shivered. "Like a demon? I know they can possess people."

"It's not a separate entity, and I'm not possessed. It's as much a part of me as my angel is."

She rubbed her arms. "*That's* why you warned me to run away from you that first night we met."

"A pity you didn't heed my advice. And no, I'm not blaming you. I came to you, after all."

"For the children. Was that real?"

"I never lied to you. And it worked, Kye. Even though it got screwed up, it worked."

"Tell me."

He could see her being drawn in, the same as when he'd approached her about the Cobra. "The best thing for you to do is back away from me, from this. Find a way to terminate our bond."

"Like I can just reach into my bag of tricks and pull out that one. I've spent all my time working on developing the bond, not on ways to break it. You brought me into this. I deserve to know."

"Yes, you do, but—"

A knock sounded on the door. Hayden. Damn. Kye had to go. If only he could have lied to her, told her the story was a farce and that he was the worst kind of man. And part of him was the worst kind of something. But he was too honorable to let her believe he'd tricked her. Or to involve her in this.

He said, "If you never see me again, maybe the bond will weaken."

"You think it's that easy?" Her laugh was bitter as she shook her head. "You can't throw people's lives into chaos, make me care about something, and just move on. There are consequences. Aftershocks. You are a frigging earthquake, Kasabian."

He tamped down the way her turmoil rocked through him, how he hated that she'd gotten hurt. "You have to leave now, Kye."

More pounding on the door. "Hey, it's Hayden."

Kasabian opened it. "Come in." He put his hand to Kye's back and urged her toward the door. "My friend was just leaving."

Hayden could no doubt pick up Kye's seething emotions, enough that he winced.

Kye dug in her heels and faced Hayden. "I'm Kye, the one who's life got screwed up because of all this. I'm not leaving until I know what's going on." She planted her hands on her hips and shifted her gaze to Kasabian. Oh, yeah, he could feel her stubbornness.

Kasabian wrestled with the prospect of physically ousting her, but no, it would be wrong and ugly. He introduced them and told Hayden about the Cobra, omitting the Shadow aspect. Thankfully she also kept that to herself.

Hayden dragged his gaze from Kye to Kasabian. "Get to it. Tell me what you saw. I've waited long enough." The strain of all those years of wondering stretched his voice thin.

"It was my father who ran the program."

Hayden's eyes widened. "Your *father* did that to you? To us?"

Kasabian still couldn't quite grasp that. "My parents separated when I was four, and my mother kept him out of our lives. All I knew of my father was that his competitive nature drove him to do crazy and dangerous things. Like mortgaging the house to fund an expedition to find Lucifera. I can remember overhearing my mom calling him a glory whore. I thought she said 'horse.'"

Many fools had tried to find Lucifera, the legendary island in the Bermuda Triangle on which their ancestors, both human and god, had lived. Before the two gods and the angel that made up the Tryah instigated a war that ultimately sank the island hundreds of years earlier.

"So when I saw him outside my school, I was wary but not afraid. He told me what I wanted—needed—to hear, that he missed me and wanted to spend time with me. His devastation at losing touch with me had inspired him to take in homeless children. He assured me that my mother had given him permission to bring me for a visit.

"The secluded estate was beautiful, but something felt off. I met you and another Caido our age named Silva. The first night I spent there, I sneaked into the wing my father had forbade me to enter and found several non-Caido Crescent kids locked in rooms. They told me they'd been kidnapped. Then my father discovered me and that's when he explained that they were part of an important program to find a way to break the Caido curse. And now I would be, too."

"He was experimenting with kids just so you all could get off?" Kye's outrage sang through him. At Hayden's surprised expression, she explained how she knew about desire causing Caidos pain.

"It wasn't just about sexual desire," Kasabian said. "It was about freeing us from the effect of all emotions, so we could be a part of society. He made it sound altruistic and promised that no one would be harmed in the process. But that was a lie. It hurt the Caidos, who were channeling the kids' essence to some kind of vessel." He rubbed the place where the scar resided, now remembering the searing heat. "And it drained the non-Caidos. All the kids were too young to be Awakened to their powers. My father believed our untapped magick was purer, therefore stronger."

"Why were they filling a vessel?" Kye asked.

"I don't know the exact mechanism, but an angel told my father that filling this vessel would free them from their ties to this plane. And that would break our curse." Kasabian turned to Hayden. "The reason you and I crave emotions is because we were flooded by them during our captivity. We could feel everything without pain. But after our escape, we no longer had the protection of the Essex that we got every day. And we wanted to feel again."

Hayden gripped the back of the chair he was standing near. "What happened to the kids?"

"My father said he returned them to the parents he'd 'borrowed' them from when they started to weaken. We'd wake up and one or more would be gone. I regularly crept into their wing to check on them. One Deuce girl was fading fast. I gathered her in my arms and meant to beg my father to send her home."

Such a small girl, looking at him with hope in her glazed blue eyes. "She died in my arms. I couldn't help her, couldn't…" The grief and helplessness washed over him anew. He cleared his throat. "To test my father, I laid her back in her bed. The next day when I saw her empty room, I asked where she was. He told me she'd gone home to recover. I started making an escape plan right then."

Kye's eyes glittered with tears. Could she feel his pain at that memory? She swiped them away. *"He just let them die?"*

"He kept saying our suffering was a small price to pay for releasing the pain of a whole race of Crescents. Wasn't that, after all, what wars were about? Sacrificing our soldiers' lives to win freedom? He didn't want to hear my point that today's soldiers voluntarily sign up for the dangers when they're of legal adult age. He believed that what he was doing was justified."

He tore his gaze from her to Hayden. "You and I conspired to escape. I didn't trust Silva. He was sucking up to my father as well as to me. You were the only Caido I could trust. We took the three non-Caidos who were in the worst shape. I figured we'd expose my father's operation, and all of the children would be safe. But we never got back to them." They'd been left there, abandoned to a fate Kasabian could well imagine. A flicker of hope lit his heavy heart as a memory resurfaced. "A Dragon woman escaped. She was the oldest of the captives."

"The oldest..." Hayden tapped his mouth as he seemed to ponder that. "There was a story circulating around the Guard when I joined ten years ago. A woman who called herself Willow accused someone on the Concilium of imprisoning her, along with several children. She said she'd been there the longest. Her story couldn't be substantiated, though, so they locked her in the psych ward. Another member of the Concilium tried to break her out, and they were both killed."

Kasabian ran his hand back over his hair. "From what I understand, my father was on the Concilium once."

"The man who tried to help her was Kade Kavanaugh's father. Kade is a fellow Vega, which probably keeps the story alive. Probably every new Vega hears, 'See that guy. His father...' I'll take him aside at headquarters and find out what I can." Hayden's voice went softer. "So you remember your mother getting killed?"

Kye's head snapped toward Kasabian. "What?"

All these years he had only known the bare facts. Now he had the images to go with them. "I called her as soon as we could get to a pay phone. She arrived, saying that others were on their way to help. My father showed up, killed her, then turned to us. But he hesitated. We heard others coming, footsteps pounding the pavement, so he memory-locked us instead."

Kye put her hand to her heart. "I'm so sorry."

Could she feel his ache at his mother's loss, the guilt that he had caused it? And he had. "I'm going to find Trey-lon Grey."

"Have you tried Leaping to him?" Hayden asked.

Kye stepped closer. "Isn't that where you can pop in to some other place? So you just think of your father and you're there?"

"Only if we know the exact location or have an emotional connection to the person, which acts as a touch-stone," Kasabian explained. "I've already tried to find the bastard, but I keep hitting a barrier. That's an invisible force field we can erect to keep another Caido out."

"I asked Cecily at the Guard to check into missing Crescent children reports," Hayden said. "There were an extraordinary number of them in the last year. I could ask her to do a search on your father's name, but it will raise red flags."

Kasabian shook his head. "We don't want to do that. See if there are any other ways for her to search. In the meantime, I'm going to keep trying my father. If he put the barrier over his location, I can catch him when he leaves." He turned to Kye. "And when I do…this is why we have to sever this bond."

Her beautiful face was even more pale. "I'll try."

"Excuse us for a minute, Hayden." Kasabian led Kye to his bedroom for privacy, turning her to face him once they were closed inside. "Do it." The words were hard to push out, because a part of him craved this bond.

"Relax, like you did before. Let me take control." Her fingers wrapped around his, linking them. She closed her eyes and inhaled deeply, determination tightening the lush mouth that was recently plastered against his. His gaze drifted down her long, graceful neck, the curves of her breasts, and the hint of cleavage. His Shadow thrummed.

Her jaw flexed, and her eyebrows pulled down in a frown. Agony filled her eyes. "I can't summon my Zensu magick. Before, when I felt romantically drawn to a guy, I got static. Now I get nothing!" Her panic plowed into him as she drove her fingers into her hair and turned away. "What am I going to do? Without my abilities, I'm worthless."

"Why would you say that?"

She was going to cry. He felt it before even glimpsing the first glistening tear on her eyelashes. The sight of a woman or child crying wrecked him, but it was much worse because he'd caused her angst.

He pulled her close, keeping his hands on her shoulders. "I'm sorry, Kye. I take full responsibility. But in my defense, the Shadow has never done something against my will before. I wouldn't have taken a chance otherwise. But now that we're bonded, the Shadow is growing stronger, its whispers more fervent."

"What is it whispering?"

"It wants me to throw you onto that bed, tear off your clothes, and take you. It wants to devour you. The worst part is, I don't know how much is the Shadow and how much is me." He took in the swirl of mist in her eyes. "When I kissed you just now, you should have immediately shoved me away. You should be putting distance between us right now. But you're drawn to it, too. And that is the most dangerous aspect of all."

"I...I'll look through my notes and see if there's something that will give me a clue."

He forced himself to open the door. Kye darted down the hallway toward the living room. By the time he got there, she was already at the door. Smart girl.

"I'll let you know if I find something," she said, then gave Hayden a nod before leaving.

"Did it work?" Hayden asked when the door closed behind her.

"No."

"I wouldn't mind being bonded to her. I'd—whoa, dude. Your eyes went *black* for a second."

Rage had roared through Kasabian at the flippant comment. He had no right to feel possessive of her. He rubbed his eyes. "It's been a long night, an even longer morning." Had his eyes really gone black? Somehow his feelings for Kye had given this thing inside him more power. It scared him.

Hayden was keeping a bit more distance between them now. "I'll do some quiet checking, see if I can find where your father is these days."

"Very quiet. He's willing to kill children to attain his goal. That day we escaped, he struggled with whether to kill us. Maybe because I was his son. This time I guarantee he won't hestitate."

Chapter 5

———

Kasabian closed the blinds, stripped off his shirt, and bowed as he Invoked his angel essence. Caidos' wings were not made of feathers but an energy that resembled wings. That energy tore through his back like butcher knives, making him hiss with pain. Once the Transformation was complete, the Light pulsing inside him chased away the pain.

He straightened, focused on his father, and slammed up against the barrier again. Kasabian kept trying every few minutes throughout the day, exhausting himself with the effort. Finally he felt himself transport.

He arrived outside a residential entrance, the curved concrete walls bearing a discreet shell-shaped sign but no words. In those first few seconds after Leaping, he was invisible, long enough to pull in his wings in case anyone was standing nearby. But he left the shield and his wings in place as he surveyed the property in front of him. Down a long drive, he could see one of the old, Florida mansions. And coming up the drive was a black Mercedes. The gates began to open. Kasabian stood off to the side as the car drove out a few seconds later. He knew his father was inside, felt him, but he was more interested in the mansion at the moment. Kasabian slipped inside just before the gate clanged shut. Beyond the mansion, he spotted an assortment of smaller buildings. A salty breeze rustled the leaves, indicating that the ocean was nearby.

The air in front of him shimmered, and he felt the tightness in his gut as he neared the Caido barrier. He could see beyond but couldn't pass it. He felt along its edge as he followed it toward the back of the property. He saw no sign of any children, but last time his father hadn't allowed outdoor toys or play equipment.

Kasabian needed to get a feel for the scope of the operation. How many kids held captive? How many adults involved? He kept close to the tall, thick hedge that separated this property from the next. The windows were all blocked by blinds. He dropped his invisibility cloak, which was cumbersome to maintain, and crouched near a cluster of hibiscus bushes to wait.

Twenty minutes later, one of the back doors opened, and a man herded a boy of about ten to some vegetation, where he proceeded to vomit. Kasabian remembered when the channeling got too much for his body. He strained to throw himself through the barrier and strangle the adult. He had to suck in deep breaths to pull his Shadow back.

The adult gave the boy a small towel to wipe his mouth. The vomiting was only the beginning. Early in Kasabian's captivity, two Caido boys started getting sick. His father told him that, regrettably, he had to slow the pace at which the boys channeled the essence.

Kasabian watched as the man escorted the boy back to the house. The kid was gaunt, his movements listless. Like all of the children had been before they "went home."

He knew where "home" really was. Death.

There were only two ways to get through a barrier. Be invited in or go through with someone who was allowed. He made his way to the front of the property and waited for his father to return.

Silva watched the intruder slither among the landscaping toward the back of the property. He might have not seen him at all but for the fact that he was staring out between the narrow slits of the blinds daydreaming.

Who would dare come onto the property? And how had he gotten through the front gate? Not that he'd get past the barrier, but still, an intruder had to be dealt with.

Silva waved his hand, creating a cloak that rendered him invisible. This shouldn't have anything to do with the mess he'd inadvertently caused. Could the man be the Caido whose wings he recently Stripped? Silva flexed his hands at the sweet memory. He had powers not many did, and he was finding new ways to use them.

He slipped out the side door on the other side of the house. The intruder was hunkered down near some bushes, his face hidden by the pink flowers.

Silva passed through the barrier, stepping lightly on the grass as he neared his quarry. When the man stood, Silva nearly dropped the cloak in his shock at seeing him here. Kasabian. That he *was* here meant the memory lock had failed after all these years. But how? Had it just gone *poof*?

It also meant he was investigating what those memories meant. He was once again a threat to their operation. And that couldn't happen. Treylon had questioned the wisdom of letting him live after his escape, regretting his weakness. It was Silva who had convinced him that Kasabian posed no threat if he remembered nothing. Treylon would kill him on the spot now.

As much as Silva had wished Kasabian dead for abandoning him and nearly destroying Treylon's work, he did not actually want him dead. He wanted him broken and bleeding and under his control. He had dreamed of it for so long, Kasabian begging for mercy, then forgiveness, then for Silva's gentle caresses. In contrast to the pain, Kasabian would accept, even welcome, Silva's hands on his muscular, tanned body.

Kasabian was intently watching Beldeen taking one of the young Caidos out back to puke. Treylon was pushing them too hard now that the solar storm was approaching. Silva touched the starburst scar. It still burned from his last session. He was doing it voluntarily now, but he remembered how helpless he'd felt when Treylon had first brought him to his estate all those years ago. Kids couldn't comprehend what was at stake. Now he did, and he would give everything to see it through. Well, everything but his life.

Kasabian's jaw tightened, his mouth tight with his anger. He looked dangerously beautiful. Only inches away, Silva reached out, straining to touch him. He held back, unsure how to deal with this particular intruder.

Kasabian headed toward the front of the property. Was he leaving? If he told the Crescent authorities some crazy tale about a former Concilium member holding children, he would be ushered away. Like the boy who'd recently escaped. Or he would be made insane, like the woman who had escaped many years ago.

Kasabian ducked back into the hedges near the front of the property by the gate. No, he was waiting. He'd probably seen Treylon leave and was waiting for him to return. Silva wasn't ready to reveal his presence yet, but he couldn't let Kasabian ambush the man who was like a father to him. Could not let him destroy the program that would release all Caidos from their torment.

He returned to the house and summoned Gren. The tall, lean Caido met him in the foyer, a coy smile on his face. "You have need of me, my master?" He was twenty, pretty, and a new recruit in the program. "You look tense. Need some tension release?" He ran his tongue over his full lower lip. "A suck, a f—"

"A detainment," Silva interrupted. "A discreet one. We have an intruder lying in wait near the front gate. You'll have the element of surprise, but be careful. He's like me."

"You don't want him killed?"

"No. I want him incapacitated and put in the white room."

Gren's mouth curved into a smile. "Your will is my command."

That had been nice at first. Now Silva wanted more of a challenge. He wanted the one man he could not have. Kasabian.

Gren pulled on his invisible cloak, and they made their way along the hedge line.

Kasabian heard the footsteps coming up behind him. He spun but saw nothing. No, not true. The air wavered. The cloak dropped, and a male Caido in full wing dove at him. Kasabian shifted, but the Caido got him in the side and sent them both to the ground. Kasabian used his Light to knock the other Caido on his ass. In seconds, the Caido was on him again, slapping his hand on his forehead. Kasabian felt the stun Light flash against his skin and pulse into his brain. He twisted before it penetrated, wrenching the guy's wrist and making him scream in pain. But that didn't stop him from smacking his head against Kasabian's temple, knocking him senseless for a moment. The Caido shoved him backward, flat on the ground, then straddled him. His thighs tightened on Kasabian's sides to pin him.

Kasabian bucked him off, sending him rolling over his head. As soon as Kasabian got to his feet, he was tackled and pinned between the guy and a banyan tree. He shoved his knee into the guy's solar plexus, right below the starburst.

"They're using you," Kasabian said as he landed another blow. "I don't want to hurt you. Let me help you get away from this insanity."

The Caido laughed as he shot a beam of Light at Kasabian. "I'm here of my own volition. I don't want to be *rescued.*"

Kasabian felt the searing heat slice his neck even as he ducked to the side. "What do you get out of torturing children?" He threw the Caido, where he landed in a clump of bushes.

"I get to be part of something that matters. *I* matter."

The guy came at him again, his patrician features distorted in rage. The Shadow grew inside him, fueled by the fight. Hungry for it. Kasabian met the Caido halfway, tossing him over his head with a strength that surpassed even his angel essence. He saw black, just for a second, as he grabbed the guy before he could stagger to his feet. The Caido tried to kick free, but Kasabian deflected the blows as he threw him at a massive oak tree. The impact left a perfect impression of his body on the trunk. The guy crumpled to the ground, blood smearing the crushed lines of bark. He panted, his breath sawing in and out as he tried to get to his feet.

The desire to kill the son of a bitch roared through Kasabian like a flash fire. He wrapped his hand around the guy's throat. "How many kids are in there?"

The guy spit blood on his shoe. Then he thrust his hand out to shoot Light at Kasabian, who snagged the man's arm and wrenched until he heard the bone snap. The guy started to scream in pain, and Kasabian slapped his hand over his mouth to shut him up.

More, more, more. He wanted to crack, crush, pulverize every bone in his body. The bloodlust roared through Kasabian. The Shadow's bloodlust.

Even with his mouth broken and bleeding, the guy sneered with contempt. "I'm going to kill you," he said, holding out his good arm to use his Light weapon.

Kasabian grabbed that hand, crushing his bones. "Tell me how many or your neck is next."

Searing pain stabbed Kasabian all across his back. Little black bird-like creatures tore at his wings the way a disturbed nest of fire ants attacks an intruder. He swatted at them, and they tore at his fingers. They reminded him of *Mad* magazine's bird spies, with sharp-as-hell beaks and a desire to destroy. He staggered around to come face-to-face with another Caido.

No, not just any Caido. *Daniel*. Daniel, with a mix of emotions crossing his face. Regret. Anger. "I didn't want you to know I was here," he said, coming closer. "But I couldn't let you kill Gren. And now I can't let you leave."

Then Kasabian saw it, the similarities between the boy Silva and the man who'd become his friend. It hit him as hard as any physical blow. "And I can't let you continue to do what you're doing." Kasabian pushed past the shock and used his Light like a saber to fry the birds.

"It's only for another day or two, Kasabian. Then we will be free of the pain we live in. A few lives impacted, yes, but kids whose fates are to be used, abused, destined to end up overdosed on some street corner, or sliced and diced in a motel room. Can you put away your self-righteousness for just a minute and think about what it means for all of us?"

Kasabian swung at Silva. "Their fates are not sealed because of their circumstances. They're not worthless."

Silva met his blow, engaging in a Light sword fight. "No, they're very valuable. I was one of those kids. Your father gave me a purpose and treated me better than anyone else had. Yes, even with the pain. I know it's hard for you to imagine, because you never had to dig through garbage cans for dinner. You never had to suck some guy off so your mama could pay the rent. This was better than anything I'd lived until then."

Kasabian sorted through Silva's words as he fought, disgust turning his stomach. "It doesn't justify using kids like that. I don't care if he gets permission from their drugged-out parents; it's still kidnapping."

"If we had some time together, I'm sure I could persuade you to see that what we're doing is justified. Sometimes what you think is wrong is perfectly right." He threw out his hand, and something that looked like a black snake coiled from his palm.

Kasabian slashed as it careened toward him, but it dove right through and wrapped around him like a python. Even with his angel strength, he couldn't budge it. A glimmer of panic ignited in him. He gripped the odd energy of the thing, sending deadly Light into it. Nothing. "What the hell kind of power do you have?"

The snake wrenched him off balance, sending him crashing to the ground.

Silva approached, a cruel smile in place as he watched Kasabian fight to free himself. "That's for me to know and you to find out."

Black rage saturated Kasabian's mind. He felt the same sensation, heat passing through his eyes, as when Hayden told him his eyes had darkened. The Shadow. It moved closer to the surface and whispered seductively: *Use me.*

The shock of hearing it, the feeling that it was a separate, sentient entity, completely threw him.

Gren was staggering to his feet. "Kill the son of a bitch." His arms hung useless, but they were no doubt already healing. His crumpled wings were straightening.

"No. He goes to the white room."

"Why the hell would you do anything but kill him?" Gren asked.

"Shut up." Silva tilted his head as he considered Kasabian. "Get the room ready. And tell no one."

Gren's sneer appeared again. "This is the one, isn't he? The one you—"

"Go," Silva ground out, and the Caido stiffly walked toward the house.

Room. Prisoner. Words that shot panic into Kasabian. He would never be held against his will again. The Shadow thrummed through him. He feared that if he let it come, it would take over.

The snake squeezed tighter, making Kasabian's voice breathless when he said, "Why did you pose as my friend?"

"Your father asked me to check on you, make sure you were still blissfully ignorant of your days with him. Your memories have recently returned. How?"

Kasabian would never bring Kye into this. "I dropped some acid last night. It uprooted everything in my brain."

Acid was a no-no for any Crescent. Kasabian had never touched a drug in his life.

"I don't believe you. We've been friends for a long time, and not once have you ever said a thing that would lead me to believe you'd do drugs."

Why his deception should piss Kasabian off, with much more pressing matters at hand, he didn't know. "So you do my father's bidding."

"I follow his orders because he has given me a life. He has been like a father to me. Because I see the value of loyalty in a world where the people who should care will toss you away or sell you for a few dollars."

Silva and Treylon believed Kasabian had betrayed *them*. "And you think I should have allowed kids to die out of *loyalty*? You of all people should have fought for those kids. Instead, you aligned with my father!"

Silva shook his head, a soft laugh on his breath. "We always differed on our ideals, even as we are alike in other ways."

"Are you kidding me? We are *nothing* alike."

Silva threw out another net of those damned birds. They tore into Kasabian's wings and back, and he couldn't do a thing about it. His arms were pinned, body immobile. He bit back screams of pain because he wasn't going to give Silva the pleasure of hearing them. But Silva was getting pleasure all the same, given the smile on his face. In fact, he knelt close to Kasabian and watched. "What would you do to convince me to stop the pain? Beg? Suck me off? Maybe you'll understand me better if you're desperate to escape your circumstances."

"Fuck you," was all Kasabian could manage.

Hell, Silva's smile grew even bigger. When the birds were done, he released the snake with a snap. The snake and birds evaporated.

Kasabian arched in pain, the sensation of a thousand razor cuts on his back. Something wasn't right. He felt a gaping hole in his soul. "What did you do to me?"

"I Stripped away your angel essence." Silva flexed his hands. "I haven't used the ability much, though it did come in handy not long ago. You are a mere Mundane. Well, mostly." His blue eyes twinkled with some kind of secret glee.

That's what the hole was, the lack of his essence. No wings, no Light, and no ability to Leap. All he could do was sink his fingers into the grass as he tried to hold back the pain.

"We'll get reacquainted once you're settled in." The weird gleam in his eyes disappeared, and he glanced around. "I don't want your father to find you here. He is not going to take a chance of anything jeopardizing our plan. We've had trouble recently, so he's even more on guard."

Shouting made him turn toward the house, where Gren was waving him over. "Demis is checking in for a status report, and Treylon isn't here."

Demis? Kasabian searched his pain-gutted brain for the name but nothing came to him. Hell, he could barely move.

Silva stood. "Now he'll have to talk to *me*." He nodded toward Kasabian. "Take him to the room. He has no power, so you should be able to handle him now."

Silva stalked off, and Gren turned his bitter smile on Kasabian. "Aw, been Stripped, eh? That's too bad." He kicked Kasabian in the side. "Another bruise or two won't be noticeable." His boot came at him again, and Kasabian felt his ribs crack. A sharp pain rocketed through his side. He tried to summon his healing power. Nothing happened.

He managed to reach out as Gren readied for another kick and grabbed his ankle, jerking him off balance. Gren fell, arms wheeling, landing hard on his back. Sure, it would piss him off even more than the asshole already seemed to be, but Kasabian had nothing to lose at this point.

Gren scrambled to his feet, his face red with fury. The last thing Kasabian saw was a fist coming at him.

Chapter 6

———

Sarai gave Kye an agonized look from across the table at their favorite Italian restaurant. "So tell me, is it lust or love at first sight, o wise one? I need to know if I'm going off the deep end again with this guy or if it might, maybe, possibly be the real thing."

Kye didn't want to tell Sarai that she'd lost her Zensu abilities, so she bluffed. "You know I don't believe in love at first sight."

"Not love, per se, but the way your soul is drawn to another soul. That *wow* factor that's deeper than infatuation or lust. You've never experienced it yourself, but I know you've felt it in others."

Kye had felt it. Was feeling it. Being apart from Kasabian wasn't helping one damned bit.

"Come on, Kye, tell me if it's real. Don't let me make a big mistake."

Sarai could sense trouble for others, but not for herself. Sadly, this was true of many Deuces. Their personal stake in the matter muddled their clarity or, like Kye, their ability altogether.

Shoot. Kye didn't want to be pressed, but she'd been giving Sarai advice on her roller-coaster love life for years. "All right." She held out her hands, and Sarai clasped them over the table. Kye closed her eyes and picked up...nothing. Just like she'd picked up nothing with the clients she'd met with earlier that morning.

"I think it's infatuation," Kye said, and just to be safe, added, "But don't discount that it's not the real thing. Let it develop slowly and see where it goes."

When she opened her eyes, Sarai was scowling at her. "You are so full of shit."

"What?"

"I have *nada* interest in any guy right now. I was testing you, because I suspect that you have not taken my advice about Kasabian and gotten yourself into a snarl."

"Bitch." Kye flopped back into her chair, giving her the same kind of scowl. "I didn't *not* take your advice."

"You should have seen your eyes get all misty when I talked about the *wow*."

Kye picked up her fork and forced herself to draw lines in her spaghetti sauce instead of throwing it at Sarai. "It's not quite that simple."

"Please tell me you haven't fulfilled the sex forecast I got. Tell me you haven't gone there." Something good and hot and sexy, Sarai had said it would be. Then something bad.

"I am not having sex with Kasabian." But Kye wanted to. Every cell in her body wanted to.

"You sound like President Clinton, and we know what happened there."

Kye rolled her eyes, but she was trying really hard not to think about Kasabian's mouth on hers, his hands...

Sarai obviously took her silence as confirmation. "Kye, that's how the bad part starts!"

"You'll be happy to know that we are not romantically involved. In fact, we've agreed that it would be a bad idea."

"But? I sense a 'but' in there somewhere."

"We're bonded."

"Whaaaa?"

It felt good to share this with someone. "He and I did magick to help him retrieve lost memories, very important ones. We ended up being bonded, and, yes, I've lost my abilities. For now. I'm so angry I could tear his hair out."

The image that popped into her mind, though, had nothing to do with fury and everything to do with her hands gripping his hair as he thrust into her. Kye blinked the image away.

"Wouldn't it be best to stay away from him?" Sarai asked.

"Oh, believe me, I am staying completely away from that man." The memory of his big bed popped into her mind.

Sarai was shaking her head, a grim expression on her face. "You won't. You're going to get sucked in so deep, you won't know where you end and he begins." She reached out and grabbed Kye's hand. "And you're going to get ripped to shreds."

"Uh...literally?"

"No, your soul. Your heart." Sarai sank into her thoughts. "What I get are words, ideas about what's to come. And the feelings to go with them. All I know is that if you stay with him, you're going to suffer terribly. I'll keep working on getting more."

"And I'm going to work on breaking our bond. It's the last thing I need."

Sarai was studying her with narrowed eyes. "But there's a part of you that likes it."

"No way. It's unnerving. Annoying. Disturbing." Did it count as a lie if she was telling it to herself, too?

Twenty minutes later, when Kye was back in her office going through her patient files, she got the first hint of the pain to come. Real pain, along with a spear of panic. Kasabian. She got to her feet and grabbed her phone from the credenza. But she didn't have his number. If he were involved in some kind of altercation, he couldn't answer anyway.

Suddenly the breath left her lungs, and she stumbled to her knees. Gasping, she dialed the number all Crescents had on hand—the number for the Guard. She could barely ask for Hayden.

"I'm sorry, he's not here right now. May I leave him a message?"

"No. Emergency."

"We can send someone else—"

"Need Hayden," she managed to utter. "Please, get me in touch with him."

"Give me your name and number, ma'am, and I'll do my best."

She'd no sooner given the information when excruciating pain dropped her completely to the floor. Her legs were jelly, her back on fire. What the hell was happening to Kasabian? She wasn't sure where his fear stopped and hers began.

Her phone rang a minute later, and she could barely grasp it. She didn't recognize the number, assumed it was Hayden, and answered with a gasp.

"Kye? What's going on?"

"Kasabian... in trouble. Pain." She sucked in a deep breath. "Bad."

"I'll Leap to him and try to take him to his place. Can you meet us there?"

She clutched the chair to help her to her feet. "I'm on my way."

Hayden Invoked his angelic essence, enduring the pain of his wings tearing through his flesh. Since he and Kasabian had been friends since their abduction, he should be able to Leap to him without his express permission. It took a few minutes to get a lock on him. He felt his body transport and prepared for whatever would be at his destination.

Which turned out to be a gated entrance in a high-end neighborhood. The property had several buildings set way back from the road, hidden by vegetation. Hayden stayed to the side of the ornate gate, out of view of the camera and passersby. He assessed the borders of the property, figuring out the best way to get inside. The yard, with banyans and oaks, was surrounded by a fence camouflaged by hedges. In the distance, a man kicked something on the ground. Vicious kicks.

Hayden Leaped into the yard but bounced off a barrier. He felt along the edge of it, which went to the property line, sneaking closer to the Caido who was outside the barrier. What Hayden saw tightened his lungs. Lying on the ground was a bloodied Kasabian being pummeled by a Caido who had been on the receiving end of a similar beating, judging by the blood and torn clothing.

Hayden quickly assessed the situation. No other ene-
mies in sight. The attacking Caido was too preoccupied to
notice his presence. Yet. Hayden wasn't about to let him
have that chance before he got the upper hand.

He shot him with a Light beam that threw him several
yards away. Hayden Leaped to that location before the
guy could gain his footing. He was fast, though, rolling
with Hayden's punch and landing on his feet again. Hayden used his Light to slice across the Caido's chest, but it
only caused a flesh wound. The Caido sent a concussive
beam at Hayden, throwing him back. He landed hard on
the ground, twigs scratching his back. The Caido jumped,
ready to obliterate him.

Hayden took the brunt of the man's weight, but grabbed
hold of him and shot him with Light. The Caido kicked
as his body convulsed, breaking contact. He fell to the
ground, still convulsing.

Hayden jumped to his feet and ran to Kasabian's still
form. He was in bad shape, unconscious, a gash above his
eye, his mouth a wreck. And blood on the ground around
him. Hell. Why wasn't he in angel form? Hayden ducked
as a beam of Light shot toward him, searing the tree to his
right. He didn't have time to deal with this moron. He had
to get Kasabian out of here now. Hayden put his hand on
Kasabian's chest and Leaped them back to his apartment.

Chapter 7

Kye held herself back from pounding on Kasabian's door. No need to attract attention, but the desperation to see if he was all right screamed through her. The worst of the pain had subsided, but she knew something was terribly wrong. The door opened, and a tense-looking Hayden stepped aside so she could come in.

Kasabian lay on the floor, curled up on his side. The sight of him sank her stomach. She took inventory as she rushed to him. He was bruised, his lip torn and bloody, face swollen.

She looked into his eyes. They were open, but he stared at nothing. His body trembled. "Kasabian, talk to me." His nonresponsiveness scared her. She was afraid to touch him. "Kasabian, please. Say something."

"Children there," he said on a hoarse whisper. "Have to...go back."

Hayden knelt down beside him, and it was only then that she saw him. Really saw him. He was in full wing, the beautiful silver essence spread out majestically from his shoulder blades. She had never seen a Caido in wing before, and it should have mesmerized her. But her gaze returned to Kasabian, bloody and broken on the floor. And all he cared about, even now, were the children.

"Are you crazy? You can't go back," she said. "You have to heal."

Hayden's hand glowed as he waved it over Kasabian's face. The bruises and gashes miraculously healed, leaving only blood and dirt.

"I felt his pain here, too," she said, pointing to her ribs. "I felt...everything."

Hayden moved his hand over them, and Kasabian exhaled as the Light pulsed along his skin. "Three broken ribs."

"Oh, gods," she said. "What happened?"

Kasabian's breathing eased, and his fisted hands relaxed.

"A Caido was kicking the hell out of him," Hayden said. "Kasabian had put a hurting on the other Caido, but for some reason he wasn't angel. Which doesn't make sense, because you always go angel in a fight."

"Check his back." She started to turn him. "That's where I felt the worst pain." She sucked in a breath at the sight of his raw skin. It was as though someone had branded angel wings on his back.

Hayden waved his hand over the bloodied, broken skin, but it didn't heal. He tried again, and still, nothing. "I can't heal it. Kasabian, can you Invoke?"

Kasabian managed to shake his head. "Gone. Stripped."

"Your angel essence?" Hayden asked, disbelief in his voice.

Kasabian nodded.

"What does that mean?" Kye asked.

Hayden stared, shock and outrage in his eyes. "It's the Essex on steroids. The Caido sucks all of another Caido's essence in at once. I've heard rumors of Caidos with dark powers who can do that, but I've never encountered one. Who did this to you?"

Kasabian managed to sit up, and his gaze locked onto her. His eyes were no longer empty, but they were filled with a soul pain. He turned to Hayden. "The other Caido who was in captivity with us, the one who sucked up to my father. Silva."

"Is that who was beating the crap out of you?" Hayden asked.

"No." Kasabian got to his feet, using a chair even though Kye held out her hands. He braced himself on the back of it. "Silva is Daniel. He's been posing as my friend at Harbor, keeping an eye on me. For my father." Kye could feel his sense of betrayal.

"Son of a bitch," Hayden said. "And he's one of these dark Caidos?"

"He could use his Light in ways I've never seen. Snakes. Birds." Just when Kye thought Kasabian had suffered some mental damage, he elaborated. "He created a coil of energy that bound me like a damned python. Then he threw a net of bird-like things that attacked my back." He tried to turn and look but swayed slightly and gripped the chair again. "After that, I could feel the absence of my essence."

"There has to be a way to get it back," Kye said.

"I don't know enough about being Stripped to know how to undo it," Hayden said. "But from what I've heard, it sounds like Silva is a Wraithlord."

"Wraithlord," Kasabian repeated slowly, as though he were trying out the word. "Why haven't I heard of them?"

"Because they're a mystery. They stay hidden even in the Hidden, and, fortunately, there don't seem to be many of them. They're some kind of Caido aberration. No one knows exactly what they are or how they came to be. They were dubbed Wraithlords because they can control wraiths."

"Ghosts, you mean?" Kye asked.

Kasabian turned to her with a grim expression. "Ghosts in a way, but they're vicious. And they have fangs. It's what Caidos become if they die and aren't interred properly."

Hayden rolled up his sleeve, revealing a V tattoo on his arm. "What I do know is that Wraithlords can use their Light in crazy-ass ways. I've heard stories about it becoming anything from a spear to a monster. I've never fought one, but I heard a retired Vega talk about encountering one. He barely escaped, but his partner did not. There was a brief mention in our class manual of a Vega being Stripped by a Wraithlord."

"What happened to the Vega?" Kasabian asked.

Hayden glanced away as he rolled up his other sleeve. "Every situation is different."

"He died, didn't he?" Kasabian's voice was low. "Because we can't survive for long without our essence."

Kye's heart tightened into a hard ball. "There has to be a way."

"Exactly," Hayden said. "We can't make assumptions."

Kasabian didn't look at all hopeful. "I will get weaker and weaker until I fade completely. And without my essence, I can't Leap to my father. And you don't have a connection with him to use as a touchstone. I didn't see enough of the neighborhood to recognize it. Did you?"

"I was too busy looking for you to notice any landmarks or street signs." Hayden pulled his phone from the holster at his hip and read the screen. "I've been summoned to headquarters. Kye, can you stay?"

"I just want to take a shower, and crash for a few hours," Kasabian said. "Alone."

Kye felt rooted to the spot, watching him. Hayden mouthed, *Stay*. She knew she should leave, but human decency dictated that she not leave a man in pain alone. She nodded.

Kasabian gripped Hayden's shoulder, his eyes wide. "As Daniel, Silva is involved with the Harbor. He has access to the kids."

"I'll swing by on the way to headquarters and let them know to ban Daniel from the premises."

"He's been hanging around me, biding his time for...what? Preying on the kids?" Kasabian's face went red at his words.

Hayden said, "Harbor keeps a constant guard over the children in their custody. I can't think of one who's gone missing. If they return to their homes, or go to a new one, Harbor's involved in the process from beginning to follow-up visits for a year afterward."

Relief calmed Kasabian's visible rage. "Yeah, you're right. Okay, go now, warn them."

Hayden closed the door, and she locked it. Not that it mattered. Caidos could friggin' Leap.

Kasabian stared at nothing. "I can't even wrap my head around it. Someone I trusted, thought was my friend, has been spying on me. Working with the man I consider my worst enemy." Kasabian looked shell-shocked. Distraught. She had no idea how to comfort him.

She came close, afraid to touch him like she wanted to. "You've gone through a lot. You should rest."

"I need a shower. You should go. I'm not the best of company right now." He headed toward the hallway with careful steps.

She checked the shadows in the corners of his living room, then the kitchen. The sound of the shower propelled her toward the hallway. He shouldn't be alone in there, not as off balance as he seemed.

"Kasabian," she called out softly, warning him she was coming.

She followed the hum of water to his bedroom, a tropical oasis of palms, the moss-green walls and dark mahogany furniture he seemed to prefer. It felt strangely intimate being in here. Unlike the first time when she'd been so focused on breaking their bond.

The bathroom door was partially open, and steam wafted out. She walked to the side of the opening and tried not to look inside. But her gaze went right to the reflection of his back in the mirror.

She wished the sight of his back was the reason for her sudden intake of breath, but her eyes followed the lines of his hips, his ass, and the muscles of his thighs. He bore no tan lines, just the same tone of golden skin all the way down his muscled legs.

A rush of both desire and compassion overtook her, and she turned her face toward the wall. "Kasabian," she pushed out. "Are you all right?"

"You really need to leave."

"You shouldn't take a shower alone. You're off balance."

"And that's why you should go."

She squeezed her eyes shut. Yes, she should go. Just as he'd warned from the beginning. "I can't leave you alone like this. Since Hayden couldn't stay, I am. Just..." She swallowed hard. "Just to make sure you're okay."

"I don't think that's a good idea right now, Kye."

She curled her fingers against the wall, her nails grazing the paint. "I know." Her heart was thrumming like a rabbit that had just darted across the road in front of a car. She knew it was from being alone with him. Did she like it...or fear it? Maybe a little of both. "I'm staying until you're done and settled in bed. Then I'll go."

She heard him step into the shower, the way the sound changed as the water hit his body. And she now could visualize that body very well, thank you. Of course, she knew he'd be gorgeous, perfection, other than his back. How was he going to wash those wounds? They needed to be cleaned and treated.

No, don't do it.

"Where do you keep your first aid supplies?" she called. "Kye, you don't have to—"

"Just tell me. I know I shouldn't, that I don't have to. The only way I'm going to get any peace is if you are not in pain. So consider it selfish. Where are your damned supplies?"

"In the hall bathroom."

She made quick work of finding disinfectant and antibiotic cream, returning to Kasabian's room. She caught a glimpse of him inside the glass enclosure, his hands braced on the stone wall and water sluicing down his back.

She made herself move away and waited. The shower cut off a few minutes later, and she heard the door open. Then the sound of him drying off. A few minutes later, he stepped out into the hallway, a towel wrapped around his waist. His eyes looked more green than hazel. "So you staying with me is about you then?"

"Yes. Go lie down. I'll treat you and leave."

His pain was evident as he stiffly laid down and spread his arms to the sides. The towel molded to the curve of his ass, and she thought how terrible she was to notice that when he was in such bad shape.

"Did you find a way to break our bond?" he asked, his voice muffled by the mattress.

She laid out the supplies on the bed and gingerly sat next to him. The mattress sank invitingly. "I have a call in to the medium who allows me to talk to my Babs. She might have an answer."

"Your Babs?"

"My grandmother, Ekaterina. My mother's family is from Russia, so she is—was—my babushka. She's the one I inherited my abilities from, much to my parents' chagrin. She was a master of fertility but could also diagnose a sex problem at thirty yards. She called herself a sex witch, which I could tell made my mother bristle. Babs did it on purpose. I loved her spunk and wish I had it where my parents are concerned. She died before I learned I had her ability. My mother is a medium, so in theory I could talk to Babs through her. But I don't want to get into our situation with my mother." It was times like this when she needed her Babs. "In fact, I never talk to Babs through her."

"It sucks to be alone in the world, doesn't it? Even when you've got people around."

Not only was he picking up her isolation, but he also felt the same. "Hayden doesn't know about your Shadow, does he?"

"No one but you knows."

Great. Something else that bonded them. Kye opened the disinfectant, then decided not to put him through that pain. "I'm going to put on the cream." She shuddered at the thought of touching that raw skin on his back. *Please don't let me hurt him much.* "Did the Shadow leave with your angel?"

"No." He dropped that word as though it were a heavy weight.

She put a thick layer of cream on her fingers and very gently left a trail of it across those terrible lines. His hands tensed, gripping the wrinkled sheets. "I'm sorry. I'm trying to be as gentle as possible."

"I live with pain all the time," he said. "So don't sweat it."

"And there's a part of you that likes it." She sat back, capping the tube.

He came up on his hands and knees, facing her. "The Shadow part of me likes pain but it craves sex." Like a cat, he prowled closer, until his face was only inches from hers. In his eyes, the Shadow flashed, dark and seductive. "Bloodshed." He moved even closer, forcing her to lean back. "And you, Kye. It craves you."

Her heart pulsed at his nearness, his words. "Is the Shadow in me, too? Because of the bond? Ever since we did the Cobra, I feel...different."

"Hungry? Horny? Afraid? Afraid is good. You should be pushing me away, heading to the door. But you're not."

She knew she should be, but the Shadow in his eyes held her. "No. I'm not."

His mouth came down over hers, crushing hers. She lost her balance and fell back on the bed, and he followed. He plunged his tongue inside, sucking at her. The power of him enveloped her. He captured her—mouth, body, and soul. Because even as her logical brain screamed in warning, her mouth melted beneath his, and her tongue sparred with his.

She clutched at his biceps, kneading the hard muscles that held him hovering over her. Her heart hammered in her chest. He drew one hand down the side of her neck, her collarbone, and over her breast. She arched into his touch, needing his hand to squeeze her. Oh, gods, what was happening to her? She'd never wanted like this before. No, *craved*, his word.

His thumb moved across the silky material of her blouse and circled her hardened nipple. A needy sound escaped her mouth, right into his. She slid her hands up over his shoulders. Her fingers drove into his damp, thick hair.

He moved to her other breast as though he knew it ached for the same kind of touch. Maybe he did. Because he knew her, felt her. He made love to her mouth, brutal and devouring, waking something primal in her. The hunger she'd repressed, the same way Caidos repressed their emotions. Kasabian triggered her own bombardment, except it was all sexual.

He pulled her shirt out of her waistband and slid his hand beneath it, across the heated skin of her stomach. When his hand moved under her bra and touched her skin, she shuddered. His fingers directly touching her nipple, pinching it gently, driving heat down the center of her core. She was having trouble pulling in a breath. A thought. Anything.

"Not . . . the Thrall," she managed.

"What?"

"This, what's happening to me. Not some angel hypnosis."

"I'm no angel." He took her mouth again, claiming her, then finishing the kiss and sucking on her lower lip. "Love, it's dangerous, you being here in my bed," he said between kisses. "Letting me touch you like this."

"I know," she whispered. "I can't seem to make myself leave."

"The more I touch you, the more I want." His hand now rested on her stomach. "I've always felt the Shadow was dangerous, but since the Cobra, it's growing stronger. It spoke to me when I was fighting the Caido. The first time I've ever heard it speak."

Their mouths were so close, if either of them moved forward, they'd be kissing again. She could sense him holding back, reining in a powerful urge.

She moved back an inch, and gods, his eyes were like black ice. "What did it say?"

"'Use me.' It wanted me to release it. I didn't, and I got my ass handed to me. I'm going to release it. Because it's all I have now."

"No, Kasabian. Don't do it."

"And when I release it, you cannot be anywhere near me. Because it wants you."

That statement coiled through her, scary and seductive at once. "Why? Why me?"

"Because I want you. The desire I thought I'd stuffed deep inside me came awake when we met. And so did this thing inside me."

"There were tons of beautiful women at the bar, all drooling over you. They were easy."

"I didn't want anyone." He moved his hand in small circles across her stomach, his fingers leaving dizzying trails of their own. "Their desire was pleasantly painful, yes, like a dull ache. You made me feel different. From that first time I saw you, I've been obsessed with you."

"I became obsessed with you, too, that night. Despite your warning. Maybe because of it."

"You're a beautiful and sensual creature, and your guarded smile made me want to get past your walls. Just doing this"—he trailed his hand lower, his thumb slipping beneath the waistband of her pants—"starts an inferno inside me." He brushed his cheek against hers, the slight rasp of his stubble rubbing her skin. His mouth moved against her ear. "And if I fuck you, I'll feel like I own you. And trust me, you don't want me to feel that way. Now that my angel is gone, I'm all Shadow."

Maybe he thought the raw word would repulse her. And it should. Instead it rocked through her. "You say it as though I don't have a choice."

He slid his hand all the way into her panties, palming her mound. Her breath caught as his finger slid into her folds and brushed her clit. "*Do* you have a choice, love?" His finger moved farther down, sliding over her opening. "You're wet for me."

All the control she'd held so carefully fell away at his touch, along with that endearment. He stroked her, sending shock waves to her core. *Yes*, that controlled part of her shouted, while her body melted against him. Control. It meant everything to her, the ability to shut off her feelings, to protect her ability. And herself. It took every ounce of strength to push him away. She stumbled on weak legs toward the door. How could she become so compliant, so lustful?

His chuckle was low and soft, even as his eyes shone black. "Don't be so hard on yourself. It's the Shadow. The faster you break this bond, the sooner you get your life, your control, and your magick back. And the safer you'll be. Go, Kye. And don't let me touch you again."

Chapter 8

Silva stood beside the man he considered his father—even if he never spoke the word—as the Caidos arrived for an impromptu meeting in the courtyard. Like a king and his son, the two of them hovered above the gathering men from the balcony of Treylon's suite. Except a real prince would know what the meeting was about.

Treylon turned to Silva, his voice low. "Hayden Masters, one of the Caido boys who escaped with Kasabian, has been investigating missing children. The boy who escaped stirred his interest; probably Hayden discovered they have the same mark. For now he's been circumvented, but he'll need watching. I don't like trouble when we're this close to our goal. Demis says the others are having trouble as well, but damn it, I don't want to be part of the problem. I want to be the solution."

Treylon didn't just want it, as far as Silva could tell. He ached to be the one to release the curse and prove that he was a valuable member of Caido society. Ironically, he didn't consider that the people in his life might feel the same need to feel valued.

Demis, the fallen angel from whom Treylon had descended, would not deign to talk to Silva, even when Treylon hadn't been there. Another conversation Silva had been left out of. He, with his sketchy background, had no idea which angel was his forebear. But they were all bastard children when it came down to it.

Demis was one-third of the unlikely alliance that was the Tryah—angel, Deuce god, and Dragon god. Treylon didn't like when Silva reminded him that the Tryah had tried to obliterate Crescents by inciting a war on the island more than three hundred years ago. Recently, they had hatched a scheme to free the tethered gods, enlisting the help of the very Crescents they had once been willing to kill. Demis was sure that if the angels were released, the Caidos' curse would end. But his promise to those who helped was greater and more definite: to bestow both immortality and power beyond anything they'd ever conceived.

If the gods could be trusted.

Silva had found no one in life who could be trusted completely. But he wasn't doing this for the power, since he had plenty of that. What he ached for was acceptance and respect. He wanted Treylon to see him as an equal, a valuable asset.

Treylon gave him a dark look. "Don't do anything else to botch this up."

Sure, remind him again of how he'd nearly ruined everything a few weeks ago, all to procure a newborn. "You're the one who's getting desperate, pushing everyone. I took a chance, and it backfired. But it turned out all right in the end. Only my name was implicated, and since I do not legally exist, no one can find me. Or trace me to you." Silva raised his arms to encompass everything in front of him. "And we are here, in this beautiful place."

"Our benefactor had to relocate guests to accommodate us. My connection in the Concilium had to do a quick cover-up. I don't like needing help."

"But you do need help, from me." Silva gestured to the Caidos below who had put their lives on hold to assist him. "And them."

Treylon's mouth tightened. "I mean from my peers."

Ah, the Caidos here worked *for* him, not *with* him. Even Silva, who had been with him the longest. It would have to be enough to know that the old man needed him, even if he never voiced it. Or thanked him. But it was hard not to resent being given little credit for his loyalty.

Treylon headed downstairs to the courtyard, where twenty Caidos now formed a line military-style. Most of these men, in their late teens and early twenties, had been culled from the streets as Silva had so long ago. Treylon made sure they all felt as though they owed him a debt of gratitude. Servitude. Each bore the mark on their chest as a result.

Silva traded a look with Gren, who was clearly curious about the impromptu meeting. He'd been curious about Kasabian, too, jealous that Silva wanted to keep the man whose name he'd called out once in the heat of ecstasy.

Treylon clasped his hands behind him. "A boy escaped yesterday and ended up at the Guard. Fortunately, one of our people alerted me and our contact made sure that he was extracted before he could tell them anything. He is now recuperating and will return to us before our deadline, to assist us in our task."

Treylon's cold eyes assessed the group. "Someone here allowed that boy to escape." Though his voice appeared calm, a deadliness edged his words. "Someone jeopardized the entire program. I want that person to speak up now. I will show you mercy if you confess."

The men glanced at one another, shifting nervously. No one spoke.

Treylon walked from man to man, spending several seconds staring into each of their eyes. He paused in front of Beldeen. "I know it was you."

Beldeen's face blanched. "No, sir, I—"

"You flinched when I first mentioned it. And now your expression gives you away. Tell me why you released the boy."

Beldeen swallowed hard. "He was so ill. I memory-locked him so he could not tell anyone where he'd come from. I couldn't bear his suffering anymore, and you would not let up. I'm sorry."

Treylon released a long breath. "You gave in to your nature. It is understandable. But not forgivable." He slapped his hand over Beldeen's face. The Light that came from his palm melted his face. There was only one scream, terribly short, and then blood and flesh dripped down the man's shoulders and chest. He collapsed.

"You said you would show him mercy," one of the others stammered, stumbling away from the body.

"That *was* mercy. He did not suffer much, now, did he?" He surveyed the rest of the group. "Does anyone have any other concerns?"

Silva saw Gren's eyes shift away, and in that moment,

he knew that he would tell Treylon about Kasabian's visit so that he could move to a higher position in the group. They had shared their bodies, but not a real bond. They only used each other. Gren's mouth parted, and his hand began to rise.

Silva sent a black whip at him. It wrapped around Gren's neck, strangling the words he wanted to utter. Gren clutched at the whip, his face nearly purple.

Treylon turned to Silva, still calm. "The reason for this?"

"He's a traitor," Silva said. He jerked Gren to his knees. "I saw him sneaking around the grounds earlier. I knew he was up to something. I believe he may have been working with Beldeen. They're lovers, you know."

Gren shook his head, but the only sounds he could make were grunts.

"I want to hear what he has to say," Treylon said, stepping closer to Gren. "Release him."

Silva snapped the whip, and Gren's head fell from the stump of his neck. His body followed, pouring blood onto the pristine white stones. "He was trying to send his Light into me. I had to end him."

The other Caidos had moved away from Gren, but their horrified gazes remained on the body. They would take the warning well.

"Clean this up," Treylon ordered no one in particular. "Take them to the interment room." He spun and stalked away.

They would not be interred properly, however. A dead Caido had to be sealed away in a holy crypt within twenty-four hours of death or he would turn into a wraith. Wraiths came in handy when one could control them. Silva smiled briefly, but anxiety quickly returned. He followed Treylon. Did he suspect something? Why had he wanted to hear Gren's last words?

"They were necessary kills," Silva said, coming up beside him.

"Now we are shorthanded. The solar storm erupts today. That means we have two days before the waves reach us. If we aren't prepared, we will fail." He paused just inside the doorway of the building. "We have worked a long time to make this happen. It will be a longer time before another storm of this magnitude hits. How are you doing on the new recruits?"

"I have a call in to Gemini."

Treylon grunted. "You deal with him. I've implemented the other part of the plan."

"The one I told you about?" Yes, damn it, he wanted credit.

Without warning, Treylon's hand was around Silva's throat, his thumb pulsing over his carotid artery. "Never use your power in front of the others without my permission again. You may have dark power, but I have old power. Do not make me use it."

Humiliation washed over Silva, followed by rage. It rose within him, eager to annihilate the old man.

My father. Can't kill my father.

Silva nodded his acquiescence even as he hated himself for it. Treylon released him and walked away, so unafraid of Silva's power that he left his back unprotected. Better to consider it trust rather than arrogance.

He flexed his hand, watching the black talons stretch from his fingertips. Killing Gren had fed the monster within. Unfortunately, it wasn't sated. Instead, it was as hungry as ever. He fed it images of Kasabian, bound and helpless.

Just wait. You'll have what you want soon.

Treylon stepped into the lobby of the alternative healing building where Kye Rivers had her counseling office. The building also housed massage therapists, intuitive readers, and other types of Deuce healers. But probably no one who could help him the way Kye could.

He approached the young lady at the reception desk. "I have an appointment with Kye Rivers."

"Oh, didn't you get the message? I'm so sorry. I tried to catch all of her appointments. She's having...technical difficulties and is not taking any appointments for the next couple of days. I'm happy to reschedule." She started clicking keys at the computer.

He had gotten the message. He'd just chosen to ignore it. "I really need to talk to her. Desperately," he added, holding her gaze. "And perhaps I can help her as well."

The woman hesitated, but she was caught up in the Thrall and merely nodded. "I'll ask her." She disappeared down the hallway, returning a few minutes later. "She'll be right out."

He wandered the lobby, pretending to look at the pictures of waterfalls and sunrises. Silva had relayed Kasabian's revelation about this woman's ability to inure Caidos to the pain of their lovers' emotions. Treylon found the idea interesting indeed. Thus protected, Caidos could channel even more essence without burning out. He was under so much pressure to fill the vessel, ensuring that it would be ready in time. The effort was particularly hard on the children, but even the adults were showing signs of fatigue. And at the critical time when the solar storm hit, he needed all of his Caidos in fully functioning mode if they hoped to free the angels.

Kye Rivers's supposed technical difficulties worried him.

A tall blonde with a tennis player's physique came down the hallway. For a sensual Deuce, she was dressed modestly in blue pants and a beige pleated top. She held out her hand, then let it drift down when she saw he was Caido. "Hello, I'm Kye." So she knew that Caidos didn't touch others. Did she know why? She must, to have developed such magick.

"I'm Carl Wallen. Thank you for seeing me."

"As the receptionist told you, I'm afraid my magick is on the fritz right now." This concerned her greatly. He could both feel and see it on her beautiful face. "But we can certainly talk."

Once they were settled in her office, he got right to the point. "I understand that you've developed a magick called the Cobra. I am very interested."

Her expression fell. "I have, but it's not available to the general Caido public yet. It's not even supposed to be *known* to the general public."

"M'dear, you don't think something like this will stay quiet for long, do you?"

She frowned. "I suppose not. I'm just not ready to start fielding requests yet. I want to keep it on the down low until I see some consistency with the side effects in my trials."

"Don't worry, Kasabian told me in confidence. I will keep it as such."

"Kasabian?" She nearly spit the name out. "You know him, then?"

"For a long time. How well do you know him?"

According to Silva, Kasabian had a crush on her but didn't intend to act on it.

She shrugged. "Not that well, actually."

"Please don't be upset with him for telling me. In fact, I'd rather you not say anything at all. He only said something because he's aware of my situation. Tell me about the mechanism of your magick. How does the Cobra work?"

Her mouth pursed as though weighing her words, deciding whether to trust him or not. She'd reacted to Kasabian's name, but would that influence her to help or to evict him from her office? He contemplated abducting her. Oh yes, he had ways of making a Crescent talk...

After several seconds, she heaved a deep breath. "The process is a continuation of the Essex. I'm a Zensu Deuce, and it allows me to harness certain...energies...better than other Deuces, whose powers are better suited to different spells. My magick acts as a conduit that allows a Caido and non-Caido to make the Essex permanent."

"So the Caido's essence is balanced all the time, and his lover's emotions do not harm him?" When she nodded, he said, "Interesting. You mentioned side effects."

"All the emotions the Caido has ever repressed are released, which totally overwhelmed one Caido. And the two lovers are bonded." Something about that aspect bothered her. "And it has, in two instances, unearthed lost memories. I have performed it only five times." She briskly rubbed her arms. "But as I said, I can't do anything right now."

"And that upsets you greatly." He softened his voice and

tilted his head. "I pick up a lot of turmoil. And heartache. Is that what's causing your impairment?"

She hesitated for another long moment, then nodded. "It's always been a problem."

"Perhaps I can help. Did you know that Caidos can heal emotional trauma?"

Her eyes widened. "That's right. You can take away heartache."

He felt a rush of hope from her. "Tell me about this person who has broken your heart."

She paused again, obviously not comfortable sharing personal information. "He's a...Deuce. A player who broke his promises." She wasn't going to elaborate by the way she turned away from him. "A mistake. Is your healing permanent? Will I just...forget about him? Not feel anything for him?"

Ah, he'd found the right enticement. "It will, though having any kind of interaction can reignite all those feelings. Perhaps if I heal your heartache, your abilities will return. And you can help me."

"I'm not sure healing my heartache will help in my particular situation." She rubbed at her collarbone for a moment. "You want me to perform the Cobra for you and your lover?"

"Yes, but for an unconventional reason." One that would be more likely to endear her to his request. "My Deuce lover is dying of cancer."

"Cancer? That's unusual for a Crescent."

"I'm afraid she's done the Essex with me too many times over the years, and it's sapped her magick. And made her prey to human frailty. I wish for us to be bonded so I can take some of her pain. I cannot heal her with my magick, and I'm afraid she doesn't have much time left. Maybe if my essence is permanently inside her, it will cure her. I'm sure that's untested, but you are my only hope."

He didn't need his Thrall to lure her; his expression of pain touched the compassion he sensed inside her, along with her need to help others.

"But I don't know what will happen if one half of the bonded couple dies," she said. "Fortunately, none of my test couples have dealt with that."

"I can live with whatever that is, if I can just ease her suffering. And report back to you as well, so you'll have the data going forward."

She chewed her bottom lip as she considered it. Finally she nodded. "I'll give it a try."

Chapter 9

⁓

Kasabian slammed his hands against the wall, fingers digging against the stucco, as the Shadow filled the empty space his angel had left. He let it come, because he needed it.

Whatever his father and Silva were doing was going to happen in a few days. He remembered how driven the man had been, how passionate about his goals. He'd stolen his own son to be part of it, trying to sell it as some great opportunity.

"We can be the ones who free Caidos," he'd said in the voice of a revival preacher. "We will be the ones to change the lives of all of our kind. Small sacrifices amount to huge achievement. Yes, it's hard on the children." He had placed his hand on Kasabian's cheek. "And on you. But you are a strong and noble boy, and soon you will see the payoff."

His father had obviously either given up or been stopped, since no such breakthrough ever came about. But recently he must have found a way to succeed. Started taking kids again.

Kasabian could not abide the necessary sacrifice. He would stop them, even if it killed him. And it might. That kind of sacrifice he could manage.

He thought of Kye and what that might mean to her. If it didn't hurt her, she'd be free of him.

He banged his head against the wall. Giving in to her was a bad idea. He had meant to scare her away, to show her his Shadow's lust and power. He had not expected her to fall under its spell. She was supposed to push him away, not grind her body into his and devour him back.

He had to shove her from his mind and concentrate on this *thing* that was invading his soul. He would give himself to the demon if that's what it took to defeat his father and Silva. Which meant he couldn't have anyone else around him, especially Kye.

The sensation of it squeezed his lungs, making him drag in deep breaths. It burned along the lines on his back.

"Come on out, you beast," he gritted out.

It seized him. Kasabian threw his head back and let its roar pour out of him. Its heat scorched his cold soul. He focused on the wall beneath his hands, the air he was drawing in. The room felt as though it were falling away, and he with it.

Beneath the darkness, he felt something else. Not dark or evil, but light. Warmth.

Kye.

Their connection vibrated, like a gong sounding in the dark. He homed in on it, driven by an instinct he'd never felt before. He searched in the pitch black of his mind and saw a cord spiraling into distant space, a twist of her gold and his dark silver. Their essences. It stretched so tight that he could hear it cracking beneath the pressure.

She'd found a way to break the bond. He should be relieved. A part of him was, for her. Another part railed against it as her essence began to pull away. He had to let her go. Then it would be over.

The Shadow pushed at him to follow the cord that now threatened to break apart at any second. No. He had to resist. A sense of danger and urgency pressed even harder. Was she putting herself at risk to sever the bond? He grasped the trembling cord as he struggled to get to her.

The closer he got, the stronger her presence was. Then he saw her, and the sight surprised him. She was blurry, as though he were looking through warped glass. And still, she was so beautiful it made him ache. Her head was thrown back as his had just been, her eyes squeezed shut. Her body shook as the cord began to split. He could see that her arms were stretched out and that her hands were clasped with someone else's. Had she found another Zensu Deuce? He couldn't resist seeing the person who was freeing her, shifting to see the man linked to her—his father.

The horror of it nearly pulled him away. He held on, even as the cord shook harder. How could his father know about Kye? Daniel! Hell, Kasabian had told Daniel about the Cobra, and he'd asked her name.

Kasabian jerked on the cord. *Kye! Get out, dammit!* He reached through the connection and touched her. Her eyes snapped open, and Kasabian lost the connection. He psychically groped for it, like a drowning man reaching for a rope. In the darkness, he started to spin again, to lose all sense of grounding and reality.

Have to get to her. Have to . . .

He lost complete touch with his physical self, with his thoughts, and darkness claimed him.

———

At first, Treylon sensed Kye's turmoil and the way she felt betrayed by this Deuce to whom she had clearly given her heart. He sent his essence into her and instructed it to pull out all of that angst. But Kye's attachment to the man who had her all twisted up was strong, much stronger than anything he'd ever encountered.

This has to work. I need her.

He increased the power of his magick and felt something within her start to vibrate. He sent more power, willing it to break the attachment. It began to shake apart.

Suddenly she gasped and stumbled back. Her gray eyes were wide.

No, no, no! But he kept his expression placid, concerned. "Was it too much? I had to use a lot of power to break your attachment to this man."

She nodded quickly, running her fingers through her hair. "Yes, that's what it was. Maybe…maybe I'm not ready to let him go yet."

Rage burned through him, but he maintained his cool. "That's unfortunate. I don't think my lover has much time left." As he spoke, he tried to figure some way around the annoying requirement to get her permission before he could Leap her away. "Perhaps you could come to my home and try anyway?" He hated begging. He wanted to just grab her, take her to his car. He could hardly do that without causing a stir. He started to use the Thrall, but she closed her eyes and took a deep breath.

"I'll see if that was enough to restore it." After a few moments, she shook her head. "We didn't go far enough."

"We could try again." He held out his hands, using the Thrall again. "That man has done terrible things to you. If you get rid of your connection to him, you'll feel so much better."

Even though Kye was looking right into his eyes, her pupils weren't dilating. The Thrall wasn't working.

"I just need to talk to him one last time. Say goodbye, clear the air. Give me your number and I'll call you back tomorrow. I promise."

Her intent was true, that much he could tell. Damn, he wanted to shake her. But he couldn't do anything that might make her wary of him. "I understand what you're feeling," he said instead. "I suffered this kind of heartbreak when my wife ordered me to move out many years ago. And I felt the same longing you do as I tried to change her mind. Ultimately, I failed to win her back and held on to my attachment to her for longer than I should have. I beg of you, don't make the same mistake."

She nodded, giving him a soft smile. "It's kind of you to think of me when you have your own pain."

Patience. He'd suffered through enough of that virtue in the last few years. He could wait a few more hours. He recited the number of a throwaway cell phone he'd procured for this appointment. "Please, call me soon. I can't stand to see her suffer anymore."

Compassion filled Kye's eyes. "I will."

She was clearly distracted as she gathered her purse and escorted him out of the office. He would follow her, and find out where she lived. If it came down to it, he would kidnap her. It wasn't an ideal plan. Possible witnesses. Injury to her or the staff he would send to do the deed.

She walked down the hall and disappeared from sight. He went out to his car and waited for her. Ten, fifteen minutes passed. He drove around to the back side of the two-story building's lot, where he saw the employee parking area—and another exit. She was gone.

He could use his contacts to find out where she lived, no doubt. But he would give her a day, all he had to spare. He would rather have her come willingly...at least until she learned the real reason he needed her.

A pounding sound stirred Kasabian from the dark pit in which he'd fallen. *Kye.* His first thought as he became aware of his physical self again. He used the wall to brace himself as he got to his feet. The pounding continued. Someone at the door.

He jerked the door open and found Kye, dressed all demure and professional. And pissed as hell.

She burst in, full of glorious fury, alive. And none of it caused him any psychic pain, which meant they were still bound. That pleased the dark part of him.

She slammed the door shut and jabbed her finger at him. "I had almost broken our bond! You told me to find a way, and yes, you proved how dangerous this connection between us is. And I did find a way. Then you sabotaged it, you son of a bitch!"

The Shadow swept through him, and he gripped her arms and shoved her against the wall. His thigh moved between her legs. Fully pinned by his hips, she could not miss his body's reaction to her proximity. Or her body's counter-reaction to it.

His mouth came to within an inch of hers. "You will never be free of me," he said in a low and guttural voice he'd never used before.

Her eyes widened, and apprehension filled them as she looked into his. "Let me go." She tried to wriggle free, to no avail.

Her attempt at escape fueled the Shadow more, just as her effort to break the bond had. He slid his hands down to her wrists, linking their fingers together, and pinned her hands against the wall by her head. "You are *mine*." The fierce possessiveness was as foreign, as crazy, as what he was doing.

She was breathing hard, which made her breasts brush against his chest with every exhale. "You let it in, didn't you?"

"I had to."

"Kasabian, don't give in to it. You're stronger than it is."

He pressed his forehead to hers, fighting the urge to take her mouth. "I told you not to come near me."

"I was angry at you. I want answers."

She smelled so good, warm and sweet, and he took a deeper breath to calm himself. He needed to back away from her. He managed to pull away an inch, ready to fight for another one.

But she kissed him tenderly, meeting his gaze. "You're not going to let it turn you into a killing machine. Or a lust machine." Her voice was strong and clear. She believed in him, even after everything he'd done to her.

Or she's just trying to get away. The Shadow's whisper. He could still taste her, and she was looking at him with confidence that he would not hurt her. He wished he could be so sure. His body trembled with the need to make that possession complete.

He loosened his hold on her hands, rubbing her palms with his thumbs because he couldn't bear to release her yet. His eyes felt heavy with wanting her. He could feel desire freely now, and it throbbed through him like a current. So sweet. So electrifying.

"I see you fighting it, Kasabian," she whispered, watching his face. "You will win."

With a sharp exhale, he released her and stepped back, bowing his head. "Jesus, I'm sorry, Kye." He ran his hand back through his hair. "What I said about you being mine..."

She took a step away from him. "It wasn't you. I know you didn't mean that."

"Don't fool yourself, Kye. This thing inside me does feel that way."

She stepped farther away, her posture going defensive again. "Is that why you stopped me from breaking the bond? Because you think you own me?"

That's how crazy he'd gotten, losing sight of why he'd stopped her. "No, getting free of me is the best thing you could do. And yes, I do mean that. Tell me about the man who was helping you."

"How did you know—"

"I followed our bond when I felt it breaking. I could see you."

"I don't get you, Kasabian. You say I should get away from you, and then you want to do the Cobra. You promise you won't complete the bond, then you do. And now you're saying I should be free of you, yet you stopped me from escaping. What the frigging hell?"

He rubbed the back of his neck, feeling every bit of her frustration himself. "Tell me about the man, and I'll tell you why I stopped it."

She looked as though she were going to argue, but she released a breath and walked to the sofa. Her arms were crossed in front of her as she sank onto the cushion. "His name is Carl Wallen, and he said he heard about the Cobra from you and came in because he wants to try to ease his dying lover's pain with the bond. It's an intriguing proposition. I explained that my magick was on the fritz, and he offered to heal the cause of it." She arched her eyebrow. "That would be you. I didn't tell him we were bonded. In fact, I said that the guy who had me all tangled up was a Deuce, and he seemed to take that at face value. He offered to heal my heartache if I would try to help him. I wanted my Zensu magick back. I need it."

He took the chair across from her. "Because you feel worthless without it." He wanted to know why, wanted to tell her how utterly wrong she was. *Focus.* "So he was going to heal your heart and then what?"

"He didn't say exactly, but I imagine he would have taken me to his lover."

"Ah. Son of a bitch."

"All right, spill. Who is Carl? Is he some kind of lecherous Caido who lures women to his lair?"

"His goal, with his sob story, was for you to give him permission to take you to where he's keeping the children. That man was my father."

Her expression darkened as the implications set in. "The one who's been doing the experiments? Who kidnapped you?"

"The same. What I want to know is, why is he after

you? I only mentioned to Daniel that you'd created the Cobra. Treylon has no reason to connect us in any meaningful way. We don't live together; we're not dating." He couldn't know that Kasabian would go after anyone who threatened her. "So I doubt he was going to use you as a lure to get to me. And hell, he could probably get to me anytime. So clearly he wants you for something."

She shuddered visibly so that Kasabian had to fight the urge to put his arms around her and tell her he would never let anything happen to her.

"And I was going to go," she said, a quiver in her voice. "He totally fooled me."

"Kye, your need to feel worthwhile, and to help others, could be your downfall."

She didn't argue. "He seemed genuinely interested in the mechanism of the Cobra."

It hit him then why his father wanted her. Kasabian gestured to his scar. "The Caido kids who were channeling the other kids' essence got this starburst because this is where we take it in. While they were drained, the Caidos were overcharged, and some got burned out, just like the boy who ended up at the Guard. I bet Treylon thinks the Cobra will allow the Caidos to channel more essence without burning out. And that would kill the other Crescents even faster."

"If he thinks I'd do the Cobra with kids, he's sorely mistaken."

"You would, Kye. You would look at their drawn, haggard little faces and you would do anything to protect them. I know, because I've seen those faces."

That softened her outraged expression. "Like you taking the chance of getting caught when you planned your escape."

He nodded, the memory now burning in his chest. "My father will try to get you to cooperate, one way or the other. I'm not going to let him." The thought of that burned even more. "I can put a barrier around your apartment so no one without permission can Leap in. Except I can't create a barrier, because I have no angel in me." He paced, pinching the bridge of his nose. "I'll ask Hayden." He snatched up his phone and, when Hayden answered, said, "I need your help."

"I can't get away at the moment." He lowered his voice. "I'm on a bullshit assignment with my sergeant."

"They're on to you."

"The Concilium idiots grilled me on why I had an associate look up missing kids. I gave them some inane reason, but they were suspicious. What's up?"

"I need you to put a barrier around Kye's apartment." He explained why.

"Hell. All right, I'll come as soon as I can."

"Use me as a touchstone. I'm glued to her until you get here." Kasabian disconnected.

"So now we're going to be physically bonded as well."

He felt a stirring at those words. "Just until Hayden gets there. Then we are staying away from each other."

"Yeah, that doesn't seem to work very well, does it?" She wandered around the apartment, looking everywhere but at him. And that ended up being his computer monitor, which showed a satellite view of Miami.

Kasabian came up behind her. "I've been trying to find my father's compound through Google Earth. I know, a needle in a haystack."

"Yeah, I understand. It's better than doing nothing." She twisted her fingers together. "All I can think of are those children, and not being able to do something is driving me crazy." She waved to the computer. "Go on, keep looking."

She pulled up a chair a safe distance away and watched him find and then discount area after area. Finally, she said, "Oh, shoot. I've got to get home and feed my cat. I never hear the end of it if I'm late with his dinner."

"Ruled by your cat, eh?"

"I'm *his* pet, actually. I never understood that until I got him, how there's some part of you that wants to please him, to earn that bit of affection he throws your way. He always seems happy when I come home, and he likes to snuggle. He's the best thing that ever happened to me."

Kasabian loved her smile as she talked about her cat. He couldn't help but think, *And I'm the worst thing.* "Let me grab some things, and we will save you from a cat thrashing."

He threw on a shirt, grabbed some clothes, and followed her to her apartment. On the way, they picked up Chinese food for dinner.

Kasabian had to keep from whistling when he walked into her apartment. Everything about Kye saturated the place, from the black carpet in the living area to the red sofa that looked as though it had come out of a bordello. Old horror movie posters adorned the walls, all professionally framed. The place was neat and comfortable and, yeah, sexy.

"You think I'm weird," she said, setting her bag on the desk.

"The more I know about you, the more you fascinate me." He purposely didn't look her way as he said that, instead focusing on an Andy Warhol–style painting of Frankenstein.

A black cat jumped up on the back of the sofa where Kye stood. "This is Vlad. I named him for the man who inspired Dracula because he's got huge incisors. Smile, Vlad."

The cat meowed, and yes, he did have long-ass fangs. Kye stroked Vlad, her fingers and red nails contrasting with his dark fur.

"He's beautiful," Kasabian said, finding his gaze moving to Kye's face.

"He was at the shelter. The guy working there said that people were freaked out about his fangs, afraid he'd be vicious. And the volunteer at the shelter said that black cats are usually the last to be adopted because people are still superstitious." She picked up the cat and rubbed her cheek against his. "He's the sweetest thing ever, aren't you, lover kitty?"

Kasabian ached at the sight of her snuggling the cat and the affection he felt from her. The bond still allowed him to pick up her emotions. To divert his thoughts, he walked into the kitchen nook and set the bag of takeout food on the table. She fed the cat, then ducked into her room to change. When she emerged, she wore a white skirt and a red tank top. She washed her hands and got out utensils and plates.

He watched her eat, the way she deftly used the wooden chopsticks. Especially the way they slid in and out of her mouth. Her tongue flicked at a drop of soy sauce on her lip. She suddenly stopped and looked at him.

"You're making this a lot harder, eating like that." He had to shift to accommodate what was getting physically harder.

"Eating like what? This is how I always eat Chinese."

He couldn't help chuckling. She really had no idea. He opened the second package of chopsticks and broke them apart. "Allow me to demonstrate." First, he mirrored what she'd been doing. "Maybe you'll understand better if I do this." He slipped his tongue between them and drew it slowly up and down, thinking of the way his finger had slid between her folds. Her cheeks reddened, and she set her chopsticks down and picked up a fork. But the beast of desire had been woken. In him and in her.

He felt the glorious rush of it seductively twining inside him. "You seem to be enjoying the idea of my tongue moving up something that's much softer than these sticks."

The mist churned in eyes that grew heavier with her lust. She squirmed in her seat and gave her shoulders a shake. "And you would know, having stuck your hand down my pants."

He rode the wave of desire, giving in to the thrill of it. "Go ahead and sound indignant, but I know you enjoyed it. At first you felt a jolt of shock, but it changed to desire. You were wet, love, and I hadn't even touched you yet."

She clamped her teeth on the edge of the fork. Her cheeks were getting even more red. "While you were warning me away. Telling me how dangerous it is for us to be together." She squirmed again.

"And you see that I was right. That part of me is still saying it, way in the recesses of my soul. But the Shadow part wants you right here." He unbuttoned his jeans and pulled the zipper down an inch. "Straddling me. Naked." His cock throbbed for her. Now she shivered, but her struggle for control was clear on her face. *Good girl,* that distant, logical part of his brain said.

"Then you'll own me. You got control of the Shadow before. You can do it again."

He gave her a grin he knew was devilish. "I don't want to gain control of it at the moment. Do you know how good it feels to lust for you without pain?" He tilted his head back and tunneled his fingers through his hair. "Kye, you can't imagine having repressed desire your whole life and then suddenly be able to feel it." He met her gaze. "Or maybe you can."

She drew her hand to her collarbone. "Too well. But I'm afraid to go...there with you. Your eyes are glittering black. I can feel the power of the Shadow, like the dangerous energy that comes off a wild animal just before it attacks."

He turned his chair and stretched one leg toward her. "You're both afraid and turned on. Tell me, which is stronger?"

She took in the length of his leg, as though it were a barrier to escaping. A sheen of perspiration created a dewy glow on her face. "Unbutton your shirt."

He arched an eyebrow but complied with her command. Mmm, where was she going? "As you wish."

Those words seem to fire her even more. "Unzip your jeans." So did the sight of his erection straining past the top of his blue briefs. She seemed to force her gaze up to his chest. "You have no tan lines. I noticed that when you were taking a shower."

"I Leap up to the roof. There's a private spot where I can grab some sun in an unrestricted way." He shrugged. "It's my one small vanity." He hitched his fingers over the waistband of his jeans. "Shall I take these off, too?"

Her pupils dilated. "No! I mean, it's not necessary. Just sit back and relax."

He felt the most curious sensation, like a magic glove wrapping around his cock. A glove with a thousand electrical points that sent a wave of heat and...hell, he didn't know how to describe it. Other than amazing, incredible, and yes, magick. Now *he* was squirming.

"What in all that's decadent is *that*?" he ground out, trying to control his physical reaction.

"Sex magick." She tilted her head, a deliciously coy smile on her face. "Is it working?"

"Gods, yes." He shoved his jeans and briefs down and gripped his cock. "Why are you tormenting me? I'm already on the edge."

"I'm not tormenting you." The sensations increased, and so did her smile. "I'm protecting myself. If you get release, you won't be so scary. And obviously you need release."

His body bucked. "Holy Zensu."

"It's not actually Zensu magick. All Deuces have sex magick," she said, before continuing to torture him.

He arched in his seat as pleasure pushed him closer to the edge. And she watched, wisely using her magick from a safe distance. Maybe it would work. Except as he let out a hoarse moan and brought his hand down as the orgasm seized him, he could feel her desire as much as his own. Hell. He didn't think this was going to work.

He threw his head back and shuddered. Gods, it had been forever since he'd come. He felt her magick rolling through his body as viscerally as if she were physically touching him.

When he drifted back to himself, he caught her gaze riveted on his hand gripping his stiff cock. Her eyes were as heated as his own. With a small gasp, she met his gaze and her cheeks reddened even more.

"Watching you come was…" She shifted her gaze away. "Interesting."

When she looked back, he was zipping his jeans.

"Interesting like, weird, ew, yuck? Or interesting like mmm, watching someone else get off makes me want to get off, too?" He already knew the answer, but he wanted her to say it.

"Yeah, more like the latter. Not that I want…that I need…"

He approached her. "I think you do want. And need. I can help you."

She furrowed her eyebrows, but he saw a spark of desire in her eyes. "How?"

He wiggled his fingers. "The old-fashioned way."

She licked her lips. Flicked her gaze to the kitchen. A lovely pink glow flushed along her cheeks. Finally she met his eyes. "Okay, but this is about release, not sex. No kissing or making love in any way that will get out of control, right?"

Even though he'd gotten off, he still craved more of her. But he would stick to their agreement. "Just that."

"All right. Then we can get this blasted desire out of our systems."

"Yeah, sure we can." Let her think that. Because he wasn't going to let her leave this table without experiencing the pleasure of letting go. "Unbutton your shirt."

She arched an eyebrow at him.

He shrugged. "Just a suggestion."

"And no watching."

"You liked watching me come."

"It's too embarrassing. Too personal. Promise me."

Damn. She was invoking the promise. "I promise to keep my eyes closed. Under duress. Now, relax."

She was wound up tighter than a coil, her fingers linked in her lap. If he had his magick, he would wave his hands over her. So, he'd have to do it the Mundane way. He came up behind her and started slowly rubbing her shoulders. Her body obeyed, sagging back against the chair. Her eyes drifted closed. She trusted him. Silly girl. But something deep in him wanted to earn that trust.

His hands moved down her arms, his thumbs grazing the edge of her breasts. Her bra was thin so that he felt her curves and saw her nipples tighten. Damn, he wanted to touch those beautiful mounds. Leaning forward put his cheek next to hers, and it was all he could do not to kiss the creamy length of her neck.

He restrained himself and moved his hand down to her wrists. Damn, it was hard to make this just about release. Sure, she wanted it to sound clinical, like something she would tell her clients to do. He wasn't going to let her get away with that.

Kasabian came around and knelt in front of her. He ran his hands from her ankles up to her thighs beneath the skirt, this time letting his thumbs trail along the sensitive skin of her inner thighs. Every time he stroked up and down, he got a little closer to her apex. She tilted her hips up and let out a soft breath. Oh, yeah, she was aroused.

"Spread your legs, love," he whispered.

As she did, he pushed her skirt up to her hips. He moved his hand over her sex, cupping it gently. She pressed against his palm, and her mouth was turned up in a soft smile. He lightly ran his nails across the silky fabric over her nub, and her breath hitched.

Her fingers tightened on the edge of the chair as he continued to stroke her. He could feel the dampness of her arousal through the fabric. Her head rocked back, and she inhaled deeply. He kissed her knee, moving up her thigh as he tugged at her panties. "These are in the way."

She made some faint protest right before he slid his finger beneath the fabric and touched that slick flesh. Even better, she started unbuttoning her skirt and pushed it past her hips. He grabbed it and her panties and pulled them down in one move, setting them aside. She was beautiful, half naked, her hair trimmed into a small triangle. Then he touched her again. Her breath came erratically as he dipped one finger inside her incredibly tight entrance, while his thumb stroked her nub. So wet.

The more he touched her, the more her body took over. She shifted, lifting her hips, spreading her legs even more to give him access. He inhaled her beautiful scent, sweet and musky, feeling it coil inside him. He kept kissing the soft skin of her inner thighs, moving closer to the sacred V. His cock was not sated apparently, because it throbbed to drive into the slick opening his finger stroked. He found the place inside her that made her gasp.

Maybe the *G* in *G*-spot meant *gasp*. He smiled at the thought, and the way she was moving into his strokes. Sensing that she was on the precipice, he pulled his thumb away and touched his lips to her nub. Her body jerked slightly when she realized it was his mouth on her now, and then her hips pushed even closer. Adhering to his promise, he closed his eyes. There was plenty to lose himself in outside his visual senses.

He parted her folds and gave the swollen nub a gentle laving that had her breath coming faster. His finger kept sliding in and out, simulating the thrust of his cock. She moved with him, faster, and then she convulsed with her orgasm.

He rode her through it, savoring every contraction and shudder and pulse around his finger. Gods, he wished he was inside her, thrusting hard into her tight heat, finding his own release alongside hers.

"Holy shit," she muttered as her body contorted with pleasure. Her body gradually relaxed, and her breathing calmed. It was amazing how giving her pleasure had felt as good as receiving it had earlier.

"Holy shit," she said again, this time with more force. She wriggled away, stumbling out of the chair and grabbing up her skirt and panties and pulling them on. She pushed her hand through her hair, genuinely stunned. "How did we go from eating to ... this?"

"I gave in to the Shadow. Just a little. And so did you."

She still looked shaken up. "You're a bad man, Kasabian."

"Yes, love. But you knew that from the beginning."

Chapter 10

Hayden Leaped in just before Kye was about to turn in for the night. He took in their positions on opposite sides of the room with a curious glance. Or likely he picked up on the tension between them. "Everything okay?"

"Peachy," Kye said, setting her book aside. Her body felt great, revitalized, and it wanted more. She kept imagining Kasabian's hand around his big shaft, the way his muscles tightened when he came.

"Fantastic," Kasabian said in that same terse tone, sitting up from his sprawled position on her couch.

"Okay, then. I finally broke away, claiming exhaustion. Truth is, Cecily called with some registration information about the Hummer that took the missing boy away. She's an information analyst at work, the one who looked up the stats on the missing kids. She has a bit of a crush on me, and yeah, I'm being an asshole and using that to get her to help me." He smiled. "For a good cause. She peeled back two layers of false corporations connected to the vehicle that took him away. I have every confidence that she'll find what we need."

"Is Cecily Caido?" Kasabian set Jonathan's picture on the coffee table, having been staring at it for the last twenty minutes.

"She's Dragon. Cute thing. Reminds me of a kid sister. Anyway, she's been helping me dig up information on the sly. But someone is obviously monitoring her activities. Her superior asked her why she was doing queries on missing children. She circumvented the question, but if she does more digging on the Guard's computers, they're going to know she's involved. She did a manual search and found out that Treylon's dead."

"Officially," Kasabian said. "What about Silva?"

"Doesn't exist. I've been trying to talk to Kade Kavanaugh about his father and the supposedly crazy woman, but he's been out of pocket."

Kasabian stood. "I'll feel a lot better when this barrier's in place."

Hayden started to raise his hand to create the barrier but stopped as his gaze drew to the picture on the coffee table. He snatched it up. "Where'd you get this?"

"That's Lyle's little brother, Jonathan. The one who's missing. Why?"

"This is the boy who was found and is now with the Concilium. How did Jonathan go missing? When?"

"He went to some government-assisted camp a year ago. Soon after, Lyle and his mother were relocated to the Bend."

"The Bend?" Kye asked.

Hayden kept staring at the picture. "Crescent housing

for single mothers to raise their kids and get clean if they need to. It's run by a private nonprofit group and is very secure. I can tell you, I never hear about any incidents there."

"Supposedly this boy was adopted," Kasabian said. "Lyle thinks he was sold because right after Jonathan went to this supposed camp, his mother moved to the Bend and suddenly had a nice home and money to spend."

Now that Kye had seen Jonathan's big brown eyes and cupid's-bow mouth, this felt much more personal. She wanted to reach right into that photograph and pull him out. Hold him close. "Maybe the mother agreed to a deal with Treylon, and he made arrangements to get her into the Bend."

"I think we start there." Kasabian looked at Hayden. "Put up the shield, and then you and Cecily keep looking for Jonathan on your end."

Hayden held out his hand, palm up. "One barrier coming up."

The Light looked a bit like a Deuce orb at first, a small burst of brilliance. It morphed into what appeared to be a wall of water that the wind had ruffled at its surface. He slowly waved his hand in a circle, encompassing the entire apartment. She watched it in awe as it moved to the walls and disappeared.

Kasabian watched it, too, but his expression was bereft. She felt the depth of his failure to protect her.

Hayden lowered his hand. "Done."

She could barely see any disturbance in the air. "How does it work exactly?"

"No one can come in unless you invite them. However, once you invite someone in, they are permanently exempt."

He gave Kasabian a grave look. "You know the other way in."

Kasabian nodded, his expression just as solemn. "Thank you, my friend. Go find the boy."

Hayden disappeared.

"What's the other way in?" Kye asked.

"If one of us is killed, someone can use our body to get through the barrier."

Cold dread clamped around her heart. "Oh, that's lovely." Another thought clamped even tighter. "So this barrier means it's safe for me to be here alone?"

"Yes. And you'll be safer yet if I'm gone." He wasn't moving to leave. He seemed to be gripping the back of the sofa, and then she realized it was because he was swaying on his feet.

"Are you all right?"

He blinked, nodded, and headed to the door like a zombie. No wonder. He'd been beaten, Stripped.

"You shouldn't be driving. Sleep here." How dangerous could he be in his state of exhaustion?

"No." But his body stopped.

She placed her hands on his shoulders and steered him to a sitting position on the couch. "You'll sleep here." When he looked as though he were going to protest again, she said, "I don't want you to leave. I think . . . I'll feel safer if you're here."

Kye tossed and turned in her bed despite her exhaustion. She threw on a robe and wandered down the hallway to get a glass of water. Kasabian was lying amid a tangle of sheets on the floor looking very much asleep. He was on his stomach, arms outstretched. His drawstring pants sat low on his hips, making his torso look long and lean.

In the dim light coming from the kitchen's night-light, she could see the bloody etch of his wings across his broad back. His beautiful essence gone, stripped away. And now something dark was taking its place.

She sank to her knees, studying his face for any sign of wakefulness. In sleep, he didn't seem so dangerous. His mouth was relaxed, soft and curved up at the corners.

Like an alligator.

He had amazing cheekbones, and she fought the urge to trace along the ridge and down his jawline. The compulsion to run her fingers through his hair was just as strong. She let her gaze draw down past that horrible wound. His back rose and fell with his deep, even breathing. She ached for him, for his losses and betrayals. Her hand drifted toward his lower back, where he was unmarred. She let it hover an inch above the indent of his spine at his waistband. His body heat radiated into her palm.

She should not be here. What if he woke? Danger crackled along her senses, beckoning her like a siren. She had talked him down earlier, even as she'd been scared to death that he might overpower her. She'd never been one to have domination fantasies, or any fantasies, really. But his dark power woke something inside her she didn't want to evaluate too closely.

She who lies with a wild animal will be eaten by one.

But now he was dormant, safe, locked away in sleep. His fingers twitched with whatever dream he was having. Given recent events, it probably wasn't a good one.

"Emma," he whispered, agony lacing his voice that sounded younger than his years. "Don't die."

The little girl who died in his arms? His breath heaved in something like a sob. He'd been but a boy then, caught in a terrible situation. She let her hand rest on him lightly, hoping to bring him out of REM at least.

The connection sucked her into his nightmare instead. The scene, hazy and too bright, exploded into her mind, seen through a young Kasabian's eyes. He sat on a small bed holding a girl, a wall of grief breaking him down. She had long blond hair, like Kye's; her blue eyes were pale and lifeless. He gently closed her eyes with his fingers and sat with her in a nearly bare room with hardly a toy or a splash of color. On another bed, a Deuce boy comforted a crying girl.

He met Kasabian's gaze. "She'll be next. She's as weak as Emma was. Your father's killing us, you know."

He'd suspected. Feared it. Now the realization weighed heavy as Kasabian nodded. "How many have died?"

"Four that I know of. The rest just disappear. He says they go home. But I know what that means." Panic seized the boy's face. "Emma will be taken, too, and the others will be told the same."

Kasabian slid out from beneath the girl's small body. "I'm going to get you out of here. All of you."

He closed the door behind him and checked the other rooms in the hallway. Each held two or more children, their eyes gaunt, mouths in frowns. She felt her own heart cave at the sight, twisting with Kasabian's grief and resoluteness. So many to save. Too many.

He ducked around the corner as an adult came down the hallway and passed by. A door opened, and a dark-haired boy with vivid blue eyes whispered, "What are you doing out? It's after bedtime."

Kasabian swiped at his eyes. "I was thirsty."

The boy touched his hand. "You're crying? That's right. You have a home to be sick for. I could make you feel better."

Kasabian pulled away from his clammy grip. "We'll get into trouble. I'm going to bed."

The boy looked angry and hurt. "Why aren't you my friend anymore?"

"Because you're a suck-up to the man who's keeping us captive and hurting us." Kasabian's anger and disgust swirled inside him as he continued down the hall. When the door slammed closed, he went three doors down and slipped into a room where a young Hayden sat reading on the bed.

"He's killing the children," Kasabian said as he sat next to him. "We have to get them out of here."

A blast of chilled air swept through the dream. The haziness cleared, and a dark-haired man appeared. She thought it might be the spurned boy down the hall, his features now lean with maturity.

He looked around. "Ah, the good old days. Before you left me."

"The good old days? When my father held us prisoner? Murdered children?" Kasabian was still the twelve-year-old, yet he squared his shoulders. "Get the hell out of my dream, Silva."

The man who'd posed as Kasabian's friend! He could get into other people's dreams?

"So touchy. I merely came to see if you wanted your wings back."

Kye remained very still in the dream, unsure if it *was* a dream anymore.

Kasabian stood warily, his eyes narrowed. "And how do I do that?"

"Come and get me. Let's play at Kennedy Park on Bayshore." Silva disappeared.

Kye lurched up as Kasabian stirred awake. She had just enough time to get behind the couch before he sprang to his feet. He threw on his shirt, slipped into his shoes, and scribbled a note that he left for her on the table. The barrier shimmered as he went through.

It shimmered as she went through, too.

Chapter 11

Kasabian knew it could be a trap. Was probably a trap. He also knew that, for some reason, Silva wasn't intent on killing him. He'd already had the chance. No, he wanted to keep him in some room to...what, convince him that what they were doing was right? That would never happen. Kasabian did not have his Caido abilities, but he had the Shadow. It unfurled like a battle flag inside him as he walked into the park.

He felt the barrier form soon after he crossed the boundary, no surprise. Silva would not choose a public place like this without ensuring that they weren't disturbed. Or seen. This kind of barrier made everything look like it was supposed to from the outside. Mundanes would feel a revulsion about entering the park and turn away. Crescents would know it was something supernatural and decide it was better to leave.

The moon silvered the dewy grass and made the black pathways even darker. Kasabian crept along the inner edge of mangroves, silent as an assassin. And he *did* want to kill Silva. His blood burned with the need; his back stung with it. The rage at his betrayal resurfaced, surging through his system with such force that his vision dimmed for a moment.

A figure dropped down from a lower branch of a tree several yards away. The man wore black, but his pale skin reflected the moonlight. Silva walked out in the open. "Kasabian."

Kasabian stepped onto the dark path, pulling back the rage at seeing the man who'd Stripped him. For now. "Silva." It took all of his control to hold back the vitriol he felt in saying his name.

Silva smiled. "It's been a long time since you've said my name. My real name."

His deception burned, but Kasabian held that back, too. "That's not your real name either."

Silva waved his hand dismissively. "I don't even remember my original name. When our father gave me a new start, he allowed me to choose a name."

Our father. "You feel a great deal of loyalty toward Treylon." Kasabian didn't want to use that familial title because he did not feel the man was his father. "Is that why you go along with his plans?"

Silva's mouth tightened. "Loyalty is a valuable thing, Kasabian. A rare and beautiful concept that most don't understand."

For some reason, Kasabian thought of Kye. No, sensed her. Not panic or pain, just her. He focused on Silva. "You're angry that I left seventeen years ago." Kasabian didn't phrase it as a question, and he didn't need to.

Silva's expression caved for a moment, revealing the

pain. "We were friends, the oldest of the Caido children."

"Then you joined the other side. I couldn't let you be my friend and my father's number one helper at the same time. Now I wonder if it's Stockholm syndrome."

Silva sputtered. "It's very simple. Treylon treated me better than any adult ever had. And I liked being important. The night you were dreaming about, you went to Hayden. Not me, *Hayden*. You shut me out." Bitterness seeped into his words.

"You were my father's pet. I couldn't trust you. We could only take a few of the kids with us, the ones who were in the worst shape." He'd left many more behind. "I had every intention of bringing back the authorities to release everyone there. Including you." It was too late to ask now, but he would anyway. "Would you have gone to him with my plan?"

"Of course. I didn't want you to leave me."

Silva would make this about him, no matter what Kasabian said. He needed to put aside his disgust—his pity—and find out what he could. "I wasn't leaving *you*. I was going to save everyone and shut Treylon's operation down."

"What a hero," Silva sneered. "If you hadn't interfered, we could be free of this curse, able to love and feel without pain. Things got shaky after your escape. Our benefactors told us to pull back. They couldn't protect us if it went public. Father had to shut it down and go away for a while. You are very shortsighted."

"Perhaps." Kasabian shrugged. "I don't think we should use animals to test products and procedures either. Call me a softie." He walked over to one of the bars where runners could stretch. *Keep calm, control yourself. For now.*

He focused on the cold metal beneath his fingers. "Treylon restarted the program. Why?"

"Because we can." And that was all Silva was going to tell him, by the smug expression on his face.

"You said you'd restore my Caido. I assume you want something in return."

Silva smiled, making him look like the Joker in the moonlight. "Let me fuck you. Here. Now."

The words thumped against Kasabian. "You're kidding."

Silva's smile vanished. "Do I look like I'm trying to be amusing? Strip, bend over." He tapped the bars. "And let me drive into you. I know you think you don't go that way, but I promise you'll like it."

The Shadow reared up in anger. Kasabian let it out. He felt its "wings" fully extend without pain. Silva hunched over as his Caido wings tore through his shirt, and Kasabian lunged for his neck. Silva flipped backward over the bars and hit the ground hard, smashing his wings. Kasabian stopped when the image of talons overlaying his hands snagged his attention. *What the hell?*

Silva took advantage of his shock, throwing him several yards. Kasabian landed on the grass, though it was still not a soft landing. He'd only just gotten to his feet when Silva knocked him back again and jumped on him. His weight propelled the air from his lungs.

Silva's eyes flashed black, hints of red undulating within as he straddled Kasabian. "So beautiful when you're angry."

Kasabian reached for his throat again, but he was three inches short of contact. Rage engulfed him with heat as Silva's thighs tightened on Kasabian's hips. Magick tingled along his outstretched fingers, pooling at the ends. The black talons grew into tendrils, stretching from his fingertips and wrapping around Silva's throat like five thin snakes.

Like Silva's magick.

Silva's words came back to him: *We always differed on our ideals, even as we are alike in other ways.*

"Son of a bitch. I'm a Wraithlord."

"I wondered if you knew," Silva gritted out. "Because...you didn't use it last time."

Silva's magick sliced through the elongated talons, severing them. Once released, he extended claws toward Kasabian. Caidos used their Light as weapons, sometimes as swords. Kasabian didn't know how to use the dark, but he would improvise. He envisioned a hatchet, and it appeared from the palm of his hand. *This is cool. I can work with this.* He swung it at Silva, who scrambled away. The blade nicked his back, leaving a long red line that oozed blood.

Silva got to his feet and faced Kasabian, arms akimbo. From his hands sprang two whips, which he wielded. The two faced off.

"How do we get this way?" Kasabian asked. "Is Treylon one?"

"No. It's a random genetic mutation, passed down from someone in your family."

Kasabian stalked closer, swinging the hatchet. As he advanced, the blade grew larger, the sharp point at the top longer.

Silva watched, his eyes widening. "You obviously know how to use your dark magick." He flicked the whip, and Kasabian swung. The fringed tip fell to the ground. "But I've been working with it longer, I bet."

His other whip snapped, wrapping around the base of the hatchet's blade. Kasabian held on, but Silva's magick was better honed. The whip turned to flame, shooting heat up the handle. Kasabian struggled to yank it away as his palms blistered. He released it when the pain became too much.

Silva looked dreamily at Kasabian. "How I've longed to look at you like this, to see the Shadow in your eyes."

Shadow. Exactly what Kasabian had called it. "Are we part demon?"

Silva laughed. "Part angel, part demon. Wouldn't that be quaint? But no. We are part Obsidian Dragon. Our Light has the abilities of their Breath weapon. We harbor the beast's hunger and fire, but we cannot turn into one. Too bad, that. When the gods became physical on Lucifera, an angel or two must have unknowingly mated with an Obsidian in human form." He arched one of his fine eyebrows. "We might even be related if we traced our ancestry back several generations."

Kasabian liked the idea of harboring a Dragon as opposed to a demon. "But that doesn't explain how we can control wraiths."

Silva seemed eager to share information about their heritage, probably thinking it might bond them. "That, from what I understand, comes from the unique combination of power. Though a Caido isn't strong enough, the added power allows us to have control."

"Nice to know. I'll keep that in mind the next time I run across some wraiths." Kasabian created a sword that he thrust at Silva. The tip sunk in before Silva lurched backward, his hands covering the wound. Blood poured out between his fingers. Then Light emanated from his hand,

and the bleeding stopped. Kasabian was ready when that bloodied hand shot toward him, sending a spear sailing at his shoulder. He shifted, and it missed by inches.

Frustration set Silva's face in a tight mask. He wind-milled his hands, drawing several swirls of smoke into a tornado. Kasabian cut through it before it could fully form, slicing across Silva's arms in the process.

"I don't want to hurt you!" Silva shouted. "I just want..."

"What? Me helpless, submitting to your lust while you convince me that what Treylon is doing is right?"

Again, Kye's presence and energy filled him. Now was not the time to be thinking about her. Why was she popping into his mind?

Silva's laugh was harsh this time. "Lust? You think I merely lust for you? I have others to sate my base needs."

Kasabian pulled the sword in an arc to the right, willing it to extend as he did. The blade sang as it sailed toward Silva's neck. He dove at Kasabian, rolling up to his feet in front of him. Smiling. The sword was torn from Kasabian's hands and flew over his head. Something pulled at him from behind. Kasabian spun to face a black tornado. It had been silently forming behind him all along. It sucked him in, pinning him as though it were made of glue. He summoned his power, feeling the tornado crack against his skin. But it wouldn't break apart.

A blue orb streaked past like a comet and crashed into the side of Silva's head. He stumbled, and his tornado splintered.

Orb. Deuce. Kasabian spun to the right, shocked to find Kye at the edge of the mangroves working up another orb on her palm. *Use Silva's surprise.* He threw a magick cloud at him, keeping him from getting to his feet. Using his hands the way Silva had in forming the tornado, Kasabian turned the cloud into bars that imprisoned his opponent. Silva tried to wrench them apart and hissed when they burned his hands.

Kasabian glanced at his own blistered palm. Whatever this magick was, however wicked, it was amazing. And dangerous as it pulsed through him, wanting to destroy. He looked Kye's way, taking in her silk pajamas, the tangle of her long hair.

What the hell was she doing here? *Focus on your enemy.* He walked toward Silva, who was using his magick to saw through the bars. Kasabian summoned one of the bars to thrust down and press into Silva's chest. Every time he exhaled, the point dug in.

"Restore my Caido," Kasabian said.

"You brought a woman to the fight?" Silva said, disgust in his voice. "You needed a woman to distract me so you could get the upper hand?"

Did he not know who Kye was? Silva had obviously never seen her. Kasabian decided to play the same angle and keep her out. "I didn't bring her. She must have slipped past your barrier." He shot her a menacing look. "Or came in right before you erected it." That she'd followed him, and put herself in danger, infuriated him. "Just an innocent bystander, but nevertheless, you screwed up." He turned back to Silva, pressing the bar harder. It punctured his skin. "Restore me. Now. Give me your word that is what you will do, and nothing more."

Silva released a long breath, his gaze sliding to Kye. Kasabian followed his gaze. She stood several yards away, a blue orb floating above her open palm, still looking murderous. But the shock of what she'd seen was clear in the pallor of her face. And he felt it now that he could sort through his own reactions and emotions.

"I give you my word," Silva said, releasing a silvery black mist from his hand that floated through the bars. Once outside them, it formed into angel wings. Kasabian's apprehension tightened every muscle in his body as the wings came to rest against his tender back. Could he count on the promise of someone like Silva? He felt ice saturate every cell. His hands glowed briefly as his Caido essence settled back inside him. He felt it tip the balance again. But Kasabian knew the two energies would fight for control.

He Invoked, and his wings tore through his back. The pain was a relief, along with the feeling of angel that surged through him.

The bars disintegrated, and Silva got to his feet. "The woman must be memory-locked or killed."

"Do not touch her." Kasabian walked closer to Kye, fastening his hand over her wrist. He gave her a slight shake of his head—*Don't let him know we're connected*—before turning his attention back on Silva. "I'll take care of her."

Silva's expression changed to one of deadly interest. "You know her. I sense her emotions where you're concerned. Worry. Fear, both *of* you and *for* you. She cares about you." He made a tsking sound. "So sweet."

Kasabian doubted she still cared after what she'd seen.

Silva's eyes narrowed. "Wait. This is Kye, isn't it?" He approached, his gaze on her while Kasabian pulled her close. "How can you still care about him now that you know he's some freak of nature?"

Kasabian cast the hatchet out again, letting the blade

rest against Silva's neck. "You will not go anywhere near her."

Silva didn't appear to be worried. "Do you see how you reach for the dark side of your nature, even when you have the Light back? You felt the dark when we were kids, yet you never sensed our kinship. So sad. I did, but I didn't know what it was. I just knew I was drawn to you. It wasn't until years later that someone explained what I was. What *we* are, Kasabian."

Kasabian let the blade cut into Silva's neck. "Tell me where Treylon's operation is."

Silva smiled. "See you in your dreams."

Then he Leaped.

Chapter 12

Kye had said nothing to Kasabian, merely walking to her car. Kasabian followed her to her apartment as dawn broke across the sky behind him. She had sensed his seething anger at her. Could he sense how freaked out she was by what she'd seen? Probably.

The moment they closed the door of her apartment, he said, "What the hell were you doing out there?"

"Saving your ass, as it turned out. 'Why, thank you, Kye, for distracting him so I could get the upper hand.' 'You're welcome, Kasabian.'"

"You could have gotten killed!" His face flushed red, but the black Shadow crossed his eyes.

She took an involuntary step back. "You could have, too! You sneak out of here, leaving a damned note." She gestured to the kitchen. "If he'd gotten hold of you, taken you to his lair, I would have had only a vague idea where you'd gone. So very nice of you."

Kasabian stepped right in front of her and forced her to

look at him. "This doesn't concern you. You see what I'm dealing with." His expression darkened. "What I am. He could have incinerated you."

Vlad rubbed against her calves, and she reached down and stroked his back. "Excuse me for caring about you."

"You shouldn't care. Don't you get that? You should get the hell away from me, from this."

She should. Of course she should. "You're a Wraithlord."

He gave a low nod. "Apparently."

She could sense his shock and unease, despite his cavalier response. "You have an answer now."

He seemed to settle into the reality. "Yeah, I do. I have a name to go with my abomination. Bottom line, I harbor a Dragon." Disbelief and awe filled that one word.

"Half heat and fire and passion, half cool Caido. Then again, you were never cool and unemotional."

"Thanks to my father's project, no. It explains why I've always felt tangled up inside, though."

"Silva's in love with you. And obsessed."

Kasabian grunted. "I never gave him any indication that I swung that way." He seemed to just realize the back of his shirt was torn. He ripped if off and shoved it into the garbage can in the corner. The soft under-counter lights washed over the contours of his muscles. He was lean and lethal, all hard angles and muscles like a gymnast.

Kye spun her finger in a circle. "Turn around." He did, and she had to resist touching the black wings that stretched across his broad back. "Your wing tattoo is completely back to normal. Not even a sign of the torn flesh."

When he'd brought forth his angelic essence, she had to catch her breath at the magnificence of it. Of him.

He spun around, facing her. "Kye."

Desire heated his eyes as he dropped his gaze down over her. She was suddenly aware that the silk of her pajamas wouldn't hide her tightening nipples. Not that it mattered, she realized. She was naked to him, or at least her soul was.

His gaze snapped to hers. "Knowing what I am doesn't change a thing."

"It explains why you feel possessive. That's definitely a Dragon trait. I've worked with enough to know that."

"And the fact that I can desire you without pain, you don't know how tantalizing that is. How tantalizing you are. From that first moment I set my eyes on you. And every second I'm with you."

She could see his agony, agony she knew well. Her resistance melted. She was tired of fighting it. Gods, did she want him.

"Kye, you're tormenting me again."

She stepped closer, sliding her arms around his neck. "And do you remember what happened the last time I tormented you?"

He circled her waist. "Mmm, I do. And as good as that felt, I want more than that. Much, much more."

His words sinuously wrapped around her. "Me, too."

She felt the moment he broke, unleashing a torrent of heat and passion as he tightened his hold on her and devoured her. Within seconds, he'd pulled off her silk top. His fingers slid between hers, intimately binding their hands and holding them behind her back. He liked controlling her physically, she realized. The idea of it spiraled through her, trust and fear and arousal. She tilted her chin and exposed her neck in symbolic surrender.

"You sure you want to incite the Shadow?" he said in a low, dangerous voice. "That's what it wants, you fully surrendering to me."

"Yes," she whispered.

"Oh, love, I wish you wouldn't."

"I've never wanted someone like this before. I have to trust my feelings."

She felt his teeth graze her skin, nip, and then his tongue traced up to her ear. He bit the lobe softly and growled. She found herself growling back, shivering as his hot breath spilled into the shell of her ear. He moved down the length of her throat, kissing the indent of her collarbone, and then his mouth closed over her nipple.

She gasped as her whole body came alive, right down between her legs. His tongue circled her nipple, making the muscles in her thighs quiver and curling her toes. Then he sucked hard enough to make her cry out softly.

"How can something hurt and feel good at the same time?" she gasped.

"That's how I felt when I watched you at the club." He kept sucking. "Is it too much?" But he didn't let up.

"Yes, but keep doing it. I want to know what you experienced."

He moved to the other one. Pleasure and pain, oh yes, he knew it well. She dug her fingers into his shoulders, her breath coming quicker.

So fast that the world spun, he threw her over his shoulder and hauled her to her bedroom. He released her to the bed, and the heated way he looked at her shivered down to her bones. He shucked his pants and briefs in one move, and the glory of him thrust out straight and hard. She kept revisiting the memory of him gripping himself. Something about his strong fingers wrapped around himself was oddly arousing. She had imagined her fingers wrapped around its girth.

The early morning sun slanted in through the wooden blinds and gilded his body in stripes. As lethally beautiful as a tiger, he stalked toward her on hands and knees across the bed.

He pushed her flat on the bed and touched every inch of her. She saw the beast in his hazel eyes as he claimed her with his gaze. *Mine*, it said, and she felt his possession of her. And some primitive part of her responded with *yours*. That scared and aroused her, too, how she'd fallen under his seductive spell. Trusting a man who'd told her he couldn't be trusted. Wanting a man she shouldn't want.

He pushed her legs apart and touched the heat of his mouth to her core. She had craved this since the last time and gave herself to him and the pleasure he sent coursing through her. She gripped his hair as his tongue licked and tickled and gently sucked, making her hips move in a sensuous rolling motion. As she was about to fall into the chasm, he backed off, planting chaste kisses along her inner thighs. Just when she was about to beg—*beg*, for gods' sake!—he slowly, agonizingly made his way back to the part of her that ached for more. Finally, she arched as wave after wave crashed over her. And still he stroked her thighs as she slowly came down and calmed her breathing. He rolled her over and nipped, kissed, and licked his way across her back and ass. His hands followed, squeezing, stroking.

Kye would not let him control everything, rolling over and pushing him back the same way he'd done with her. She straddled him, her thighs tight on his hips, her sex pressing against his hard ridge as she planted soft kisses across his chest. He was tanned, golden and perfect. He arched up into her, molding their bodies even closer. She nipped harder than he had as she moved down his body, leaving red marks across his abs, driven mad by hunger. He liked it, if his low groan was any indication. And somewhere in that groan lay buried her name.

She traced her teeth across his nipples, squeezing her thighs even tighter, running her hands along his arms. She swooped in and kissed him hard and quick, retreating before he could fully engage.

"Witch," he whispered, but he was smiling. "The only magick I want is you wrapped around my cock."

She drew her fingers down his chest, then beneath him to squeeze his tight ass. Her mouth moved across his ridged stomach, feeling the slick tip of his cock graze her chin. "Mmm, want to fuck me, do you?" She didn't like the word, but when he'd used it, its raw sexuality had stoked her.

He tangled his fingers in her hair. "Very much."

She drew the magick into her mouth, swirling it around like a good wine, and then took him in. The magick tingled across his skin and over his head, swirling around his cock with hot vibrations. She sensed when he was about to lose it and withdrew, then left a trail of kisses along the faint line of hair leading up to his chest. Yeah, two could play that game. His body was trembling, his breaths coming in short pants.

He pulled her up for a long kiss. She tasted their mingled essences, somehow erotic, as he devoured her with his tongue. When he finished kissing her, he sat up and pulled her pelvis against his.

"I know you want to drive, my sex witch," he murmured against the inner curve of one breast. "Because you're already driving me crazy."

She couldn't help the smile at driving Kasabian to the brink. She eased onto his large erection, glad that he'd made her nice and slick. His arms slid around her back, fingers splayed as he urged her on. Her knees gripped his hips, hands squeezing his shoulders. She threw her head back and let out a long, soft groan as he filled her. Years of abstinence, and now complete fulfillment. It was almost too much to handle. Too right. Too good. She loved this position, facing each other and allowing her to wrap her arms around him. Their bodies brushed as they moved together.

She never felt like this, hungry and full, satiated and craving more. She raked her fingernails up and down his back out of a need to express some of that craziness zinging through her.

He gripped her hard and uttered, "Oh. My. Gods."

"Any particular one?"

"All of them. To experience this without pain or muting of desire…"

She let the goddess lead her, leaning back and bracing her hands on his hard thighs. Kye was rewarded by the wild kisses Kasabian planted over her breasts. He gently took one of her legs and put it over his shoulder, opening her more to him. He thrust even deeper into her. When she thought she couldn't take the intense pressure, she exploded into a thousand sparks of light. At least that's how it felt; she'd never experienced anything like it before.

He laid her down and drove into her again, surrounding her with his body, his heat and intensity. He kissed her and touched her and spun her like flotsam in a tornado. She scrabbled for a sense of up and down, left and right. Wrong and right.

"You have sex magick, too," she managed to utter. She could feel his essence flowing through her, a river of Light and stars and galaxies, with meteors flying past.

"It's the bond." His breath was coming heavily as he thrust into her harder and harder. "Combined with the Shadow and our desire, it's powerful."

What did he feel? She couldn't speak anymore, could barely gather her thoughts when his body shuddered. He clutched her to him as his orgasm claimed him—and her. It rocked her through their bond and their physical connection.

Kasabian was a tornado, no doubt about it. He'd said that once he tasted her, he would want her always. She knew what he meant, because she had tasted him, and she could now only have this. Nothing else—no one else—would ever be enough.

He collapsed, half on and half off her, his arm slung over her middle. His leg lay over hers, pinning her to the spot. Not that it mattered. She couldn't move. Her body had melted into a puddle.

All she could hear was him catching his breath and a vague buzzing in her head. Slowly she began to pull her thoughts together. It took a while longer to work them into coherent spoken words.

When he finally came back and met her eyes, she said, "I *felt* you come. It was crazy."

The corner of his mouth twitched, probably as close

to a smile as he could muster. "I felt you, too." He rolled his eyes. "Mind-blowing. It seemed almost selfish to make you come again and again. But I worked through that."

She giggled. "You can be selfish anytime."

His laugh was smoky, like the finest whiskey she'd ever had. His eyes glimmered, dancing with a rare smile. His hand slid down between her legs, stroking the now very sensitive nub. "I'll keep that in mind."

Tina Arena's song "Chains" played on her mental radio. Kye was in chains, held by nothing more than that smile, those eyes.

"Kasabian."

"Mmm."

"Do you feel like you own me? You were worried about that."

He wrapped his leg over hers, pinning her to the bed. All trace of playfulness fled his expression. "My angel is keeping the balance inside me between dark and light. Barely. Even before I was Stripped, I nearly bit Hayden's head off, because he said he wouldn't mind being bonded to you. I don't trust myself. And I don't deserve your trust either." He placed his palm against her cheek. "Look what I've already done to your life."

Not to mention what he was doing to her heart. She saw and felt his remorse. "Kasabian—"

"Don't let me off the hook by blaming my Shadow. I had as much to do with giving in as it did. Maybe more." He rubbed his thumb over her lower lip. "I know the best thing I can do for you is to send you away. I just don't know if I can."

To illustrate that, he pulled her close, nestling her face

against his shoulder. At the moment, what felt like the best thing for her was being right there in his arms.

A knock on the door jerked her out of her sleep. Kye groped for wakefulness, realizing she was still in Kasabian's embrace.

Another knock. "Kye? It's Mom."

Kye's eyes widened as she sat up. "Stay here." No way did she want to explain him.

He grabbed up his pants. "When you open the door, invite her in before she feels the barrier."

"Hold on a minute, Mom," Kye called out as she hastily pulled on her clothing. It was ten in the morning. She opened the door, and her mom gave her a soft smile. "Come in."

"I woke you. I'm sorry. I forget that you stay at that awful nightclub so late."

"Half of my client base goes there," Kye said for the umpteenth time. "Is everything okay?" Her mom rarely stopped by unannounced.

She inspected the apartment as she always did, probably finding several things she didn't like within her first few steps. This time she didn't mention them. She sank to the sofa, twisting her ring. "I haven't fully supported your... gift. I had hoped for something more respectable."

"Like talking to the dead," Kye said.

The haughty tone returned when she said, "It's a lot more respectable than divining people's sexuality." She shook her head. "I didn't come here to denigrate you. I came...for help."

Oh no. Please don't ask me about your sex life. "I don't think I can—"

"I might be in love with another man."

Kye's protest dropped like a heavy stone. "What?"

"I want you to read my feelings for this man. He's come to me for a few readings to talk to his deceased wife. We have become friends, and I have developed feelings for him. Right now it's just friendship, but he makes me laugh. I feel good when I'm with him. I need to know if these feelings will develop into something romantic. If so, I will back off."

Kye could barely process it. Beyond the fact that her mother seemed on the verge of a possible affair, she'd come to Kye for the first time. If Kye could help her, she could show her mother the validity of her gift. Maybe she would say "gift" without the pause.

And Kye didn't have her ability. *Please, please come back just for a few minutes.* Kye sat down next to her and took her hands. "Think about the man."

Usually the feelings tingled through Kye's hands, pooling into her in waves of colors she could see in her mind's eye. She tried so hard to tune in, to coax the feelings. All she could think about was Kasabian in her bedroom, him in angel form. Him. Damn it.

She considered lying and telling her mother that yes, she'd picked up romantic love. That it would be foolish and dangerous to pursue a relationship. Of course, she was thinking of Kasabian again. She simply couldn't focus on anything but him when it came to romantic feelings.

Kye's eyes opened. No way could she make up something. It went against everything that was in her, everything she subscribed to in regard to her profession.

Her mother was waiting, worry on her normally placid expression. "Well?"

Kye released her hands. "I can't read you."

Her mother blew out a frustrated breath. "The one time I need your ability and you won't—"

"Can't, Mom. I can't, because my Zensu ability is not working. I can't pick up anything at all."

Her mother narrowed her eyes. "The only time you have trouble with that is when you've been romantically involved with a man."

No way could Kye explain what had happened. "I'm a little tangled up about someone right now," she admitted in a soft voice.

"Who?"

"You don't know him."

Her mother's gaze went to the duffel bag tucked to the side of the living room. "He's here, isn't he?" She shot to her feet. "He's here, and you let me go on about my personal issue. I am beyond mortified."

Join the crowd. Kye didn't think it was possible to shrink anymore, but she did. "I'm sorry. I just didn't want to get into that situation with you." Kye had seen that disappointed look so many times, yet she never became inured to it.

Her mother planted her hands on her hips. "Well, bring him out of hiding, where he's been listening the whole time." She called down the hallway, "Come out."

Kye wanted to drop through a hole. Instead, she said, "Kasabian."

He stepped into the hallway from her home office, still shirtless, his hair tousled. She tried to view him through her mother's eyes. Bad boy, with his confident gait and smile that failed at being anything but sexy. Even though he hadn't come from her bedroom, it looked as though they'd recently had sex. And she saw the exact moment her mother realized he was Caido.

Kasabian held out his hand. "Nice to meet you, Mrs. Rivers." He briefly kissed the back of her hand and then gestured to himself. "Sorry for the lack of attire." He ruffled through his bag and donned a shirt. "I was checking my stocks." He gave Kye a guileless look. "Sorry, love, I didn't know anyone was here."

He was good, assuring her mother that he'd heard nothing. Maybe he'd tuned out once he'd heard the reason for her visit.

Her mother's mind was clearly grinding through all the possibilities, and she didn't like any of them if her eyes were any indication. "Kye, walk me to my car."

Kasabian gave Kye the slightest nod. He'd be watching over her.

"What have you gotten yourself into?" her mother hissed the moment they walked away from her door. "He looks like all kinds of bad news. And he's a Caido!"

"I knew you'd disapprove, like you disapprove of all of my life choices." Kye glanced back to find him watching from the distance, surveying the surroundings.

"He's all wrong for you."

"I know."

"He's dangerous. I can see it written all over him."

"I know."

Her mother stopped next to her Mercedes-Benz. "Are you in love with him, or is it infatuation?"

"It's lust." That's all it was, right? Just as he'd said, combined with their bond and the lure of his Shadow. "I don't plan on marrying him, but I feel a connection to him

I can't explain. I did from the first time we met." That was true, having nothing to do with their bond.

"What does he do for a living?"

"Of course you'd ask that. He's a bartender at the Witch's Brew. And he volunteers at a youth center."

Her mother sneered. "A bartender." She didn't comment on the second part. "You know what kind of men tend bars at clubs like that?"

"Men like Kasabian. He has a good heart. He volunteers with disadvantaged kids."

Her mother clapped her hands in front of her face. "Snap out of the spell. Men work at bars because they're looking for one thing."

Kasabian did want one thing—to feel emotion. But Kye couldn't exactly explain that. "Uh, yeah...income. He excels at his job. He's entertainment, the way he mixes the drinks and flips the bottles."

"But is he worth giving up your abilities for? You've told me and your father how much your precious abilities mean to you, how helping people is more important than even your self-respect. Or ours." She flicked her gaze to the apartment building. "Now something else is more important." She shook her head. "A Caido," she muttered, getting into her car.

Kye stood there as her mother pulled away, feeling again like a fourteen-year-old who'd just discovered she'd inherited the wrong kind of ability.

"You all right?"

She spun to find Kasabian behind her, a sympathetic expression on his face. "No, I'm not all right. I finally had the chance to show my mother the value of my abilities." It stunned her, that her mother had come to her. "And I couldn't help her. Because of you." She pushed at him, needing to vent. Her hands connected with his hard chest. He barely took a step back. "You came into my life and messed everything up. Just like you said."

He clamped his hands over hers. "Your mother's right. You're caught in a spell. You can't resist any more than I can. And we're going to drown in it."

A breeze blew a lock of her hair across her cheek.

"She's not right. She's self-righteous and prejudiced." Kye brushed her hair back with her hand. "I'm sorry I took it out on you. She's been making me crazy for so long. I just wanted to prove to her that I have value."

He started to step forward, perhaps to put his arms around her, but visibly pulled back. "You do have value, Kye. Not because of your abilities. Just for yourself. Don't listen to all of that denigrating stuff she says." Before her heart could fully open to those words, he went on. "But she's right about me. I am wrong for you. I am danger-ous. She probably senses the darkness in me. I'm trying to keep the balance between my humanity, my angel, and the Shadow, but where you're concerned, I'm mostly the hun-gry, possessive Shadow. I couldn't stop us from giving in to this desire between us. I'm ashamed to admit I didn't even want to. If I hope to have any control, any sense of right and wrong, we have to stop this."

She saw the agony in his expression, felt his regret. Control. She had lost hers, too, and they both needed it now more than ever. She walked to the apartment. He followed, but she kept her gaze straight ahead. The moment the door closed behind him, she turned to him. "How do we stop this pull we have? Even losing my abilities doesn't keep me from wanting you."

"The only way is for us to stay away from each other. You need to remain here until I determine it's safe."

"And where are you going?"

"To the Bend. If Jonathan ended up with my father, he may have come through this supposedly safe community. I need to find out everything I can about the place."

"Then that's where I'm going, too."

He crossed his arms over his chest and shook his head. "Uh, no, you're not. Remember, we just agreed it would be best to stay apart."

"I saw your dream, Kasabian. I was *in* your dream, and I saw what those kids went through. What they're probably suffering now. If you think I'm going to sit in this bubble while you figure it out, you're sorely mistaken."

———

The moment Lyle's eyes lit upon Kasabian, he rushed forward. "Did you find him?"

"Yes and no." Kasabian told him everything. "Hayden is making it his top priority to find him, I promise you that." Kasabian introduced Kye. "We're working on another angle, and we need to get into the Bend. You've been there. Tell us the best way to get inside."

He jabbed his chest. "Me."

Kasabian shook his head. "The people I'm dealing with are very dangerous. One of them has dark powers. I can't afford to get you involved in this."

"Didn't you just tell me that sometimes you have to let others help? I kept thinking about that all night, how you offered to help me. I didn't want to let anyone into my problems. My life. But I need help, and it's stupid not to take it when it's offered."

Kasabian couldn't help meeting Kye's gaze, and yeah, she was gloating.

"He's right," she said.

He focused on Lyle. Nothing like having a mirror thrust at you in the guise of a young man. "I can't endanger a minor."

"It's the Bend, a gated community. How dangerous can it be? I can get in because my mother lives there. You can accompany me because of your affiliation with the Harbor."

Kye's face lit. "Smart kid. Kasabian, you can pretend to be his guidance counselor. He's having problems in school."

Lyle lifted one shoulder. "That's the truth. But you know why."

Kasabian leaned toward Kye, sensing her body heat, her scent. *Distance*. They had to maintain distance. He moved back. "Lyle's been spending every spare minute of his time looking for Jonathan. So what's your role?"

"I'm his therapist." She brushed her hand over Lyle's unruly hair. "I'm sensing some behavioral issues stemming from his brother's absence. Perhaps we can get some answers, resolution."

Kasabian was surrounded by brilliance. "All right, we'll start there." As long as they didn't look too closely at her credentials, considering that she was a sex therapist.

Cory, who was leaning against the door, said, "There won't be any danger, right? I can't send one of the Harbor kids into an iffy situation."

Lyle stepped forward. "The Bend is nothing compared

to the places I've been looking for Jonathan. If I can get a clue, just a clue, to where he is, I'd go to the Dark Side."

Where demons lived in a plane adjacent to this one.

"He won't be going to the Dark Side," Kasabian assured Cory. "I'll protect them with my life. Can you work up some business cards that show we're affiliated with Harbor?"

Ten minutes later, Cory had printed out a page full of cards for Kasabian and Kye. "If they call, I'll cover for you." His expression grew somber. "Be careful."

"It's a gated community," Kasabian said. "What could go wrong?"

Kasabian borrowed one of Harbor's vehicles, since the Lotus had no backseat, and they had lunch at a little Cuban café before heading to the Bend. It took fifteen minutes for the gatehouse to clear Lyle, and they were sent directly to a building that looked a bit too secure and foreboding to be the community center it pretended to be. The receptionist seemed benign enough as she told them to wait in the lobby for Paul Porter.

A tall, older Deuce came out, his gaze on Lyle. The man seemed unassuming, but his eyes were sharp and calculating. "Yes, I remember you. Your mother has been very worried." He focused on Kasabian and Kye. "Lyle ran away soon after his mother relocated here. He's clearly a troubled young man." Porter spread his arms. "To run away from all this."

What if Lyle's mother insisted on keeping her son with her? After all, she could provide a safe environment for him now, at least on the surface. The Mundane courts would certainly deem her fit, as would the Crescent government. The thought struck deep in Kasabian's stomach. He would not let them keep this kid.

Kasabian held out his hand. "I'm John Thorpe, Lyle's guidance counselor." He gestured to Kye. "This is Mary James, the Harbor's staff therapist."

Kye, in professional attire, handed him a card with her credentials spelled out—minus any reference to sexuality, of course. She gave the man a firm handshake. "Psychologically, Lyle is doing very well at Harbor. But he's struggling with issues I feel can be helped with some answers from his mother. We can then talk about his future."

Paul referred to a folder he'd brought out with him. "I've asked that his mother join us. She should be"—he glanced up as the door opened—"ah, here she is now. Lisa."

A very pregnant woman waddled in and paused as she took in the three of them. Kasabian paused, too. It was always a surprise to see a Caido female.

She pasted a smile on her apprehensive face and gathered Lyle in an awkward hug. "Lyle! I've missed you so much." She stepped back too quickly, her arms crossed over her belly and then loose, obviously not sure what to do with them. She assessed him, but not in the hungry way a mother would, had she been truly eager to see her son. "You ran off, saying all those crazy things." She gave a nervous laugh. "I was terribly worried."

Kasabian wondered if she'd been worried about her son or what he might tell others. "He's been safe and sound at Youth Harbor."

"He would have been safe and sound here, too." Her

expression hardened as she met Kasabian's gaze, but she turned back to Lyle. "But it doesn't matter now. You've come back." She flicked a glance at Porter that sent apprehension through Kasabian again.

Kye must have felt it also, either through their bond or on her own. She put her hand on Lyle's shoulder. Surprisingly, Lyle moved closer to her.

Porter stepped forward. "We've been looking for him. He made some wild accusations. Is that why you're here?"

Lyle's mother's laugh was so phony it grated on Kasabian's nerves. "He's always had a vivid imagination. Add in puberty hormones, and . . ." She shrugged.

So that was her story. Kasabian needed to allay her concerns and put her at ease. "He hasn't told us anything other than that he's heartsick over the loss of his brother. He needs answers so he can move on with his life. His preoccupation with finding Jonathan is not only holding him back, but it's also putting him in precarious situations." Kasabian turned to Porter. "Give us the name of the family who adopted Jonathan. If Lyle can talk to the boy, that will help immensely."

Porter stiffened. "All adoptions are private. But let me assure you that Jonathan is a happy, well-adjusted boy. Why, I did a post-adoption visit just last week, and I've never seen him so content." An outright lie. His smile was even phonier than Lisa's laugh had been. "But perhaps I can arrange to get you a picture. If you come back here to stay, we can keep you updated."

Son of a bitch.

Lyle's expression shuttered again, seeing the trap for what it was. "I want to talk to my mom. In private."

They wandered outside, leaving Porter to watch from

the window. Kye and Kasabian followed at a discreet distance. Lyle couldn't keep his gaze from his mother's belly. "Who's the father?"

Lisa's eyes flicked toward the office as her hand rubbed her distended belly. A subconscious giveaway. Porter.

"When you left, I was distraught," she said. "I turned to someone for comfort."

Kasabian's fingers twitched with rage. She was using Lyle's escape to manipulate his feelings, make him feel guilty. Kasabian couldn't tell whether Lyle was buying into it or not. That his expression was still shuttered was a good sign.

"You sold my brother," Lyle said, his own anger just beneath the surface.

"I didn't sell him, sweetheart." She lifted her hands to encompass the Bend just as Porter had done. "I came here for all of us. I needed time to get straightened out. Jonathan was so young and impressionable. I hurt him." Lisa put on an appropriately bereft expression. "So I let him go to a camp where he could emotionally detox. The people who run the camp fell in love with him. They had the ability to offer him so much more than I could, even living here. They could give him a family."

Did she believe that? Maybe she'd convinced herself. "Did you meet this family?" Kasabian asked when Lyle went silent.

"Yes." She kept her gaze on her son, even though Kasabian had asked the question. "They seemed like a wonderful couple."

She was in on whatever was going on here, had to be.

"If they're so wonderful, why won't they let their new son see his brother?" Kasabian asked.

Lisa's mouth worked but no words came out. *Can't come up with an answer for that, can you?* Finally, seeing that Lyle was waiting for an answer, too, she said, "They want him to have a fresh start."

Lyle tentatively put his hand on her belly. "And what will happen to this baby? My half brother or half sister?"

Lisa placed her hand over his. "If you stay, you can help me raise it. Be a big brother."

Holy hell, she was good. Kasabian clamped a hand on Lyle's shoulder at the same time that Lyle withdrew his hand from beneath hers. He gave Lyle a warning look. *Don't buy this load of bullshit.*

As they wandered the sidewalks, Kasabian studied their surroundings. The Bend certainly seemed like a normal community. The sidewalks could use pressure washing, yards were overgrown here and there, but overall it was well maintained. He saw mostly women, many of them in various stages of pregnancy from baby bumps to due-any-second. That was odd enough. What he didn't see were a lot of children's toys, swing sets, or other evidence that these women kept the children they carried.

What was this place, a breeding farm? The thought gave him a sick feeling.

They passed an unmarked, utilitarian building. "What's this?" Kasabian asked Lisa.

"Security. Administration. Job training and child care."

"Funny, Lisa, I don't see a lot of evidence of children here," Kasabian said.

"They're here," she said in a rush of words, regarding him warily. "No, not a lot of them. Some of the women find themselves in, uh, unfortunate situations." She rubbed her belly. "The Bend finds good homes for their babies."

"They must do a hell of a job," he muttered. He sensed that pressing Lisa would get him nowhere. "I'll be right back. I spotted an old friend. Lisa, if you're hoping to lure—I mean, to convince Lyle to live with you again, it would ease our minds to see where he'd be staying. Why don't you show Ms. James?"

Kye's eyes widened in question, but she nodded. "Yes, that would be helpful."

He watched them head off, wanting a bead on the direction they were going. Then he ducked into the building. The lady at the front desk looked a bit startled when Kasabian approached and loudly asked, "Do you have any children who need a home? My wife and I are unable to conceive, and I understand you facilitate adoptions."

"Sir, this is not—"

"I see lots of pregnant women here," he interrupted. "Surely one of them is ready to pop out a baby she has no plans to raise on her own?"

Two men came out of their offices, drawn by Kasabian's desperate and rude plea. The thinner of the two said, "You got this, Gemini?"

The big, beefy Caido with a white trimmed goatee and mustache stalked toward Kasabian. "Your father just doesn't give up, does he?"

Now it was Kasabian's turn to be startled.

"You are Treylon's son, aren't you?" Gemini asked.

How much did this guy know? Kasabian was going to have to tread carefully. "I am. How did you know?"

"It was a guess. You look like him, and considering he's been here bugging us so much lately, it wasn't hard to put together." Gemini came to a stop mere inches away. "So he's sucked you into this whole"—he made finger quotes—"getting ready for the big, bad solar storm, huh?" He gestured for Kasabian to follow him outside, where they didn't have the receptionist for an audience. "Does he know something we don't, or is he just panicking like all those preppers? He seems to have the inside track on the storm, when it's coming, how strong it's going to be."

Kasabian decided to bluff. "He's serious enough to be stockpiling kids. How many has he gotten from you?"

Gemini shrugged. "I'm not sure exactly, maybe a dozen in the last few months. He's made some special arrangement with my boss, borrowing them until the storm passes. Supposedly he's using their essence to keep the *Deus Vis* even during the storm for his friends and family. Using it like the Essex, right? Son of a bitch has wiped us out."

He was talking about children as though they were merchandise. Kasabian swallowed back his outrage, and the implications of what he was saying. "The people who run this place are okay with him using them like that?" His shock and disgust was leaking through, and he could see that it was putting Gemini on guard by his closed expression. He tempered his voice when he asked, "Is that what you do here? Sell kids?"

Gemini sounded almost robotic. "We don't sell children. We find loving homes for them with Caidos who want a child. We give unwed mothers a safe place to have their baby." There wasn't a speck of concern or warmth, no indication that he cared at all what happened to the kids who were born here.

"Yet, you let one man borrow a dozen so he can prepare for the solar storm?"

"You'll have to take that up with your father." Gemini's

eyes narrowed. "How'd you get in here, anyway? All outside guests come through the office."

"I'm here to talk to a resident about her preteen son. This kid's been at a youth center, and we're trying to negotiate his...adoption. My father thinks getting older ones may work better, because there's more availability."

Gemini's mouth tightened. "You're trying to work around our office?"

"The kid's not part of the Bend, so we aren't violating any rules." Whatever those might be.

"And I say he is."

Kasabian felt Kye before he saw her. She came up beside him, Lyle at her side. "We should go." Her wary gaze settled on Gemini.

Gemini clamped his big hand on Lyle's shoulder. "If he's a resident's son, he's technically ours."

Kasabian gripped Gemini's wrist and let the Shadow cross his eyes at the same moment he sent a magick jolt into Gemini's skin. "He came in with us, and he leaves with us."

The man jerked back with a hiss. "What the fuck?"

Kasabian anchored his hands on Lyle's shoulders. "We're leaving now." He steered the boy toward the small parking lot, keeping his eye on Gemini.

As soon as they were inside the car, Kasabian headed toward the gate. "Forgive me for not making introductions. That was Gemini, a cog in the Bend's organization."

Kye rubbed her arms. "This place is more like the Bent. Something's wrong here. Very wrong."

Lyle looked behind them where Gemini simply watched them leave. "Dude's scary."

Kasabian watched their surroundings as he drove. No

sign of movement or people gathering. He'd feel much better once they cleared the heavy iron gate. Except it wasn't opening. His chest tightened. He'd brought Kye and Lyle to a potential prison. The guard in the gatehouse held out his hand in a *Wait* motion.

Kasabian put the car into reverse, ready to ram it. He was so focused on the guard, the tap on the window made him jump. Gemini motioned for him to roll the window down. He did, ready for anything.

Gemini was breathing heavily, obviously having run here. "If your father does know something about the storm, would you let me know?" He thrust his card at Kasabian. "With the news talking about it, and Treylon...well, it can make one a bit paranoid, if you know what I mean."

Relief swamped Kasabian as he took it, followed by anger. The guy wasn't worried about all those kids he'd farmed out, but he sure was worried about his own ass. "Yeah, sure."

The gate opened, and it felt like ten minutes passed before it was wide enough to drive through. Everyone in the car collectively blew out a breath once they turned onto the road.

"You're right about this place being bent," Kasabian said. "It's definitely twisted. I think it's a breeding farm that supplies kids for Caidos as their own personal Essex device. Most of the women there were Dragon or Crescent."

"What's an Essex device?" Lyle asked.

Kasabian met Lyle's gaze in the rearview mirror. "You know how it's uncomfortable to pick up Dragons' and Deuces' emotions? It gets worse once you hit puberty and you're Awakened."

"That's when I come into my full Caidoness, right? When Dragons can become all beastly and Deuces find out what their magick is. Cory's been preparing all of the twelve-year-olds for that."

"Exactly. Then it will be a lot harder to be around other types of Crescents, and Mundanes as well. The Essex is a way to alleviate that pain temporarily." He explained how it worked. "Caidos can't take someone's essence without their permission, but children don't have to give permission. If a Caido adopts, say, a Dragon child, he can do the Essex with the child as often as he wants." Kasabian didn't say that it could drain that child to the point of death. Like the children who'd been rescued with him.

Kye looked horrified. "And if that child was raised from birth with the Caido, he wouldn't know any different. All those pregnant women are breeders..."

"Like my mom." Lyle's face blanched. "So everything she said about wanting me in her life, me being with my half sibling..."

"I'm sorry." Kasabian had to tell Lyle the truth so he wouldn't be ensnared by the rosy picture she was painting. "I know how it feels to be betrayed by the one person who should be doing everything in his or her power to protect you."

Kye gave Kasabian an empathetic look before turning to run her hand down Lyle's arm. "The lure of money can be very strong. This is about her, not you or Jonathan." She looked at Kasabian. "From the outside, her little house was unassuming. Inside, she had a high-end surround sound system, a huge television. Everything I saw was first class. And no sign of a nursery. I told her she'd have to set up a room for Lyle before he could come back. She would have to dismantle her elaborate gym in the second bedroom."

"I'm not going back to her." Lyle's cheeks were blotchy, his eyes puffy. "But I am going to get my half brother or sister out of there."

"And we will," Kasabian said. "We'll crack open that whole place. At the moment, we have more immediate concerns. Silva said this would be over in a day or two, meaning sometime tomorrow. I don't think it's a coincidence that the solar storm effects are supposed to hit around the same time. Years ago, when I was in Treylon's captivity, he didn't have enough power to use the accumulated essences in whatever way he needed. Given the Crescent scientific theory that a major solar storm triggered the gods' ability to become physical in the first place, I think Treylon is hoping this one will give him the boost he'll need to pull off his scheme."

Kye chewed the tip of her finger. "Which means we don't have much time."

A few minutes later, they pulled into Harbor. Kasabian and Kye escorted Lyle back to his empty room. Lyle just stood there, the strain clear on his face. All it took was for Kasabian to put his hand on the kid's back, and he collapsed against him, sobbing. Kasabian had healed many a Crescent of heartbreak, had been torn in half by tears, but he'd never given physical comfort before.

Kye came up behind Lyle and pressed her cheek against his bony shoulder. She whispered words of comfort. It made Kasabian realize he needed soothing, too. Lyle turned into Kye's embrace, and she hugged him fully. Her eyes were squeezed shut as she held him.

Lyle finally gained control over himself and stepped

back. "That was so not cool," he said in a thick voice, rubbing away his tears.

Kye brushed his damp hair from his forehead. "You'll be stronger for it, not weaker."

Lyle looked at her as though she'd caught *him* in Thrall. "I wish my mom were like you."

Bittersweet sadness filled Kye's smile. "My mom's no loving cup either. We get what we're dealt. It's our job to make the best of it."

Lyle gave her an imploring look. "Let me help with this. I need to help."

Kye's smile was soft and regretful as she smoothed back his hair. "I know the feeling. But you're only a child, and we can't put you in danger."

Kasabian kept his hand on Lyle's back. "I will let you help where it's safe. You'll have to trust me. I want to find him almost as much as you do."

Lyle nodded, his eyes still wet. "I trust you."

Those simple words made him smile. "Thank you."

After they headed out, Kasabian walked to the Lotus's passenger side to open the car door for her.

Kye paused before getting in. "I trust you, too."

She was close enough that he brushed a stray lock of hair from her forehead. "Now that's a mistake, love."

Her mouth curved in a smile. "Mmm, it's 'love' again."

The endearment had slipped out, despite his order not to use it on her. "It rolled off my tongue that first night we met."

"I figured you probably called every woman that."

He could lie and say he did. But she'd just said she trusted him, and so in the end, he admitted, "I've never called any woman 'love.'" He leaned against the roof of the car, facing her. "Don't look at me like maybe, just maybe, I'm not so bad because I let some kid cry all over me. I'm not good, Kye. I used you, made you lose your abilities, and I want to possess you despite all of that. And that's not even the Shadow part of me. Don't ever trust me, Kye."

Chapter 13

Sarai had been getting terrible feelings about Kye all morning. She'd been trying to call her for just as long. On the third try, Kye answered.

"Thank gods! Have you been ignoring my calls?" Sarai had to tamp down her ire.

"No, of course not." Sarai could hear her friend's genuine contriteness. "I've just been, well, caught up in something."

"Something called Kasabian?"

"We're involved in a...project."

Sarai leaned back in her chair, crossing her arms over her chest. "Oh, is that what they're calling it nowadays?"

"It's serious. I don't want to drag you into this any more than you are. Excuse me for a moment," Kye told someone and then a moment later said, "Look, Sarai—"

"I've been worried about you. Remember that forecast I got when you first met him? Well, I'm getting more. But I need to ask you something first, and I'm not being nosy. Did the first part of my forecast come true?"

Silence for a few moments. "You mean the good and hot and sexy part?" she asked at last.

"Yes. I need confirmation that I'm accurate. Because frankly, I'm a bit confused."

Another moment of silence. "Yes. It was all of that, Sarai, and don't lecture me."

Sarai closed her mouth on what would have been just that. She was concerned for her friend, for so many reasons. Kye had always been the levelheaded one. While Sarai fell in love willy-nilly, Kye was the voice of reason. To throw away her abilities, her sanity, to chase Kasabian and some *project* wasn't like her. She'd heard that Caidos could hold others in Thrall, and that had to be what Kye was under.

Kye broke into her thoughts. "I know it's hard for you to trust my judgment when it feels like I've gone off the deep end. I'm asking you to anyway. What are you seeing? No matter how crazy it sounds, I need to know. Maybe it could help."

Sarai didn't trust her judgment, but she would tell her what she knew. "Are you dealing with any Dragons right now? Because I'm seeing some dark Dragon energy."

"Sort of. Go on."

"I still see you in a very bad place, and whatever's going on there is tearing your heart out. I keep getting the phrase 'sleeping with the enemy.' Does any of that mean something to you? Particularly the 'sleeping with' part?"

"Kasabian is not the enemy, and I'm certainly not sleeping with anyone else. That expression can mean working with the enemy, too."

Sarai mulled that over. "Something about that phrase resonates. Yeah, working with the enemy will move things forward. That's what I'm getting, though I'm not sure what it means. What in the hell are you two up to?"

"I have to go, hon. Thank you. For the information and for your confidence in me. Let me know if you get anything else. I'll talk to you soon."

Sarai sank down on her couch. Her best friend was sliding down a very slippery slope. Sarai needed to call in reinforcements if she was going to save her from whatever was at the bottom.

Hayden was about to drop from exhaustion. For hours, he'd been staking out the estate where he thought the Hummer was registered. It wasn't the same place where he'd found Kasabian being beaten. That would have been too easy.

The gate opened, and the black Hummer pulled out. Suddenly Hayden wasn't tired anymore. Was Jonathan inside? The windows were too dark to see anyone, but he thought he saw a head that was shorter than the rest in the backseat. He waited for several heartbeats and followed.

Fifteen minutes later, the Hummer pulled into the secured garage of the White Tower, an exclusive and secure high-rise with residences above the ground-level shops. The estate had been impossible to Leap into because of a barrier—the Tower would be even harder.

Kasabian had just updated him on their visit to the Bend. Or the Bent, as he heard Kye call it in the background.

The place had always given him the creeps, and he never knew why. Now he did. That boy who'd been sold and

used, who still lived deep inside him, must have sensed
that something wasn't right. Once they were finished with
Treylon's operation, he was going to shut down that dis-
gusting madness.

He called Kasabian and reported, "The Hummer finally
left. I'm not sure if Jonathan was inside, but I have a feeling he was. I followed it to the White Tower."

Kasabian took a second to digest that. "Where the
Elders are rumored to live." The elite group of the oldest
Caidos. "Which makes sense, since at least one Concilium
member is obviously involved in my father's scheme. The
one who arranged for Jonathan to be taken from Guard custody. Find Jonathan and we find that person."

Hayden leaned forward and scanned the side of the
building that rose up some twenty-five stories. "Exactly
what I was thinking. Other than the small issue of getting
inside the most secure building in Miami. I was part of a
team that responded when a Caido took a woman hostage
here. Even then I had to be double cleared."

"Come on, you're super Vega man. Are you saying that
getting in is going to be a problem for you?"

Smart-ass. "I'll just scale the outside and bust into one
of the windows."

"I have an easier way to get us in."

"The super-secret password?"

"Yeah. Muse."

Hayden curled his fingers over the bottom of the steering wheel. "Come again?"

"You've heard of Muses?"

"Only that they're a small group of female Caidos with
that geisha mystique. From what I've heard, they're basi-
cally high-priced call girls who only service the Elders."

Kasabian made some kind of grunting sound. "They're not *call girls*."

"Sounds like they're just taking advantage of being a rare female and making men pay for it. Which makes them call girls."

The Caido male who snagged a female Caido could manage to have a marriage, even a sex life, because Caidos couldn't sense each other's feelings. On top of that, they suppressed their emotions, so they felt no true desire and thus no pain. It ended up being more of a partnership, a way to perpetuate the small population of Caidos.

"They've been revered and protected by Caido Elders since the beginning of our kind," Kasabian said. "They are treated like goddesses. If she sees a non-Elder as a client, he usually showers her with gifts. Men go to them to be inspired. They're like the Greek muses. And they live in the Tower."

"And this helps us how? Because I don't know about you, but I don't have any Muses in *my* phone directory."

"*I* do."

Hayden slapped the wheel now. "You've been getting it on with some sex goddess, and you never *told* me?"

"We haven't been *getting it on*. Mallory and I kept running into each other at a coffee shop. We became friends, and she confided about the Muse thing. Before that, I thought they were high-priced call girls, too."

"Hey, if she can help us get to that kid, I'll kiss her feet."

"All right, I'll set up an introduction. Foot fetish then. Call you right back."

"I hope you're kidding," Hayden said, but Kasabian had already hung up. He sat back in the seat and released an impatient breath. Now that he'd potentially located

Jonathan, it was hard to stay still and wait. A Muse would get him in. Figured. He didn't have anything against Muses morally. Well, maybe he did. He remembered the Crescent men who came to his mother's run-down apartment and paid for the novelty of fucking an angel. There were Caido men, too. She'd told him that the pressures of being one of the few females had messed her up. She never knew if a man wanted her for her or because she was Caido. So she sold herself and kept the boundaries clear. And her bank account full.

His phone rang. Kasabian.

"You're in. I told her you were desperate."

"Nice. So I have to act desperately horny?"

Kasabian laughed, the bastard. "You've got to get the whole prostitute thing out of your head. I told her you're a writer, and you've been suffering major writer's block. You have a deadline, and you're desperate for inspiration."

"Ha-ha."

"I'll give you something to laugh about. You've got a couple of sex scenes you need help with because you're a virgin and have no idea what actually goes on. That should give you something to talk about until Kye and I can get over there. We got stuck in a traffic jam, so we pulled off so Kye could run into a Starbucks. I'll have to figure out another way to get to you, but it may be a while. You can start checking out the place. Maybe even find out if Mallory's seen any kids."

"This is getting better and better. So I have to ask her about sex. That won't be awkward."

"Buck up, my friend. You've been in tighter situations than this."

Well, that was true. Hayden grunted and hung up. Great.

Time to pose as a john. He wasn't buying the inspiration thing for a second.

The security guard at the desk checked his ID, then summoned another guy, who escorted him to the twelfth floor. Hayden wanted to knock the guy out and start exploring the floors, but he was sure the guard manning the security cameras would put a stop to that soon enough.

"Muses have panic buttons all over their condos," the escort said in a droll voice. "If I have to come up, prepare to be hurt very bad. You do not pressure, coerce, or threaten the Muse. No pictures or video. And you do not leave the residence on your own. When you are finished, I escort you back down again. Understand?"

"Perfectly. But thanks for explaining it so well."

The guy's eyes narrowed at Hayden's sarcastic comment. "You ought to be grateful she's seeing someone like you."

"Like me? And what's that, exactly?"

The elevator door opened, and the man pointed for Hayden to go first.

"You're not coming in with me, are you?"

The guy ignored the question and pressed the doorbell. Pleasant chimes sounded on the inside. The door opened, and Hayden's first thought was, damn, Mallory had a helper or chaperone. The woman at the door wore little makeup, and her long, dark brown hair wasn't fluffed or arranged to be seductive. Her red jeans were tight enough to show toned legs and slim hips, but they didn't scream *sensuous* or *inspiring*.

"Welcome, Hayden," she said, giving the escort a polite nod before gesturing for Hayden to come in and closing the door.

Hayden took in the spacious condo, then the windows that showcased the city beyond. The walls, painted in shades of light rose and beige, were punctuated by original paintings by a Caido artist known as Callo. Little was known about him, other than that he was reclusive, insanely talented, and painted scenes of exquisite sensuality. Painful sensuality. A song he'd never heard before played on the stereo, something he'd categorize as soulful electronica.

"Would you like a drink?" the woman asked. Her glossy hair draped over the swells of her breasts, concealing what little the loose black top revealed. "Absinthe?"

"Please. Is Mallory here?" Maybe she'd had to run out, which would buy him more time before he had to pretend.

Her mouth quirked. "I'm Mallory."

"Oh." The word drew out of his mouth, a long vowel of embarrassment and surprise. "I was expecting…"

"Flowing gown? Rose petals in my hair?" She went to work setting two bell-shaped glasses on the granite counter of an incredible custom wet bar situated off to the side of the living room.

He couldn't help smiling. "Yeah, something like that."

"Sorry to disappoint. This kind of first encounter is unusual, but Kasabian is very persuasive. Usually it would be more like a business meeting. We discuss your goals, expectations, that sort of thing. If I accept you as a client, we decide on the specifics."

"Is that a euphemism for sex?"

Her beautiful face remained placid as she poured liquid over a sugar cube, but the shimmer in her eyes spoke of fire and not ice. "I do not have sex with my clients at their whim. It is always my choice to proceed in that direction,

and I rarely do." She handed him one of the glasses, bringing with her the scent of the anise. "Kasabian did tell you
about the nature of what I do, didn't he? And what I don't."

"Sure, of course. I don't have, er, anything to offer. I understand that's customary."

"It's fine. I don't require a gift. That's a very old custom." She lifted her glass in a toast. "To your first time."
Their glasses touched. After taking a sip, her mouth curved
in the slightest smile. "I'll be gentle with you."

Something tickled through his stomach. Okay, he took
it back. She *was* provocative.

The song was the perfect backdrop for Mallory. The female singer was asking why he couldn't like her like the
other boys did. They stared at her, but she craved him.

"Interesting song," he said. The syncopation of the bass
line pulsed through his body.

"It's 'Crave You,' by Flight Facilities. I like the Adventure Club dub mix." She took another sip and swirled the
liquid around in her mouth before swallowing. "So, Hayden, what is it that you want from me?"

He was annoyed to find the prickle of desire stampeding
right down to his cock as his wayward mind supplied an
answer or two. He trained his gaze behind her, to a picture
frame that was turned away and out of view.

"Tell me why you do this." He wandered over to the
picture, turning it to see Mallory and a young girl on the
beach. Both were covered in sand and grinning.

She followed him, taking the picture from his hand. The
softness had left her eyes. She set the frame facedown with
a *clack*. "Let's focus on your writing."

Hayden couldn't miss the edge in her voice. "I'm just
making conversation, getting to know you. As a writer, I'm

interested in what motivates people." He took in the things that probably weren't expensive gifts: a shell necklace dangling from a statue, a collection of feathers in a tall, fluted glass, and a picture of dolphins breaking the surface all spoke of the real Mallory. "What moves you?"

"This is about you, not me."

He plucked one of the feathers from the glass. "But if you're my inspiration, it's about you."

"Only as it pertains to you." Her fingers twitched as she eyed the feather in his hand. He liked ruffling her placid exterior. He tipped his chin toward the picture. "Who's the girl? Your daughter?"

Mallory's cheeks flamed hot. "My niece. And that's all I'm saying about her."

He sauntered over to one of the paintings, a male angel kneeling before a seated female angel, his face buried in her upturned hands. Her long, dark hair spilled down over his bowed back, catching the light coming from a window.

Hayden couldn't keep from feeling pulled into the scene. She stepped up beside him, her gaze on the painting, too. Her eyes softened and shimmered. It moved her, even though she saw it all the time. His gaze went back to the woman in the painting, and it hit him. "That's you." She looked so beautiful and innocent, it almost hurt.

She merely shrugged. "I pose for him sometimes."

She obviously inspired the artist to the greatest of heights. Every shadow, every wash of light over skin and hair, perfection.

Hayden kept his gaze on the innocent version of Mallory. "What do you think this scene is about? Supplication?"

"It depends on my mood. Sometimes I think he's begging her to love him back. Other times I think he's bidding her goodbye."

He obviously did feel inspired in her presence, or at least his mouth did, because he had no intention of voicing the question that popped into his head: "Have you ever begged someone to love you back?" He met her gaze, at the same moment the woman on the stereo sang, "I crave you."

Her gaze dropped to his mouth for just a second before she turned back to the painting. "Kasabian said you have writer's block. Let's talk about that."

"All right. I'm writing a story about a Muse who falls in love with one of her clients. So, of course, I need to know what motivates a woman like you. What moves you."

She aimed an irritated look at him and opened her mouth to no doubt tell him off. The phone rang, silencing her. Kasabian.

Chapter 14

We're going to see a Caido *hooker*?" Kye traced her finger along the stitching on the seat of Kasabian's Lotus.

Kasabian made a turn toward the ocean. "She's not a hooker; she's a Muse. Didn't you hear what I said? Muse, for their ability to inspire. Mallory is a professional, as dedicated to her craft as you are to yours. She stays unemotionally involved for the same reasons you do."

Yeah, and look how that turned out. "I guess I got hung up on the 'inspire with sensuality' part. I, of all people, shouldn't judge. I know how folks misconstrue the word *sensuality* for *sex*." She wanted to pretend she didn't want to know, but the words "Have you been, uh, inspired by her?" came out.

"I did not go to her as a client, no. We became friends." He shrugged, which meant *And more*, but he was too nice to say.

She wasn't nice. "Can you give me a definition of 'friends'? Yes, I'm being nosy."

His eyebrows raised. "Muses can take lovers, but they aren't allowed to get emotionally involved or married. It has nothing to do with their abilities being impaired, like you, but more about their obligations to Muse-hood. My word, not hers. We were hanging out a little too much. She said she was starting to have feelings, and we backed off. That was about five years ago."

"She fell in love with you." Oh, yeah, Kye was liking this woman less and less.

He lifted his shoulder in a shrug. "We have lunch once in a while, and that's it."

Kye hated to admit it, but Mallory *was* like her in some ways. Helping people with their issues, staying emotionally uninvolved for fear of losing her career. Damn, she wanted to dislike her on principle. Not for what she did, but for her history with Kasabian.

"Do you visit other Muses then?" She gave him a stern look. "And don't say a word about me being jealous. I'm just…curious."

He gave her a sly smile. "Of course you are. For the record, I haven't had empty, meaningless sex in a long time. It was easier to not think about that aspect of my life."

Was easier. Her ego was eating up the fact that he was obsessed with her, that she was the one who'd awakened that part of him. *Bad ego. Bad, bad ego.*

She sank into the memory of his hand squeezing her breast and skimming her skin, the way her body had come to life beneath his touch. He had awakened a savage beast in her, too, though hers wasn't the Dragon kind.

Those thoughts sparked the memory of him pinning her against the wall. *You are mine*, he'd growled, and some part of her had answered, *Yes, I am.*

Holy Zensu, what was happening to her? Kye stopped the thoughts before he could pick them up through their bond. *Puppies. Babies. Cleaning the litter box, Vlad supervising as always.* Anything to divert her attention.

"Kye," he said on a groan, "you're killing me."

Too late. "Sorry, my thoughts tend to run away from me sometimes. What do you pick up exactly?" *Please, not images or specifics.*

"Your desire. Like you're getting aroused by the idea of meaningless sex."

Yeah, you keep thinking it's that. "But I thought desire wasn't painful when it came from me because of the bond."

He pulled into the parking lot of a huge high-rise building and found a visitor's parking space. His fingers tightened over the shifter as he pinned her with a look of heat and agony. "It's not the same kind of pain. It's more like…mass frustration. Because I can have it, and I can't have it."

Kye understood too well. She shoved back all those thoughts. It was easy to quell the desire when she was about to face a woman who'd fallen in love with him. It shouldn't matter at all. But it did.

Kasabian phoned Hayden. "How's it going?"

"I think it might help if you come over. Us writer types, we're a little awkward socially. At least for me, it's easier to talk to my characters than a…beautiful woman." His voice got a little fainter. "Mallory, is it all right if Kasabian comes up? He's in the neighborhood."

"Yes," she said from a short distance away. "*Please*, have him come up."

Kasabian chuckled as he disconnected. "Hayden's playing his role well, I think. Maybe too well."

"Or she's just eager to see you," Kye said, getting out of the car.

Kasabian looked at her from across the roof as he got out. "Not that you're jealous or anything."

She narrowed her eyes, but what could she say? This was a foreign feeling. She'd never had anyone to be jealous over.

Mallory had already notified the man behind the security desk, so within a minute they were being escorted to the elevator. A few seconds later, a woman who looked nothing like Kye expected answered the door. Not seductive and overly made up, but clean and fresh, like the girl next door. If that girl were ethereally stunning.

Mallory's tense expression immediately melted, and she hugged Kasabian. For a moment her eyes squeezed shut. She seemed to reluctantly let go and invited them in. Kasabian rested his hand in the middle of Kye's back as he made introductions. It felt faintly proprietary, and a part of her liked that. *Mine,* echoed in her mind again. Her voice or his, flowing through their connection?

Mallory took the two of them in with even more curiosity but was too polite to voice the questions that were on her face. Kye wondered what Mallory picked up from her. Mallory focused on Kasabian. "I'm not sure your friend is ready to do this." She gave Hayden a backward glance.

"He's not." Kasabian led Mallory to her sofa by the hand, sitting down on the arm once she was settled. "I'm sorry to deceive you, but this isn't about creative inspiration."

Mallory almost looked relieved, but then she turned to Hayden. "So all your harassment was what? A way to pass the time?"

Kasabian gave Hayden a stern look. "You were harassing her?"

Hayden shrugged. "I was probing her. I mean, prodding. I was just asking her some questions. Yeah, to pass the time." But he looked a bit flustered.

Mallory turned her now irritated expression to Kasabian. "What the hell is going on?"

He pulled out the picture of Jonathan. "Have you seen this boy in the Tower?"

Mallory studied the picture. "Cute kid, but no. I rarely see children here."

"Who owns the black Hummer?"

"Kasabian, you know the identity of those who live here is sacrosanct. What is this about?"

He tapped the picture. "Whoever owns that Hummer has this kid. And he shouldn't."

Compassion glittered in her eyes. "Has he been kidnapped?"

"In a manner of speaking. He's being used in a program that at least one member of the Concilium is sanctioning. I don't know who, so we can't go to the authorities." He settled his hands on her shoulders. "I don't want to drag you into this. If it causes any trouble, tell them I tricked you, that we forced the information out of you, whatever you have to say. But I need the name and the floor he lives on or this kid dies."

"You're serious?" Mallory asked.

"Very."

"Richard Talbot owns the Hummer. He lives on the eighteenth floor. I don't know much about him, other than he's an arrogant ass and a very old Caido. He was trying to get me to work with his son, Kevin, who's Arrogant Ass, Junior."

Kasabian planted a kiss on her forehead. "Thank you." He opened the French doors leading out to her balcony and went out, Hayden right behind. They seemed to be sizing up the distance between balconies.

Mallory leaned up on tiptoe, balancing herself by putting her hands on Kasabian's arm, and whispered, "You are *not* going to scale six floors."

There was no easy way to get from one floor to the next, and the thought of them trying tightened Kye's stomach.

"And you can't Leap either," Mallory added. "There are barriers all over the building. You'd be shot down the moment you were spotted. These old Caidos have awesome powers. A few years ago, some guy tried to break in." She grimaced. "It wasn't pretty."

Kye waved them inside, and once the doors were closed, said, "We need to find out if Jonathan's in there first. I can send a scry orb up to look in the windows."

Kasabian and Mallory looked at her with puzzled expressions.

"It's a spy orb, a tiny thing that looks like a bug unless you know what you're looking at."

"Great idea," Kasabian said, looping his arm around her and pulling her close for a moment. "This is why I brought her," he said to the others. "She's brilliant."

She arched an eyebrow at him. *As if you had a choice.*

Kye held out her hand, palm up. "It's been forever since I've made one. It's one of the first bits of magick we learn. Then we discover it's intrusive to, say, spy on your best friend's conversations or your parents when you think they're Christmas shopping." She shuddered at the memory of catching her father stuffing more than the stockings.

Hayden said, "The Deuces in the Guard use them a lot. Sometimes they really come in handy."

Mallory's mouth dropped open. *"You're with the Guard?"*

Hayden's shoulders widened just a bit, his pride showing. "Vega."

Mallory spun to Kasabian. "You sent a Vega to me? They're incompetent, egotistical, corrupt—"

Hayden held out his hand as though he could physically stop her words. "Whoa. We're not all that way." He paused. "What happened?"

Mallory glanced behind her at a shelving unit. A picture on the unit, Kye thought. "The Guard was useless when I needed them." She pinned Hayden with a hard look and huffed. "That explains a lot."

"Mal, please?" Kasabian said. "Work with us."

Mallory's eyes got sort of shimmery as they locked onto Kasabian's. Though Kye couldn't pick up one damned feeling, she knew Mallory was still a little in love with Kasabian.

"All right," Mallory said. "For you."

At least she hadn't said, *Anything for you, Kasabian.* Kye would have gagged.

Kye focused on the magick that spiraled from the center of her palm and swirled into a small gray orb. "It's not tight enough." The orb was fraying at the edges, barely holding together. It had been nearly as hard to create the blue orb she'd used when Kasabian was fighting Silva. "I'm so out of practice. Tighter. Come on, tighter."

The orb snapped together, shiny and gray like a metallic beetle. She directed it to float upward and then into the kitchen. She created a holographic window to see through the orb. Sleek shell-pink granite and opalescent cabinets, a black granite sink. She brought the orb back. "It's working."

The four of them returned to the balcony. Kye released the orb and directed it to the eighteenth floor. They all watched it fly up and out of sight, then turned to the window that hovered in the air. Balconies and French doors whizzed by as they all counted the stories out loud. Once the orb reached the right floor, she directed it to land on the balcony railing. Its legs clamped onto the smooth concrete. The windows reflected the sun, making it difficult to see inside, so she sent it closer to the French doors, where it landed on a mullion.

A man was on the phone, pacing and clearly arguing, though she couldn't hear his words. He jammed the phone into his pocket and stalked into the interior of the condominium. Another man was in the kitchen pouring a glass of milk. She watched him carry it into the living room and hand it to...a boy. Jonathan!

"He's there," she said on a long breath of relief, resolve, and trepidation.

The man looked up, staring at the doors. Then he started walking toward them. She called the orb back, and it disintegrated as it reached her.

"Good job." Kasabian gently squeezed the back of her neck. "How do we get to him?"

I want a kiss, too. It was a silly and childish thought, but there it was.

"I can make an orb to destroy the door," Kye said, mentally sorting through the various orbs she could create. "Of course, that would draw attention. I could create a bubble orb. It creates the illusion of invisibility. We could knock on the door and go inside when someone opens it."

"I can get us into his son's residence," Mallory said. "I could apologize for being rude to him." She grimaced. "Tell him I've been thinking about all those freaky, jacked up muscles of his, the insane edge to his laugh, and the endearing way he stares at my boobs as though he expects them to move of their own volition."

She seemed to shake off the memory of that encounter. "He leers at me every time we pass in the lobby or out by the pool, so I think he'd buy it. If he invites me in, I'll make some excuse to go to the bathroom and Leap you in. I'll have permission to enter, and you'll be coming in with me, so we should be able to bypass any barriers on that floor." This she said to Kasabian, no surprise. "Which covers Talbot's unit as well, since he and Kevin have units on the same floor. We subdue Kevin and climb over to Talbot's balcony. Not easy, but doable."

We. She'd inserted herself into the action. Kye took a better look at the shelving unit, seeing a picture of Mallory and a little girl. Maybe she had a personal reason to get involved.

"I like it," Kasabian said, getting agreement from Hayden. "I know you can pull off the seduction, but are you ready for combat?"

Mallory's shoulders stiffened. "I have to be ready all the time. I can't rely on some security guy to come to my aid. One of the Muses here was taken hostage by a Caido blissed out on Abyss. He beat her up pretty bad, and the Guard had to come in and rescue her. That was one time they got it right."

"That was me," Hayden said.

Just for a second there, admiration crossed Mallory's face. Then she returned to her determined expression. "You were her hero. I'm not willing to wait for my prince to come. I take care of myself."

Hayden gave her a wooden smile. "Duly noted. In case I get any ill-conceived notions of saving you or anything."

They sparked off each other. *Hmm, it'd be interesting to sense what's going on between those two.* Damn it, she wanted her Zensu ability back. Not only were her feelings for Kasabian short-circuiting them, but now new ones were also coming in. Jealousy? *Really*?

Not to mention lust, of all things. Especially when Kasabian took off his shirt in preparation for Invoking his angelic essence. Holy Zensu, mother of all things sensual. His black wings tattoo shimmered. The hard lines of his back, the indent of his spine that begged for her to run her finger all the way down to the waistband of his jeans, made her want to touch him.

Kasabian turned, catching her looking with the aforementioned lust. Busted. She shifted her gaze to Hayden, finding him also shirtless. His physique was on the other end of the ridiculously gorgeous spectrum. He was a big farm boy built with an enormous chest and biceps that made one think he could lift a house from its foundation. Still, her eyes went back to Kasabian, liking his lean physique better.

She focused instead on her upturned palm. "I'm going to send an orb down to the parking garage to keep an eye on the Hummer."

"Good idea," Kasabian said.

Kye hadn't even noticed that Mallory had left the room, what with all the masculine distraction, but now she returned wearing something a bit more provocative. While

Kye had worn her tight black skirts and fishnets to intimidate, Mallory's ruffled, deeply cut blouse and tight black pants invited. And at the moment, they invited Hayden's appreciative stare.

"Good luck," Kasabian told her, and she walked out with a solemn nod.

Hayden let out a long, low whistle. "She's something else, and I mean that in a lot of ways." He gave Kasabian a wary glance. "You're not going to get all"—he did a vague wave across his eyes—"like you did before, are you?"

Kasabian chuckled. "You may whistle all you want. It's not the same. Not even close."

What was that about?

Kye went back to her orb, releasing it off the balcony and sending it down to the garage. Through the window, she sent the orb to settle on the Hummer's back bumper. If it moved, she'd feel it.

Hayden pulled out his cell phone. "I'm going on vibrate mode. Text me if you need help."

She took the opportunity to clear her thoughts, deeply inhaling the ocean air. The breeze caressed her cheeks and toyed with the loose strands of her hair. When she opened her eyes, Kasabian was leaning on the railing next to her, and they were alone. He was going to ask her something, and it was going to be personal. She could see it in his curious expression, and it would likely be about whatever feelings he'd picked up from her earlier.

"Mallory's still in love with you," she blurted out before he could question her. "You two seem good together, you know. I mean, other than the fact that she's a Muse." When Kasabian gave her a baffled look, she forged on. Or rather, she babbled the words out of her mouth. "What I mean to say is, couldn't you convince her to quit? I think she'd quit for you."

He gave her a heart-stopping, roguish smile. "Trying to get rid of me?"

"I don't have you." Boy, could those words come out of her mouth any faster? She curled her fingers over the rough edge of the balcony railing, training her gaze on the distance.

Kasabian released another sigh. "Yes, you do. I just don't know what to do about it."

That made her turn to him, and for a moment, their gazes locked. Her heartbeat thrummed, pulling her toward him. Before she could even begin to think of a reply, Mallory appeared—like out of thin air—in the living area.

"I'm in. Kevin's in the bedroom waiting for me." She shuddered.

"Damn, you're good," Hayden said, admiration in his voice.

Red tinted Mallory's cheeks. She turned to Kasabian. "I need to get right back."

"The Hummer's on the move," Kye said, feeling the orb vibrating as the vehicle's engine started. They watched the Hummer pull out of its spot and stop near the elevator. "We need to get down there."

Kasabian bowed, bracing his hands on his thighs. Silvery wings emerged from his shoulder blades, catching her breath with their magnificence. His magnificence. For a moment, the pain drained the blood from his face, but he quickly recovered and looped his arm around Kye's. "Hayden, go with Mal. I'm going to take Kye down and scope out the situation with the Hummer."

Before Mallory could object, Kye felt her body evaporate in a crazy way. Nothing new there. Everything that had happened to her since meeting Kasabian had felt crazy. Especially when she was in his arms.

They landed next to the Lotus in the outside parking lot, his arm still around hers as he pulled her down behind the car. "Where's the window?"

She pulled it up and moved the orb to a nearby car for a better view of the elevator door. One of the rear doors of the Hummer was just closing.

"They just got in," she said, clutching Kasabian's arm. "I couldn't see who."

"Then we follow. Between the four of us, we have Jonathan covered."

Chapter 15

———

Silva's phone vibrated in his pocket. "Yes?" he answered.

"We're on our way back with the boy, but there's a problem."

"Not another one." He couldn't take many more.

"We're being followed by a yellow Lotus. Two people inside."

Kasabian and someone else. Hayden? Kye? Apprehension and adrenaline surged through him at once. If they were following the Hummer, they had put together too many pieces. He wasn't going to be able to hide Kasabian's interference from Treylon anymore. Or protect him.

Silva gripped the phone tight. "Leap here with the boy. I'll handle the Lotus."

The tall, thin Caido appeared, his hand on the boy's arm. Silva leaned down to the kid's level and gave him a genuine smile. "Welcome back."

Jonathan started crying. Well, Silva was happy to see *him*, anyway. The kid looked stronger than he had before his escape, enough to facilitate their final plan. The big push would no doubt be the end of him. He wasn't strong enough for that.

Kasabian's words about kids like this—like he had been—pinched his conscience. *Sorry, but this kid's fate is sealed.*

"Take him to the house and keep this incident quiet. Treylon doesn't need the stress right now. I'll take care of the problem." Silva Leaped to the passenger seat of the Hummer, startling the driver into swerving slightly. "Head to the causeway."

"Yes, sir."

Silva liked the sound of subservience. It had always been him saying "Thank you, sir, may I have another?" or doing everything Treylon asked of him so he could attain the position of his son. Not that the man had ever acknowledged that.

Bitterness seeped into his soul as he climbed into the back and spotted the Lotus following close behind. The sun gilded Kasabian's shoulder through the window, a Greek god in a little yellow car. His passenger looked like the woman in the park. Kye. What was their relationship?

He returned his focus to Kasabian. Silva had fixated on him from the first moment he'd laid eyes on him all those years ago. He just hadn't realized what the feeling was.

Damn you, Kasabian. I don't want to have to kill you.

Hayden followed Mallory out of the bathroom, staying out of sight. He needn't have worried. Kevin was lying on the rumpled bed, his arms and legs spread, his hand trying to work up an erection. Hayden could have lived his entire life without seeing that.

"I knew you wanted me," Kevin said as Mallory entered his bedroom. He had an effeminate voice with a built-in whine. "I could tell by the way you looked at me every time we saw each other. I never understood why you fought it. I've been with the other Muses, but you always refused my requests for a visit. Of course, you know that made you even more enticing." He lifted his head and frowned. "Why aren't you in some sexy outfit? You were in the bathroom for so long, I thought you were strapping on garter belts or leather straps."

Mallory knelt on the far edge of the bed, drawing the man's attention away from where Hayden maneuvered to remain hidden. "I thought you might want to undress me yourself."

Hayden clocked him from behind with a low dose of Light. Not enough to kill the bonehead, just enough to knock him out. Kevin flopped back onto the bed, his half-ass erection flopping to the side.

"Is this what you have to deal with?" he said, trying to wipe that image from his mind, too.

Her mouth tightened as she took in the man on the bed. "Sometimes. Just because he's the son of an Elder, he thinks he's entitled. He doesn't get that it's always our choice."

Hayden waved his hand over Kevin's head. "He'll be out for a while. Let's go."

They stepped onto the balcony. The ocean breeze snapped against him. Buildings, roads, and water spread out below, and he hoped no one looked up to see two people scaling the walls. Several yards away, another balcony jutted out.

Mallory's hair, caught by the breeze, washed over her shoulders as she turned to him. "See the cornices and the stone angels?" She pointed to some decorative pieces mounted to the exterior, fat cherubs in various poses. "We can use them."

"You do mean 'we' theoretically, don't you?"

"No, I don't. There could be a few Caidos in there. You might think you're a big, tough Vega, but you're only one Caido." She tapped her collarbone. "Now there are two of us."

"You must really be in love with Kasabian if you're willing to throw yourself in like this." At her surprised expression, he added, "I saw the way you held on to him for just a little too long when you greeted him."

"I care about Kasabian, but... it's not love. I'm doing it for my niece, who went missing two years ago."

The girl in the picture. "And the Guard did nothing to help." The pieces started to come together.

"That's an understatement. There was something hinky about it, because even the Elders wouldn't intercede."

She'd gone past the cool, detached woman and became a vulnerable, hurting one. He would investigate her niece's disappearance, but he wouldn't tell Mallory unless he found something. He would offer her no false hopes, no promises.

Hayden kept watching the balcony. "My plan is to grab the kid and just get him out of there. He's my first priority." But now he had Mallory's safety to keep in mind. "If either of us finds him, we yell 'target!' Then Leap him to Kasabian's apartment. Do you know where that is?"

"No. I've never been to his place."

Hmm. Maybe she was telling the truth about Kasabian. Hayden gave her the address. "If only one of us gets out—"

She put her hand on his arm. "I can take care of myself." She seemed to realize that she was touching him and jerked her hand back. "Like you said, the boy is the priority here."

Mallory pulled off her shirt, leaving her in a lacy red bra that cupped two luscious handfuls. He had to catch his breath at the sight of her willowy figure, trim hips, the way her hair brushed her waist. A script *M* graced the top curve of her breast. Her wings pushed out of her back, and she grimaced in pain. He had the absurd urge to come up behind her and wrap his hands around her waist. Pull her against his body and comfort her. That urge stabbed through him, as though a dozen knives had come flying his way.

She sucked in a breath through clenched teeth. "Damn, that hurts like a bitch every time." Her creamy flesh showed through the red lace of her bra. "I bought it at Victoria's Secret if you want one for yourself."

Yeah, he was staring. "Why don't I just take yours, save me the trip?"

She blinked, then slapped her arm over her chest. "Touch it and die."

Damn, she was feisty. Probably better to capitulate than continue to antagonize her. "Sorry, I've never seen a female Caido Invoke before. I have no interest in your bra or what's beneath it." But he did, and it rocked through him. "Let's go."

He Invoked, too, the angelic form muffling the pain of desire. Leaving only desire. *Helluva time and place for that.*

Hayden hoisted himself up over the balcony, reached for one of the decorative pieces, and took a long step. His foot barely made contact with the shallow ledge. He grabbed for the next cherub. The head broke off, and he started to pitch backward. He heard Mallory gasp, but his only focus was finding something to grab on to. That turned out to be the target balcony's banister. He climbed over it, dropping down to the floor. Through the railing, he saw Mallory's white face, her wide eyes staring at him.

Maybe she cared a little that he didn't fall and go *splat*.

Not that he would have fallen. He would have Leaped back to her condo.

This end of the balcony wasn't near any windows or doors, but he checked to make sure no one could have spotted him. He stayed tucked to the side and ready to help Mallory. She was already climbing over, agilely stepping onto the cornice with her bare feet, then grabbing on to the broken piece. He reached for her, but she sidestepped his hand—and lost her balance.

Stubborn woman.

He grabbed her, feeling that lacy material at her back and those soft mounds of flesh collide with his bare chest, and hauled her over the banister. He immediately released her. She mouthed her thanks, passed him, and crept to the edge of the window. He was right behind her, in the electric energy of her wings. Someone had likened it to the feel of running one's fingers through the arms of a sea anemone without the sting.

She peered in the window while strands of her hair wafted in front of his nose. He brushed them away, so it looked like he was playing with her hair when she turned to him. She gave him a stern shake of her head, but he wasn't sure if she meant *Stop playing with my hair* or *I don't see the kid.*

She bumped into him, forcing him to back up. "I don't see anyone," she whispered.

"I'm going in." Whether Jonathan was in there or not, Hayden was going to find some answers. His fingers clenched. And if he had to smash some heads to do it, fine by him.

"You take the right hallway, I'll take left," she whispered.

He carefully pulled the door open, relieved to find it unlocked. No one was expecting an intruder this far up. He scanned the main living room as he veered to the right, spotting a half glass of milk on the coffee table. Ahead, double doors looked like the entrance to a master bedroom. In the other hall, he heard a door fly open. A wall of Light slammed into him, making him stumble back. A man appeared behind the Light, wielding a sword. He was older and in excellent shape. Talbot, he guessed.

Hayden dodged arcs of Light as he drew his own sword. Their "blades" clashed, sending sparks that burned Hayden's skin. Talbot tried to advance and force Hayden into the open space. But Hayden whipped the sword in frenzied arcs, sending those sparks shattering over his opponent and pushing him toward the end of the hallway. Talbot obviously thought he had more room, because he looked surprised when his back hit the wall. Hayden lunged forward and thrust the blade into the man's abdomen.

He clutched the hole in his stomach with his glowing hand, already working on healing it. "Who are you and what are you doing here?"

"I've come for the boy. Where is he?"

"There's no boy here." But the man's expression betrayed his surprise. "You're the Vega who's been sniffing around where he shouldn't. Masters, right?"

Hayden hoped Mallory had found Jonathan. Why hadn't she come out of the back hall yet?

Talbot Leaped, ending up right behind Hayden and plunging forward with his sword. Hayden moved, but not fast enough. The blade sliced him across the side, sending a searing pain through him. When Talbot thrust forward again, Hayden threw him to the side with his Light. The force of it sent him hurtling toward one of the upholstered chairs, toppling it.

Hayden heard a *thump* down the other hall. That wasn't good. As Talbot bounded to his feet and came at Hayden, he maneuvered toward the opening of the hallway. No sign of Mallory or anyone else. Since she hadn't come to assist him, Hayden had to assume she was dealing with someone, too.

As confirmation, she let out a scream of pain. Hayden ran down to the open doorway on the right, driven by instinct. Immediately he realized he'd trapped himself. Talbot was advancing, his jaw rigid as he wielded his sword.

Mallory burst out of the bedroom backward, hitting the wall hard. She held her footing, bringing her sword up to deflect a hot beam of Light coming at her. She sliced it in half, sending each side arcing away from her to hit the wall.

Hayden faced Talbot, meeting his advancing sword with an upward thrust of his own. Talbot's gaze riveted on Mallory. "So that's how you got into the Tower. A clear violation of the rules, Muse."

"So is kidnapping kids," she muttered, slicing her blade

down the other Caido's arm and taking off an inch-wide swath of his skin.

He reacted with a lunge that barely missed her neck.

Talbot didn't seem concerned about his minion, not affected by his scream of pain in the least. He circled Hayden, his voice oddly calm. "I do not kidnap children."

"No, you buy them from the Bend, which is nothing more than a black market baby farm. One that I'll be shutting down." Hayden pushed Talbot back with another series of frenzied moves.

"That will be hard to do from beyond the grave. You may have wheedled your way in here, but you will not be leaving in one piece. The barriers are set to lock-down mode. Though I would like to know how you did get into my unit."

There was a pounding at the door. "Father! Father. Let me in. There's trouble."

Kevin.

"Use your key, idiot! I'm dealing with the trouble right now," Talbot yelled, lunging at Hayden with his sword.

"Key," Hayden muttered as he dodged the blade. "We could have looked for a key."

Mallory pushed back the man she was fighting, who was now trying to grab her. "That would have been boring." She brought her sword up between the guy's legs, and with a scream, he leaped backward. His pants were scorched all the way to the crotch, but he'd managed to save his junk. So far.

She pushed open one of the closed doors and peered inside. "I haven't seen the boy. He's not in either of these rooms."

"I told you, there's no boy here," Talbot said. "Whatever

heroic quest has you both addled enough to break into my home is for naught."

Because he's in that Hummer. Hayden didn't want to alert Talbot that they knew about the Hummer, so he kept that to himself. Hopefully Kye and Kasabian were following it.

The man Mallory had been fighting came out of the bedroom once again, more cautiously this time. The scent of burned fabric filled the hallway.

Hayden lifted his hands. "You're right. We've made a mistake. We heard you had kidnapped a boy. The lead was obviously wrong." He snatched Mallory's hand, yanking her closer. "I apologize." It was time to pound in some heads, but Hayden wanted the men off guard. "We'll leave now."

Just as he came even with Talbot and readied his Light, something circled his ankles and held him in place. Black vines sinuously wound up his legs, his hips. They were doing the same to Mallory. *What the hell?*

She screamed and yanked out one of her wing feathers, using the dhagger it became to cut at them. The knife worked differently than Light. It held a super-concentrated charge of power and was more precise. The vines mended as fast as she cut them. Others circled her arms and pulled them tight behind her. The dhagger fell from her fingers to the carpet, gleaming silver in the light. Hayden was just as bound, and it happened in seconds. His magick faded, and his wings sank into his back. Her wings did the same.

Wraithlord magick. Talbot was one, too.

Kevin burst in at last, panting. He took in the scene and pointed to Mallory. "She set me up!"

Talbot looked at the open French door. "So that's how they got in."

"I'm a member of the Guard," Hayden said in his most authoritative voice, struggling against the confines. "I command you to release us."

"The Guard has no say where I am concerned." Talbot's eyes flashed as black as smoke, and his smile was just as eerie. "Please, don't rush off," he said in a hospitable voice. "I'd like to chat with you about your source of information. Allegations of kidnapping are very serious, you know."

"Let her go, and I'll talk." Hayden wasn't promising to talk about anything specific. "I coerced her into helping me."

Talbot scratched his chin. "She didn't appear to be coerced when she tried to castrate my associate."

"That's because my informant alleged that you had something to do with her niece's disappearance. He used her concern about the girl's safety to fire her up."

Talbot walked closer to Mallory. "And this informant connected your missing niece to me? Interesting." He grasped her chin in his grip. "Have you met this font of information?"

At the sight of his fingers digging into her skin, Hayden jerked toward her. The vines held fast.

"Only over the phone," she lied, but that wouldn't protect Kasabian. All Talbot had to do was check with security to see who had been to visit Mallory.

"Since he misled you, I assume you'll be cooperative in telling me all about him."

"I don't know anything."

The vines pulled Hayden and Mallory together so hard that their bodies collided with a loud *whump*. His chin fit over the top of her head, filling his nose with the ginger scent of her shampoo. Her face was smashed into his chest, and she turned so that her cheek pressed against him instead of her nose.

Kevin edged in closer, reminding Hayden of a hyena circling its prey. "Let me have her." He bared his teeth. "She owes me gratification."

Hayden felt her body stiffen at the same time that his did. That he was helpless to do anything to protect her raged through him.

Talbot moved his hand, and the vine followed the motion, pulling them off their feet, and they crashed to the floor. He walked to the balcony, trailing them along behind him. "Since you like hanging out on balconies so much, you'll enjoy this."

The vine slithered up the wall and anchored on the ceiling formed by the balcony above, stringing Hayden and Mallory upside down. They swung with momentum for several seconds, the outer arc flinging them over the edge of the railing to look down eighteen stories. Hayden's cell phone fell from his pocket and landed on the tile deck.

Talbot snatched it up. "I have an important meeting with people who will be very interested in learning about this new development. Perhaps you'll be willing to share more when I return. Watch them, Brian." Kevin started to open his mouth again, but Talbot cut him off with, "It was your need for gratification, I presume, that led to this invasion of my privacy? This could have been disastrous. Go home and marinate in your idiocy."

"Can I have her?" Brian grinned as Kevin trudged toward the door. "My own personal slut, bound and gagged, legs tied to the bedposts spread-eagle."

"Shut the fuck up," Hayden said. "You don't talk about her like that."

Talbot punched Hayden, sending the two swinging again. Pain rocketed through his jaw as Talbot swung in and out of view with an amused expression. "And they say chivalry is dead."

Brian hadn't taken his eyes off Mallory. Or specifically, her body. "If you leave her bound with your magick, she won't be able to do a thing but lay there and look at me. I can do anything I want to her." He laughed and looked at Talbot. "Ever heard of someone being fucked to death?"

This time Hayden heard her soft intake of breath. Hayden wanted to kill the guy just for saying it.

The corner of Talbot's mouth twitched, but he didn't smile. "No, can't say that I have. I want to spend some time with them, find out everything they know. When I'm finished, you may have your way with her. And since the male seems bothered by the prospect, I say let him watch."

Chapter 16

⌐

Kasabian followed the Hummer across the causeway. "I'm not sure if they've made us yet. I'm going on the assumption that they have, which means we need to be ready for anything."

Kye was working on one of those spy orbs, having lost the original one when they Leaped. Using her long, graceful fingers, she coaxed her magick into something that looked like a solid object. "Good boy," she whispered, then rolled the window down and released it. "If you're adept at making orbs, you can do this remotely. Unfortunately, I'm not." She narrowed her eyes in concentration, and the orb zigged and zagged in the draft of the cars speeding by. It flew into the next lane and was hit by a car.

"Damn it." She flattened her palm and tried again. "If I knew I'd need these things, I would have practiced more."

"We do have the vehicle in sight, you know."

She gave him a *duh* look. "But if we lose them, or rather if they lose us, we'll still know where they're going."

"Brilliant."

Her smile at his admiration turned into a thoughtful look. "Why didn't you go with Mallory? I was surprised when you sent Hayden, since you and she are, well...you know."

"We're what?" He wanted her to say the words.

"Involved. Attached." She shrugged, but there was nothing casual about it. "You have a history."

She'd surprised him by suggesting that he and Mallory get together. Kye may have lost her abilities—temporarily—to sense people's sensual feelings, but surely she knew that she was the only woman he could think of in romantic terms. He hadn't meant to, but he'd made that pretty clear. Or, as he suspected, she was trying to build a protective distance between them.

"I chose you because you can make spy orbs," he said, leaving it at that. "What if I did get romantically involved with Mallory? Would that break our bond?"

"Maybe." The word popped out, hard and cold.

She released the latest scry orb out the open window. It bounced around on the drafts again, but she held it under better control. Still, she had trouble directing it to the bumper.

The Hummer suddenly shifted lanes and slowed down, dropping behind them.

"Shit. We're definitely made," Kasabian was able to say before it slammed into his car and sent it into the short guardrail.

Kye screamed as the huge vehicle started to ram his much smaller one again. He gunned the gas and slid out as the Hummer's bumper made contact. The Lotus shimmied until Kasabian got it under control again. The Hummer was coming up behind him fast.

"Get your seat belt on," he said, maneuvering around another car.

"Kasabian, watch out!"

The Hummer rammed another car, sending it spinning toward them. The cars collided, smashing the headlight and sending a spray of glass into the air. His foot jammed on the gas, but the other car involved in the crash was blocking forward movement. The short concrete guardrail blocked them in on the right. And on the left, the Hummer barreled at them.

Something black streaked toward the Lotus and split off like two tendrils. One snaked into the car, right through the glass, and wrapped around his arm. Kasabian couldn't see where the other one went, because the Hummer slammed into his car and sent them over the rail. Kasabian's arm automatically shot out to grab Kye and Leap them out. But he couldn't. Like in his altercation with Silva at the estate, Wraithlord magick had paralyzed his Caido abilities. He didn't have time to figure out how to use his own dark abilities to get them out. The blue water came up fast, and they hit nose-first and plunged into the water. The windshield shattered, obliterating his forward view. He slammed into the steering wheel.

The car sprang to the surface, throwing him back into his seat. His head was still spinning, pain radiated throughout his chest, but his gaze went to Kye. Not in the passenger seat. Slumped down, nearly folded in half. Not moving.

"Kye!" he screamed, and blood spurted from his mouth. His lip was cut so deep, it bled when he called her name.

Water sluiced into the car through the vents and broken windshield. He reached over and gently rubbed her back. "Kye, wake up."

Gods, there was blood all over her legs. The door. The seat. The car was sinking fast. He thought he had to let the water equalize the pressure before he could open the door.

Or he could Leap. The dark vine was gone, its job to keep them in the car done. The pain of Invoking paled in comparison to everything else. He put his hand on Kye and Leaped, through the barrier and into her living room. The cat let out a yowl as he launched off the back of the couch.

"Sorry to startle you, Vlad," he muttered, his gaze on Kye as she slumped onto the floor. She was unconscious, her body slack, but he sensed life in her. He would not let her go. Fear clutched him at the sight of blood pooling from a gash in her head and soaking her hair. The skin of her cheek was torn, and he thought the bone might be shattered. At the moment, he was more concerned about any internal injuries.

"Hang in there, love," he said, and more blood poured from his lip.

He waved his hands over her head, sensing swelling in her brain. His breath left him, the absence of it crushing his chest in a dull throbbing. Taking in another breath increased the pain to excruciating. Damn, broken ribs again, but this time probably paired with a side of punctured lung. He sent healing energy to her, feeling the lesions mending, the brain returning to normal size. He moved down her body, reading the numerous injuries: broken collarbone, bruised kidney, torn tendons, and general trauma. He pulled from his deepest resources and triaged.

You have to leave enough to heal yourself, a voice whispered.

Her first. Have to...

Lastly, he returned to her cheek and mended the bones, tissue, and skin.

Her eyes fluttered open, dazed and heavy. She met his gaze and then must have seen the span of his wings, because she whispered, "My beautiful angel."

He brushed his trembling fingers across her cheek. "Sleep, love."

"Love," she repeated, her voice slow and thick. "I like when you call me that."

"You shouldn't." Despite his pain, elation filled his heart.

She frowned. "I wanted you to kiss me, too."

"You're delirious, love." Damn, the word had slipped out again. *What do I know about love?* Except that he shouldn't be feeling it for her because they were supposed to be keeping a chaste distance. "Close your eyes. You need to rest." His lip split with his speech, but it wasn't bleeding anymore.

"Like you did with Mallory when she helped." Her eyes drifted closed. "On the forehead."

He didn't know whether to laugh or cry, so he did neither. "You shouldn't want me kissing you anywhere."

She mumbled something, but sleep finally claimed her. He wanted to lie there and watch her, but his strength was waning fast. Even covered in blood, she was achingly beautiful. He knew he was looking at her the same way she'd been taking in his wings—with awe. Hell, she'd caught *him* in the Thrall, and it wasn't supposed to work that way. He'd never loved someone before. Never thought he could. He wanted to think it was all lust. That he understood. But with his Dragon Shadow quiet, this felt like much more. That was scarier than the Shadow had ever been, because he wanted to be a man worthy of her. And he was far from it.

He brushed his finger across her mouth, wishing he could kiss her. She'd almost died. The reality of that crushed him as much as his punctured lung. He drew in shallow breaths, each one a knife in his chest. Then he collapsed next to her.

Treylon was sure his contact at the Bend was holding out on him, just to be difficult. And it *was* making things difficult. The Caidos were withering, the Deuces and Dragon children fading. He needed more power, and he was getting less.

His fingers gripped his phone, ready to call and...what, beg? Again? He released it, humiliation and anger washing over him. Gemini and his boss no doubt loved having this kind of sway over him, especially since they thought Treylon's panic over the solar storm was unfounded. Of course, they were right. Still, many Crescents *were* worried about the effects of the storm, just like the Mundanes had been worried about December 21, 2012, and the end of 1999. It was plausible, and the Bend had happily taken his money and supplied him with children. Until recently.

Let them laugh at him, as some had laughed when everything fell apart twenty years ago. The Dragon woman named Willow had escaped and gone to the Guard with allegations that he'd been keeping her and other children captive. While those sympathetic to the cause of freeing the gods and angels had intervened, they had also demanded that he step down from his esteemed position on the Concilium. They thought he was carrying things too far and, worse, jeopardizing their own positions. Not many Dragon and Deuce members would approve of him using their children for his goals, no matter how important.

He was exiled for a time. Only Silva had asked after his welfare, wanting desperately to play the role of son. But Treylon couldn't muster up that kind of affection, not after Kasabian had betrayed and nearly ruined him. He had no need for a son, only devoted servants.

The phone rang. Richard Talbot, an old friend who was still on the Concilium. He answered at the same time that someone knocked on his door.

"Hello, Richard," he said.

Silva opened the door and came inside. He looked pale, haggard. Treylon lifted his finger. *Wait.*

"Are you having any problems over there?" Talbot asked.

His gut tightened, and he looked at Silva. "Are we having a problem?"

Silva nodded. "Well, were having a problem, but it's been...taken care of."

Treylon turned back to the call. "What's going on over there?"

"The nosy Vega and, oddly enough, a Muse from the building broke into my condo looking for the boy. Fortunately he was already on his way to you. But then the man driving the Hummer encountered an issue. He was being followed. He could only give me cursory details, as he is now on his way back to my private estate to hide the vehicle. The police will no doubt be looking for it."

Treylon turned his attention to Silva. "What happened?"

"Kasabian...he was the one following."

Silva might as well have hit him with a two-by-four. "My son, Kasabian?"

"He knows what we're doing. His memories have returned. I was hoping to take care of him without you knowing. So you didn't have to be put in the position of killing him."

"You knew he was going to cause trouble and *you didn't tell me*?"

Silva winced at his booming voice. "I was protecting you."

Treylon had forgotten momentarily that Talbot was on the line. He told him, "Let me know what you find out from the Vega."

"I'm heading to a Concilium meeting so I can't interrogate them right now. But I'll see to it as soon as I return."

Treylon disconnected, steepling his fingers on his desk. "I don't need to be protected. Or spared difficult decisions." It had been embarrassing, his indecision when he'd been faced with terminating Kasabian and the other runaways. He had taken a big chance by relying on the memory lock. Now it had blown up in his face. "Tell me everything."

Like a child admitting his transgressions, Silva relayed Kasabian's intrusion at the facility. "I ordered the driver to ram Kasabian's car, and I used my magick to send it over the railing. He's...dead."

That word traveled through Treylon's veins like poison, leaving a cold trail in its path. "How can you be sure? He could have Leaped out."

"My magick followed him all the way down, keeping him from Invoking. It's been on the news, a bystander's recording of the accident being played ad nauseam. The car hit hard and sank fast. I don't think he or the person with him could have survived. I checked his apartment and there's no sign of him. Nor was I able to Leap to him."

Treylon couldn't let himself think about Kasabian's death, not right now. He focused on Silva. "If you ever keep important details from me again, I will kill you."

Chapter 17

⌒

Kye was on a wide and nearly deserted beach. Heat rose from the sand, and the sun seared her from above. She felt the weight of a hand resting on her stomach and looked over to see Kasabian lying on a towel next to her.

He smiled, and her heart flipped over. When she thought he would say something endearing, he said, "You shouldn't want me kissing you anywhere."

Huh?

Suddenly the beach lurched sideways, and he threw his arm out to try to keep her from falling forward. Her eyes opened, and she gasped at the sudden change of scenery. Nothing was moving now. And she wasn't on the beach but on the floor of her living room. Vlad was reclining on the top of the sofa watching her.

The weight of the hand on her stomach was real, though. Kasabian's arm lay across her. She visually followed that arm to his bare shoulder, his ethereal wings. A faint current of energy pulsed over him, casting a glimmer across his skin. She felt it flow from his hand into her.

He was asleep, or unconscious, but alive. She could see his chest rise and fall, feel the heat from his hand. Dried blood covered his lips and matted his hair. The coppery scent filled the air. Panic jumped her heartbeat as she searched for the source of the blood. His lower lip bore a faint gash, but it was healing as she watched. Stunning.

He had healed her. Kye didn't remember it but sensed that he had. She lifted her hand to her cheek, feeling dried blood there, too. Her pants were damp and cool and smelled salty. The pieces began to knit together, driving across the causeway, getting rammed and going over the edge. The heart-stopping feeling of falling and then nothing. She couldn't recall hitting the water or anything after that.

Kasabian had Leaped them back here. Healed her first, no doubt. And now he was lying on his back, his body repairing itself. She studied his face, so beautiful and innocent. He was only one of those things. But he drew her very soul as no one ever had.

Vlad meowed as he jumped to the floor. She stroked his back, but her gaze remained on Kasabian. She hadn't realized how long his eyelashes were, how perfect his cheekbones. His lip was now fully healed, and the bruise on his chest the size of the steering wheel was fading.

His fingers twitched, then tightened against her skin. He took a deep breath and opened his eyes. She saw the relief on his face, felt it surge through her.

"We're all right," she said in a soft voice. "Thanks to you."

He searched her face. "I thought I'd lost you."

Because he had her. Those earlier words came back, filling her with the same deep sense of connectedness as the first time.

His expression sobered. "Jonathan. We did lose him."

That piece fell into place in the remnants of her memories just prior to the crash. Her heart ached at being so close and losing him. "*If* he was in the vehicle." She looked at the clock. "It's been a couple of hours since we followed the Hummer."

Kasabian got to his feet, looking like something from a dream in only jeans and those wings.

"Stay there for a moment," she asked. "I just want to soak you in."

"Kye," he said, the word laced with a plea. Agony.

She tried to lighten the moment. "You're eye candy. Don't read too much into it."

"I want to read too much into everything. That's the problem." He bowed his shoulders and pulled in his wings where they settled across his back. He took his cell phone from his pocket. "It still works." He ran his hands down his jeans. "They only got wet up to my thighs. No message from Hayden. They might be hiding, waiting for the right time to act. We can't even get back into the Tower to find out what happened. Or help."

He sent a short text, and then his phone rang. "It's Cory, one of the guys who runs Harbor. Yeah?" he said into the phone.

Kye started to rise, and Kasabian held out his hand to help. She took it, feeling his fingers close over hers. As soon as she was on her feet, he released her.

"I'm fine," he was saying. Kasabian whispered to her, "Turn on the news... Yeah, that was my car. Look, don't say anything to anyone. We're fine...yes, it's related to the missing kids." He ran his fingers back through his hair. "I'll be in touch."

Kye found one of the local channels and sucked in a breath at the shaky video coverage of the Hummer smashing into their car. She could see the line of black magick snaking from the Hummer to the Lotus, but it would look like smoke to any Mundane.

The person who'd taken the video on his cell phone had captured the car hitting the water. Kye dropped down onto the coffee table, her legs unable to hold her up.

Kasabian disconnected and came over, squeezing her shoulder. "I suppose the police will track the car to me. Until then, let them sort out the mystery. They won't be able to bring the car up for a while. If ever."

"Your car..."

"It's only a car."

The news camera panned the sparkling water that showed no signs of the car now. According to the anchor, they were looking for the Hummer and any information as to the owner of the Lotus. Was it an execution? Road rage?

Kye tuned out the witnesses excitedly relaying what they'd seen. "What do we do now? Besides taking a shower. Separate showers," she added when a voice in her head had added *together.* "Just in case you were thinking..." She had a feeling that his Shadow had been thinking the same thing by the glimmer in his eyes.

"Yes, separate. Definitely separate." And she could tell he hated the idea as much as she did.

"Go ahead and use the bathroom down the hall. I'm sure you want to get this blood off you as much as I do."

Once under the hot water, Kye inspected her body,

amazed that Kasabian had healed every injury, even bruises. And she must have had plenty if the blood was any indication. She washed, scrubbing her hair three times to remove the evidence of what had to have been a severe head injury.

Staring at the blood as it swirled down the drain made reality crash in on her. She could have died. They'd lost Jonathan. She hadn't seen him, but she felt that he'd been in the Hummer. Scenes flashed in her mind, the boy's picture with those haunted brown eyes. Smashing into the concrete barrier and then flying over. The damned orb not sticking. She started shaking.

Shock, fear, and failure pushed up inside her like a volcano and then erupted. The tears got lost in the water. She hoped the shower covered the sound of her crying. She leaned against the cool tile, pressing her cheek against it.

The door to the bathroom opened, and she saw Kasabian's silhouette leaning in through the steamy shower door. "You okay?"

Of course, he could feel her grief. But by the alarm in his voice, he wasn't sure what was causing it.

"I need to...cry. Release. I'm okay." She didn't sound the least bit convincing to her own ears. "Just go."

Those moments in the living room with Kasabian had weakened her. This situation had weakened her. And mostly, *he* weakened her. She closed her eyes, willing him to leave. The door closed softly. Thank goodness. She couldn't fight her need right then. She turned and nearly gasped.

He was leaning against the glass door, his back to her. "Kye, talk to me."

Why didn't she feel annoyed that he hadn't listened to her? At least he was giving her visual privacy. She could see that he wore a towel and nothing else. He'd come directly from his shower when he'd felt her distress.

"You don't have to fix me. I just need to process my feelings."

"So process them with me. Remember how you stayed with me after I'd been Stripped? It's my turn now."

His offer made her choke back a sob. Maybe if she stopped crying, he'd leave. *Breathe, breathe, suck it in.* "I'm not comfortable sharing my feelings."

"Let me get this straight: you're all right with people sharing their intimate thoughts and feelings with you, but you don't like to do the same."

She wrapped her arms around her waist. "Exactly." She laughed. "Ironic, isn't it?"

"Just a little. But you can't hide from me. I feel you, your joy and darkness, and all those other things you'd rather not feel. And right now you're in the dark. Tell me why, and I'll go away."

Fine. She'd pour out her guts. "I failed Jonathan."

"No, you didn't."

"If I'd been able to make the orb stick, we'd know where he was. We'd know where all the children are. I couldn't use a stupid, simple scry orb." Tears surged again, making her choke out the words, "See, I *am* worthless."

He stepped inside the shower and gathered her in his arms. He held her so tenderly, so chastely, it made her cry even more.

He smoothed his hand down the length of her hair with one hand while the other held her close. "You're the reason we even knew about the Hummer leaving. You're very worthwhile." He continued stroking her hair. "If you only knew how much you mean to me."

His words settled in her soul like a hot coal melting away the chill. Meant how? Her hands had automatically moved to his back when he'd pulled her close. She felt his muscles moving beneath his skin as he stroked her hair.

"I wasn't thinking about you being naked when I came in here. I just wanted to make sure you were all right. I'd better go. I'm trying to be good, like you told your mother I was," he murmured, and she could hear his struggle. "I want to be good. I don't want to mess up your life any more than I already have." He started to back away, proving that he was a much better man than he thought.

She didn't let him go. "Don't be good. Love me." She met his eyes. "Can you love me?"

He made a sound deep in his throat as he brushed wet hair from her cheek. "Too much."

She couldn't interpret that or the feelings coursing from him. Lust was easy to identify, but not this deep warmth. *I want to matter to you.* She reached toward his face, impossibly beautiful as all Caidos were, and yet, even more so. Because she saw his strength and his weakness... for her.

She threaded her fingers through his wet hair, around the back of his neck, and pulled his mouth down to hers. His kiss was ardent at first, but he kept it to a slow, sensual dance. He gathered her long hair in one hand, tugging her head back for a better angle. Now she could feel his erection, but he wasn't grinding it into her. Its hard length only brushed against her stomach. She resisted the urge to press closer.

He turned off the shower and stepped out, leading her with him. His wet towel fell away, leaving him naked. He reached for another towel and dried her. She closed her eyes and sank into the feeling of the terry cloth rubbing across her skin, wrapping around her hair, and then scrubbing her scalp.

He grabbed another towel from the stack and started to dry himself. She took it from him and did the same for him. It was a selfish act, as it turned out. She soaked in his beauty the same way the towel soaked up the beads of water.

Now he led her to the bedroom, to the bed. The muscles of his jaw ticked as he visibly held back the Dragon Shadow from pouncing. He lay down next to her, his appreciative gaze taking her in. "You are so beautiful," he whispered, mirroring her thoughts about him. He moved his mouth down her body, leaving a trail of devastatingly tender kisses across her breasts, her stomach, her thigh, all the way down to her ankle. Then he bent her knee and kissed the bottom of her foot. He kissed each toe, so tenderly, with such care, that she saw her feet in a whole new way—as cherished.

His eyes took in each part of her as he moved up her thigh, as though she were the most precious object he had ever seen and handled. He sent waves of pleasure through her even though he'd not touched her intimately.

After he had treated her other leg with the same exquisite care, he rolled her onto her stomach. His hands massaged her shoulders, arms, and down her back. He worked her muscles, turning them to jelly beneath his agile hands. Inside, desire built like a smoldering fire. His fingers worked her scalp, then circled her ears. Even though she could feel the tip of his erection against her thigh, he took his time...loving her. She wanted him. Not just physically, but his heart, his soul. Everything. And that was much scarier than wanting sex.

She rolled over and tugged him down to the bed next to

her. He stretched out, still running his hand along her side. His thumb brushed the outer swell of her breast, and he let it linger before continuing to draw his fingers down to her hip.

"Kye," he whispered, but said nothing else. As though he was content just to speak her name.

She traced her finger along the planes of his face, the silky arch of his eyebrows, the bridge of his nose. When she reached his lips, he sucked her finger in and touched the tip with his tongue. She inhaled at the sensation, of how it correlated directly to her private region. He slowly drew it out and kissed her palm, her wrist.

She wanted his mouth on hers, and she leaned forward and kissed him. A slow, sweet kiss at first. He captured her mouth with his, drawing her lower lip gently between his teeth. She opened to him, sliding her tongue inside to trace the edge of those perfect, straight teeth. He slid his hand around the back of her neck and deepened the kiss. He made slow, seductive love to her mouth. Not driven by mindless lust or an out-of-control passion.

"Kye," he said on a long breath, wrapping his leg around her to pin her close. Now she felt the evidence of the desire he was reining in. She rocked against his erection, touching off her own fire.

He found evidence of that when his fingers slid into her intimate folds. "So wet for me," he whispered, making her breath catch as he circled her sensitive nub.

She wrapped her fingers around his penis, rubbing her thumb across his slick tip. "Mmm, you, too."

"Always," he said on a low chuckle. "Every time I look at you, I want you. I don't think I could ever get enough of you."

She closed her eyes on those words, spoken from his heart. "Me, either." But she had to know, and so she met his gaze. "When you say you want me, that you could love me too much, do you mean sex? Or...more?"

"More. Much more."

He dipped his finger into her entrance, sliding it back and forth while he let his thumb graze her nub. She rocked her hips against his hand, and he kissed her deeply, moving his tongue in the same rhythm as his fingers. The sensation built, her thighs tightened, and she screamed her pleasure into his mouth. And he seemed to swallow it, growling and tightening his hand on her.

He gently pushed her back, nudged her thighs apart, and guided his erection to her slick entrance. He teased her, moving the tip all around her already sensitive nub, and then she gripped his arms and fell to her pleasure again. When she opened her eyes a minute later, he was watching her with a cat-that-ate-the-canary grin.

"I love watching you come," he said without apology.

Kye realized she felt no embarrassment. She reached down and took him in hand, relishing the long, hard feel of him as she stroked. "And I love coming for you." Her legs wrapped around his waist, and he sank his shaft into her. She shifted her hips up high so that he drove in to the hilt. Gripping his shoulders, she moved her hips to match his rhythm, his fervor. "I also love the look on your face right now."

He rolled his head back, his eyes closing for a second, giving himself to the satisfaction she felt coming from him. No, completion. And he hadn't even come yet. His eyes were on her again, intense, effervescent as they moved together. No hint of black, no Dragon Shadow. This was all Kasabian.

All mine.

He rolled over so that she was on top, letting her control their movements for a while. She planted her hands on his chest, hard muscle and soft skin, and lost herself in the feel of him filling her so perfectly, so exquisitely. He gripped her hips, sinking deeper still, until she shattered. She threw her head back and lost herself to it. Then she got to watch him come. The tendons in his neck tensed, he let out the most delicious groan, and all the while his eyes held hers.

When he caught his breath, he moved his hand down over her breasts and across her stomach. He gave her a heart-stopping grin. "I like watching you when I come, too."

She lay down on his chest, careful not to disengage. She looked at that gorgeous face and felt him in her heart. "What are you doing to me?" she whispered.

"Making you mine," he said simply, running his hand across her back in slow strokes.

His. Every cell, every thought, every inch of her, his.

The smile faded to something else. He stroked his thumb down her cheek, to her jaw. "I've never belonged anywhere. Not with Caidos, not with Deuces. But when I'm with you, I belong here." And when those eyes locked onto hers... *Omigods, I'm so in love with this half angel, half devil, all thief.* He'd stolen her heart from its secure place behind stone walls and laser alarms. She would never get her abilities back because all she'd be thinking about would be him. In bed like this. But also the way he was looking at her now, as though he needed her. Not just her body, but all of her.

"I already am," she whispered. "Yours, I mean."

Those words stole his smile altogether. He took her

hand and pressed it against his mouth, his eyes intense and fierce. "What *have* I done to you?"

Loved me.

Before she could speak the words, he answered. "Screwed up your life. Someday you're going to realize that. But I'll take this until you do." He took a ragged breath, then looked at the clock. "I need to check in with Hayden. Maybe he called while we were in here losing our minds."

He got out of bed and walked over to his discarded clothing. She let her gaze linger on his backside before getting up and dressed. The woman in her bathroom mirror looked trippy. Loopy.

In love.

Shit. That's what he was doing, making her fall in love with him. She should be thinking about their next step, not how delicious he looked wearing only jeans as he thumbed through the texts on his phone.

"Hear from him?" she asked, pulling her shirt over her head as she walked over.

He shook his head. "Something's wrong. He would have checked in by now, even just a text. They got caught. It's the only explanation." He rubbed the back of his neck. "Damn it, how do we help them?"

"Hayden's a Vega in the Guard. It's not like he can't take care of himself and Mallory."

"He's capable." Kasabian seemed to grab on to that. "And Mallory's no slouch either."

Worry permeated his expression, and Kye wrapped her arms around his waist. He surprised her by crushing her to him. She heard his heart beating furiously.

"Are you all right?" she asked.

His hands tightened on her, and she thought he shook his head. "I know you're capable, that you have lethal magick. But the thought of something happening to you..."

She leaned back to look at his face and saw the terror of the thought. "I'll be all right. I'm strong."

He gathered her face in his hands. "You're in me now, in a way I can't even describe. You flow in my veins; you're settled into my bones. The thought of something happening to you sucks the breath right out of my chest. If you were hurt, it would make me beyond crazy." His eyes shimmered black.

The intensity of him enveloped her, unnerving and calming at once. She'd never been consumed and possessed like this. Now she craved all of that. All of Kasabian.

Kye recognized the knock on the door, three quick raps followed by three more. "Sarai. Maybe she's seen something that will help."

Kasabian pulled on a shirt as Kye went to the door.

Sarai's gaze went right to him, her blue eyes hard. She steered her gaze to Kye. "I need to talk to you. Alone."

"Kasabian can hear whatever it is you have to say."

"No, he can't." Sarai clamped Kye's arm in her grip. "Excuse us for a few minutes."

Kye shrugged as her friend led her out the door. She knew Kasabian would be watching, keeping her safe. "What's going on?"

Sarai kept steering her farther away, heading to the parking area designated for visitors. "Come sit in my car with me."

Except they didn't make it to the car. Doors on a van slid open, and arms grabbed Kye and pulled her inside.

Panic choked her as she fought, getting in a solid kick at her captor's stomach. He grunted but remained in control, tying her wrists behind her. She was gagged and unceremoniously dumped on the floor of the van as the door slid closed. Someone was already in the driver's seat, easing out of the parking spot. *Oh, my gods!* What was going on? What had happened to Sarai?

Wait. She was in the van. Sitting next to her looking worried and chagrined, not at all like someone who'd just been kidnapped.

"I'm sorry we had to do it like this," Sarai said.

We? Kye strained to see the person who'd gagged her mouth. *"Dad?"* she managed through the thick material.

And her mother was driving. Kye had fallen into a bizarre nightmare. Her parents and best friend had gone psychotic!

"I'm sorry, honey," her mother said. "This wasn't my idea, but I agree that it's the best way to handle this."

"Handle *what*?" Kye tried to ask.

Her father untied her mouth. "I didn't like the gagging part at all, but we couldn't have you screaming and attracting attention." He grimaced, holding his side. "I'm happy to know you're a fighter."

Her mother drove calmly down the street. "You'll understand all of this once we explain. Explain it, honey."

"It was my doing," Sarai said, pulling her knees up to hug them to her chest. "My visions. I told your parents. They were getting scarier, Kye, and nothing seemed to deter you from doing whatever it is that's putting you in danger. Kasabian has you under his Thrall."

"He does not." Kye couldn't say how it was so much deeper than that.

"I saw it, too," her mother said.

"It's not the Thrall. I'm in love with him. There's a difference."

Her mother threw up one hand. "It's even worse than we thought."

Kye tried to wriggle free. "This is ridiculous. Untie me."

"Not yet," Sarai said to her father. "She still looks like she's going to kill me."

Kye narrowed her eyes and gave her a rigid smile. "With love. I'm going to kill you with love. Take me back. Kasabian is going to freak."

Her father put his arms on her shoulders. "This is an intervention. When Sarai told us her latest vision, we knew we all had to act together."

Kye worked the rope around her wrists. "What was the latest one?"

Sarai's voice went very low. "I saw a Caido—not a Caido, exactly. He had wings like a Caido but a face like a Dragon. Remember that I sensed Dragon energy. Well this Caido was sort of both, which I know doesn't make any sense. He was killing you in a jealous rage. And it was Kasabian."

No one there knew about Kasabian being a Wraithlord. They probably didn't even know there were Wraithlords, and yet Sarai had seen one. But not Kasabian.

Kasabian appeared in the van in full wing, frantically looking around. His black gaze locked onto her, noting the gag still around her neck and her father's hands on her shoulders. He lunged. Kye only saw a dark blur and claws reaching for her father's neck as he was slammed into the side of the van. She could feel Kasabian's murderous rage, his capacity for violence.

Kye screamed, "Stop! Kasabian, it's my father!"

Her mother slammed on the brakes and pulled into a parking lot, tires screeching.

"That's what I saw!" Sarai stuttered, pointing at him and shrinking away at the same time.

Kye saw Kasabian struggle to pull his Wraithlord back under control. "You're all right?" he asked her, shadows moving across his eyes.

"I'm fine. Sarai saw a vision of—"

"You, Kasabian! I saw you killing Kye in a jealous rage. Like you're doing to her father. Let him go!"

Kasabian finally reined in his power and released him. He looked Kye over again, surveying her with his now hazel eyes. He shifted that gaze to Sarai. "Tell me about the vision."

Sarai, who'd shrunk against the back of the passenger seat, regained her courage and described the vision.

"You're sure it was me?"

"I didn't see your face clearly, but I sensed that it was you. Seeing you now...yes, it was you."

Kye saw the horror of that possibility cross his face, felt his pain in thinking he would hurt her. "Kasabian, you would never do that to me."

Her father was rubbing his neck. "Did you see what he just did? Of course he could kill you." He positioned himself between Kasabian and Kye. "What are you?"

"That's not important," Kye said. "You saw how he pulled it back in." She turned to Kasabian. "You controlled it."

He was still trying to catch his breath. He met Sarai's gaze. "I've heard about your visions. You have true foresight."

Sarai nodded. "That first night you met at the club, I warned her about getting involved with you. I saw it then, something bad."

"And something good," Kye said. "You saw that it was good between us."

Kasabian's focus was on Sarai. "What was the bad?"

"Danger. I felt flashes of fear. Something about Kye's heart being ripped out, though I didn't take it literally at the time. Then I got the Dragon-Caido vision and knew I had to take desperate measures. I went to her parents and implored them to stage an intervention. They were completely on board, especially when I told them about that last vision."

"Of me hurting her." Kasabian's voice was soft, dead calm. His expression changed in a way Kye couldn't understand. She saw—and felt—his relief. He met her father's gaze. "Keep her locked up, like a princess in a tower. Away from me."

"Oh, no you don't," Kye said. "You are not shutting me out of this. You need my help!"

"It's the only way to keep her safe," he said to her father, ignoring her.

She knew he could feel her outrage, her anger. And she let him have it. "You will not—"

Kasabian pulled the gag back up over her mouth. He kept looking right past her toward her father. "I only need her to stay in your custody for a day. Can you manage that?"

Her father nodded. "Anything for my girl."

Those words might have warmed her if Kasabian wasn't totally pissing her off. He finally dared to meet her eyes. "You know it's for the best."

"It is not," she ranted, but it came out muffled. She struggled, wanting to shake and smack him. "You need me."

His eyes became a slate of gray. "No, Kye, I don't. As you said, you're worthless as far as your magick goes. There's nothing you can do to help." The word _worthless_ hit her like a slap in the face. It dug at the core of her insecurity. He met her father's gaze. "If something happened to your daughter because of me..." He meant him hurting her. Sarai's vision had scared him. "She is out of her element, and I haven't been able to convince her otherwise. As much as it pains me, she's better off far away from me."

"Permanently," Sarai said. "She's better off away from you permanently, you mean."

"I'm right here," Kye tried to say, furious. The knucklehead was trying to protect her, and Sarai had just handed him the perfect reason. And damn it, he'd lanced her in the most tender spot of her psyche, trying to widen that distance between them.

"Yes, permanently." He looked at her for a moment. "I don't think that will be a problem." Kasabian kissed her forehead. _Now he does it!_ "Mmm, your rage is lovely." He brushed her tangled hair from her face, the tips of his fingers lingering against her skin. "I love how you believe in me. I wish I could believe in myself the same way."

He disappeared. Kye kicked and screamed. He would not leave her out of this. And damn it, without Hayden, didn't he realize he was entirely on his own?

Chapter 18

Kasabian returned to Kye's apartment to get his things. The barrier was still in place, which meant Hayden was alive. Kasabian tried to Leap to him, but his soul hit a barrier that threw him back to the living room. He tried Mallory, too, with the same result. They must still be at the Tower.

Kye's anger radiated directly into him through their bond.

Sorry, love. It was a golden opportunity to keep you out of Treylon's grasp. Hell, out of my grasp. Now that he'd been intimate with her, the possessiveness was even stronger. The need for her consumed him.

Mine, mine, mine, the refrain kept chanting.

He'd almost killed her father. Had wanted to tear out Hayden's throat for his comment about her. Just a freakin' comment. It made Sarai's vision even more likely to come true.

Kye's phone rang. He paused to listen to her outgoing

message, the light cadence of her voice both soothing and painful.

"Kasabian? Are you there? This is Sarai."

He picked up the phone. "Yes, I'm here."

"I got a vision of something else that I think is tied to what you're involved in. Maybe it'll make sense to you, because it seems bizarre to me. I'm seeing children who are fading. Like they're becoming invisible."

Kasabian's heart tightened. "That's what's happening, though not in a literal sense. Can you see anything around them?"

"At first I thought it was an estate, but it looks more like a small resort with a handful of medium-sized buildings and concrete pathways connecting them. I see a hallway with many doors that have numbers on them. And one of those signs that shows you how to get out in case of a fire. That's all."

He'd take any clue at this point, even a scrap. It corroborated what he'd seen. "That may be enough. I'm going to give you my cell number, in case you find anything else." After he did, he couldn't help asking, "How's Kye doing?"

"She's pissed."

"Good." It would help her separate from him.

After he disconnected, he soaked in the details of Kye's space one last time. The cat watched him from the window seat in the kitchen nook. At least *he* had the good sense to stay away. "Your mistress, not so much." Would Kasabian be strong enough to stay away from her? He knew better. That's why he'd tried to made her angry, though using the word *worthless* had hurt him as much as it had hurt her.

He grabbed his duffel bag and Leaped to Cory's office at Harbor.

Cory yelped before catching himself. "Dude, are you trying to give me a heart attack?"

"I need to borrow the car again."

Cory's expression darkened. "This is some pretty serious shit you're into."

Several kids trudged by with suitcases and bags, talking about getting eaten by alligators. One girl was whining about mosquitoes.

Kasabian let himself enjoy the banter for a second before answering. "You wouldn't believe how serious. Right now I need transportation. Do you have anything I can use for a day?"

"Dude, I'm afraid to loan you anything. But I do feel an obligation since you did donate the sedan to Harbor." He unlocked a cabinet and handed him the keys.

"I'll bring it back in one piece or replace it." Kasabian started heading out.

"I just hope you're alive to honor that promise."

"Me, too."

Lyle spotted him from down the hallway and ran over, his backpack flopping from left to right. "Any news?" Delicate hope tensed his mouth and raised his eyebrows high on his forehead.

Kasabian put his hand on the kid's bony shoulder. "We were close." He shook his head, unable to say how they'd lost him. "But I'm working on it. I will bring him home, I promise." He should know better than to make promises like that. But the words had come out, and he would honor them. *One way or another.*

Lyle clutched Kasabian's arm. "Let me help."

Kasabian wanted to tell him how brave he was, wanted to share his own story of leading the kids out of the hell

his father had put them through. But that would only encourage the kid, and Kasabian couldn't be responsible for
spurring him into action that would put him into danger.
"You go on the trip, have fun."

"Fun. Yeah, like I'm even going to be able to concentrate on collecting samples of swamp water and document-
ing the wildlife." He stared past Kasabian, clenching his
fist to his chest. "I want to see him again so bad it hurts."

"I know the feeling." Unfortunately, he did. The need to
see Kye, to touch her again, raged through him. "I'll update
you as soon as you return. Right now I've got to run."

Kasabian sorted through his options as he headed toward the parking lot. He needed to make sure that Hayden
hadn't been detained at work. Hayden trusted his boss,
but the man seemed bound to superiors who couldn't be
trusted. Kasabian would talk to Hayden's sergeant and very
carefully find out what he needed to know.

Kasabian was escorted to Bane's office thirty minutes after
arriving at Guard headquarters. There was an odd tension
in the air. Officers were standing around talking in low,
somber tones, and they seemed shaken.

Brian Bane bore the same kind of morose expression as
he stood up from behind his desk. He didn't even try to
paste on a cordial look. "You said you wanted to see me
about Hayden?"

Kasabian didn't like the combination of Hayden being
missing and something off happening here. He nodded toward the pit of desks in the center of the building. "What's
going on?"

Bane gave away nothing, not even a twitch. "Nothing that concerns you."

So not related to Hayden. "I'm a close friend of Hayden's. I've known him since we were kids. We were both kidnapped, and we escaped together." He touched the center of his chest, drawing his finger and thumb down to the scar. "I need to know if you've sent him on one of those highly secretive, important missions he's been working on lately." Kasabian gave him a look to convey *one of those bullshit missions*. "Because I can't get hold of him, and it's imperative that I do so."

Bane looked at the clock. "He's late for work, actually, which is unlike him." He picked up his phone and dialed. "It's Bane. Any word from Masters?... Okay, thank you. Let me know immediately if you do." He hung up. "What are you and Masters involved in?"

"It's probably better if you don't know. But I'm concerned about him." More like worried as hell.

Bane dropped down into his chair, staring blankly into space. "What is going on around here?" he asked no one in particular, then seemed to realize he'd spoken aloud. "It must be the *Deus Vis* fluctuations. Since the solar storm flares started hitting, we're seeing some bizarre behavior. Like Vegas digging into things they shouldn't." Now he gave Kasabian a pointed look.

"Understood. I'll let you know when I find him."

"I didn't agree to see you so you could ask me questions and then just leave. Hayden's one of my best men, and we don't have a lot of Caidos in the Guard as it is. Not only am I worried about him, I'm worried also about my own ass. If he gets into trouble—or worse—I have to answer for it. I don't like when the Concilium big shots whose names I don't even know come in asking questions, especially when I have no answers. I could detain you, have you interrogated."

"That will open a box you don't want opened. You can let me leave and remain blissfully in the dark or face knowing something that requires you to risk everything you've worked for to do the right thing."

Bane's mouth tightened. "I always do the right thing."

"With all due respect, you do what you're told. Something seems to happen when an officer gets elevated from Vega to the higher positions. Maybe you have more prestige and income to lose. But you lose something much more precious." *Balls.*

Kasabian turned to leave before Bane could spew the words that he was trying so hard to contain. The officer who had escorted him to the inner sanctum was ready to lead him out. Kasabian took in the paintings of the various gods of the island of Lucifera staring at him from their gilded frames. Many Crescents could trace their ancestry back to their godly sire. It was a matter of pride to come from a Dragon god of war or a Deuce goddess of sensuality, for instance. Like Kye.

Kye.

He pushed her from his mind even as he looked for Zensu. He stopped at a painting of an angel who was depicted as giant and glowering. DEMIS, the nameplate at the bottom read. Kasabian had heard it in the distant past. And the recent past. One of Treylon's minions had come out to tell Silva that Demis was checking in for a status report. Silva had run to the building like an eager child with the same suck-up expression he'd had for Treylon all those years ago.

A memory, this one buried in childhood, surfaced. His father crying out to Demis, beseeching him for a way to not feel the pain of a broken heart. His parents were together but fighting all the time. Right before his father moved out.

"Sir?"

The officer was waiting, and not patiently. Kasabian took several more steps but stopped at the sight of another familiar name: Cecily.

"Excuse me for a second," Kasabian said. "I need to say hello to Cecily." He ducked into her office and closed the door before the officer could object.

She started, her fingers poised over her keyboard. "Who are you?"

"Kasabian. I'm a close friend of Hayden's."

Her long ponytail draped over her shoulder, and her eyes were bright and fiery behind stylish glasses.

She swiveled her chair to face him. "I've heard him mention you. Where is he? I've been trying to get hold of him."

"Something happened here. Everybody's on edge." Kasabian's gaze locked onto hers, and her pupils dilated. He used the fact that she was dazed. "What happened?"

"One of our Vegas tried to attack his superior, right in his office. He was taken down to the psych ward. This guy, he was very good. Very by-the-book. They're not telling us much, just speculating that he fell to the fluctuations. But no one else is going mad like that." She blinked, giving her head a shake. "I really hate how you guys use that Thrall thing. I shouldn't have told you any of that."

"Sorry. I just needed to make sure it didn't have anything to do with Hayden. I can't connect with him either."

"It's this thing he's been investigating on the side, isn't it? The boy."

Kasabian nodded. "We almost had him, thanks to your help." Losing Jonathan touched on the same raw nerve as leaving all those kids behind years ago. "Hayden went into Talbot's unit in the Tower. I haven't heard from him since."

Worry tightened Cecily's forehead. "That's a high-security building, isn't it?"

"Very. There's no way to get inside now that Talbot has likely discovered the intrusion. Best case scenario, Hayden's in hiding, waiting for an opportunity to get out."

"And worst case?" Her fear radiated out to him.

"Let's not go there."

"How can I help?"

Kasabian was counting on her crush on Hayden. "I understand you're the information guru around here. Hayden sings your praises. Especially lately."

That got a small smile out of her. "I help him whenever I can."

The officer knocked on the door. "Sir, I must insist that you leave now."

"One more minute," Kasabian called. "I need a list of small to medium resorts in Miami that are owned by Caidos, if you can get that specific."

"I'll see what I can dig up. But I'll have to do it at home. They're watching me here." They exchanged numbers, and she glanced at her watch. "I get off duty in two hours."

"The sooner the better."

"Can I help in a way other than sitting at a computer?" She removed her glasses. "I'm in the Argus training program now."

"Have you been trained in combat? Use of deadly magick?"

She nodded.

"Could you kill someone if you needed to? If it meant saving a child's life? Hayden's life?"

"Yes."

"Think about that. Because I may just take you up on it."

Chapter 19

———

"You know we only did this because we love you," Sarai said for the umpteenth time.

Kye sat at her parents' kitchen table, a Whis-Kye that was supposed to be some kind of peace offering sitting on the thick wood table in front of her. She wasn't touching it on principle. They were watching her, waiting for the Thrall to wear off. Even though they knew it only worked while the Crescent was looking into the Caido's eyes. But she wasn't looking into his eyes, because he'd kicked her to the curb.

Her mother's hands were wrapped around a coffee mug. "Ohhhhh."

Everyone turned to her, and for a moment, Kye hoped it had finally dawned on them that Kye *needed* to help Kasabian save those children.

"What?" her father asked when her mother didn't elaborate on her drawn-out word.

"We saved Kye because we love her. That man could

have killed all of us. He was furious that we'd taken Kye, and then suddenly, he backed off. He left because he wanted her safe, too. You saw his face, Sarai, when you told him about the vision. Does that mean he loves her, too?"

The question hit Kye squarely in the chest. She'd been so angry, so humiliated that Kasabian didn't think she was capable of helping, that she hadn't considered any other reason for his shutting her out. But yes, of course. He was trying to protect her. From the danger of this mission he was undertaking. And himself.

"No way," Sarai said. "They only met, what, a few days ago." She studied Kye. "Oh, hon, you're in love with him. He really got to you, didn't he?"

In more ways than one. But she wasn't about to admit that to anyone, especially her parents. "Right now all I want to do is throttle him." That his Wraithlord would hurt her terrified him, and Sarai's vision—along with her parents' rash plan—had given him the opportunity to shut her out.

"He cares about me." Kye met all of their gazes. "Like you care about me. I understand." It still pissed her off.

Her mother draped her hand over Kye's. "And hopefully you understand why we had to take such drastic action." She rolled her eyes, shaking her head. "Kidnapping our own daughter. Luca, forgive us."

"We watched a *20/20* episode about a couple who hired someone to kidnap their daughter after she got sucked into a cult," her father said. "That's where we got the idea. Then she had to be deprogrammed."

Kye narrowed her eyes at them. "I'm *not* getting deprogrammed. And this isn't just about Kasabian and me. Children's lives are at stake." She gave them an overview of Treylon's plan. "That's why I've been involved in this. Why I need to still be involved."

"And why you should stay far away from it," her mother said. "Kye, you're a therapist, not some caped avenger. You could get yourself killed! And the visions Sarai's been having prove that's a real possibility."

Sarai rubbed Kye's arm. "Kasabian will get the help he needs."

"Did you get a vision about that?" At the shake of her head, Kye said, "Then get one!"

Her laugh was bitter. "If I could produce the damned things on command, do you think I'd be a cocktail waitress? I only base that statement on what I know about Kasabian. When he appeared in the van, I knew he would do anything, even kill, to save you."

"He's a good man," Kye grumbled.

"What is he?" her mother asked. "He's no ordinary Caido."

"He's not," Kye said, leaving it at that. There was nothing ordinary about Kasabian. Hadn't she known that the first moment she'd laid eyes on him? "Mom, ask Babs what she thinks about all this."

Her mother's eyes blinked like an owl's. "Now?"

"Yes. I want her opinion." Kye wasn't going to admit that she'd talked to Babs before, using another medium. "You owe me that much."

Her mother inhaled softly, deeply. "She's already here."

Kye crossed her arms over her chest. "What did she think about you kidnapping me?"

"She says I've always been so reserved, she's shocked. But you're safe, and that's all that matters."

"And what does she say about Kasabian? Us?"

After a moment, her mother said, "She says you should be committed. She's shaking her finger, the way she used to do when she wanted to make a point. 'She should be committed, that girl. It will solve the problem.'"

Kye could well see Babs doing it, but the words hurt. So she was crazy for thinking there might be hope for her and Kasabian. Or for thinking she could help him. Because she wasn't equipped to help.

Yet, something inside her strained against that. If she slunk away, she would never regain that sense of worthiness for which she longed. If she left kids to suffer without even trying, she could never forgive herself. "There's no need to commit me. It's better that I'm away from him. Forever."

Relief washed over everyone's eyes. She meant it, too. For about one second. Then she remembered something. Treylon obviously needed her skills. And hadn't Sarai said that sleeping with the enemy would help?

Kye stood. "He'll let me know what happens. I need to get back to work, get Kasabian out of my system. My head. And I know exactly how."

"How?" Sarai asked, her eyebrows furrowed. Suspicious? Of course, Sarai saw the real Kye, while her parents saw the daughter who rarely spoke her mind.

"I met a client a few days ago. A Caido. You know they can heal heartache and grief, right? I explained that my powers weren't working, and he took away my turmoil over Kasabian. It was gone, just like that." She snapped her fingers. "And my abilities returned. Unfortunately, because I saw Kasabian again, the turmoil returned." Kye gave her mom a meaningful look. "I'm going to erase Kasabian from my system so I can resume my work."

Her father gave her a hug. "Smart girl. You take after me." It was probably a good thing he couldn't see her surprise at that statement. All she ever heard was "oh, the tragedy" that she hadn't taken after him or her mother. He stepped back. "But you know that we're not letting you just go off. See, I'm smart, too."

"Fine. You can accompany me to my office, but obviously you can't sit in on my session."

"We'll wait in the lobby," her mother said, patting her arm.

"I'll watch her window," Sarai said.

Kye tried to look indignant at their distrust, but they were right, after all. She called the secretary that all the therapists shared. "Can you please pull up Carl Wallen's number for me?" She jotted it down and then called him. "It's Kye Rivers, the Zensu therapist you met the other day." He paused, perhaps surprised she'd survived the car's plunge off the bridge. When he acknowledged remembering her, she said, "I'm ready to move ahead with our session, if you still have need of my services."

"Yes, I do. Very much so. You are ready this time?"

"Yes. The man I'm in love with has left me, the bond is broken, and I'm ready to move on. I need to get back to work, and your case is my most important."

"That is gratifying to hear. When can we meet? The sooner the better."

"How about in thirty minutes at my office?"

They ended the call, and she met everyone's gaze. "It'll be good to get back to my life. At the least, I need a diversion until I hear what's happening on Kasabian's end."

"What did you mean by 'the bond is broken'?" her mother asked.

Crap. She didn't want to get into that. "Emotional bond. Let's get going."

Treylon needed her for something. *He* saw value in her abilities. She would go with him and do what she could for the children. The bond between her and Kasabian would alert him to where she was. And she would become a touchstone for him to Leap to the resort.

She arrived at the office building with her entourage. They perused her collection of books on the massive shelving unit and flipped through her issues of *Psychology Today,* while Kye pretended to make notations in client files. What she was really doing was composing a note. Backup in case Kasabian couldn't make sense of what was going on.

Kye's phone beeped, and the receptionist's voice said, "Your appointment is here."

"Thank you. I'll be right out."

Kye waited for her entourage to head toward the door before situating the envelope on her keyboard. Kasabian would feel her fear the moment Treylon revealed his reason for bringing her to the resort. Even if she was expecting it, the reality would cause all kinds of anxiety.

She now saw the man in the lobby in a whole new way. The dying lover was a lie. Kye felt stupid falling for it. Kasabian was right; her need to help others did make her vulnerable.

"I appreciate you seeing me," he said, preceding her into the office.

She closed the door behind him.

He rubbed his hands together. "I'm so excited to finally do this." She'd never seen a Caido excited before. He was like a boy about to see Santa.

Now that she was looking for it, she could see where Kasabian got his jawline, his cheekbones. The man removed his shirt and Invoked. She saw no beauty in his angelic form, felt no sense of wonder. She allowed herself to feel all the turmoil Kasabian caused. That was easy. Treylon didn't flinch at her emotions, which meant he'd probably recently used the children's essence in an Essex to protect himself.

Bastard.

He took her hands in his, and everything she felt for Kasabian slid away. A trill of panic filled the empty space left behind. What if Treylon erased all of her feelings? What if she couldn't love Kasabian anymore?

"That's much better," she lied, pulling her hands away as fast as she could.

"Good. As I said last time, the easiest way is to Leap you to where my lover is. You can bond us, and then I'll bring you back."

He sounded so convincing that she wondered if maybe that was his intent after all. Or was it the Thrall that helped her to believe?

He reached for her hands again. Her body evaporated, then reappeared in a beautiful garden with concrete paths stamped with the patterns of leaves. Several two-story buildings blended into the natural landscape with neutral colors.

Kasabian, see through my eyes. She spun in a slow circle. "It's a lovely place. Where are we?"

"A private facility for rehabilitation." He was giving nothing away.

Kasabian had described a cord that connected them, but she couldn't see it. She groped for the connection but could feel nothing of him. The panic returned. Had Treylon cut the bond after all?

"This way, m'dear." Treylon led her to the nearest building, upstairs to one of the rooms at the end. He opened the door to a luxury suite with a view of the water. An ocean breeze wafted through the open French doors, making the sheer curtains dance. "She's in the bedroom," Treylon said, taking her arm and leading her to the doorway. Where Silva sat, his blue eyes bright with...anticipation?

She tried to act surprised to see him, not wanting them to know that she'd come willingly. With a plan.

He stood and approached her. "Were you in the car with Kasabian when it went over the bridge? Never mind answering. I can feel your fear over it."

Treylon's mouth tightened. "Since you're alive, so is Kasabian, I presume." Unfortunately, he sounded disappointed, not relieved. "I suppose you thought you'd lead him here. Didn't he tell you that the barrier keeps him from sensing where you are? And Leaping here?"

Her heart froze. But they were bonded. Kasabian would feel her fear and know something was up. Then he'd tune in and see her, like he'd done before. He could pick up some clue from her surroundings, so she would search for visual landmarks. Their bond would save them.

⌒

By the time Kasabian arrived back at his apartment, he felt a strange absence of Kye's anger. She'd accepted his abandonment of her then. Maybe even realized it was for the best.

Can you?

He had to. Separating from her *was* for the best. The thought of it hurt like hell, but he'd already started the process. Seeing Kye's face when she realized he was shutting her out stabbed him in the heart. That she'd believed in him made it even worse. The problem was that he didn't believe in his ability to control his Wraithlord Shadow. Especially with Sarai's vision of him killing Kye.

He dropped down onto his bed and dug into his psyche for that cord that bound them. Could he sever it? His father had been about to, so Kasabian should have that ability as well. In his mind, he grasped the cord. He wanted to follow it to her, to see her. The need clawed through him.

He sucked in a deep breath. *No.* He would weaken, falter.

The Dragon Shadow fought him, sending bursts of pain through his psyche. He summoned his Light, creating a knife that gleamed silver. This was a bond she never wanted, one that had been forced upon her. She'd tried to break it herself. He prepared to slice the knife across the cord, gently, so the connection didn't shake. He didn't want to startle her.

His hand trembled, even though it was in the psychic space of his mind. The Shadow pummeled him, trying to wrench him back. He fought against it, pulling the blade across the cord and severing it.

Chapter 20

Kye searched as the two men led her outside and toward the building closest to the water. Small signs identified the various buildings, and on one was the logo of a nautilus shell. She summoned all her fear and focused on that logo.

Come on, Kasabian, connect.

She remembered feeling him coming through the connection before, though she hadn't known what it was until Kasabian yelled at her. He would yell again, once he realized what she'd done. Then he'd see what an opportunity it was. Maybe he could bypass the barrier because of their bond. Finally she spotted a sign with the likely name of the facility: Wildwood. She stared, willing Kasabian to see it.

Why couldn't she feel him? Angry, scared, she'd take anything at this point. But Kasabian was...gone. Now that she was tuning in, she could feel his absence.

Don't panic. He'll get your note.

A lot of good that would do if he couldn't find this place. She'd put herself in danger for nothing. She had to still her breaths as full-scale panic set in. *Stop. They'll feel it.*

The men were talking about timelines and names, and though they were watching her, it was mostly out of the corner of their eyes. Maybe this wouldn't be for nothing after all. If she could escape, she would be able to tell Kasabian where this place was. She surreptitiously scanned the property and began working up two blue orbs in the palms of her hands. At one end, she could see a tall fence behind overgrown hedges. She didn't think she could scale the fence before her captors would stop her. She knew their power, especially Silva's. Escape was unlikely, but she had to try. In fact, she had nothing to lose. They needed her, so they wouldn't kill her. At least she hoped not.

Toward the back of the property was the ocean. No fences, just a dock. And lots of water. And they were headed right to it. The orbs grew hot in her hands, still small enough to conceal. She'd been able to surprise Silva before, when he hadn't been expecting an orb to slam into him.

As they started to turn toward the building that was closest to the ocean, she turned and threw the orbs at them. They smashed into each man's face. Then she ran like hell. They shouted, at first in surprise; then she heard Treylon ordering Silva to stop her. If only she had the breath to scream. Her plan was to dive as far out into the water as she could, where she'd be potentially in sight of the general public—people on boats or in the surrounding houses.

Something grabbed her, something definitely not human. She saw black fingers clutching at her shoulders. She dropped and rolled, and the grip loosened. The water was only a few yards away now. She didn't dare look back, zigzagging in case Silva was aiming that black magick at her. A spear shot past her, then curved around in front of her. Not a spear but more of a rope, aiming to loop around her as though she were a runaway horse. She ducked, nearly losing her balance, and veered away from the dock.

She reached the seawall and prepared to dive. Her burning calf muscles coiled in preparation. Footsteps pounded behind her. Her feet braced on the concrete. Just as she launched, ropes slithered around her body and pulled her back, throwing her to the ground.

The sky swam in front of her, and then Silva's piqued expression as he leaned over her. She gasped, trying to catch her breath.

"Nice try, Ms. Rivers," he said. "But no cigar."

Treylon came into view, huffing and puffing. "Keep her bound and take her inside."

She could barely walk, what with her gasping breaths and aching muscles. It didn't help that those horrid magick ropes wrapped around her all the way to her knees, making her shuffle. The Caidos escorted her into the first room on the ground floor and only then released her. Four children sat inside, two Caidos, a Deuce, and a Dragon, all huddled on one bed. No hope glimmered in their eyes, even as they turned to her. Their eyes were empty and so, so sad. Kasabian was right. Kye would do anything to help them. Anything at all.

Silva opened his mouth, but Treylon cut him off. "We have been working with these four for a while now. The Caidos channel the Crescents' essence and send it upward, where it accumulates in a vessel. But it drains the children so quickly." Treylon actually looked sympathetic. "If you bond one Caido to one Crescent, both will continue to be strong."

Kye's throat tightened painfully at the thought. "I can't bond children."

"They only need to last until the solar storm wave rolls through. You can help them survive. Once we've filled the vessel, we can break the bond and release them unharmed."

He wouldn't care that she had no idea how to unbond them. She met Treylon's gaze. Could she believe that he'd release them?

"Memory-locked, of course," he added. "You, too. But you can all survive if you cooperate. If you don't, we'll simply kill you now." He gave a baleful look at the kids. "And the Crescents will likely die."

The children sucked in a breath, and one made a sobbing noise.

"You give your oath?" she asked.

"I do. I have no ill will toward the children. They are only tools for a very important purpose."

"To free Caidos from the curse."

His eyes glittered with passion. "Do you know the pain we live in? Unable to work and play among others. To love."

"It's a worthy goal." She looked at the children. "But the cost is too high. And that cost includes your own son."

"He is already dead to me."

"Because he's trying to save these children." She could vividly imagine him as a boy, leading those children to safety. "It was the right thing to do. He's a good man."

Silva snarled. "He was only saving his own ass."

"If that's true, he would have left alone. But he took

children who slowed him down, no doubt." Admiration swelled in her heart. "It was risky."

"He's no hero to *me*." Silva's bitterness tainted his words.

Treylon made a huffing sound. "He was blinded by their suffering and couldn't see the bigger picture. If the Caido population knew what they lost, they would not see Kasabian as a hero."

"But they'll see you as a hero," she said.

Treylon raised his fist. "I will be a god among my people instead of a laughable failure. Even the angels will bow to me."

"Why?"

"Because once the vessel is filled with essence, the additional power of the solar storm will free them from this plane. Which will break our connection with them and free us as well."

"I think having the angels in your debt, garnering their respect and admiration, is more important to you than freeing your fellow Caidos."

Treylon's smile was fleeting. "That does motivate me, yes. One gets tired of being looked down upon and disparaged."

Kye could relate to that, but she would never go to the insane lengths Treylon had. "Getting respect is never worth such a sacrifice."

He pinned her with a look. "Will you be a hero to these children?"

She fought his attempt to Thrall her. He didn't need to. "Yes." *And then I will kill you.* "After one more promise. That you won't hurt Kasabian."

"She's in love with him," Silva said, grit in his voice.

All of her anger and angst over Kasabian was gone, courtesy of Treylon. But her feelings were not. She faced Silva. "And so are you."

His scoffing laugh was hollow. "Ridiculous."

"Then why did you offer to restore Kasabian's Caido essence only if he would submit to you sexually?"

Treylon's eyes narrowed. "Restore his essence?"

"Because he Stripped him," Kye said.

"Stripped... when did this happen?"

"When he came here yesterday," Kye answered, cutting off Silva's words just as Treylon had earlier. "Silva lured him to Kennedy Park early this morning, where they fought." She gave Treylon a puzzled look. "Doesn't he tell you anything?"

Silva's eyes flashed black as he glared at her. "You will shut up now." He lifted his hand.

Treylon gripped his wrist. "No, she has so much to say." His eyes narrowed. "That's why you killed Gren, isn't it? Because he knew and was about to tell me. You killed one of our assets to cover your tracks."

Silva had murdered one of their own? Cold chills washed over Kye. And he would kill her, too. She could see it in his eyes.

"It wasn't like that," Silva said, the submissive boy edging into his voice. "Gren was defecting, just as Beldeen did."

"You didn't tell me you'd Stripped him. Or about your meeting in the park."

Silva crossed his arms over his chest, as regal as a prince defending his actions. "Details. You give her pleasure driving a wedge between us. That's all she's doing."

Damn, she forgot how Caidos could pick up emotions.

She turned to Treylon "You haven't promised not to kill Kasabian."

"I will not kill him," Treylon bit out.

Both men felt righteous in their motives, and both felt that Kasabian had been the betrayer, albeit for different reasons.

Treylon put his hand to her back. "You will begin bonding the children."

"I will have to rest between them. It takes a lot out of me. When does it need to be finished?" She looked out at the dying light of day.

"The solar storm is predicted to arrive full force sometime tomorrow." He waved his hand in front of the window. Suddenly, a tall tube was visible in the sky, the image wavering against reality. A blue substance filled the tube nearly to the top. "That must be completely full by morning."

Kye glanced at the children on the twin beds. Jonathan was here somewhere. She wanted to find him. "Let's get started." She approached the nearest Caido boy, who she guessed was about ten. All of them so young, so vulnerable, with their pallid complexions and shadows beneath their eyes. "I'm Kye," she said. "What's your name?"

"Evan," he whispered.

"I know this whole situation sucks. I'd love to bust you right out of here." She turned toward the Deuce girl squished into the back corner. "What's your name?"

"Cassie," she whispered.

"I'm going to form a bond between you two. It will make the channeling easier." She wasn't going to say that it would mostly help Evan. The drain would be the same for Cassie unfortunately. "It won't hurt." She turned to Evan.

"You may feel a lot of emotions washing over you. It'll go on for a little while, and it might be scary. I'll be here if you need me."

"We don't have time for that," Silva said.

She shot him a hard look. "Yes, we do." She took each of their hands in hers. Because these children weren't old enough to be romantically interested in anyone, they shouldn't bond on that level. *Forgive me*, she asked no one in particular, and began the Cobra.

The children took the bonding well. She held their hands throughout the process and rested for a while between the two pairs here. Silva glared at her the entire time, checking his watch.

Kye released the second pair's hands and approached the two men. "How many children are there altogether?"

"Eighteen, for now."

For now. They were working on getting more. *Please, please let them fail.*

They led her to the next room, and then the next. Her bones felt weak, her soul stretched thin, until she saw that familiar face with the big brown eyes. Jonathan. She had thought of him so much that she expected him to recognize her. He buried his face against his bent knees. He had almost gotten away. To be that close and then returned here must have been hell.

She sat on the bed and ran her hand down Jonathan's back. "Hi, sweetheart. I'm sorry that you're here. I'm going to try to make this a little better, so you won't get as weak." She leaned closer and whispered, "Lyle has been trying to find you. He loves you very much."

The boy lifted his head, surprise and hope in his eyes. She wasn't sure there was reason to hope, but she wanted

him to know someone loved him. Cared. She had failed
him, though he didn't know that. By not sticking that orb
to the Hummer. By making the decision to come here without knowing the rules of Leaping. All she could do was
save him some suffering. Despite Treylon's promise, she
couldn't be sure any of them would survive once this was
over.

The receptionist left for the day, leaving Sarai alone with
Kye's parents in the waiting room. The building was quiet,
other than the soothing music still flowing from the hidden
speakers and the distant sound of conversation. Kye's office was very quiet, but Sarai figured the room was soundproofed for privacy.

Mrs. Rivers sat ramrod straight in the chair, her mouth
moving silently. Probably talking to a spirit. *Thank the
gods I didn't get that kind of ability.*

The visions were bad enough, though when they saved
people's lives, it was worth it. Sarai had met Kye's parents
only a few times, when Kye had included her in holiday
celebrations. Then she'd seen the other side of her friend,
the one that quietly put up with her parents' subtle put-
downs, their obvious disappointment. But now Sarai could
see how much they loved their daughter.

"*You* tell her then," Mrs. Rivers said, her voice going a
hair louder in agitation. "It's a bad idea."

"Uh-oh," Mr. Rivers said. "Must be your mother."

Mrs. Rivers rolled her eyes. "She hasn't left me alone
since I gave Kye the message." She looked at something—
some*one*—about two feet in front of her, her expression

one of a girl who was being chewed out by her mother. "I told her exactly what you said!"

"Was that the thing about her being committed?" Sarai asked, feeling as though she were intruding on a private conversation.

Mrs. Rivers nodded sharply. "My mother said it. I can't help it if Kye took it the crazy committed way."

"How was it meant?" In the context of these circumstances, crazy made sense, Kye throwing herself into a dangerous situation with a dangerous man.

"She meant to commit to someone. If Kye commits herself to that deranged Caido, her abilities will come back. *That* sounds crazy!"

"Are you sure she means Kasabian?"

"Yes, she keeps saying he's 'the one.' He will love her. He will…" She narrowed her eyes. "What? Why do you keep talking about the time?"

They all glanced at the clock on the wall. Kye had been in there for more than an hour.

Sarai's chest tightened as she came to her feet. She quietly walked to the door and listened. Not a sound. Seconds ticked by as she tried to wait out perhaps a thoughtful silence. Still nothing.

She knocked. "Kye?"

Her parents now stood behind her, their scared expressions mirroring her own, no doubt. Sarai opened the door to find her worries substantiated. The office was empty.

They rushed inside and stupidly checked in places where Kye and her client would not be, like beneath her desk and in the small supply closet.

"The window's closed," Mrs. Rivers said, trying it. "It's locked. She didn't climb out."

Sarai had watched the window for forty-five minutes, finally deciding that Kye wasn't going to escape. "Her client is missing, too. Caidos can Leap to other places. And they can take people with them."

"Why didn't you see this?" Mrs. Rivers said in a high-pitched voice.

Oh, yes, Sarai totally got how Kye's mother dumped her disappointment onto her daughter. "It doesn't work that way. I get—" Her gaze fell on the envelope propped on the keyboard. She lunged for it and tore it open.

I'm sorry to do this to you. I have to make myself useful. I have to DO something. Tell Kasabian I met with Treylon, that I'm in, and to Leap to me. Remind him he can see through our connection. He'll know what it means.

Chapter 21

———

Y ou smell nice, at least."

Every time Mallory spoke, her warm breath washed against Hayden's neck. Considering they were hanging upside down and very likely about to die, it was odd to notice the pleasant sensation. Or the way her breasts, firm and ample, fit just below his rib cage. Even if the lace scratched every time she twisted in an attempt to free herself.

"Why, thank you," he said. "It's probably my aftershave you're getting up close and personal with."

"It's all of you I'm getting up close and personal with." So she'd noticed the rub of their skin against skin, too. "It's Versace, isn't it?"

"Yep. I guess you're familiar with all of them."

She stiffened. "I can hear your disdain, even now. I don't give a flying fig what you think about me. I don't think much of you Guard people, either. At least I have principles. Boundaries. You Vegas just follow orders like hound dogs, chasing down prey and killing it."

"Yes, some of them are like dogs, blindly following orders. If I were one of them, I wouldn't be here hanging out with you. I'd probably be at my desk or sniffing down some criminal. Woof woof."

"Okay, maybe you're different." Just when he thought he'd get a concession from her, she went on. "Maybe you think you're better than everybody else. More self-righteous than the masses, Dudley Do-Right, looking down from his pedestal."

"I think it just slays you that I'm not falling all over myself at your Muse-ness."

Her husky laugh held all kinds of challenge. "That's because you haven't seen the full extent of my magick."

"Hah, I knew it. Kasabian told me it's not about sex, that it's about *inspiration*, but I didn't buy that for a second. Why would you subject yourself to your chosen career? You're beautiful, smart, and..."

She tilted her head away enough that he could see her narrowed eyes. "And what?"

Sexy. Fascinating. Fortunately he reined in those words and simply said, "Interesting."

She relaxed again, letting her face rest against him. "You don't know enough about me to make that kind of statement."

"By design, since there's a mystique purposely built around your profession."

She made a scoffing sound. "It's not a mystique. Why publicize what most can't have?"

"But we of the unwashed masses want to know what we're missing."

"It's not like that. We have always belonged to the Elders."

"Since we're probably going to die here, can you tell me what I'm missing then?"

"There's even less point telling you now," she said.

"You are a cruel woman, Mallory. Can you at least tell me why you chose your profession?"

"You're exasperating."

"Probably."

"Annoying. Nosy."

"And? I could hear an 'and' in there."

"Interesting," she said at last.

He laughed. Amazing that he could find a speck of amusement. "Touché. So indulge my nosiness."

"I didn't choose to be a Muse. I was born into it, as my mother, and her mother, and so on. It's all I know. For as long as I can remember, I heard that I could never be sure if a man truly loved me for me or if he just wanted one of the few Caido females. As a Muse, I would never have to wonder, because I would not ever fall in love or marry. I would be held up as a goddess, revered and protected."

And yet, she didn't sound full of herself about being considered a goddess. "I would be surrounded only by the best, smartest, most talented men, who would never ask more of me than I wanted to give." She paused, as though considering how much more to tell him. Probably figuring he'd continue prodding her, she said, "And yes, some Muses do offer physical interaction as part of their services. I focus on the inspiration aspect of my gifts, working primarily with artists, songwriters, and other creative types. Their desire for me allows them to create in a way they can't in their otherwise repressed state. I hope that sates your curiosity, because that's all I'm saying about it." The edge in her voice was clear.

He absorbed all of that. It was more than he could wrap his head around, and yet he wanted to know more.

The French door opened, and the minion stepped out. He was holding Hayden's phone and had a smug smile on his pretty-boy face. "Your friend Kasabian texted you a question mark. Guess he's wondering how things are going. Talbot said to invite him to the party."

The sound of his phone ringing pushed Kasabian to wakefulness. He felt like he'd been Stripped again. Hell, he must have passed out from the force of severing the connection. It took all of his energy to run to the living room and find the phone before the call rolled over to voice mail. "Yeah?" His voice sounded hoarse, thick.

"Kasabian?"

A woman's voice, but not Kye's. "Yes."

"It's Sarai. Kye's gone." Before those words could fully wrap around his heart, she went on. "She wanted to meet with a client, to get her head back into her life. We were waiting outside her office as her chaperones. We just realized she's gone! She left a note telling us to let you know that she's with Treylon. You're supposed to Leap to her. Or at least see through your connection."

"Oh, hell. Oh, *hell*." He scrubbed his hand down his face, panic gripping him. "Treylon's the enemy. What is she thinking?"

"Oh, no, this is my fault. I told her that sleeping with the enemy would be helpful. But it can't be good that she's with him, not by your reaction."

Kye had met with Treylon. She was at the resort,

thinking he could Leap to her because of their connection.

"You can go to her, right?" Sarai said. "You can do that Caido thing and instantly be where she is."

"It's complicated, but yes, I can. It's going to take time though." He didn't want to dash her hopes with the truth.

"She said she had to *do* something. And I understand that, because we're feeling the same way, me and her parents."

Kye needed to feel valuable. He should have seen this coming. And he had no doubt he had helped spur that need with his attempt to keep her out. With his cruelty in calling her worthless. No way was he involving her parents or Sarai.

"Please, Kasabian. Please don't let anything happen to her."

"I promise I'll bring her back safe and sound." Another promise.

After a pause, Sarai said, "I know you will." Another pause. "You love her, don't you? I know it sounds crazy, but in the van—"

"I'd better go." He had to hang up before his voice cracked. He dropped to the floor and, in that dark space in his mind, searched for the cord. He would stitch it back together, glue it, anything. But there was nothing. No sign of it. *Gone!* Sarai's voice echoed, her grief apparent.

He called Silva, getting his voice mail. "She can't help you. Her magick is gone. Let her go. I'll come in her place. I'll channel the energy. You hurt her, and I will tear you apart."

Just as he disconnected, someone knocked on his door. Cecily started at the abrupt way he opened the door, and no doubt the ashen look on his face. "Come in, quick."

"What's wrong?" she asked, loping inside with a stack of papers.

"My . . ." What was Kye to him? Friend seemed a ridiculous assessment. But not girlfriend either. *Mine,* some part of him whispered. *Just mine.* "Someone I care about has thrown herself into the lion's den." The thought of it tore him apart all over again.

"I know the feeling. Have you heard from Hayden?"

Her Dragon eyes flared, and Kasabian felt an answering call to the embers burning deep within. "I broke down and sent him a text a short time ago, just a question mark. But I haven't heard anything yet. Let's start calling this list. This very long list," he added when he saw the pages. "We're looking for resorts that are fully booked or have some other reason for not accepting a reservation. At this time of year, off-season, it would be rare for a resort to be fully booked."

"I was able to pull together a list of all the resorts in the Miami/Fort Lauderdale area, but I couldn't cross-reference the owners' names with the database of all Crescents without raising any flags."

As frustrating as that was for Kasabian, if their enemy were monitoring Cecily, they would know he was close to finding their operation. And they might hurt her. "I think that was smart."

They sat down and divided up the list. He could Leap to each one, but that would be too taxing. He needed to conserve his power. So they both went to work calling each resort.

He kept catching her watching him as they made their fake inquiries. She would avert her gaze quickly, guiltily. Finally, she blew out a breath. "It's not fair, you guys being so . . . so gorgeous. Beyond gorgeous. Every time I'm around Hayden, I get giddy. Giddy! I haven't been giddy since I was a teenager. And no, I'm not a teenager." She obviously got that a lot.

Kasabian shrugged. "It's just the Thrall."

"I wanted to think that, believe me. But I'm afraid it's more than that. He's a good guy, very nice, but he cuts off any bit of flirting. Yet, I know he likes me."

Kasabian wasn't going there. "It's complicated." He called the next number on the list, and she went back to hers.

A half hour into their effort, Kasabian's phone dinged. His pulse jumped as he looked at the screen. "It's Hayden. He says they have the boy, the scene is secure, and I should come to the Tower right away."

Cecily actually jumped up and down, her long ponytail slapping her shoulder. "That's wonderful! Let's go."

"You keep going down that list of resorts."

"But I want to help in a real way."

He tapped the papers she held. "Kye is being held at one of those resorts. By narrowing it down to a handful that we can check out physically, you're being a huge help."

"Can you tell me what's going on here? All I know is that it has something to do with that little boy who was found and then taken away again. And that someone high up is involved."

Someone should know what was going on. He gave her a thumbnail version. "Stay here, work on this. Security at the Tower isn't going to let you in." Hayden would be furious if Kasabian involved Cecily. He knew exactly how it felt to have someone you cared about in danger. "Help me find Kye."

She brushed loose strands of hair from her face. "So Caidos *can* fall in love with non-Caidos."

He had to dampen the hope flickering in her eyes. "It's very complicated." There was a way, of course, but he couldn't get into the whole Cobra thing because then he'd have to say *if* Kye survived, and he couldn't fathom that *if*. At least they'd have Jonathan in their custody. So why was a dark feeling dampening *his* hope? He stopped. "It's a trap."

"What, the text? How can you be sure?"

"I can't." He read the text again. "But it doesn't sound like Hayden. He'd have said, 'I have Jonathan,' not 'the boy.' He would have called because he'd be so freakin' excited to get that kid back, and he'd want to tell me the details. Or he would just Leap here with him. Plus, we're pretty sure Jonathan was in the Hummer."

Kasabian was actually sorry to have crushed her hope that Hayden was all right. But hey, it sucked for him, too. He continued to the door.

"You're still going?" she asked.

"It's a way into the Tower. Jonathan may not be there, but Hayden and Mallory are."

"What should I do if you don't return?"

"Is there anyone in the Guard that you trust implicitly?"

"I would have said Kade Kavanaugh, but he's the one who went crazy today. And then his sister, who's an Argus, broke him out. Things are weird at work right now. I'll give it some thought."

"I have to go. Let me know if you find a likely resort." Kasabian Leaped to the corner of the Tower's parking lot and walked into the lobby, appearing for all intents and purposes to be about to meet up with his triumphant buddy. The man at the desk gave him a curious look. "Didn't you come in earlier? I don't remember you leaving." He checked the computer.

"I had to Leap out, urgent business."

"And now you're here to see Mr. Talbot?"

Kasabian gave him a wooden smile. "For completely different reasons."

The man cleared his throat. "Well, I would assume so." He glanced over at a man wearing a suit. "Take him up to Talbot's."

Kasabian gauged the escort's body language. He wasn't involved in this, so Kasabian would not kill him unless absolutely necessary. But he would have to incapacitate him if his initial plan didn't work.

He let the Wraithlord magick curl from his hand as the elevator soared upward. It heated his palm, tickled along his skin. He'd had no time to work with this new ability. But he knew what it could do, thanks to Silva.

As soon as they exited the elevator and the escort headed to the door on the left, Kasabian brushed his hand against the back of the man's head.

"You delivered me," he whispered, staring into the Caido's eyes as he implanted a false memory into his mind. "Now go back down to the lobby."

The man faced the elevator, waiting for it to arrive. *Hurry*. He didn't want this guy here when Talbot opened the door. The elevator arrived with a soft *ding*. The escort stepped into the car. Kasabian put a visual shield over himself and Invoked. As the elevator doors slid closed, Kasabian heard the condo's door unlock. A Caido in full wing lunged out with his sword of Light, ready to launch a surprise attack—on no one. He stared at the empty foyer as the elevator doors closed. The man, who was too young to be Talbot, started to go back inside.

Kasabian dropped the shield and rushed him, shoving

him backward into the condominium. They tumbled to the floor, Kasabian on top. He knew all too well that Wraithlord magick curtailed Caido abilities. The Dragon Shadow reared up, fueled even more when the Caido scorched his side with Light. He sent dark magick to curl around the man's throat. "Where are they?"

He didn't have to wait for an answer from the red-faced, gasping man. Kasabian's gaze moved up, through the glass doors and out to the balcony. Hayden, Mallory, alive. Hanging upside down and oblivious to his presence since the doors were closed.

The guy beneath him took advantage of his distraction and threw him off. In the seconds it took for Kasabian to gain his balance, the Caido pulled a feather from his wings. It instantly solidified into a dhagger. As Kasabian lunged for him, the knife came flying at him, hitting him in the arm and slicing out a nice-sized chunk of flesh. Fired by his success, his opponent called the dhagger back for another shot. "Screw your dark magick!"

Kasabian let the Shadow take over and released a shower of darts at the man's chest. With a hiss of pain, the Caido threw the dhagger again. While Kasabian ducked to the side to avoid it, another one buried itself in his abdomen. Pain lanced right through to his back. He grasped the knife, careful of the sharp edges, and pulled it out. His blood coated the feather-etched blade.

The Caido plucked the darts from his body, each one unleashing a gush of blood before the wound started sealing up again. All the while, he kept an eye on Kasabian, and his wounds, reaching back to grab another feather.

"You'll be featherless before you kill me," Kasabian growled.

He caught the knife just as it was about to puncture his chest. The blade cut into his palm, slicing even more as he released it with the kind of spin he used with liquor bottles at the bar. The knife hit the Caido in the chest, making him stagger back. Kasabian released vines to force him to tumble over the coffee table to the floor. The Caido screamed like a girl, grasping at the vines that wound around his neck. He finished him, pulling so hard that the Caido's neck snapped.

He spotted Hayden's phone on the coffee table, grabbed it, and stuffed it into his pocket. As he started to head to the French doors, he felt a presence behind him. He spun to find a man who *was* old enough to be Talbot. He was tall, lean, and muscular, with a narrow face and a mouth that looked like a slash. A shadow flashed across his eyes as he took in his dead associate. Another Wraithlord. *Hell.*

"You have no idea what you're messing with, boy," Talbot growled.

Oh, yes, he did. Kasabian could say the same, and he was going to take advantage of that lack of knowledge. He threw out his hand and sent a Shadow spear at Talbot's chest. His shock registered a millisecond before the spear hit, throwing him back several steps. Kasabian didn't give him time to react. He created a lasso and tossed it toward him.

Talbot had already recovered, though. He jerked the spear out, and dodged the lasso, leaving a trail as blood poured out of the hole in his chest.

"Does your father know you've inherited the Wraithlord DNA?" Talbot used both his hands to send a rolling wave of smoke at him. It left a trail of blackened carpet and burned the edge of the couch. Kasabian Leaped out of its path, landing behind Talbot.

"No, but he's going to find out."

Talbot spun, swinging a magick weapon that looked like a scythe at head level. Kasabian ducked, feeling it whip just an inch over his head. He barreled into Talbot's stomach, gripping his waist as he drove the man toward the far wall—and right through it. Drywall dust created a white cloud that tickled Kasabian's throat. He created several spikes that shot out and punctured Talbot's innards.

The man screamed in pain, loud and guttural. A long black arm clamped around Kasabian's neck and propelled him clear across the room, where he crashed into another wall. Talbot's arm, extended with dark magick, still gripped him. His hand tightened, cutting off Kasabian's air, as Talbot stalked toward him. The multiple puncture wounds were already mending, as was the hole in his chest. His other hand morphed into a drill bit, its sharp tip spinning as he drew closer.

Kasabian summoned the Shadow's strength. It vibrated from the center of his being, but he couldn't break free of Talbot's hold. The drill pierced Kasabian's skin, sending pain screaming through him.

Kasabian's Shadow broke loose, Transforming him into the half angel, half Dragon he'd seen Silva become. The force of it blew Talbot back a few steps, enough for Kasabian to break free. He sent thick vines to wrap Talbot in a tight grip, lift him up, and thrust him down on top of the glass coffee table. Wood splintered and glass flew, the shards slicing into Talbot's body. In a dark flash, he disappeared.

Kasabian spun to find Talbot plunging his dark fist right into Kasabian's chest. He staggered back, feeling his heart trip at the injury. He sucked in a deep breath as he met the

next punch with his hand, then squeezed Talbot's fist until
he felt it crumble in his grip.

Kasabian's body healed even faster in Wraithlord form
than it would have in Caido form. Unfortunately, so did
Talbot's. How the hell was he going to kill this bastard?
He glanced out at the balcony. Hayden was looking in
their direction, obviously having heard the commotion. If
Kasabian didn't kill Talbot, his friends would die.

That's when it hit him. Talbot knew where his father
was. Where Kye was.

Talbot's arm stretched out across the room, aiming for
a red button near the front door. A panic button that would
bring others. Kasabian sliced at his arm, severing it. His
forearm fell to the floor, turning back to human form.

Talbot used his magick to make a tourniquet near the
end of the stump. His mouth was set in a grim line. His
dark eyes held Kasabian's gaze so that he didn't even see
the razor-sharp whip that lashed at his neck. Kasabian
shifted, missing the brunt of it but feeling the sting as it
grazed him. Talbot wanted to pay Kasabian back by taking
his head.

Kasabian willed his fingernails to become long spikes.
As Talbot cracked his whip again, Kasabian waited until it
reached the downward snap. Then he lunged at Talbot and
drove the spikes into his head. The force threw them both
back, until Talbot hit the wall.

Kasabian wrapped his other hand around Talbot's neck,
pinning him the same way Talbot had done to him. "Tell
me where my father is."

Kye. She popped into his mind, her beautiful face full of
fear as she realized that he could not help her. What would
she think if she saw him now?

"Where is this resort? The place you sent Jonathan." He pushed harder, feeling the tips of his claws touch the wall. "Tell me, and I'll release you." Not that he'd let him just go free.

The shadows in Talbot's eyes dissipated. He managed a shaky smile, his eyes glazing. "You'll never...find it in time." And he sagged.

Kasabian retracted the spikes, and the man fell to the floor. Kasabian checked his pulse. Nothing. He pulled the Wraithlord back, but left his wings intact. He might still need them. Then he ran to the balcony.

It might have been a funny sight under different circumstances, the two of them hanging like a pair of bats. "You all right?"

"Peachy," Hayden said in a smart-assed tone that told Kasabian, yeah, he was fine. "Though any assistance would be appreciated. This is that fucked-up Wraithlord magick."

"We haven't been able to budge it. Or Leap," Mallory said, trying to turn her head to see him.

The same kind of fucked-up magick he'd just used. Oh, yeah, Wraithlords were turning out to be a stellar example of Crescent goodness. He wondered why the magick persisted when the Wraithlord was dead. Lingering energy? Kasabian glanced back at the French door that was still closed. The sky's reflection obliterated any view of the interior, so they hadn't seen a thing.

Kasabian met Hayden's gaze. "Brace yourself." He summoned his Shadow and willed it to undo the magick. It became like those damn birds that Stripped him, darting toward Hayden and Mallory in a swarm. Kasabian used his will to corral them to the vines that wound around them.

The magick obeyed, though he watched carefully to make sure it didn't harm his friends.

Mallory couldn't see what he was doing from her angle, but Hayden simply stared. Great. Now he was going to think Kasabian was a freak. Or rather, *know* he was.

"I'll explain later." Kasabian guided his magick up the vine that attached to the ceiling, though he could see that it was starting to disintegrate on its own. He gave it a final zap. The moment they started to fall, Kasabian slapped his hands on them and Leaped to his apartment.

Cecily let out a gasp when the three landed in a heap only feet away. Then her gaze zeroed in on Hayden and Mallory, chest to chest, his arms around her.

Hayden and Mallory stumbled to their feet as the blood drained from their heads. Hayden automatically steadied Mallory with his big hands on her bare shoulders, even while he was wavering.

"Major headache," Mallory said, bending over and clutching her head. "Ouch, ouch, ouch."

Hayden braced one hand on the back of the nearby chair, squinting in his own pain. Then his gaze found Cecily, who was gaining her ground as she took the two of them in. Her gaze lingered on Hayden's hand still gripping Mallory's shoulder and then the lacy bra that didn't conceal much.

Hayden looked just as surprised to see her. "Cecily? What are you doing here?"

"Helping me," Kasabian answered to give her a few more seconds to compose herself. Gods help her, she was big-time infatuated with Hayden. "Mallory, I'll get you a shirt." He ran to his room and grabbed a T-shirt.

While she slipped into it, Kasabian redirected their attention. "Let me get you up to speed with what's been happening while you two were hanging around doing nothing."

He didn't give Hayden time to shoot back anything sarcastic because he told them about Kye.

"I'll help." Mallory dropped into the chair and seemed to just realize Cecily was standing nearby. "Hey. I'm Mallory."

"Cecily," she managed. She lowered herself to her chair. "I'll show you what we're doing."

Kasabian nodded for Hayden to follow him into the room he'd converted to a home gym. Hayden closed the door behind him and leaned back against it. "Explain." His expression was a wary mask.

The thought of losing his friendship hurt more than the punch through his chest had. "I'm a Wraithlord," Kasabian said. "But you probably figured that out."

The muscles in Hayden's jaw twitched, like they always did when he was pissed. "Yeah, I got that. Why didn't you tell me?"

"I found out when I fought Silva and got my Caido back."

"But you must have sensed it long before that. I saw a shadow in your eyes that day I mentioned how hot Kye was. You've never shown a hint of being jealous, and for you to do it over a woman who's not even yours was weird. With everything else going on, I pushed it to the back of my mind. Because I thought I knew who you were. But I don't. And you never said a thing." And that, Kasabian suspected, was the worst part for Hayden.

"I didn't know what *it* was. I just sensed something dark inside of me, and I was ashamed of it. Scared of it. I didn't tell anyone, didn't want to acknowledge it myself. I didn't want you, of all people, looking at me like I was an aberration. But that's what I am. You can't take that? Fine." Kasabian shrugged, even though it wasn't fine. Not at all. "But I need your help. I can't do this without you."

Hayden had perfected that Guard poker face. "I bet you said the same thing to me all those years ago when you had this cockeyed idea of escaping."

Kasabian nodded. "I knew I could trust you. Count on you. That's never changed."

"You can." Hayden started to turn toward the door but stopped. "Does Kye know?"

Kasabian leaned back against the weight machine. "She was there when Silva told me."

"And what does she think?"

His chest caved in when he pictured her surrendering to him. He tore himself from the image. "She's not afraid. Stupid girl."

"She's in love with you. It makes her blind."

The way she believed he could control the Wraithlord...she thought he was good. *Then you raked her wound and proved you're not.* "What about you?"

Hayden's laugh lacked humor. "Well, I'm definitely not in love with you." The poker face disintegrated, breached by the pain of Kasabian's secret. "You've been like a brother to me. I need time to process this. But first we find Kye and those kids."

Chapter 22

Silva watched Kye sleeping. She had bonded all the kids and had literally crawled into a bed in one of the empty rooms. This rehab facility had ended up being perfect for their use, with its secure buildings and separate rooms. He wasn't sure what the owner had done with all of the wealthy patients.

Kye's thick braid was frayed. She had rammed her fingers into her hair every time she saw the next pair of children. Silva had felt her heartache and sympathy for them. No one had ever felt that for him. She certainly radiated nothing but hatred toward him. Fortunately the Caidos here regularly did the Essex with the children to protect against all their emotions, so her animosity didn't hurt.

Kye was pretty, he'd give her that, though not as pretty as he. She had a big heart, comforting the kids with her soft words. He could imagine a man falling for her, a man inclined toward that sort of thing. Kasabian would fall for her courageousness alone, since he harbored that trait, too.

Silva dialed into his voice mail and listened to Kasabian's phone message for the fourth time. The rawness of his voice, the intensity of his plea. He had definitely fallen for this woman. His devotion to her grated.

It was tempting to take Kasabian up on that offer, even though they could not let Kye go. How far would Kasabian go to save her? Oh, to be loved like that. He found little satisfaction with Gren or the others who had participated in a mutual use-use relationship with him.

All his life he'd been used. For his body. For his assistance and powers. Years ago, Kasabian had shown him kindness without asking anything in return. Kasabian had encouraged Silva to stand up to Treylon, but that was more than a father-deprived boy could comprehend.

Well, Silva had gone against the old man at last. Had hidden secrets from him. Treylon had ripped Silva a new one for those secrets and called him weak and soft. A failure. Now Treylon watched him with suspicion.

"Kasabian," Kye mumbled, rolling to her side.

Silva closed his eyes and dove into her dream. Immediately he wished he hadn't, and yet he watched as Kasabian kissed her, calling her "love." Then they were fucking, but no, that wasn't the right word. It was raw, yet tender. Passionate. Everything Silva longed for. Jealousy consumed him in its fire. He imagined himself in his Wraithlord form, tearing her apart with his bare hands, clawing at her flesh. He felt it overtake him, the darkness transforming him to monster.

Footsteps echoed down the hall. Treylon. He knew the sound of those expensive leather shoes on the tile floors.

Silva pulled his magick back and quelled his rage, grateful for the interruption. He could not lose his head. They needed her, at least for now.

Treylon entered the room and closed the door behind him, an odd mix of emotions in his expression. "Demis just informed me that the others have failed. It's up to us now. Our first priority is, of course, to free the angels. We don't even know if we have enough power to do that. But the Tryah is looking to us to help free the Dragon and Deuce gods as well." His face fairly glowed. "We are their last hope."

Treylon clenched his fist to his chest. "Imagine, all of the freed gods being indebted to us. We could rule Miami— the world!" His eyes glittered in the same way they often did when he talked of victory and glory. His expression sobered. "Which means we need more children, more essence. And we have very little time left to procure it."

Silva did not share his enthusiasm. "Well, unfortunately there aren't a lot of children roaming around at two in the morning."

"They'll be heading to school in the morning. We're stationing our people near Crescent schools—"

Silva raised his hand as an idea struck. "Buses. The Harbor is sending a bunch of the kids on a trip to the Everglades in the morning. And they're going with a group of students from the Deuce Academy, most pre-Awakened. A charter busload of children all in one vehicle. There will be forty, maybe fifty kids. And if I wait until the bus is on its way out to the swamp, it's possible that no one will know they're gone for a while." Finally Silva felt the flush of his own power. "I will disguise myself and pose as one of the kids. The Academy kids will assume I'm with the Harbor and vice versa. When the time is right, I'll kill the adults and Leap the whole bus here."

"It is a brilliant idea," Treylon said.

As much as Silva hated himself for it, he soaked in the compliment. He would make up for his mistakes and secrets. They would succeed because of his plan. All he asked in return was the opportunity to kill Kye. Then he would take up Kasabian's offer to trade himself for her. Of course, he'd leave out the part about her being dead.

Kasabian Leaped back from the last resort on the list. The others had already returned, and he could tell by their expressions that they'd had no luck either.

Astrophysicist Michio Kaku was on Fox News talking about the ability of the storm to wipe out power grids, satellites, and life as they knew it. Kaku referenced the massive storm in 1859 that wiped out telegraph poles, high technology at the time.

Kasabian pulled in his wings and dropped to the couch. Frustration swamped him. As powerful as he was, he couldn't find one woman. One incredibly brave woman.

Mallory, Hayden, and Cecily were sitting as far apart as they could manage. Mallory, unwittingly, was the stick of dynamite in the room. He'd picked up the same female territoriality from Kye back at Mallory's condominium.

"What now?" Mallory asked. "We're not giving up, are we?"

"I will never give up." Kasabian bowed his head, rubbing the bridge of his nose as the tension pinched it tight. Kye, his beautiful Deuce. She'd found her value all right.

He studied Cecily, who sat stiffly and tried to focus on the newscast. They were playing REM's "It's the End of the World as We Know It" in the background. She looked young and vulnerable, with little makeup and her hair pulled back in a ponytail.

So young. But not vulnerable.

"Why are you looking at Cecily like you're going to eat her as a snack?" Hayden asked.

Kasabian would have laughed at the protective posturing if he'd been in a better mood. "More like, I'm considering throwing her to the wolves. With her assent, of course."

Hayden stood in full *You're not endangering my sister* mode. "Come again?"

Cecily killed the television and came to her feet, too. "What do you mean, throw me to the wolves?"

"They needed Kye for her magick, and she used that to get inside. What else do they desperately need?"

"Children," Cecily said, and then she got it by the way her face lit up. "Or maybe someone who people assume is, like, fourteen all the time. I get carded every time I try to buy a four-pack of Guinness. Yes, I'll go in."

"No way." Hayden shook his head. "You're not trained for this kind of thing."

"Kye wasn't trained, but that didn't stop her from doing whatever she could to help." Cecily planted her hands on her hips. "And you don't get to say what I do and don't do." She looked at Kasabian. "How do I get in?"

"That's the shaky part of the plan. The only way I can think of is convincing a Caido named Gemini to present you to them. He's not exactly trustworthy."

"Considering the guy trades in children," Hayden added, his mouth in a tight line as he aimed a hard look at

Kasabian. "You are *not* putting her in that cretin's hands."

Cecily waved in Hayden's direction. "Hello? Again, you're not the boss of me. And I'm a Dragon. I'm not exactly helpless."

"What do you mean, he trades in children?" Mallory asked.

Kasabian said, "We discovered an operation that masquerades as a community for troubled mothers. They set them up with a nice house if they let their children be adopted. We think they also encourage women to breed children for Caidos to supposedly adopt and use as their own personal Essex."

"We're going to shut that down next," Hayden said, studying the dawning expression on Mallory's face. "You're thinking of your niece, aren't you?"

"Maybe that's where my sister went. I could go."

Kasabian shook his head. "Mallory, we may not find her. I don't want you putting yourself in danger for a possibility."

"A possibility is more than I've had since she went missing."

He could see determination glittering in her eyes. "But Cecily looks much more convincing as a pre-teen than Mallory."

"Most fourteen-year-olds don't have racks like that." Cecily tapped her own modest chest. "So the job is mine."

"Gemini delivers you to Silva, and we follow. I'll make sure Gemini doesn't Leap you there. We find this place the old-fashioned way."

Hayden started to object, but he must have realized he wasn't going to convince Cecily to back down. "We follow in two different vehicles. That way if one of us loses Gemini, we have someone else on the trail."

"Agreed." Kasabian pulled out the card Gemini gave him and touched the numbers on his phone's screen. When he answered, Kasabian said, "Gemini, it's Kasabian, Treylon's son." Gods, he hated identifying himself that way. "You wanted me to let you know if my father was on to something. Well, he definitely is. And if he succeeds, it's going to put you out of business."

Kasabian had run through different scenarios that didn't involve having to, well, involve Gemini. One was absconding with his phone and calling Silva as Gemini, but there was no getting around it. Gemini was going to have to make the drop, because Silva might get suspicious if someone he'd never seen before showed up.

As soon as he pulled into the parking lot, Gemini got out of his old Cadillac and headed over. Good. He was taking this seriously. Now to enlist his help.

The big Caido stopped a couple of feet in front of Kasabian. "All right, you got my attention."

Kasabian closed the door and settled against his car, arms loosely crossed in front of him. He had to remember how he'd felt when he first figured out what his father was doing. "I'll be honest. I don't like what you're doing at the Bend, and I personally don't care if you go out of business." An enormous understatement. "But I imagine you do."

"Hey, we're providing a valuable commodity to our kind. You must know how difficult it is to find people to do the Essex with on a continual basis. The kids get a home, and Caidos live their lives relatively pain free."

It was no use trying to convince people to stop doing horrible things they believed were justified. Righteous, even. Kasabian had to bite back his disgust, as well as the vitriolic words that wanted to spew out. "The only reason I'm cluing you in is because I need your help to shut my father's operation down. I tell you what he's doing, and you do me a favor. Deal?"

"What kind of favor?"

"Believe me, it's right up your alley."

Gemini considered it for a moment. "All right. But this better be real information."

"Treylon is not using those kids to shore up extra *Deus Vis* for the storm. He's draining their essences so that he can combine it with the power of the solar storm to free the tethered angels. Which will break our curse. And yeah, I think he may succeed. My problem with it is that he's killing children, draining so much of their essence that they're dying. Your problem is that once he breaks the curse, Caidos won't need to give those children 'loving' homes. *Comprende*?"

Gemini seemed to mull that over. "What does your father get out of breaking the curse?"

"He's always been a glory whore, and he's been trying to break the curse for decades. His success gets him accolades for freeing Caidos and proves that he's not a failure." Kasabian shrugged. "Maybe there's more to it than that."

Gemini's face settled into grim lines. "I knew that guy was lying, but my boss is greedier than I am. He kept filling Treylon's orders until there was nothing to fill them with. Man, he's going to be pissed."

"You have to promise me that this stays between us for now. I don't want Treylon tipped off."

"And you have to promise you won't try to shut us down or drag us into this if it goes public. We have protection in high places, but I don't want any trouble."

That was a harder proposition. Gemini was waiting for the Caido oath. Kasabian could promise, but that didn't prevent Hayden from doing it. "I promise not to shut you down or drag you in." The whole operation would be covered up by the Guard and Concilium in any case. No way could the Mundane world know about the nature of Treylon's scheme...or the Bend's. "You haven't given me your word yet."

"You have my word that I won't alert my boss. I want all of our kids back."

"No deal." Kasabian didn't want to push his luck, but no way in hell was he letting the Bend have these kids. Especially after all they had gone through. "The kids go to Youth Harbor where they'll have a chance at a normal life."

"What are you, some kind of crusader?"

Well, I'm not some asshole who profits from children, that's for sure. "I have humanity. Compassion."

Gemini sneered. "Quaint. So, what's this favor you want?"

"The easiest way to pay me back is to tell me where Treylon's operation is. If you can do that, your part is over."

Gemini's eyes narrowed. "You don't know where he is?"

Of course, Kasabian being the man's son, Gemini would assume he'd have been there. "I only recently reunited with my father. He doesn't trust me enough to bring me in. Now I know why."

"He's the same way with us. He had his people Leap us

to his compound when we asked to see where these kids are going. All I can tell you is it's in a residential neighborhood."

Kasabian already knew that much. "And?"

"It's not a residence. My guess is it's a small, private hotel. I saw a sign pointing to the laundry room, for instance." He started to walk away. "If that's all..."

"If you can't supply me with an address or specific location, I want you to call Silva and tell him you have a girl for him. She's newly Awakened, but assure him she's no threat. And you will not Leap her to him or vice versa. Make up some reason that you have to physically deliver her."

"You're providing this girl, I presume?"

"Yes. As a bonus, you can keep the money Silva pays for her."

Gemini gave a slow nod. "All right."

"Call him now. We need to get this in motion. And put it on speaker."

"Man, you're as pushy as your old man." He pulled out his cell phone and thumbed down his phone directory. Then he initiated the call.

Silva answered. "Yes?"

"It's Gemini. I have a teenage girl, about fourteen. A runaway looking for a better situation. You still interested?"

"Is she Awakened?"

"Yes, but only recently. She has no handle on her power. She's shy, meek, won't cause any problems."

Kasabian nodded his approval at the improvisation.

"Sure," Silva said.

"The fee is double."

Kasabian lunged forward and twisted his hands in Gemini's shirt. He did not approve of that improvisation. *Take it back*, he mouthed.

Silva said, "You know what? We're good. Thanks anyway." He hung up.

Kasabian shoved Gemini back, his Shadow pressing close to the surface. "You son of a bitch! You just fucked the whole deal. Call him back and tell him it's the normal price."

Gemini fumbled with his phone and redialed, watching Kasabian closely. No doubt watching the shadows cross his eyes. "All right, normal price."

Silva paused, making them wait a few seconds. "Is she at the Bend?"

"No, she's with me and she does not want to be Leaped. The thought terrifies her. I can meet you anywhere."

"I'll call when I'm available." And Silva disconnected.

Kasabian paced the living room, waiting for Gemini's call. Why wasn't Silva jumping at the bait? At least it had given them time to buy a Hello Kitty shirt for Cecily and a grown-up shirt for Mallory.

Kasabian's phone rang, and he saw Gemini's name on the screen. "Finally."

"Silva just called back. We meet in thirty minutes."

Kasabian took down the details, set up an interim meeting place, and hung up. "We're on," he told the others. The need to get to Kye and make sure she was all right raged through him. His phone rang again: Cory at Harbor. "Yeah?"

"Someone took the bus," he said, words spilling out in

a breathless gush. "A Deuce couple just brought four of the kids back, said they were found on Alligator Alley waving down cars. The kids wouldn't talk until we were alone. Steven said that Lyle pushed him and some other kids off the bus to save them. He stayed on board. Then the bus disappeared. I don't know what to do. Call the Guard?"

The whole bus. Kasabian fell back against the wall, his knees weak.

"Okay, tell him," Cory was saying to someone else. A kid came on the line. "Lyle told the kids to tell you it was Daniel. And that he was going to find his brother."

Lyle had gone willingly.

"Kasabian?" Cory asked, sounding lost.

"Don't tell anyone at the Guard for now. The last kid who escaped and ended up at headquarters was taken back. Calm the kids, tell them we're on the case. We have to go."

He could barely breathe or tell the others what had happened.

Cecily's eyes ignited. "I hate that the Guard can't be trusted. But we will find these kids. We'll bring them home."

Kasabian rested his hand on Cecily's back. "I need to ask you a big favor."

"You mean besides handing myself over to the enemy?" She gave him a grin.

"This is a little easier. Have you ever heard of an Essex?" At her puzzled expression, he said, "It's where we exchange a little of our essences." Normally Kasabian didn't explain why he needed their essence, only that it was part of the healing process for the Crescent.

Now she frowned. "This hardly seems the time for any kind of weird sex play."

Hayden came over and held out his hands. She slid hers into his, clearly perplexed. "We've been friends for a while now," he said.

"Friends," she echoed. "Yeah, sure."

"I know I can trust you with a big secret. The well-being of all Caidos depends on it. When we go to the resort, we will be bombarded by the children's fear and pain. Because Caidos feel it. I can feel your emotions now, your apprehension, the way my holding your hand makes you..." He let that hang.

"You feel what I feel? When I've been angry or happy or..." She let that hang, too.

"Emotions are like a knife cutting into my soul. Good or bad, doesn't matter. It's why most Caidos don't associate with non-Caidos."

Her expression fell. "So every time I flirted with you, it hurt?"

He gave her a long, slow nod. "You didn't know."

Cecily glanced at Kasabian. "That's what you meant by 'it's complicated'?"

"Yep."

She turned back to Hayden. "It's fracked up is what it is. And sad. Of course, if you're rescuing scared children, it will be debilitating. And I'm also guessing there's something I can do to help."

"The Essex is a temporary balm," Hayden said. "Your essence balances ours so we're not as sensitive."

"And you need me to do it with all of you?" When he nodded, she said, "All right."

"We do it through our linked hands." Hayden tightened

his hold on her. "Just relax and let me pull your essence toward me. You'll feel mine going into you."

"Sounds rather intimate." She closed her eyes and took
a deep breath.

Hayden threw his head back and sank into it. His body
shuddered, and he pulled her flush against him and
wrapped his arms around her. "Thank you," he whispered,
now sinking into the bliss of being able to feel without
pain. He would feel Cecily's rush of joy at being held in
Hayden's arms at last. Kasabian felt it prickling along his
skin.

Her arms had gone around his waist. "You're welcome,"
she whispered back.

They stepped apart, and Hayden said, "Next."

Once Mallory and Kasabian had done the Essex as well,
they headed out to their cars. Cecily rode with Kasabian.
He didn't want Gemini to know that someone else was following. They met up with him twenty minutes later.

"Anything happens to her, we'll tango," Kasabian said.

Gemini lifted his hands. "I can only keep her safe until
I hand her off."

"Until then, I hold you responsible. No games like you
tried to pull earlier. No last-minute bids for more money.
Play it straight."

"Yeah, yeah." But when he saw the Shadow rolling
across Kasabian's eyes, his cavalier smirk disappeared.
"Straight. Got it."

Kasabian followed from a safe distance, his gaze never
leaving Gemini's Cadillac. It pulled into a parking lot, and
a Caido gestured for him to park next to his car. It wasn't
Silva or either of the Caidos he'd seen at the resort. Cecily played the part of a scared girl about to start a new

life. Gemini accepted a manila envelope that was no doubt filled with cash and got back into his car. Cecily eased into the Caido's car, and Kasabian followed them out of the lot.

Kasabian kept his focus glued on the car taking Cecily to his father. Hayden had pulled in the lane next to the car. Good, they had her covered. So why was he finding it hard to breathe? It wasn't, he realized, from the tension of what lay ahead. The air shimmered, the way the heat did as it radiated off an asphalt road.

The storm. Invisible particles rushing into the earth's atmosphere. It was beginning.

Chapter 23

———

Kye was jarred from sleep by a hand shaking her. "Wake up. We have more kids."

She sat up so fast that her head swam for a few seconds. The morning light spilled in through the drapes, casting lines across the bed from the bars on the window. Silva stood beside her, his eyes bright and triumphant. More kids. Is that what she'd heard?

"You have more bonding to do," he said.

"Can't." She couldn't get her mouth to work right. Exhaustion still clung to her.

"You can and you will. Do you want those kids to die? Are you so selfish that you'd put your comfort before their lives?"

"You already know I'm not." *Bastard*.

It hit her then, that the plan was still moving forward. She wanted to ask if Kasabian had come but held the question. Silva would have told her. She pushed herself to the edge of the bed, preparing to stand on legs that felt like strands of cooked spaghetti.

"You were dreaming about Kasabian," Silva said, a bite to his voice.

"How do you know? Oh, that's right. You can creep into people's dreams, you voyeuristic son of a bitch." She was so tired she wasn't even censoring herself.

He narrowed his eyes. "How do you know? Did Kasabian tell you?"

"I was there when you poked into his dream about the past. When you were sad that he didn't want to be your friend. That's how I knew you were meeting."

"How? Can you dream walk?"

"I was bonded to him."

"You did the Cobra with him. Because you and he are...lovers?" It seemed that he could barely say the word.

"Yes." Suddenly she wanted to hurt Silva, to drive home that he could never possess Kasabian. She could see how Silva ached for that, how fragile he was when it came to his obsession. Kasabian was his weakness, and Kye would use it. "We made love all night long, and he could enjoy it without any pain because of our bond."

A Shadow crossed his eyes, the same one she'd seen in Kasabian's. "Shut up."

"I touched him everywhere, and he adored my body with his hands, his mouth. He said that with me, he felt like he belonged for the first time."

Remembering brought it all back, his hands on her, the taste of him, and the perfection of him buried inside her. But his confession moved her the most. She knew Silva could feel the emotions the memories evoked.

Silva flew at her so fast she didn't even see him move. He body-slammed her into the wall, his arm pressed against her throat. The Wraithlord pulled away, a dark and violent Shadow with the snout of a Dragon. She had miscalculated his reaction. He had become stronger, not weaker. Damn it, she couldn't get anything right.

"I. Said. Shut. Up," he ground out, barely reining the beast within. "I will rip you to pieces when this is over so you will never experience any of that with him again."

Killed in a jealous rage. Sarai hadn't seen Kasabian; she'd seen Silva!

"I won't experience it again," she managed. "We are no longer bonded. He left me the same way he left you."

He narrowed his eyes in suspicion, but at least he pulled his arm back so she could breathe. "How?"

"He cut the cord."

"He found you wanting? Lost interest?"

She gathered her thoughts quickly. Which tack to try? She went with the truth because the rage thing wasn't exactly working. "He's not a callous person. Everything he does, he does for the good. He left you to save the children, but he intended to save you, too. He left me so I would not get hurt. He is blinded by his love for others."

"He does not love me, never did. But I thought he cared about me, a long time ago."

Silva's pain and emptiness went far beyond his obsession for Kasabian. Her anger had made her miscalculate. His weakness could not be mined by taunting him with what he couldn't have, but by seeing his humanity. The speck of it she could find, anyway. He wanted to matter to someone. Wasn't that what she wanted, too? It pained her to realize that they had something in common. That they both had gone to great lengths to feel valued. *That* was something she could mine.

"Silva!" Treylon's voice boomed from down the hallway. Damn, she needed more time.

Silva gripped her wrist and pulled her with him. He still longed for a father's love and approval. She doubted he got it much.

Silva followed Treylon upstairs, where two of their minions opened the first door. Six kids huddled together inside, Caido and non-Caido. Her stomach turned. Then it leaped when she saw Lyle. His eyes widened as he saw her in the same moment.

"Kye? What are you doing here . . . with *them*?" Then he saw Silva's grip on her wrist, must have seen the fear in her own eyes.

"You know this boy?" Treylon asked.

"From Harbor," she said simply. She pulled away from Silva and approached Lyle, taking his hands in hers. "How did you get here?"

"They took our bus."

The trip to the Everglades. So many kids at once. Lyle had mentioned it during their ride to the Bend. She really thought she would be sick, but she held back the nausea. "Jonathan's here," she whispered. "He's all right." For now.

Lyle's eyes filled with emotion. "Where?" he whispered.

"Bond him and the Dragon over there," Treylon said, pulling the girl over. "There will be no time for resting in between."

Kye could feel a difference in the air. The storm's effects had arrived. But there was something else going on, too. Through the window, she could see the vessel, not quite full enough.

Treylon told the kids how the bonding worked and that the Caidos would draw their essence to send to the angels above. He clasped his hands together and smiled. "You will help free them. They will be very grateful."

The children would never understand his way of thinking. She took Lyle's hand and that of the girl. She needed to protect them, all of them, as fast as she could.

Kasabian and the others gathered outside the gate. "We incapacitate when we can, kill only when necessary," Kasabian reminded them. "Some of these minions could have been taken the same way I was, against their will. One of them helped a boy escape. At least that's what I suspect."

"But there's only one way to get inside the barrier," Hayden reminded him.

"We kill one to get in and play the rest by ear."

Their plan was simple. Disable as many minions as possible. Kill Treylon and Silva. "We gather all the kids together and Leap them to Harbor. We'll get them all home from there. No one gets left behind."

Hayden looked at the buildings in the distance, his expression tense with worry. "And we find Cecily."

"She'll be with the kids," Kasabian said, but his mind kept chanting, *Kye, Kye, Kye.* Finding her, laying eyes on her, pounded through his head.

He led them around to the right, where he'd been caught before. They stripped off their shirts and Invoked. He spot-

ted one of the minions in the distance and made a sound
to draw his attention. The guy headed over on full alert.
The three were hidden, leaving only Kasabian visible. He
ducked behind a bush just as the Caido headed over.

The Caido passed through the barrier to investigate the
shape he saw in hiding. The Caido who would die to allow
him passage inside. Kasabian didn't recognize the man
whose own wings were out, his Light ready to annihilate.
Kasabian released his Wraithlord, lunging at the Caido and
whipping black vines all around him. One slapped over his
mouth just as the man was about to scream.

Kasabian leaned close. "Where is the woman Treylon
brought here?" He loosened the cord.

"Another demon freak," he spat out. "Go to hell where
you belong."

"You first." Kasabian drew the vines so tight that the
man's flesh bulged between them. Something popped inside him, and he fell still. Kasabian released him and
turned to the three who stood in silence watching.

Hayden cleared his throat. "Glad you're on our side."

Mallory stepped closer to Hayden, her eyes wide. Great.
Kasabian had lost both his friends.

The power of his Wraithlord pulsed through him. He
hoisted the body over his shoulder and held out his hand to
Mallory, who was the closest. "We have to link together to
get through."

She stared at his hand for a second, then clasped it. Hayden took hers, and they passed through.

Mallory pointed up. "What is *that*?"

They all turned to a formation of clouds moving in
unnatural ways above the compound. No, not clouds but
forms that were stretching, pulling. Angels, he realized,

their enormous wings smashed against one another's as they crammed into this one space.

"It's happening," Kasabian whispered. "They're freeing the angels." Kye would be with the kids. "I'll take the building in the center. Mallory, go right. Hayden, left." He shot toward the pathway, staying close to the lush foliage. Another Caido patrolled the path, approaching from the right.

Kill.

The urge to take him out rushed through him, fed from his last kill. Kasabian crouched like a predator, waiting for the Caido to come near. He was barely out of childhood himself, brainwashed into loyalty. And he would kill Kasabian if given the chance. But Kasabian would not kill him if he could help it. He waited until the young man was nearly even with him and then sent out the vines to snag him around the ankles and jerk him off his feet.

The Caido sent a jolt of Light at him as he fell, his expression angry and determined. Kasabian shifted out of the bolt's way and Leaped to the Caido just as he hit the ground, gagging him with more magick. His Wraithlord strained to eviscerate the terrified Caido. Kasabian stuffed the urge back and sent a benign blast of Light into his head, putting him into a deep sleep. He pulled the young man into the bushes and continued toward the building.

The windows had bars on them. So not a resort. He dashed toward the blind corner and peered around the edge of one of those windows. Children were sprawled on the beds like rag dolls. One boy was curled up in a chair crying. They were too late.

No.

The boy looked up. A Caido who had been spared by

Kye's magick. Kasabian pressed his finger to his mouth. He would be back. His wings brushed against the bushes as he moved on. The next room held more children, all asleep. He had to believe they were asleep and not...

The memory of that girl dying in his arms rose like a treacherous swell, threatening to suck him under.

A rattling sound came from the next window, and the sound of labored breathing. Kasabian inched over slowly, stopping when a bloody hand thrust out through the broken glass and curled around the bars. A child's hand. Kasabian stepped into view, his finger over his mouth. He came face-to-face with Lyle.

Relief suffused the kid's face. "You're here! I have to get to Jonathan. Kye said he's here."

Kye, alive. Close by. "You saw her?"

"She did some kind of magick to help us, but it only helped me. Not her." He nodded toward the girl lying on the bed.

Kasabian's chest squeezed so tight he could hardly breathe. "Is she dead?"

"No, but she's dying. And I can't help her."

"Back away from the bars." Kasabian sent power surging through his hands. Black tendrils coiled around the bars, bending and melting them.

Lyle just stared. "Dude, that's sick."

Kasabian didn't get some of the kids' lingo these days, but he thought that was a good thing. The bars sagged to allow space enough for Kasabian to climb inside. He pressed his fingers against the girl's forehead, sending her a dose of healing Light.

Her eyes fluttered, and she tried in vain to open them. It wasn't enough. She needed her essence back. He went to the door and listened for sound in the hallway. "How long ago was Kye here?"

"A while. She looked tired. And really sad."

She would use up all her magick, her life force, to save the kids. Because that's who she was.

Kasabian heard nothing in the hallway. They'd come and gone, at least from this floor. "I know you're desperate to find Jonathan." As desperate as he was to find Kye. "And we will find him and bring him to Harbor. But you running all over the place is only going to alert the scumbags that something's going on. So I need you to be cool and logical. Can you do that?"

"I think so. Yes. I can do it."

"I'm going to open all the doors on this floor. I need you to corral the kids in here, close the door, and wait for me, Hayden, or a female Caido named Mallory. One of us will come and get you." He gripped the kid's shoulders. "I need to be able to count on you, Lyle."

The kid was shaking with fear and adrenaline. "You can."

"I'm going upstairs. I'll call for you if it's clear. Then you can bring any kids who are up there down to this room. Got it?"

Lyle nodded.

He rubbed the kid's head and worked on the doorknob. The metal bubbled and melted away, dripping down to the floor.

He stepped into the hallway, Lyle right behind. One of the minions stood just outside the building's glass door, his back to Kasabian. He Leaped, landing right behind him. The Caido turned just as he materialized. Kasabian had to silence him immediately. He tried to shoot him with the same sleep jolt, but the minion took him by surprise and shot Kasabian in the legs with searing Light. The minion started to open his mouth to scream, forcing Kasabian to slice Light across his throat. He collapsed into Kasabian's arms, and he pulled him into the foliage by the building. At least this one wasn't young.

Lyle continued gaping, even when Kasabian Leaped back to where he stood.

"I'm sorry you had to see that."

"No, I'm glad I saw it. I wish I could do it and kill these bastards." He mimicked the action.

Kasabian worked on the doorknob to the room closest to them. "Get the Caidos to help you with the Dragon and Deuce kids. You've got some strength left."

He disabled all the doors. Gods, so many children. Would his own magick dry up before he could Leap them out of here?

Chapter 24

Treylon watched Kye pull the last vestiges of her magick to bond two more children. Demis had told him they were close to having enough power thirty minutes earlier. The angels were beginning to pull free. Victory, finally!

Only two more rooms of children remained. Demis thought that would be enough. The Dragon and Deuce gods would get any leftover power. As much as Treylon liked the idea of having them indebted to him, or at least grateful, the angels were his first priority.

He felt the familiar prickle of Demis's presence. A summons. "I have to talk with Demis," he told Silva. "Take her to the next room."

Kye slid to the floor as though her bones had disintegrated. Tears streamed down her face. "I can't," she said on a hoarse voice. "I can't help anymore. I don't have anything left."

"Make her," Treylon mouthed to Silva, who eagerly nodded. He seemed to have some personal aversion to the woman. As long as he didn't kill her before her usefulness was through, Treylon didn't care.

Demis usually wanted to see Treylon alone, a request he was glad to honor. The angel did not like to deal with the more diluted versions of his progeny. Treylon went down the stairs and out the front door. Where was the guy who was supposed to be guarding it? A quick glance didn't find him, but nothing looked out of sorts, so he continued.

Maybe Demis was going to tell him it was done. Treylon's chest swelled just imagining it. He searched the sky, seeing the angels pulling against some unseen bond. Not yet then. As the solar storm approached, the angels, and now the gods, had to come close to receive the power.

"Sir!" A member of his staff ran toward him. "Dragon...girl." The Caido heaved in deep breaths. "One of the new arrivals turned Dragon and killed a worker. She's at large." Another breath. "What do we do with her?"

One of his people, dead. That was annoying. Silva was supposed to make sure the kids were too young to be Awakened. He called Silva. "A girl Catalyzed to Dragon and is on the loose. I need you to send the wraiths after her. I can't afford to take any of our people away from their duties."

Silva grunted. "That must be the girl Gemini just brought us. I knew she was Awakened, but I didn't think she'd be a problem, being new and meek. I'll take care of her."

"If she's newly Awakened, you should be able to get her under control quickly. Kill her only if necessary."

He continued heading toward his suite. Demis was already waiting, his ethereal image filling the room. It was translucent, probably because Demis was projecting from his place near the vessel. "Trouble," he said. "We have intruders."

Silva hung up with Treylon. "I have to attend to a matter."

Kye didn't appear to be at risk of running again, but he couldn't take any chances at this point. He stepped out in the hallway and asked the Caido standing guard to watch her.

He would no doubt hear about the Awakened Dragon later. Hopefully Treylon would be so happy at his success that he'd forget the incident.

Silva Leaped to the cafeteria, where a bubble of Light contained two black beasts. They had once been Gren and Beldeen but were now soulless spirits—shorter and looking vaguely like gargoyles.

"I am your Wraithlord," he said to the horrid little beasts.

They scurried to his side of their prison cell, awaiting his orders. Without wills of their own, they drifted aimlessly. If they had no master, they created their own kind of mayhem, sometimes being mistaken for ghosts or demons. Wraithlords could command their will. He had used them before on another pesky female Dragon and her Caido cohort. Hopefully they would succeed this time.

"There is a Dragon on the property. You will hunt her down and bring her here. If she resists, tear her limb from limb."

They clawed the side of their cell, eager to do his bidding. He opened the door of the bubble, and they loped off. He watched them disappear around the corner. Then he looked up to the mass of angels hovering above the grounds. They had made themselves visible, and Silva could see the ties that bound them to their progeny. His life—all Caidos' lives—would be different once the curse was lifted.

Even if it worked, Silva would still be in pain. A pain that had nothing to do with the curse and everything to do with Kasabian.

Silva returned to Kye and dragged her to the next room; dragged because she could barely stand, much less walk. He wasn't brutal, just impatient. She couldn't stand the feel of his hands around her waist as he guided her to the door. There was something she'd wanted to say to him, but she couldn't seem to remember.

A quick blast of an alarm shook her. "What was that?"

"One of the kids went Dragon on us. They'll find her."

Fear squeezed Kye's throat. "What will they do to her?"

"She'll be killed," he told her in a flat tone. He opened the door and led her inside the next room. He gave the children his standard speech.

Kye could barely focus on the two children holding each other in the far corner. Choked sobs erupted from her throat as she sank to the side of the bed. "I can't do it."

Silva sat on the bed beside her. He waved his hands, and a warmth stole over her. That took away a little of her fatigue. In a low voice, he said, "We have to use them one way or the other. In five minutes, I must start them channeling."

Kye managed to push herself up. She wiped at her face, not wanting the kids to see her like this. Poor things were already terrified.

Silva tilted his head, studying her as though she were some curiosity. "You would sacrifice yourself to save one more child."

"They're innocent, and it's our responsibility, as a race, to protect. To cherish and love them."

Silva's face twisted in a grimace of pain. "No one protected me for most of my so-called childhood." He removed the emotion from his expression. "Just as you would sacrifice your soul for them, I would do the same for my father. He was the only one who protected me."

"He *kidnapped* you."

"He took me out of my own personal hell."

"Treylon used you, just like he used his own son. The same as he uses all of these children."

"No, it's different with me. He . . ." Silva couldn't say the word.

"Loves you? Is that what you believe?"

The muscles in his jaw twitched. "Love is a silly concept that belongs on greeting cards and in empty promises. What matters is loyalty. Dedication. But I don't understand what drives you to squeeze out the last of your magick to save people you don't even know." His dark blue eyes implored hers. "Can you explain that to me?" His gaze flicked to his watch. "In two minutes or less."

She nearly laughed, despite the tricky conversation. "I'm not sure I could explain it in a day. Love is not some concept. It's real. First you have to love yourself, despite your faults and the shadows you harbor. Like my Cobra, love is about giving away part of yourself and accepting a part of someone else. It's never about giving away all of yourself. Or taking all of someone."

She forced herself to place her hand over his. "You're in love with Kasabian because he's a Wraithlord like you, and you think that alone should bond you. You want to possess him, to force him into submission and salve those old wounds of betrayal. But he never betrayed you, Silva. You placed your need for acceptance by Treylon above everything else. Kasabian placed the safety of a group of children above all. You know him. Could he have done anything else?"

Her heart swelled with affection and admiration for Kasabian. She knew he was doing everything in his power to find this place. "You've placed your affection, hopes, and fantasies on two very different men. One as a father figure and one as a love interest. Think about who they are and what they've done in their lives." She gestured to the kids. "What kind of *father* subjects children to torture?"

"But it's for the good of all Caidos."

"That's what Hitler said. Not the Caidos part, of course, but he believed that killing all those innocent people was for the good of mankind. Do you believe that, or are you just repeating what you've been told for so long?"

Silva slowly blinked as her words seemed to register, saying nothing.

"But isn't he really after the gratitude of the angels?" she continued. "Even he admitted that motivates him. You've no doubt suspected that his real cause is self-serving."

"He wants the respect of all the Caidos," Silva said. "Maybe even more than the angels' gratitude."

"You have pledged your allegiance to a man who would

allow children to die for their freedom. But does he care about you beyond what you can do for the cause? Or are you only rewarded with affection when you please him?"

She had seen enough of their dynamic to feel comfortable with that guess. And by the way Silva's expression crumbled she knew she was right. Suddenly he was the sad, needy boy in the dream who craved love and approval. Reaching Silva's humanity was the key to gaining him as an ally. If that were even possible. "I took my value from what I could do for others. I'm only now realizing that I'm valuable just as I am. So are you."

Silva's mouth tightened, and his chin trembled. As he started to say something, the guy outside banged on the door. "Are you finished? We need to move to the next room."

"In a minute," Silva said, his voice hoarse.

She thought maybe she was getting through, but then he said, "It's easier to come to that conclusion when the person you most want in the world loves you back. The way Kasabian looked at you, the way he shifted his body to protect you, that's why I wanted to kill you earlier." He reached out, grazing her neck. "Why I want to kill you..."

A *thump* sounded in the hallway, and the door flew open. Kasabian stood there, in all of his winged glory—and Wraithlord rage. As scary as he looked, relief and a whole range of emotions bombarded her. His eyes flashed black when he saw Silva's hand at her neck, and the Dragon Shadow took him over. He threw Silva into the wall so hard the drywall cracked. Black ropes bound him before he could even try to extricate himself.

"No!" Kye pulled herself from the bed and fell against Kasabian. "He wasn't..."

Kasabian wrapped his arm around her and held her up. He took in the sight of her, relief on his face. The rage returned though. "I heard him say he was going to kill you."

"Before," Silva said, struggling to get free. "I wanted to kill her before."

"That isn't helping your case," Kasabian said, curling his fingers into fists that made the ropes pull tighter.

"The vision," Kye whispered. "That's what Sarai saw, a Wraithlord about to kill me in a jealous rage. Only it was Silva who was jealous." She wrapped her fingers over Kasabian's arm, feeling the barely restrained rage pulsing through him. "Pull yourself back. Silva and I were coming to an understanding."

Movement made her turn to the hallway to find Lyle stepping over a Caido's body and rushing in. He came to an abrupt stop at the scene before him.

"Get the kids out," Kasabian told him.

Lyle nodded and urged the two kids to go with him. They would escape the channeling. She hadn't failed them after all.

While keeping Silva pinned, Kasabian asked, "What kind of understanding could you possibly come to with this man?"

"We have something in common. We didn't get the approval we needed. I found people who appreciated me because of it. Treylon used Silva's needs to brainwash him into—"

"A sadistic monster who kills children," Kasabian finished.

"Into what Treylon needed."

"I can't just let him go, Kye. We have to get these kids

out of here, and he'll stop us. Like he would have stopped me before."

Lyle rushed back in. "I've got them all downstairs, but the Dragons and Deuces are fading fast."

Kye shook her head. "No. Not after getting this far."

Kasabian brushed his hand against her cheek. "You did everything you could. Don't blame yourself."

"She was willing to sacrifice the last of herself to save them," Silva said, admiration in his voice. "I thought what Treylon was doing was noble. Maybe...I was wrong."

Kye gained her balance, standing on her own. "Taking the kids out of here isn't going to help. They've lost their essence, and there's no essence transfusion."

Lyle looked as though he was about to cry. "So... there's no hope?"

"Yes. Yes, there is," Kye said as an idea formed. "We reverse the essence channeling. The Caidos sent it up to the vessel. We get them to channel it back to the children." She looked at Lyle. "Could you manage to do that? I know you're exhausted—"

"We could," Lyle said. "We could try."

"Rally the Caidos," she told him.

Kasabian used that strange black magick to lasso Silva and pull him away from the wall. "You're coming with us." He shot Kye a look that clearly said, *Though I'd rather kill him.*

Hayden started when an alarm squawked once. Enough to warn the Caidos that there was trouble, but not enough to bring outside attention. Damn, their element of surprise was gone.

As he swept the grounds, he'd dropped four minions, only one fatally. He understood Kasabian's directive to leave as many unharmed as possible. But it went against Hayden's instincts and training not to whack some asshole who was trying to whack you. They were no doubt being told that they were part of some grand plan, and the intruders were threatening that plan.

Movement in the sky caught his eye. He could see the angels trying to pull free of what looked like ropes that were binding them. The vessel was almost full.

An ungodly sound rent the air. Then a roar. A Dragon roar. He raced toward its source, searching the lush grounds as he went. A flash of deep, verdant green didn't fit in with the rest of the foliage. It moved too fast for something shifting in a breeze. He came up on a scene that twisted his heart. A deep green Dragon, scales shimmering the way the sun did as it streamed down into the water, and two black creatures attacking her.

What the hell were they? Not demons. Not Elementals. Wraiths. Roughly the size and shape of gorillas, they moved with speed and agility. They looked shadowy, but their talons and teeth were very real, given the bleeding cuts on the Dragon. Hayden tried to remember what the old textbook had said about how to fight them as he inched forward. The Dragon spun around to fend off another attack, and he saw a nasty gash on her side.

Cecily. He could see her in those cat-like irises, in the delicate jawline. It was the first time he'd seen her in Dragon form, and she took his breath away. Especially since she was under attack.

Her deep green eyes locked onto him, fear and gratitude in them. "Hayden," she said, and the growly word reflected both emotions as well.

She turned back to her attackers and blew a torrent of steam at the two wraiths. She was a water Dragon, using her breath to steam or drown her victims. Neither would work on the wraiths beyond holding them back until they found a way around her defenses. As they'd obviously done before.

It was also difficult to kill them with Light. He reached back to the electric energy of his wings and pulled one of the feathers. Like tearing out a lock of his hair and a bit of scalp, it hurt like a bitch. The feather solidified into a dhagger as he raced up behind one of the wraiths.

The wraith turned just as Hayden reached it, slashing at him with its talons. Hayden punctured the wraith's chest, but it moved out of reach before his knife could do any damage. Damn, they were as fast as cockroaches.

The other wraith took advantage of Cecily's diverted attention as she watched him and Leaped onto her tail, scrambling along the thick spines of her back. She smashed at it—and herself—with her tail to knock it off, but it skirted her. It reached her graceful neck and wrapped its lanky arms around it. The wraith readied its talons, about to drive one right up into her kill spot beneath her chin.

No.

He Leaped onto her back next to the wraith, grabbing her neck to keep from falling on the other side. He settled between the deep grooves of spines that reminded him of shark fins. He'd barely gotten his balance when the wraith grabbed his wrist with its spindly fingers. He had to strugglc to hold on as the wraith's teeth speared right through bone and flesh.

The wraith's gaping eye sockets seemed to stare him down. Hayden was losing his grip on her. Pain radiated down his arm and numbed his fingers. The slippery blood made it even harder to hold on. Cecily wasn't making it any easier, thrashing as she fought the other entity in front of her. He could use some of Kasabian's freaky magick about now.

Hayden sent a blast of Light from his good hand, punching holes in the wraith's arm. It loosened its grip just enough for Hayden to plunge the dhagger into the wraith's indistinct face. It squealed and tried to wrestle the knife from Hayden's control. He held on with a death grip, and finally the wraith disintegrated. He had to wrap his good arm around the base of Cecily's neck, flattening himself to the right of the hard spikes.

The second wraith skittered around behind them and lashed at the wound Cecily had already sustained. She screamed in pain and stumbled. His thighs tightened against her smooth scales, but not fast enough. He slid to the side and, without two operable hands, fell to the ground.

Fuck, his hand was useless until it healed. He raced around to the side. Cecily's fangs snapped at the wraith, sinking into its shadowy body. It was staying too close for her to steam it.

Hayden came up beneath her, sliding against her belly, and plunged his knife into the wraith from below. He twisted it as the wraith struggled, and then it disintegrated. Cecily staggered, and Hayden moved out of the way a second before she collapsed to the ground.

Dragons could heal themselves if they remained in their form, but that could take time. And time was one thing they didn't have a lot of.

He searched the surroundings and spotted a Caido who'd been watching the whole thing. He started to run off, and Hayden held out his good hand and shot him down with a lethal dose of Light. With a gasp, he fell.

He turned back to Cecily, who'd Catalyzed to human. She didn't even have the strength to maintain her Dragon form. Not good. The gaping wound along her side looked even worse now that it contrasted her human skin. The wraith had cut through the muscle, and blood poured out with her every gasping breath. He dropped down beside her and drew the Light to heal her.

She was shivering, her eyes wide and unfocused, hands curling into the grass. He pulled her into his arms with his good hand, settled her across his lap, and held that hand over her wound.

"Hold on, Cecily. I'm healing you, but you have to do your part and stay with me." He bent over her and cradled her, breathing through the gut-searing pain that now manifested in his side. His other hand throbbed in pain. He couldn't heal her and himself at the same time, and her wound was life-threatening.

Her breathing evened out, and her shivering lessened. He watched the torn flesh mend without leaving so much as a scar. She should sleep, continue to heal, but there wasn't time for either.

She met his gaze and smiled, the most beautiful thing he'd ever seen. Her gaze went just beyond him where she could no doubt see his wings. Or a semblance of them, since she didn't have her glasses. "My angel," she whispered, reaching up to touch his cheek. Her pupils were dilated.

He took her hand. "You gave me a hell of a scare."

"You've never seen me as Dragon before."

He chuckled. "Not your Dragon, silly girl. The wraiths attacking you."

She blinked, coming more fully back. "Is that what those things were? They were horrible."

"Wraiths are rare, so there's not a lot about them in the training manuals."

Her gaze locked onto his hand holding hers. "I can feel your heartbeat. I guess you *were* scared."

Caidos tried to keep their emotions neutral, but he'd come to care about Cecily. Especially since he and Kasabian had put her in danger. "I have to heal my other hand." He raised it, and she gasped.

"Oh, my gods. You must be in terrible pain."

"It's just a scrape." He pulled the Light and focused on the splintered bones, shredded tendons, and ripped skin. Now she watched in fascination as it healed before her eyes.

"You're amazing," she said, awe in her soft voice.

"Ditto." And now he became aware of her nudity as she lay in his lap. Her light straight blond hair fell over her breasts, not thick enough to conceal the curves. "We need to get you some clothes and find the others."

"Always the pain-in-the-ass thing about Catalyzing when you're not prepared."

He helped her to her feet, and he pulled the shirt and pants from the Caido he'd just killed. When she shrank back at the clothing, he told her, "Standard operating procedure for Dragon Vegas and Arguses in these kinds of situations."

She slid into them, an expression of disgust on her face, and they ran down the pathways. He searched for any sign of minions. A woman with long brown hair shifted into view up ahead, just before she ducked out of sight. Mallory.

He made a soft sound that had her peering around the bush. Her expression softened in relief as she ran toward them. "I haven't seen Kasabian."

"We're going to Leap to him." He nodded toward the angels that were beginning to pull free of their bonds. "We're just about out of time."

Chapter 25

Kasabian knew the only reason the Caido kids were willing to put their exhausted little bodies through more was because Kye had done the same to protect them. Lyle, holding Jonathan's hand tight in his, had made them very aware of what she'd gone through.

Kasabian felt every bit of her fear that they wouldn't succeed. They'd gathered the children in a courtyard, directly beneath the nearly full vessel that held their essences.

Three people materialized next to him. Kasabian held out his hands, until he saw that it was Hayden, Cecily, and Mallory. They all jumped at the sight of Silva, now bound to a tree with Wraithlord magick.

Hayden met Kasabian's gaze. "I'm beginning to appreciate that dark magick of yours." He looked at the group of children, and his expression fell. "We got this far. Now what?" He could probably feel their life force ebbing, just as Kasabian could.

Kasabian stroked Kye's arm. "All of the Caidos are going to draw the kids' essence back into them."

Cecily stepped forward, wearing ridiculously oversized clothing. "How can I help?"

"Catch the kids when they fall," Kasabian said. This was going to take everything out of the few who were still standing or sitting.

"I can help," Silva said.

"I'm not releasing you." Or trusting him. Kasabian gathered the kids in a semicircle. "You're going to do what you did earlier, only this time you're pulling it from up there." He pointed to the sky. "Are you ready?"

As fatigued as they looked, they nodded eagerly and went to work. It was the Essex times a thousand, not a coaxing but a tug-of-war. The angels fought to pull it back, selfish bastards, making the vessel tremble.

Kye was kneeling down next to some of the children who were barely hanging on, encouraging them. She was also watching Silva, who was trying to free himself. The Caido kids were grimacing in their efforts, their eyes squeezed shut, hands physically pulling at the air. Kasabian could see when they'd get the upper hand; a trickle of blue would start streaming down to earth. Then the angels would get a surge of strength and gain control again.

"Come on, one big pull." Kasabian could see the essence in the vessel coming down, like a tornado beginning to descend from the clouds. "Yes," he gritted out. "We're doing it."

Movement out of the corner of his eye drew his gaze to Treylon, who was stepping into the courtyard. "No." The man's eyes glittered with anger as he glared at Kasabian.

"You will not do this to me again!" He shot a beam of Light at Kasabian, who dodged it.

Kasabian's lost concentration made the streams pause, but he focused on it again. "Look at the cost to free a bunch of fallen angels!" He pointed toward the children on the ground.

"I'm also freeing Caidos from the curse!"

"Are you sure that will happen?" Kasabian asked. "Or is that what the angels told you?"

"I trust them more than anyone else."

"You trust angels who approve the sacrifice of children?" Kasabian looked at the downward flowing stream, now back to a trickle. Damn. He spun around to see that Silva had escaped his magick bindings.

Treylon pulled his Light in the shape of a sword, swinging it back and forth. He looked at Silva, his mouth twisted with cruel taunting. "Do you have the guts to kill Kasabian, or will your *feelings* get in the way?"

Silva seemed to wrestle with the answer. He looked at the children, then back to Treylon. "The question that plagues me more is do I trust angels who sanction the death of children to live up to their promises? More importantly, do I trust a man who would kill his own son, especially when that man has shown me little regard? You threatened to kill me just for using my power in front of others without your permission."

"I don't care about the questions that reflect your insecurity," Treylon bit out. "I only care that you do the right thing."

"I have the guts to do the right thing, yes." Silva stepped up next to Kasabian and added his efforts to their cause, bringing the blue light down in a steady stream.

Treylon's eyes bulged in anger. Silva gave Kasabian a meaningful look. He didn't see Treylon's anger. Or the sword that he threw at Silva. Kasabian tried to shove Silva to the side, but the sword pierced him anyway. He gasped, staring at the glistening red blade of Light protruding from his chest, and fell to the ground.

No! Not when they were this close. Kasabian felt the Wraithlord rise, and he let it take over. In a blur, he flew at Treylon and dragged him out of sight of the children. He heard Kye's voice call out, "Keep going, keep going!"

Kasabian shoved the man to the ground, seeing the shadow of a Dragon's hand over his own as it plunged into Treylon's chest. It took everything in Kasabian to muster the energy, drained as he was from drawing the essence down. Treylon reached a shaking arm out and clamped his hand on Kasabian's shoulder. Pain rocketed through him as the Light charged through flesh and bone.

"You won't win," Treylon uttered. "You don't have enough power."

"Together we do." Kasabian clutched Treylon's heart and squeezed just enough to keep Treylon inert, but not enough to kill him. Kasabian used Treylon to help pull down the essence, while adding his effort. He turned to look at the cloud, where Treylon's attention was riveted. The stream now reached the ground right where the children were.

"No," Treylon said on a faint voice. "Kill me now."

"Not a chance. I will use you like you have used all of those children. I will use you until you serve your purpose, and then you can die."

Treylon lifted his hand and aimed for his throat. He was

going to kill himself. Kasabian sent the vines to grasp his wrists and hold them.

Goose bumps prickled along Kasabian's skin. He looked up to see one angel looming above them. "Stop them!" he commanded Treylon.

"I...cannot," he said.

The sky shuddered with the sound of thunder. No, the sound of angels screaming in anger. "I am your sire," the angel told Kasabian. "You owe me your life."

Demis. Kasabian faced the angry, beautiful face. "I owe *you* for the pain and suffering that you cause all of us every day of our lives."

Demis threw his hands toward Kasabian, who braced for some kind of blast while holding his power to continue assisting the tug-of-war. Electricity filled the air and seared Kasabian's back. It felt like his skin was being flayed. He held on, panting through the pain.

Demis looked beyond Kasabian. "The wave. It's here," he called to the others. "It will be enough. It has to be enough!"

It was barely visible, a shimmering wall that rushed toward them. Demis reached toward it now. For a few moments, the *Deus Vis* vanished, leaving Kasabian breathless and empty. He felt his Caido essence wilt, his wings begin to pull in. Then the magick returned with a blast as the wave washed over and past them. Demis receded into the cloud.

Kasabian called out, "You cannot punish the innocent to free yourselves! Bastards," he added under his breath. Then he turned his anger on Treylon. "And you are the biggest bastard of them all. They have never been human, but you are. Human enough to feel empathy, to know wrong from right."

"What I'm doing *is* right," Treylon gasped. "I was trying to save us..."

His mouth went slack, and the spark of life left his eyes. Kasabian fell away from him, rolling onto his back. The vessel was gone.

Kasabian got to his feet as Kye appeared at the entrance to the courtyard. Her expression went from scared to relieved, and she threw herself into his arms. Her emotions pummeled him as their bodies collided, and he didn't care. He was alive to feel the pain... and her. His arms wrapped around her waist, and for a moment, he buried his face in the crook of her neck, breathing her in. Warm and sweet and salty from her tears. When he pulled back, he could see the faint tracks of them, fresh with her joy.

"You're okay," she whispered, running her hands over his face as though to make sure. "The kids are all right. They're starting to revive."

He could see them through a gap in the bushes, the Caidos helping them to sit up. They were rubbing their faces as though they'd woken from a long sleep. He hoped they'd see this as just a nightmare.

"Silva's in bad shape," she said. "You need to help him."

He slid his fingers through hers and let her lead him back. "He surprised me."

"Not me." Kye flashed him a sad smile. "I told you, we came to an understanding."

Yeah, he'd get to the bottom of *that* later.

"Even mortally wounded, he kept pulling down the essence," she said. "He made the difference."

Silva was sprawled on the grass, his hand over the gaping hole through his chest.

Kasabian knelt down beside him and waved his hand over

the wound, sending healing Light into it. "Why can't you heal yourself? I had a hole punched through my chest earlier, and it healed faster because I was in Wraithlord form."

Silva shook his head, his breath coming in short gasps. "I used up all of my strength to bring down the essence."

That was probably why Kasabian couldn't seem to do much to heal him either. "We're all sapped."

"I get it, why you saved the kids all those years ago. Because it feels...right." He reached toward Kasabian's hand. "I misplaced my loyalty."

Kasabian stared at it for a moment and then clasped it. "Silva, you did good today."

"Daniel."

"What?"

"My original name was Daniel. Call me that. One more time."

Kasabian wanted to hate this man who had betrayed him and caused so much pain. But now he felt sorry for him. Not because he was probably dying, but for all the things that had shaped him. And twisted his path so much. "Hold on, Daniel."

Kye put her hand on Kasabian's back, kneeling next to him. She pressed her cheek against him, the emotions she was emitting twisting like barbed wire as the Essex began to wear off.

It was worth it. What he felt was her compassion and admiration. She met his gaze, letting him know that admiration was aimed at him.

"Thank...you," Silva said. He gave Kasabian's hand a weak squeeze, took one stuttering breath, and fell silent.

Kye checked his wrist's pulse point with trembling hands. "He's gone."

Kasabian closed his eyelids, unable to look at those vacant eyes for another moment.

Hayden approached as Kasabian got to his feet, pulling Kye up with him. Mallory and Cecily were right behind him. Kasabian scanned their surroundings. "We need to sweep the grounds for any other minions."

Lyle, with his brother's hand still clutched in his, approached. "The kids want to go home."

Kasabian took them in, all of them tired and scared, but grateful. Their emotions pummeled him like fifty pairs of boxing gloves. "We have proof of what's been going on here. Hayden, Cecily, go to the Guard and tell everyone at once so nothing gets covered up. We'll take the children to Harbor and start calling parents."

Hayden put his hand on Cecily's arm. "Ready?" They disappeared.

Kasabian turned to Kye, pulling her close. "How are you holding up?"

"I'm okay. Nothing like saving lives to inject some energy into you."

He planted a soft kiss on her forehead and felt how that simple act flooded through her. It stunned him. Even without their bond, he felt connected to her. But there wasn't time to explore it right then. "Call your parents and let them know you're all right. Sarai was freaked when you pulled your disappearing act."

Her chuckle was husky. "I bet." She took the phone he pulled out of his pocket and started to make the call.

"We're going to be busy with the fallout for a while, I imagine. Tell them we'll head their way the moment we can break free."

"We?"

"I did promise I'd get you back safe and sound."

Sarai's question echoed in his mind. Did he love Kye? Could he love someone after just a few days? Could he love at all? He hadn't thought so. Until Kye.

He slid his fingers through hers and led her toward the group of restless children. "We're going to get you all home."

By the time they'd gotten every kid back where they belonged, answered thousands of questions, and walked Guard investigators through events, Kye was running on fumes. Kasabian had only been apart from her while they gave their separate statements. The moment they were released, he'd come to her side again. She could see his concern, probably worried that she'd keel over at any time. Which was a definite possibility.

Despite her exhaustion, their triumph kept her going. That and the feel of his hand clasping hers. There was something both comforting and sensual about the way he linked their hands...like he'd never let her go. Hayden had called him over though, and she felt oddly alone as she waited on one of the benches. Odd because Kasabian was in sight, only about twenty yards away. He kept glancing her way as he spoke to both Hayden and another man from the Guard.

Footsteps pounding along the pathway drew her attention to the right, where Lyle and Jonathan were running toward her. In the distance, Cory, in full wing, waited. He'd obviously brought them back.

She turned her curious gaze to them as they came screeching to a halt in front of her. "Are you all right?"

Lyle brushed his hair from his face. "That's what I wanted to make sure of, that *you* were okay. You looked...well, it was scary. I thought you might..."

Die. He'd been afraid *she* would die. That they cared about her generated a smile she couldn't contain. "I'm perfectly fine. Kasabian's been sending me doses of Light." She searched their faces, tired but bright. "And what about you?"

All of the children's bonds had broken when they briefly lost their essence during the wave. Kye had checked each one to make certain, though her feelings for Kasabian had once again started to weaken her abilities.

Lyle swallowed hard. "Thank you for everything you did. For me. For Jonathan. He said you made him feel better."

Both boys appeared to be on the verge of tears. She pulled them close, holding them as tight as she could. Their small arms squeezed her just as tight, tugging at maternal instincts she had no idea she possessed. *I'm really not a kid person. But gods, I'm in love with these boys.* They had Kasabian in their lives, but they needed a female influence, too. She caught Kasabian watching them, some unidentifiable emotion cutting across his expression even as he talked to the men. Only when the boys stepped back did she release them.

She brushed a tear from Jonathan's cheek. "How about I come visit you at Harbor? We could hang out." She gave a tug on his faded shirt. "I could take you both shopping for clothes. Sometimes you need a woman's eye." She turned her gaze to Lyle. "To coordinate the colors, patterns, that kind of thing."

"Tomorrow?" Jonathan asked, and his eagerness melted her heart.

"Yes, tomorrow. We'll have lunch and ice cream, too. I'll have to make sure it's okay with Cory though."

"That sounds fine to me." She hadn't even noticed Cory approach. "If you were willing to risk your life to save them, I figure you're safe to take them for the day." *Or forever,* a voice whispered.

Kasabian came up, and Lyle slammed his body against him, too. "Can you come, too? Kye's taking us shopping tomorrow."

"And lunch and ice cream," Jonathan added with a soft smile.

"I can manage that. You guys get checked out by the doc yet?"

"No," Cory said, his voice a bit terse. "They insisted on making sure you two were okay. Come on, boys, they're fine. Let's get back."

"See you tomorrow," Kye said as Cory put one hand on each of their shoulders and Leaped.

"We've officially been released," Kasabian said. "They're going to be doing a full-scale investigation. Hayden's already pushing them to check out the Bend. I'm sure they'll find all the evidence they need."

"If it's not covered up."

"Let's cross that bridge if we have to. I should take you to your parents. I'm sure they're anxious as hell to see you."

An ocean breeze washed stray tendrils of hair across her cheek. She turned to see a slice of blue water between the building and foliage.

"I need a few minutes of down time."

This time she linked her fingers with his and led him to the water's edge. Just seeing the expanse of wide open ocean invigorated her and cleared her mind. The dock held several lounge chairs, but Kye leaned against one of the pilings instead. She loosened her hair and let the fingers of breeze waft through it as she shook it out. Lifting her face to the sun, she filled her lungs with fresh air.

A sound, like Kasabian swallowing a groan or a growl, pulled her attention to him. He'd been watching her, hunger on his face. He shifted his troubled gaze toward the ocean.

She walked over to him, gently resting her hands on his bare shoulders. "I know what you're feeling right now. You're thinking that the right thing to do is push me away because you harbor dark magick and you don't want to hurt me. But part of you doesn't want to do the right thing."

"Your abilities work? Even with us like this?"

She shook her head. "No, they're pretty much all mucked up. That was an educated guess."

"Yes, part of me knows I should walk away because I don't know what this Wraithlord thing is capable of." He brought his hands to her face, that struggle clear on his expression. "Another part says to hell with doing the right thing. I know that's the Wraithlord, and I shouldn't listen. It whispers that none of my struggling matters because you're mine, and there's no way in hell I could walk away from you." He brushed his thumb across her lower lip, his eyes heavy with the weight of his words. "And it's right. Because the thought of that feels worse than being Stripped."

He slid his hands down her back, pulling her against his body. "That goes to show you what a terrible person I am, Kye. Driven by my dark needs, selfish beyond imagination, I would subject you to the danger of my unstable nature and the loss of what makes you feel valuable." His fingers squeezed the curve of her ass. "I would take all of you and not care what it costs." He claimed her mouth, hard and swift, giving her a taste of the violence he harbored, the possessiveness of it.

She gave it right back, matching his ardor tongue to tongue, running her hands up into his soft hair. He swiveled so that her back came up against the railing, his thighs trapping hers. He nibbled her lower lip, and she bit his back. He let out a groan of pleasure, squeezing her tighter.

"Kye, damn it." He restrained all of the energy that threatened to sweep her, and probably him, away. Agony filled his eyes as he visibly fought to pull back a few inches. "You have to tell me what a selfish bastard I am. *You* have to tell me to bug off and leave you alone so you can get back to your life, your job." He shook his head and laughed, though it came out bitter. "I can melt doorknobs, I can cut someone in half with my Light, but I'm not strong enough to walk away from you."

Save me. That's what his expression implored of her. *Save yourself.*

She ran her fingers down his cheek. "You are bad for me. Selfish, violent, possessive—"

"An aberration," he added. "Forty ways fucked up, remember?"

"I do. But here's the thing. You're more than that. You're noble and courageous. Above all, you are a good man. If you don't believe that yourself, well then, I'll believe it enough for both of us. You brought me to life, showed me passion and sacrifice and what it feels like to be cherished." She patted his cheek, giving him a chagrined smile. "So I'm not able to let you go any more than you're able to let me go."

Despite his agony, his eyes glittered with something more powerful. "Pity, love, that you're not a smarter girl."

"Yeah, pity." She gave him a sweet kiss. "And we can wallow in our stupidity as we make crazy love and annoy each other with our habits and quirks, and, oh, knowing exactly what the other is thinking because of our bond, because we are doing the Cobra again. This time on purpose."

He gathered her in his arms and spun her around, but his expression quickly sobered. "Except—"

"Crap. No abilities." She took a breath. "I'll teach another Zensu how to do it. We'll find a way."

"You'll be okay with not having your abilities to sense your clients' issues?"

She tested that idea and didn't feel that sick panic in her stomach. "Yeah, I am. I still have my counseling degree."

He pulled her close, his forehead pressed against hers, hands in her hair. "Do you know how much I fucking *love* you?"

Emotion swelled in her heart. "Why do you think I'm out here pledging myself to a slightly psychotic Dragon angel?"

He leaned back to look at her. "Because you're slightly insane?"

"I'm very crazy...over you."

He released a long breath. "I want to take you home, but I promised—"

"I know. Let's go to my parents' first."

She had stepped off a cliff, but instead of feeling scared, she was happier than she'd ever been.

Kasabian and Kye were silent as they drove, his fingers curled around hers. Kye knew her parents wouldn't be thrilled about any of this, but most especially about her falling for the monster they'd seen in the van. The one who had almost killed her father. But she had stood her ground all those years ago and pursued her Zensu career. Kasabian was worth standing that ground again.

When they pulled up to the house, Kye turned to him. "Brace yourself. Sarai's here, too."

The three surrounded Kye with hugs and frantic questions. Kasabian let her handle it, but he remained by her side once they'd settled in the living room. No one had missed their linked hands, but they didn't seem surprised or even upset about it.

There was an odd tension though, so Kye said, "Okay, out with it. You don't like that I'm with Kasabian."

Her mother traded a look with Sarai, who was silently urging her to say something. Finally her mother said, "I may have misrepresented your babushka's advice. A little." She held her finger and thumb a fraction of an inch apart.

"You mean her directive that I should be committed?" Yeah, that had stung.

"She did say you should be committed. But she meant...to him." She flicked her finger toward Kasabian. "It will solve the problem of losing your abilities. Once you commit your heart to him, the crazy feelings and doubts will settle down, and you'll get your focus back. She said he's a good man. He'll love you well."

Kye met Kasabian's gaze. Yes, he would. She pushed to her feet, which forced Kasabian to follow suit since she was gripping his hand like a vise. She gave Babs, wherever she might be, a smile of gratitude and then turned it to her parents and Sarai. "Babs is right. He is a good man. He's going to take me home and put me to bed, where I'm going to sleep for, oh, about twenty hours."

But when she woke, she would love him well, too.

Ruby Salazaar wants answers...and revenge. Her uncle has just been murdered, and the name he utters with his final breath will lead Ruby to a man with powers beyond her wildest imagination.

Please turn this page for an excerpt from

Dragon Awakened.

Ruby sat in her truck across the street from Dragon Arts. She'd changed clothes and done a quick cleanup at home. Even taking that bit of time had stretched her tight. She'd wanted to drive right over and tear out Cyntag's throat.

Those kind of thoughts usually disturbed her, hinting at a primitive violence that reared its head when someone wronged or threatened her. It throbbed inside her, curling her fingers into fists.

Get it under control. This is one bad dude. All I'm doing right now is finding out how bad.

The logical part of her brain added, *A bad dude who possibly has control of bizarre and deadly weapons while you have a gun. Hullo?*

But what else can I do, let him just get away with killing Mon and never know why? No way in hell.

Without that envelope, she had nothing but Cyntag's name and the schizophrenic thoughts bouncing around in her head.

According to their website, he was teaching a class starting in—she glanced at the clock—one minute. While he was otherwise occupied, she'd snoop and be long gone before his class was over. She had no idea how much Cyntag knew about her. Because she usually wore her hair in a braid, she left it loose and frizzy. Not a big disguise but, at a glance, different enough. She had no intention of him seeing her, but best to be prepared. Which included her gun, the metal cool against the small of her back. She'd found it useful when she started going off-site to look at people's stuff. In a city like Miami, no way was she walking into someone's garage alone and unarmed.

Warm air washed over her neck, and in the corner of her eye, something shimmered next to her. She jerked to the side but saw nothing. All her hairs sprung to attention. It had felt like a breath.

Her mystery rash, which only broke out on the right side of her stomach, burned something fierce. Doctors couldn't figure it out, and she'd tried every kind of medication to no avail. Stress always triggered it.

She stepped into the mid-September heat and humidity. The buildings in this area were old but in good repair. She spotted a Spanish/Portuguese restaurant across the way, and most of the signage was in Spanish with English subtitles. She generally felt like a foreigner in Miami, often one of the few Anglo people at any given location.

She caught sight of her reflection as she approached the glass door: cargo pants, black T sporting the Red Hot Chili Peppers' asterisk logo, and black work boots that protected her feet if something heavy fell on them. The bandage on her forehead, that had to go.

Dragon Arts was first class, with a comfortable waiting

area, natural wood floors, and halogen lights in frosted glass cones. A woman about her age, framed by a tattered pirate's flag on the wall behind her, sharpened pencils at a tall reception desk.

Her dark pink lipstick and short, white hair popped against her raven skin. "May I help you, sugar?" The small gold plaque on the desk identified her as Glesenda.

"I wanted to check the place out, see what classes you offered."

She handed Ruby a slick brochure, studying her eyes. "And not listed are..." She did a double take, her eyebrows furrowing. "Well, you can see the listing for yourself."

Well, okay then. Ruby devoured the flier, looking for one thing: a picture of the owner. No deal, same as their website. An Internet search gleaned several articles mentioning Cyntag's name in conjunction with either his studio or some competition a student had participated in, but nothing on Twitter, Facebook, or any other social networks.

Ruby caught Glesenda's eye. "I understand Cyntag Valeron teaches Cane Fighting Level One?" Whatever that was.

Glesenda nodded toward one of the large glass windows. "He's teaching in the Sapphire Room right now."

Ruby wanted to run over and finally put a face to her uncle's murderer. Her breath left her with every step toward the window. A class of ten men of various ages stood in formation as they watched two men spar at the far side of the room. One sported a shaved head, was in his fifties, and weighed about two-fifty. The other—holy Jesus in Heaven. She sucked in air and tried to pull herself together. He was whip-muscular, wearing loose white pants with a tight black sash at his waist, his ripped torso slick with sweat. Gorgeous, dangerous-looking...and the spit-and-polish image of the Dragon Prince. Even down to his dark hair and the exotic slant to his eyes.

He had a tattoo far more fantastic than any she had seen, a dragon crawling up his back. Black and blue wings spanned his shoulders, the tail sliding down his spine to disappear beneath the waistband of his pants. When he shifted, she saw that the dragon's head peered over his shoulder. It looked three-dimensional.

"Yeah, he has that effect on most women." Glesenda wore an amused expression.

Not quite this effect, Ruby bet. Her chest was so tight she had to push out the words. "That's Cyntag, the one with the dragon tat?"

"Sure is. Total hotness," she said on a sigh.

Sure, if you were into men who sent murderous orbs. The hefty guy pretended to sneak up behind Cyntag, who twisted, hooked the other guy's neck with the curved handle of the cane, and sent him flat on the mat in a flash. Unscathed, Hefty jumped to his feet and tried another attack, which was quickly thwarted with a pseudo-whack of the cane to his head. She watched, mesmerized by the stealthy grace of Cyntag's movements, the way his muscles flexed, and how damned fast he was.

"You can listen in, too." Glesenda pressed a button and then ran in five-inch heels to answer the phone.

Cyntag's voice came through the speaker. "The next counterattack we'll demonstrate is an assailant in a face-to-face assault."

Yes, the low, smooth voice she'd heard on the message. Ready to take more abuse, Hefty tried to punch Cyntag and ended up with his arm locked behind him and the cane shoving him to the floor.

Cyntag extended his hand and effortlessly pulled Hefty to his feet. "Thanks, Stephen." He raised the cane over his head, which tightened his biceps, and addressed his class. "Looks like a sign of disability or old age, right? If I'm looking for a victim, you're an easy target. Or maybe not. If you've got one of these, you have the ability to fight off an attacker with force. At all times, you can carry a weapon right out in the open, no permit needed."

At that moment, Cyntag started to look her way. Ruby moved out of view, her fingers so tight on the frame around the window that she had to pry them off. Her hands were shaking as she passed the desk where Glesenda was on the phone with someone who was obviously calling in sick. Ruby glanced at a clock. Forty-five minutes before class ended.

She'd laid her eyes on him, all right. What was she going to do about it? The only way to take him out—if she could—was to shoot him from a distance, but that wouldn't glean any answers. She was as desperate for them as she was for revenge. Maybe something here would help.

She passed a sign that read OBSIDIAN ROOM. This room bore no window. Too bad, because disturbing sounds emanated from behind the closed door. She tried the handle, ready to act contrite at interrupting.

Except, no deal. The door was locked. The thumps and growls coming from within were muffled, as though the walls were somewhat soundproofed. Those primal growls raised chill bumps on her arms. But more than that, they reached deep inside and twisted at her insides.

She rubbed her arms and wandered into the shop, pretending to look at fighting sticks, canes, and uniforms. Until she spotted a closed door with the words EMPLOYEES ONLY on it.

She pushed it open, prepared once again to feign innocence if she found someone on the other side. It appeared to be a break room and, fortunately, vacated. A door at the other end was ajar, and she could see a desk. Maybe Cyntag's office. Inside, a contemporary desk was juxtaposed with antiques, like framed compasses and maps that looked as though they'd traveled on many a high sea. No pictures of friends, family, or a special vacation. A collection of dragon figurines lined the top shelf of the bookcase, each locked in combat with either another of its kind or a man wielding a sword. Dude had a thing for dragons.

Ruby caught herself scratching the damned rash again and closed the door. She sank into the leather chair at the desk and searched for any clue to who Cyntag was and what he was involved in. Anything incriminating would be documented with her camera phone. She'd rifled through four drawers, finding nothing out of the ordinary, when the door opened. Her heartbeat shot straight up into her throat as she turned.

Because of course it had to be Cyntag standing there.

It's a fine line between love and hate. Can two adversaries team up to find the truth—and defeat a powerful force out to destroy the Dragon community?

Please turn this page for an excerpt from

Magic Possessed.

Kade drove south, through the city and toward the marsh-lands known as the Fringe. Normally, adrenaline would be shooting through his veins like a thousand Red Bulls on his way to a kill. This time he was having a hard time working up the excitement to do his job.

As he reached the edge of the Fringe, he felt a tightening in his gut. Finally. Except it wasn't eagerness or adrena-line. It was...dread? Because he didn't want to kill her. There it was.

Keep your focus. It's a job.

Each clan had a large parcel of land that was divvied up between the various subfamilies. Many had different businesses, nice legal ones like vineyards and farms. But sometimes their farms consisted of marijuana plants, one of Arlo's transgressions. The Guard cared more about the possibility of attracting the Muds' attention than the ille-gality of the farms.

Centuries of living as they saw fit gave the Fringers the

impression that they were outside the bounds of the law. Centuries of living with the threat of being extinguished by your nearest neighbor made them skilled at fighting. Violet was no delicate flower. She'd held back at Headquarters. He knew her ferocity well enough. And yeah, he knew the feel of her breast, and her body wrapped around his…though not in the good way.

Not that you want her *wrapped around you like that. Because that would make this assignment much more complicated.*

His cock had different ideas, thickening at the memory. Hell, he wasn't even experiencing physical contact and there it was, waving to get his attention. He really needed to get laid.

Violet's faced flashed in front of him.

But not with her.

Earlier, he experienced that bizarre moment of spotting someone you knew but not recognizing them. She'd cleaned up nice, dressed in white pants that made her legs go on forever and a dark blue shirt that molded to her upper body. Though he would have definitely recognized her once she gave him the *go screw yourself* look.

Kade drove down a weed-overgrown gravel road and parked his car behind a stand of Brazilian pepper bushes. Between Arlo's drug running, some assault charges, and the old coot who'd seen a gator ape, Kade had been to Castanega property enough to know his way around. There was plenty of acreage for the family's enterprises; most centered around alligators. Demons were no big deal, but those scaly, toothy creatures with perpetual grins gave him the creeps.

Kade walked the boundary between Castanega land and

the long vacant Garza land. This was not the cultivated, trimmed, and polished South Florida most people imagined. While the pepper bushes with the red berries took over open stretches of land, the tall, feathery Australian pines created dense forests elsewhere. In places where the non-native plants hadn't invaded, slash pine trees with their long needles offered more sap than shade.

A wet summer had left the ground muddy and created large marshes in some places. It was hard to walk quietly in muck. His black boots sucked free of the moist earth with every step. The smell of earth, mud, and decay filled his nostrils. Sweat trickled down his back. Even in the hot, muggy summers, Vega attire consisted of long sleeves. The black rayon allowed for movement and ventilation, but neither helped when trekking through the woods in September—a month that, in South Florida, typically was as steamy as the one before it.

Mosquitoes buzzed all around him, but none dared land on him. They seemed to sense the magick in Crescents, largely leaving them alone. But they *wanted* to suck his blood and hovered annoyingly all around. A startled hawk screeched and alighted from a branch. If he hadn't seen the hawk, he'd have suspected it was the Fringe "language," whistles and nature sounds they used to communicate over distances. Like warning of an intruder.

Two things the uniform designer did allow for were quick-drying material and ease in extracting Deuce weapons. Kade ran his fingers from wrist to inner elbow, feeling the spark of magick. The dagger "tattoo" thrummed with magick, courtesy of a specially commissioned Guard tattoo artist.

He suspected Violet's home was a cabin in the western

edge. Her face dominated his mind, the smell of her, the tingle he'd felt when her wrists were clamped in his hands, her body against the wall. A part of him had wanted her to dart off again, craving the chase. Because he knew he'd catch her.

He shook the thought away. Now he *would* catch her. And kill her. He didn't have to like or agree with the order; he simply had to carry it out. It wouldn't be the first time. Or the last.

He paralleled a gravel road, barely visible in the distance, until he spotted a burgundy Infiniti parked in the driveway. Synthetic pop music floated from somewhere beyond the house. He surveyed the area. The house was small but quaint, painted a soft yellow with white shutters and gingerbread trim. The recently mowed grass that surrounded the house in a tidy square was lush and green. Plants and flowers overran the planting beds, a wild mess. Except it wasn't, he realized, seeing a loose but deliberate arrangement of the various plants. Somehow the undisciplined aspect intrigued him more than the sculpted bushes and trimmed trees in his yard in Coral Gables.

He recognized the music now: Berlin, from the eighties. "The Metro." It fit Violet, tough and in your face. Odd, since Violet seemed too young to have been more than a child in the eighties.

Who cared what she liked to listen to? The knife tattoo came to life, filling his hand with the heavy feel of metal. He clutched the dagger as he rounded the rear corner of the house. Farther back sat a large workshop with several long tables in the center of the space and shelves that lined the walls. She was doing something at one of the tables.

He cut back into the woods and came up behind the metal building. As he sidled up along the side, he nearly gave himself away when his shoe bumped an alligator in the bushes. He slapped his hand over his mouth as he stumbled back. The alligator leered at him with glassy eyes. *Wait a minute.* Kade tapped the gator with his shoe. It was hard. Hell, the thing was stuffed. He crouched near the edge of the open bay and watched Violet.

Hopefully she was planning the next murder, doing something to prove her guilt. He tried to see inside the many clear boxes on the shelves. They looked like they were filled with colorful stones. She worked a pair of pliers on a leather strap with jerky movements, cursing when a string of beads fell and scattered all over. Damn. It wasn't destructive; it was jewelry. She bent and picked them up, her pants stretching tight over her ass. One bead bounced and landed within a few feet of him. She hadn't seen it, but a big, dopey-looking dog did. Then the dog saw him.

Uh-oh.

Its tail thumped on the floor, which was covered in outdoor carpet. Okay, not a guard dog but still problematic. He stepped out of view and heard Violet throw the beads and issue a guttural expletive.

She darted out of the workshop, her face buried in her hands, and passed within three feet of him. The dog followed, glancing back at him. Kade remained in place, watching her heaving shoulders as she reached the thicket of cypress and pine trees and fell to her knees.

The dog flopped down beside her and rested its head on her thighs. She buried her face in its fur, her fingers curling into the folds of skin. Her muffled sobs clawed right through him. These were not the cries of a woman putting on a show or upset over something that didn't go her way. This was grief, raw and keening. She said one word over and over, and finally he was able to make it out: Arlo.

She presented him with the perfect opportunity, too grief-stricken to notice if her Dragon warned of a presence coming up behind her. He scanned the surroundings as he readied his dagger for a quick, merciful kill. His pulse throbbed at the side of his throat as it did in these situations, and his fingers tightened on the hilt.

Except his body wouldn't move. Every preconceived notion he had about Violet—unkempt, untamed, violent— fled his mind, replaced by vulnerable, fiery, and innocent.

Innocent.

Former fellow Vega Cyntag Valeron had just come to him that morning, out of the blue, to decipher a magick book. He'd been cryptic about both it and the woman with him but clear about the advice he'd imparted: "Trust your gut above all else. If it doesn't feel right, it's probably not."

Kade's gut screamed, *Don't kill her.*

The oaths he'd taken as a Vega to uphold the law at any cost fell away, replaced by a conviction that Violet was not guilty of some murderous conspiracy.

One moment he stood frozen in his inner turmoil, and the next, a Dragon's gaping mouth was lunging for his throat. He twisted but still got knocked on his ass twenty feet away. He landed in a marshy area, sending a wave of muddy water spraying. His breath escaped in a hard gasp, and he hardly had time to breathe before the Dragon moved into view.

Dappled sunlight shimmered off her maroon scales. She lunged down at him, fangs stopping half an inch from evis-cerating him. Inside her open mouth, magick flares capable of inflicting any type of pain fired to life. Her cat-like eyes shrank. "You!" The fierce flames in her eyes didn't soften one bit. "How dare you sneak up on me!"

Her voice as Dragon was low and rumbly, but every bit of her anger projected through loud and clear. He rolled, coming to his feet in one swift movement. What to say? He knew she was embarrassed at being caught in such a vulnerable moment, and being Amethyst, she was all emotion, not to mention unpredictable and high-strung.

"Violet, I—"

"Idjit! People are killing each other by sneaking onto our land. So either you're here to arrest me or you've got a death wish. And if it's the latter, I'm more than happy to grant it." She charged at him again.

He pressed his hand to her forehead and "shot" her. She Catalyzed to human in the same instant that she flew backward. Her body hit with a hard thud, her arms out at her sides.

He ran toward her, calling his dagger, which had been thrown, too. It burned back into his skin as he reached her. "You okay?"

She was sprawled out, mud streaking her naked body, her eyes wide and stunned. She looked... good.

Good and mad. "What the hell was *that*?"

"Magick taser, a new Guard weapon. It sucks out your magick, which in a Dragon's case, makes you human again." He held out his hand to help her up.

She gripped it, jerking him forward and off balance. He held on to her hand and took her with him. They landed together in the mud, a tangle of bodies. His fingers slid across her skin as he got to his feet. She slugged him, catching his jaw because he was a bit too distracted by the feel of her to be as quick as he should be. She still looked as though she'd kill him.

"Why can't I Catalyze? What'd you do to me?" she screamed, gripping his shirt and shaking him.

Damn, she was strong. She reared back to hit him again, and he caught her fist. Their hands collided with a loud *slap*. She slammed him in the chest with her other hand.

He shoved her into the puddle again, trying to immobilize her. "I'm not here to hurt you. Look, I have no weapon." He held out his hands, showing her his dagger tucked away.

She kicked him in the stomach and tried to crawl away. Which left her sweet, mud-slicked ass in full view. A groan started climbing his throat but he stifled it.

"Assaulting an officer," he muttered, grabbing her around the waist. "Again."

"So it is a death wish then?" She jerked her head around, pinning him with a glare as sharp as his dagger. "Since you have no reason to arrest me."

"Settle down now, darling."

She let out a growl worthy of her Dragon and jumped on top of him, her hands around his collarbone. "Don't you dare call me 'darling.'"

"It slipped out," he grunted as she ground him into the mud. "It doesn't mean anything." But damn, that word never slipped out while on duty. She was firing up his wild side big-time. Her thighs squeezed his hips; her hands pinned his shoulders. He tried to gain control but she wouldn't budge. "Damn, woman, you an alligator wrestler?"

"Champion in the local division four years running, umpteen years ago." Her smile reeked of pride and challenge. And he always accepted a challenge. With a heave, he rolled her so he was on top. She kept the roll going, besting him again.

"Will you listen?" he said.

She grabbed a handful of his hair and jerked his head back. "I would have listened if you'd called the number on all that damned paperwork they made me fill out. While you were all inside laughing at me, I'm sure."

How to gain control of the situation without grabbing her somewhere inappropriate—somewhere that wouldn't piss her off even more? Damned tricky when she was naked. And muddy. Plus the fact that he *wanted* to touch her somewhere inappropriate. "I wasn't laughing at you."

"Sure you were. Inside. Outside you were giving me that smug smile you probably think...is...gorgeous." She fought as he tried to wrap his arms around her upper arms. "While you looked down your nose at me."

"Actually, I was looking at your tight shirt."

She slugged him in the jaw again, not really hard enough to do any damage. He threw his weight toward her, pushing her backward and coming down on top of her. Now he straddled her thighs, leaning down to hover above her.

"I was kidding," he said, his mouth only an inch from hers. "I was taking all of you in. I couldn't believe you were the same Violet Castanega I saw in muddy clothes and a tangled braid." He couldn't help the smile as he let his gaze drift from her neck down to her chest that rose and fell with deep breaths. The mud didn't cover the curve of her breasts or the hardened nipples that made him wonder if she was enjoying this on some deep level, too. "Then again, you do look extraordinary in mud."

"Let me up!" She tried to buck him off, which drove her pelvis up and dangerously close to smashing his balls.

He lay all his weight on top of her. "Not until you promise to stop fighting."

"I can't promise that. How long do the effects of your magick stun gun last?"

"Up to thirty minutes."

She bucked again, but he finally had her under his control. And he liked it. His women were always willing. Something about the fight completely turned him on, especially the way her pelvis bumped against his.

Her eyes widened. "Holy dragonfire, are you...does fighting get you...hot?"

He supposed, with all of this writhing around, it was inevitable that she'd notice his erection. "Not usually, but then again, I've never fought a feisty, naked female in the mud before. I have to admit, it's doing strange things to me." At her surprised look, he added, "Well, you asked. I answered honestly."

She took a deep breath to calm herself. "Okay then, answer this honestly. Why are you here?"

That was a bit trickier, but he could stick to the true part. "I came to ask you more about your allegations."

She just stared at him for a moment, her brown eyes disbelieving. "Instead of catching me in the parking lot, or calling, you sneak onto my land and surprise me. Are you kidding? Are you friggin' kidding me?"

"No, I'm not. Why else would I be here?"

She let out something like a growl. "After I was summarily dismissed, why would the Guard suddenly take me seriously and send someone out? And for God's sake, why *you*?"

He had those kinds of *why* questions, too, none of which he could share with her. "I'm not here on behalf of the Guard."

She furrowed her eyebrows. Mud streaked her face, her toned body, and gods help him, she was tantalizing.

"What's that supposed to mean?" she asked.

"I came on my own, because what you said piqued my interest. There's no need for the senseless deaths that would come from clan wars." He'd seen that fear in her eyes when she'd appealed to Ferro. "I want to hear everything you know."

She seemed to weigh his words. He knew how to lie well when he had to. It was part of his training, though he rarely used it in his personal life. This situation blurred the line. Violet was blurring all kinds of lines, obliterating others.

She took advantage of his introspection, because he was suddenly spinning off of her, compliments of an impressive twist and kick of her long, long legs. He came to his feet, ready for another attack.

She was stalking over to where her clothes had shredded when she'd Catalyzed. She held the remains of the nice, tight shirt she'd been wearing to her chest. Suspicion drenched her expression. "You're serious?" Kade saw a mixture of hope and skepticism in her eyes. And that eradicated any last shred of doubt that she was behind this.

"Very." He pulled off his shirt and tossed it to her.

She snatched it out of the air and wriggled into it, giving him one last heavenly view of her full breasts and flat stomach as she pulled it on. She pushed her muddy hair from her face. "Why do you care? We're all marsh trash to the likes of you."

"The likes of me? Because I'm a Vega?"

"Everything about you." She swept her gaze over him. "You move like royalty, you act like you rule the world, and you look untouchable."

Which he found amusing since he was as muddy as she was. She waited for his answer. He rubbed the mud, now itching, from his neck, buying time. Royalty, huh? He sure as hell didn't feel like any of that at the moment. At least she hadn't called him pretty. "My gut says there's something going on, just like you suspect. If the Guard won't listen, then I will."

"Why sneak up on me? You know what 'animals' we all are." She'd heard someone say it, obviously, as she mimicked it with a sneer. "We do act on instinct, at least our Dragon does. I didn't even know you were there; my Dragon did. I could have killed you."

He gave her a smile he was sure *was* smug. "No, you couldn't have."

She rolled her eyes. "This is a bet, isn't it? Can Kade Kavanaugh nail the marsh trash? You might as well go home. Ain't gonna happen. You're totally not my type."

Except those hardened nubs poking against his shirt told a different story. Of course, so did his cock, even as he said, "Neither are you, if that makes you feel any better. I'm a Deuce-gal kind of guy." Although this Dragon appealed to him more than any other Crescent—Deuce or Dragon— that he'd encountered before. And that was just...crazy. "I'd never try to nail a woman for a bet." He let his mouth curve into a smile. "Only for the mutual pleasure of both parties."

A sound escaped her throat, but she cleared it. "Are you sure you're not here to sniff out any more pot farms? Find something else to bust my brothers on?"

He didn't blame her for her distrust. She had good reason not to trust the Guard, as it turned out. "Arlo was the worst offender. He had problems, whether you want to admit it or not."

She gave a quick nod of her head. "He did."

"Now he's dead. Let's find out why." When her skepticism didn't waver, he added, "Violet, you went to the Guard for help. I'm here. Let me help."

The words broke down her resistance. The battle between distrusting him and needing him played over her expression. "You can't come in my house like that." She walked over to a faucet and turned the squeaky knob, using the hose to rinse her hair and face first. He watched, entranced, as water sluiced over her and plastered his shirt to her curves. After rinsing her legs, she headed toward him and held the stream over his head. He scrubbed his fingers through his hair, feeling the grit wash away. Then she stepped back and pressed her thumb over the end to pressurize the stream. She aimed it across his shoulders and arms first.

He swore she took vengeful pleasure in hosing him down. Or maybe it was just pleasure. Her eyes followed the mud as it slid down his bare chest. Hell, he could feel that gaze slide down his body, embers flickering in her eyes. The water was cool, the sun was hot, and he took the blast of water without giving away the war that raged through him.

Ferro's voice told him to take her out.

Cyn told him to trust his gut.

Berlin's female singer sang about flames reaching out for the sun.

Then she reached for his upper chest. "You've got a

scratch. I must have done that." She gently brushed her fingers across it beneath the water's flow. A wake of sensation followed her caress.

"Violet," he said, cursing himself for the hitch in his voice.

That got her attention. "Am I hurting you?"

He took the hand at his chest and drew it down to the front of his wet pants. "This much." He thought she'd give him hell for being so brazen, slap him silly, and that would break them out of this moment of insanity. Because that was the only explanation, that the situation and adrenaline had tilted them right into crazy territory.

Instead, her eyes fired up, and he swore she actually *squeezed* his erection just a tiny bit. *Holy shit.* She angled one of her legs between his, her hands sliding to his hips. Her thigh moved up along his, and he bit back a curse. This *was* insanity. Not seconds before he'd proclaimed he was a Deuce-only kind of guy. But right now, he was feeling all of her Dragon heat. The directive from his superior officer, the insanity of this attraction, the danger he saw simmering in her eyes, not even the cool water that continued to bathe him did a damn thing to douse his ardor.

He took the hose from her hand and let the water wash over her. When his free hand traced her collarbone, she closed her eyes, her head lolling back. He suspected that surrender wasn't something Violet often did, which only made the gesture more profound. How the hell was he supposed to grasp for any last thread of sanity now?

"Violet," he whispered her name this time. He meant it to sound like a call to logic, but it came out as more of a plea. For more.

His shirt was plastered over her firm breasts, clinging to

her hardened nipples. Damn, she was hot, all sleek skin and toned muscle. With her eyes on his, she peeled off the shirt.

Kade didn't stop to think; he just reacted. He dropped the hose, grasped her by the waist, and lifted her up. Her legs went around him, and their mouths collided. Her lips were soft against his, her tongue sliding in and tangling with his own. She made these little mewling sounds as she pressed closer, her legs tightening around his waist, her hands kneading the muscles of his shoulders and back. His hands slid from her hips to palm her perfect ass. Damn. Just *damn*.

She did some kind of sucking move with her mouth that traveled all the way down to his cock and made it twitch. His pants were the only thing separating them, and if she kept up this rodeo ride, it wouldn't take magick to bust through that barrier. His fingers tightened on her smooth, wet flesh, and he switched to hold her with one arm, moving his other hand to her firm, round breasts. Her small nipples were pink, beaded, and his mouth actually watered at the thought of sucking on them. Before he could claim one of those glistening peaks, she was kissing him again so he plucked at her nipples instead. Her moan of pleasure vibrated through him, clear to the soles of his feet.

She was fire in his arms, a breathing, writhing enchantress. The sun beat down on them, burning his back and heating her dark hair, fueling the already raging fire between them. She ground against him again, increasing the friction. If he didn't get inside her soon, he was going to lose it right there. With rough hands, he stilled her hips.

His mouth trailed kisses along her cheek and throat, and with a deep breath, he took in her scent, all nature and wild and free. His lips found her nipple, tugging on the bead.

His free hand trailed under her firm ass. His fingers found her wet, hot center, making her hips buck against his cock and pushing him closer to the edge. Getting a woman hot and bothered was nothing new, but this was Violet. Wild. Forbidden. Somehow that made it astounding. He slid his finger all around her swollen nub, wringing a cry from her lips.

He had skills, magickal ones, too, but she flew apart before he had the chance to use them. He rode her through the tempest, touching and stroking in a way that maximized her pleasure. She arched and screamed, held him, no, *hugged* him close. Her head rested against his shoulder as she caught her breath.

Then her whole body tightened in a different way. "Oh, my gods, what are we *doing*?"

"Well, I just made you come and—"

She slid to her feet and stumbled back, grabbing up the shirt. "No, I mean, what are we doing? This is—"

"Crazy. Insane." He raked his fingers back through his hair. "And amazing." He still had a raging hard-on, and his body fairly thrummed with the need for release, but what...the...hell?

"No, let's stick to the crazy insane part." She pulled on the shirt, shock in her eyes. "If my brothers had come up on us..."

"That would have been awkward."

"Awkward? They would have killed you."

THE DISH

Where Authors Give You the Inside Scoop

From the desk of Marilyn Pappano

Dear Reader,

One of the pluses of writing the Tallgrass series was one I didn't anticipate until I was neck-deep in the process, but it's been a great one: unearthing old memories. Our Navy career was filled with laugh-out-loud moments, but there were also plenty of the laugh-or-you'll-cry moments, too. We did a lot of laughing. Most of our tears were reserved for later.

Like our very first move to South Carolina, when the movers lost our furniture for weeks, and the day after it was finally delivered, my husband got orders to Alabama. On our second move, the delivery guys perfected their truck-unloading routine: three boxes into the apartment, one box into the front of their truck. (Fortunately, Bob had perfected his watch-the-unloaders routine and recovered it all.)

For our first apartment move-out inspection, we had scrubbed ourselves to nubbins all through the night. The manager did the walk-through, commented on how impeccably clean everything was, and offered me the paperwork to sign. I signed it, turned around to hand it to her, and walked into the low-hanging chandelier where the dining table used to sit, breaking a bulb with my head. Silently she took back the papers, thumbed through to the deduction sheet, and charged us sixty cents for a new bulb.

There's something about being told my Oklahoma accent is funny by multi-generation Americans with accents so heavy that I just guessed at the context of our conversations. Or hearing our two-year-old Oklahoma-born son, home for Christmas, proudly singing, "Jaaan-gle baaaa-ulllz! Jaaan-gle baaaa-ulllz! Jaaan-gle *alllll* the waaaay-uh!"

Bob and I still trade stories. *Remember when we did that self-move to San Diego and the brakes went out on the rental truck in 5:00 traffic in Memphis at the start of a holiday weekend? Remember that pumpkin pie on the first Thanksgiving we couldn't go home—the one I forgot to put the spices in? Remember dropping the kiddo off at the base day care while we got groceries and having to pay the grand sum of fifty cents two hours later? How about when you had to report to the commanding general for joint-service duty at Fort Gordon and we couldn't find your Dixie cup anywhere in the truck crammed with boxes—and at an Army post, no less, that didn't stock Navy uniforms?*

Sea life was great. We watched ships leaving and, months later, come home again. On one homecoming, the kiddo and I watched Daddy's ship run aground. We learned that all sailors look alike when they're dressed in the same uniform and seen from a distance. We spied submarines stealthing out of their bases and toured warships—American, British, French, Canadian—and even got to board one of our own nuclear subs for a private look around.

The Navy gave us a lot to remember and a lot to learn. (Example: all those birthdays and anniversaries

Bob missed didn't mean a thing. It was the fact that he came home that mattered.) I still have a few dried petals from the flowers given to me by the command each time Bob reenlisted, as well the ones I got when he retired. We have a flag, like the one each of the widows in Tallgrass received, and a display box of medals and ribbons, but filled with much happier memories.

I can't wait to see which old *remember when* the next book in this series brings us! I hope you love reading A MAN TO ON HOLD TO as much as I loved writing it.

Sincerely,

Marilyn Pappano

MarilynPappano.com
Twitter @MarilynPappano
Facebook.com/MarilynPappanoFanPage

From the desk of Jaime Rush

Dear Reader,

Much has been written about angels. When I realized that angels would be part of my mythology and hidden world, I knew I needed to make mine different. I didn't want to use the religious mythos or pair them with demons. Many authors have done a fantastic job of this already.

In fact, I felt this way about my world in general. I started with the concept that a confluence of nature and the energy in the Bermuda Triangle had allowed gods and angels to take human form. They procreated with the humans living on the island and were eventually sent back to their plane of existence. But I didn't want to draw on Greek, Roman, or Atlantean mythology, so I made up my own pantheon of gods. I narrowed them down to three different types: Dragons, sorcerers, and angels. Their progeny continue to live in the area of the Triangle, tethered there by their need to be near their energy source.

My angels come from this pantheon, without the constraints of traditional religious roles. They were sent down to the island to police the wayward gods, but succumbed to human temptation. And their progeny pay the price. I'm afraid my angels' descendents, called Caidos, suffer terribly for their fathers' sins. This was not something I contrived; these concepts often just come to me as the truths of my stories.

Caidos are preternaturally beautiful, drawing the desire of those who see them. But desire, their own and others', causes them physical pain. As do the emotions of all but their own kind. They guard their secret, for their lives depend on it. To keep pain at bay, they isolate themselves from the world and shut down their sexuality. Which, of course, makes it all the more fun when they are thrown together with women they find attractive. Pleasure and pain is a fine line, and Kasabian treads it in a different way than other Caidos. Then again, he is different, harboring a dark secret that compounds his sense of isolation.

Perhaps it was slightly sadistic to pair him with a woman who holds the essence of the goddess of sensuality.

Kye is his greatest temptation, but she may also be his salvation. He needs to form a bond with the woman who can release his dark shadow. I don't make it easy on Kye, either. She must lose everything to find her soul. I love to dig deep into my characters' psyches and mine their darkest shadows. Only then can they come into the light.

And isn't that something we all can learn? To face our shadows so that we can walk in the light? That's what I love most about writing: that readers, too, can take the journey of self discovery, self love, right along with my characters. They face their demons and come out on the other end having survived.

We all have magic in our imaginations. Mine has always contained murder, mayhem, and romance. Feel free to wander through the madness of my mind any time. A good place to start is my website, www.jaimerush .com, or that of my romantic suspense alter ego, www .tinawainscott.com.

Jaime Rush

♥ ♥ ♥ ♥ ♥ ♥ ♥ ♥ ♥ ♥ ♥ ♥ ♥ ♥ ♥ ♥ ♥

From the desk of Kate Brady

Dear Reader,

People ask me all the time, "What do you like about writing romantic suspense?" It's a great question, and it always seems like sort of a copout to say, "Everything!" But it's true. Writing novels is the greatest job in the world. And romantic suspense, in particular, allows my favorite elements to exist in a single story: adventure, danger, thrills, chills, romance, and the gratifying knowledge that good will triumph over evil and love will win the day.

Weaving all those elements together is, for me, a labor of love. I love being able to work with something straight from my own mind, without having to footnote and document sources all the time. (In my other career—academia—they frown upon letting the voices in my head do the writing!) I love the flexibility of where and when I can indulge myself in a story—the deck, the kitchen island, the car, the beach, and any number of recliners are my favorite "offices." I love seeing the stories unfold, being surprised by the twists and turns they take, and ultimately coming across them in their finished forms on the bookstore shelves. I love hearing from readers and being privy to their take on the story line or a character. I love meeting other writers and hobnobbing with the huge network of readers and writers out there who still love romantic suspense.

And I *love* getting to know new characters. I don't create these people; they already exist when a story begins and it becomes my job to reveal them. I just go along for the ride as they play out their roles, and I'm repeatedly surprised and delighted by what they prove to be. And it never fails: I always fall in love.

Luke Mann, the hero in WHERE EVIL WAITS, was one of the most intriguing characters I have met and he turned out to be one of my all-time favorites. He first appeared in his brother's book, *Where Angels Rest*, so I knew his hometown, his upbringing, his parents, and his siblings. But Luke himself came to me shrouded in shadows. I couldn't wait to write his story; he was dark and fascinating and intense (not to mention gorgeous) and I knew from the start that his adventure would be a whirlwind ride. When I put him in an alley with his soon-to-be heroine, Kara Chandler—who shocked both Luke and me with a boldness I hadn't expected—I fell in love with both of them. From that point on, WHERE EVIL WAITS was off and running, as Luke and Kara tried to elude and capture a killer as twisted and dangerous as the barbed wire that was his trademark.

The time Luke and Kara spend together is brief, but jam-packed with action, heat, and, ultimately, affection. I hope you enjoy reading their story as much as I enjoyed writing it!

Happy Reading!

Kate Brady

♥ ♥ ♥ ♥ ♥ ♥ ♥ ♥ ♥ ♥ ♥ ♥ ♥ ♥ ♥

From the desk of Amanda Scott

Dear Reader,

The plot of THE WARRIOR'S BRIDE, set in the fourteenth-century Scottish Highlands near Loch Lomond, grew from a law pertaining to abduction that must have seemed logical to its ancient Celtic lawmakers.

I have little doubt that they intended that law to protect women.

However, I grew up in a family descended from a long line of lawyers, including my father, my grandfather, and two of the latter's great-grandfathers, one of whom was the first Supreme Court justice for the state of Arkansas (an arrangement made by his brother, the first senator from Missouri, who also named Arkansas—so just a little nepotism there). My brother is a judge. His son and one of our cousins are defense attorneys. So, as you might imagine, laws and the history of law have stirred many a dinner-table conversation throughout my life.

When I was young, I spent countless summer hours traveling with my paternal grandmother and grandfather in their car, listening to him tell stories as he drove. Once, when I pointed out brown cows on a hillside, he said, "Well, they're brown on this side, anyhow."

That was my first lesson in looking at both sides of any argument, and it has served me well in my profession. This is by no means the first time I've met a law that sowed the seeds for an entire book.

Women, as we all know, are unpredictable creatures who have often taken matters into their own hands in ways of which men—especially in olden times—have disapproved. Thanks to our unpredictability, many laws that men have made to "protect" us have had the opposite effect.

The heroine of THE WARRIOR'S BRIDE is the lady Muriella MacFarlan, whose father, Andrew, is the rightful chief of Clan Farlan. A traitorous cousin has usurped Andrew's chiefdom and murdered his sons, so Andrew means to win his chiefdom back by marrying his daughters to warriors from powerful clans, who will help him.

Muriella, however, intends *never* to marry. I based her character on Clotho, youngest of the three Fates and the one who is responsible for spinning the thread of life. So Murie is a spinner of threads, yarns…and stories.

Blessed with a flawless memory, Muriella aspires to be a *seanachie*, responsible for passing the tales of Highland folklore and history on to future generations. She has already developed a reputation for her storytelling and takes that responsibility seriously.

She seeks truth in her tales of historical events. However, in her personal life, Murie enjoys a more flexible notion of truth. She doesn't lie, exactly. She spins.

Enter blunt-spoken warrior Robert MacAulay, a man of honor with a clear sense of honor, duty, and truth. Rob also has a vision that, at least for the near future, does not include marriage. Nor does he approve of truth-spinning.

Consequently, sparks fly between the two of them even *before* Murie runs afoul of the crazy law. I think you will enjoy THE WARRIOR'S BRIDE.

Meantime, *Suas Alba!*

Sincerely,

Amanda Scott

www.amandascottauthor.com

♥ ♥ ♥ ♥ ♥ ♥ ♥ ♥ ♥ ♥ ♥ ♥ ♥ ♥ ♥ ♥ ♥

From the desk of Mimi Jean Pamfiloff

Dear People Pets—Oops, sorry—I meant, Dear Readers,

Ever wonder what's like to be God of the Sun, Ruler of the House of Gods, and the only deity against procreation with humans (an act against nature)?

Nah. Me neither. I want to know what it's like to be his girlfriend. After all, how many guys house the power of the sun inside their seven-foot frames? And that hair. Long thick ribbons of sun-streaked caramel. And those muscles. Not an ounce of fat to be found on that insanely ripped body. As for the…eh-hem, the *performance* part, well, I'd like to know all about that, too.

Actually, so would Penelope. Especially after spending the evening with him, sipping champagne in his hotel room, and then waking up buck naked. Yes. In his bed. And yes, he's naked, too. Yeah, she'd love to remember what happened. He wouldn't mind, either.

But it seems that the only one who might know anything is Cimil, Goddess of the Underworld, instigator of all things naughty, and she's nowhere to be found. I guess Kinich and Penelope will have to figure this out for themselves. So what will be the consequence of breaking these "rules" of nature Kinich fears so much? Perhaps the price will be Penelope's life. But perhaps, just maybe, the price will be his…

Happy Reading!

Mimi

♥ ♥ ♥ ♥ ♥ ♥ ♥ ♥ ♥ ♥ ♥ ♥ ♥ ♥ ♥

From the desk of Shannon Richard

Dear Reader,

I knew how Brendan and Paige were going to meet from the very start. It was the first scene that played out in my mind. Paige was going to be having a very bad day on top of a very bad couple of months. Her Jeep breaks down in the middle of nowhere Florida, during a sweltering day, and she was to call someone for help. It's when she's at her lowest that she meets the love of her life; she just doesn't know it at the time. As for Brendan, he isn't expecting anyone like Paige to come along. Not now, not ever. But he knows pretty quickly that he has feelings for her, and that they're serious feelings.

Paige can be a little sassy, and Brendan can be a little cocky, so during their first encounter sparks are flying all over the place. Things start to get hot quickly, and it has very little to do with summer in the South (which is hot and miserable, I can tell you from over twenty years of experience). But at the end of the day, and no matter the confrontation, Brendan is Paige's white knight. He comes to her rescue in more ways than one.

The inspiration behind Brendan is a very laid-back Southern guy. He's easygoing (for the most part) and charming. He hasn't been one for long-term serious relationships, but when it comes to Paige he jumps right on in. There's just something about a guy who knows exactly what he wants, who meets the girl and doesn't hesitate. Yeah, it makes me swoon more than just a little. I hoped that readers would appreciate that aspect of him. The diving in headfirst and not looking back, and Brendan doesn't look back.

As for Paige, she's dealing with a lot and is more than a little scared about getting involved with another guy. Her wounds are too fresh and deep from her recent heartbreak. Brendan knows all about pain and suffering. Instead of turning his back on her, he steps up to the plate. He helps Paige heal, helps her get a job and friends, helps her find a place in the little town of Mirabelle. It just so happens that her place is right next to his.

So yes, Brendan is this big, tough, alpha man who comes to the rescue of the damsel in distress. But Paige isn't exactly a weak little thing. No, she's pretty strong herself. It's part of that strength that Brendan is so drawn to. He loves her passion and how fierce she is. But really, he just loves her.

I'm a fan of the happily ever after. Always have been, always will be. I love my characters; they're part of me. They might exist in black and white on the page, but to me they're real. At the end of the day, I just want them to be happy.

Cheers,

ShannonRichard.net
Twitter @Shan_Richard
Facebook.com/ShannonNRichard

Find out more about Forever Romance!

Visit us at
www.hachettebookgroup.com/publishing_forever.aspx

Find us on Facebook
http://www.facebook.com/ForeverRomance

Follow us on Twitter
http://twitter.com/ForeverRomance

NEW AND UPCOMING TITLES

Each month we feature our new titles
and reader favorites.

CONTESTS AND GIVEAWAYS

We give away galleys, autographed copies,
and all kinds of exclusive items.

AUTHOR INFO

You'll find bios, articles, and links to personal websites
for all your favorite authors—and so much more.

GET SOCIAL

Connect with your favorite authors, editors, and
other Forever fans, and share what's important to you.

THE BUZZ

Sign up for our monthly romance newsletter,
and be the first to read all about it.